Gilded

Gilded

MARISSA MEYER

FEIWEL AND FRIENDS
New York

A FEIWEL AND FRIENDS BOOK
An imprint of Macmillan Publishing Group, LLC
120 Broadway, New York, NY 10271
fiercereads.com

Library of Congress Cataloging-in-Publication Data is available.

First edition, 2021
Book design by Michelle Gengaro-Kokmen
Printed in the United States of America
Feiwel and Friends logo designed by Filomena Tuosto

ISBN 978-1-250-61884-9 (hardcover) / 978-1-250-84230-5 (international edition)
1   3   5   7   9   10   8   6   4   2

For Jill and Liz—
Ten years and fifteen books together.
Your continuous support, encouragement,
and friendship are worth so much more than gold.

All right. I will tell you the tale, how it happened in truth.

The first thing you ought to know is that it wasn't my father's fault. Not the bad luck, not the lies. Certainly not the curse. I know some will try to blame him, but he had little to do with it.

And I want to be clear that it wasn't entirely my fault, either. Not the bad luck, not the lies. Certainly not the curse.

Well.

Maybe some of the lies.

But I should start at the beginning. The true beginning.

Our story began on the winter solstice nineteen years ago, during a rare Endless Moon.

Or, I should say, the true beginning was in the beforetimes, when monsters roamed freely outside the veil that now separates them from mortals, and demons sometimes fell in love.

But for our purposes, it started during that Endless Moon. The sky was slate gray and a blizzard was being heralded across the land by the chilling howls of the hounds, the thunder of hooves. The wild hunt had emerged, but this year they were not only seeking lost souls and aimless drunkards and naughty children who had risked misbehaving at a most inopportune time. This year was different, for an Endless Moon only occurs when the winter solstice coincides with a bright moon in all its fullness. This is the only night when the great gods are forced to take their beastly forms. Enormous. Powerful. Almost impossible to catch.

But if you should be lucky enough, or skilled enough, to capture such a prize, the god will be forced to grant a wish.

It was this wish the Erlking sought that fateful night. His hounds howled and burned as they chased down one of the monstrous creatures. The Erlking himself shot the arrow that pierced the beast's massive golden wing. He was sure the wish would be his.

But with remarkable strength and grace, the beast, although wounded, was able to break through the circle of hounds. It fled, deep into the Aschen Wood. The hunters again made chase, but too late. The monster was gone, and with sunlight nearing, the hunt was forced to retreat behind the veil.

As morning light shimmered off a blanket of snow, it so happened that a young miller arose early to check on the river that turned his waterwheel, concerned that it would soon freeze over in the winter cold. That is when he spied the monster, hidden in the shadows of the wheel. It might have been dying, if gods could die. It had grown weak. The gold-tipped arrow still jutted from between bloodied feathers.

The miller, cautious and afraid but courageous all the same, approached the beast and, with much effort, snapped the arrow in two and pulled it free. No sooner had he done so than the beast transformed into the god of stories. Expressing much gratitude for the miller's help, they offered to grant a single wish.

The miller thought on this for a long while, until finally he confessed that he had recently fallen in love with a maiden from the village, a girl who was both warm of heart and free of spirit. He wished that the god would grant them a child, one who was healthy and strong.

The god bowed, and said it was to be.

By the following winter solstice, the miller had married the village maiden and together they brought a baby girl into the world. She was indeed healthy and strong, and in that, the god of stories had granted the wish precisely as requested.

But there are two sides to every story. The hero and the villain. The dark and the light. The blessing and the curse. And what the miller had not understood is that the god of stories is also the god of lies.

A trickster god.

Having been blessed by such a godparent, the child was forever marked with untrustworthy eyes—pitch-black irises, each overlaid by a golden wheel with eight tiny golden spokes. The wheel of fate and fortune, which, if you are wise, you know is the greatest deception of all.

Such a peculiar gaze ensured that all who saw her would know she had been touched by old magic. As she grew, the child was often shunned by the suspicious villagers for her strange gaze and the bouts of misfortune that seemed to follow in her wake. Terrible storms in the winter. Droughts in the summer. Diseased crops and missing livestock. And her mother vanishing in the night with no explanation.

These and all manner of horrible things for which blame could easily be thrust onto the peculiar, motherless child with the unholy eyes.

Perhaps most condemning of all was the habit she developed as soon as she learned her first words. When she talked, she could hardly keep herself from telling the most outlandish tales, as though her tongue could not tell the difference between truth and falsehoods. She began to trade in stories and lies herself, and while the other children delighted in her tales—so full of whimsy and enchantment—the elders knew better.

She was blasphemous, they said. A most despicable liar, which everyone knows is nearly as bad as being a murderer or the sort of person who repeatedly invites themselves over for a pint of ale but never repays the favor.

In a word, the child was cursed, and everyone knew it.

And now that I've told the story, I fear I may have misled you before.

In hindsight, perhaps it was a bit my father's fault. Perhaps he should have known better than to accept a wish from a god.

After all . . . wouldn't you?

New Year's Day

THE
SNOW
MOON

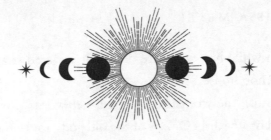

Chapter 1

Madam Sauer was a witch. A real witch—not the way some petty people use the word to describe an unlikeable woman with a haggard appearance, though she was that, too. No, Serilda was convinced Madam Sauer was hiding ancient powers and enjoyed communion with the field spirits in the darkness of each new moon.

She had little evidence. Just a hunch, really. But what else could the old teacher be, with that surly disposition and those yellowish, slightly pointed teeth? (Truly—look closer, they have an unmistakable needle-like quality to them, at least when the light hits them in a certain way, or when she is complaining about her flock of wretched schoolchildren *again*.) The townspeople might insist on blaming Serilda for every tiny misfortune that befell them, but she knew better. If anyone was to blame, it was Madam Sauer.

She probably crafted potions from toenails and had an alpine newt for a familiar. Icky, slimy things. It would fit her temperament just right.

No, no, no. She didn't mean that. Serilda was fond of the alpine newt. She would never wish such a horrible thing upon them as being spiritually attached to this abhorrent human.

"Serilda," said Madam Sauer, with her favorite scowl. At least, Serilda had to assume she was wearing her favorite scowl. She couldn't actually see the witch while her eyes were demurely lowered toward the dirt floor of the schoolhouse.

"You are not," the woman continued, her words slow and sharp, "the godchild of Wyrdith. Or *any* of the old gods, for that matter. Your father may be a respected and honorable man, but he did not rescue a mythical beast who had been wounded by the wild hunt! These things you tell the children, they are . . . they are . . ."

Preposterous?

Absurd?

Sort of amusing?

"Wicked!" Madam Sauer blurted, with bits of spittle flying onto Serilda's cheek. "What does it teach them, to believe that you are special? That your stories are a god's gift, when we should be instilling them with virtues of honesty and humility. An hour spent listening to you and you've managed to tarnish everything I've striven for all year!"

Serilda screwed her mouth to one side and waited a beat. When it seemed that Madam Sauer had run out of accusations, she opened her mouth and inhaled deeply, prepared to defend herself—it had only been a story after all, and what did Madam Sauer know of it? Maybe her father really had rescued the god of lies on the winter solstice. He had told her the story himself when she was younger, and she had checked the astronomy charts. It *had* been an Endless Moon that year—as it would be again this coming winter.

But that was nearly an entire year away. An entire year to dream up delectable, fanciful tales to awe and frighten the little goslings who were forced to attend this soulless school.

Poor things.

"Madam Sauer—"

"Not a word!"

Serilda's mouth slammed shut.

"I have heard enough out of that blasphemous mouth of yours to last a lifetime," roared the witch, before releasing a frustrated huff. "Would that the gods had saved me from such a pupil."

Serilda cleared her throat and tried to continue with a quiet, sensible tone. "I am not precisely a pupil anymore. Though you seem to forget that I volunteer my time here. I'm more of an assistant than a student. And . . . you must find some value in my presence, as you haven't told me to stop coming. Yet?"

She dared to lift her gaze, smiling hopefully.

She had no love for the witch, and was well aware that Madam Sauer had no love for her. But visiting with the schoolchildren, helping them with their work—telling them stories when Madam Sauer wasn't listening—these were some of the few things that brought her joy. If Madam Sauer did tell her to stop coming, she would be devastated. The children, all five of them, were the only people in this town who didn't look at Serilda like she was a blight on their otherwise respectable community.

In fact, they were the few who regularly dared to look at Serilda at all. The golden spokes radiating across her gaze made most people uncomfortable. She had sometimes wondered if the god chose to mark her irises because you're not supposed to be able to look someone in the eye when you're lying to them. But Serilda had never had any trouble holding someone's gaze, whether she was lying or not. It was everyone else in this town who struggled to hold hers.

Except the children.

She couldn't leave. She needed them. She liked to think they might need her back.

Plus, if Madam Sauer did send her away, it would mean that she would be forced to get a job in town, and to her knowledge, the only available work was . . . *spinning*.

Blech.

But Madam Sauer's expression was solemn. Cold. Even bordering on angry. The skin under her left eye was twitching, a sure sign that Serilda had crossed a line.

With a whip of her hand, Madam Sauer grabbed the willow branch she kept on her desk and held it up.

Serilda shrank back, an instinct that lingered from all the years she *had* been one of the school's pupils. She hadn't had the backs of her hands struck in years, but she still felt the ghost of the stinging branch whenever she saw it. She still remembered the words she'd been told to repeat with every swish of the branch.

Lying is evil.

Lying is the work of demons.

My stories are lies, therefore I am a liar.

It might not have been so awful, except that when people didn't trust you to tell the truth, they inevitably stopped trusting you in other matters as well. They didn't trust you not to steal from them. They didn't trust you not to cheat. They didn't believe you could be responsible or thoughtful. It tarnished all elements of your reputation, in a way that Serilda found remarkably unfair.

"Do not think," said Madam Sauer, "that just because you are of age, I will not strike the wickedness from you yet. Once my pupil, always my pupil, Miss Moller."

She bowed her head. "Forgive me. It won't happen again."

The witch scoffed. "Unfortunately, you and I both know that is just one more lie."

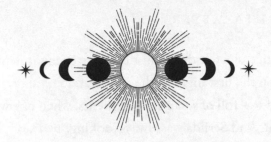

Chapter 2

Serilda drew her cloak tight as she left the schoolhouse. There was still an hour of daylight—plenty of time to get home to the mill—but this winter had been colder than any she could remember, with snow nearly to her knees and dangerous patches of ice where wagon wheels had cut slushy grooves along the roads. The wetness was sure to have soaked through her boots and into her stockings long before she got home, and she was dreading the misery of it just as much as she was looking forward to the fire her father would have started in the hearth and the bowl of steaming broth she would drink while she warmed her toes.

These midwinter walks home from the school were the only times Serilda wished they didn't live quite so far outside of town.

Bracing herself against the cold, she pulled up the hood and surged forward. Head lowered, arms crossed, pace as quick as she would allow while trying not to slip on the treacherous ice lurking under the most recent layer of feather-soft snow. The crisp air mingled with the smell of wood smoke from nearby chimneys.

At least they weren't meant to have more snow tonight. The sky was clear of threatening gray clouds. The Snow Moon would be on full display, and though it wasn't as notable as when the full moon crossed with the solstice, she felt there must be some enchantment tethered to a full moon on the first night of the new year.

The world was full of small enchantments, when one was willing to look for them. And Serilda was always looking.

"The hunt will be celebrating the change of the calendar, as are we all," she whispered, distracting herself as her teeth began to chatter. "After their demonic ride, there will be feasting on what beasts they've captured, and drinking of mulled wine spiced with the blood—"

Something hard hit Serilda on the back, right between her shoulder blades. She yelped and spun around, her foot slipping. She tumbled backward, her rump landing in a cushion of snow.

"I got her!" came Anna's delighted cry. It was met with an eruption of cheers and laughter as the children emerged from their hiding places, five small figures padded in layers of wool and fur. They popped out from behind tree trunks and wagon wheels and an overgrown shrub weighed down with icicles.

"What took you so long?" said Fricz, a snowball ready in his mittened hand, while at his side, Anna busily started scraping together another one. "We've been waiting to ambush you near an hour. Nickel's started complaining of frostbite!"

"It's unmerciful cold out here," said Nickel, Fricz's twin, hopping from foot to foot.

"Oh, shut your whistler. Even the baby's not complaining, you old cogwheel."

Gerdrut, the youngest at five years old, turned to Fricz with an annoyed scowl. "I'm not a baby!" she shouted, hurling a snowball at him. And though her aim was good, it still landed with a sad *kerfluff* at his feet.

"Aw, I was just making a point," said Fricz, which was as close as he ever got to an apology. "I know you're about to be a big sister and all."

This easily assuaged Gerdrut's anger and she stuck up her nose with a proud huff. It wasn't just being the youngest that made the others think of her as the baby of their group. She was particularly small for her age, and particularly precious, with a sprinkling of freckles across her round cheeks and strawberry ringlets that never seemed to tangle, no matter how much she tried to keep up with Anna's acrobatics.

"The point is," snapped Hans, "we're all shivering. There's no need to act the dying swan." At eleven, Hans was the oldest of their group. As such, he liked to overplay his role of leader and protector around the schoolhouse, a role the others had seemed content to let him claim.

"Speak for yourself," said Anna, winding up her arm before throwing her new snowball at the abandoned wagon wheel off the side of the road. It hit the center dead-on. "I'm not cold."

"Only because you've been doing cartwheels for the past hour," muttered Nickel.

Anna grinned, her smile gapped with a number of missing teeth, and launched herself into a somersault. Gerdrut squealed delightedly—somersaults were so far the only trick she'd mastered—and hurried to join her, both of them leaving trails in the snow.

"And just why were you all waiting to ambush me?" asked Serilda. "Don't any of you have a nice warm fire waiting for you at home?"

Gerdrut stopped, legs splayed in front of her and snow clinging to her hair. "We were waiting for you to finish the story." She liked the scary stories more than any of them, though she couldn't listen without burying her nose into Hans's shoulder. "About the wild hunt and the god of lies and—"

"Nope." Serilda shook her head. "Nope, nope, nope. I've been scolded by Madam Sauer for the last time. I'm done telling tales. Starting today, you'll get nothing but boring news and the most trivial of facts. For example, did you know that playing three particular notes on the hackbrett will summon a demon?"

"You are definitely making that up," said Nickel.

"Am not. It's true. Ask anyone. Oh! Also, the only way to kill off a nachzehrer is by putting a stone into its mouth. That will keep it from gnawing on its own flesh while you cut off the head."

"Now, that's the sort of education that might come in handy some-day," said Fricz with an impish grin. Though he and his brother were identical on the outside—same blue eyes and fluffy blond hair and dimpled chins—it was never difficult to tell them apart. Fricz was always the one looking for trouble, and Nickel was always the one look-ing embarrassed that they were related.

Serilda gave a sage nod. "My job is to prepare you for adulthood."

"Ugh," said Hans. "You're playing at teacher, aren't you?"

"I am your teacher."

"No, you're not. You're barely Madam Sauer's assistant. She only lets you around because you can get the littles to quiet down when she can't."

"You mean us?" asked Nickel, gesturing around to himself and the others. "Are we the littles?"

"We're almost as old as you!" added Fricz.

Hans snorted. "You're nine. That's two whole years. It's an eternity."

"It's not two years," said Nickel, starting to count off on his thumb. "Our birthday is in August and yours—"

"All right, all right," interrupted Serilda, who had heard this argu-ment too many times. "You're *all* littles to me, and it's time for me to start taking your education more seriously. To stop filling your heads with nonsense. I'm afraid that story time has ended."

This proclamation was met with a chorus of melodramatic groans, whining, pleas. Fricz even fell face-first into the snow and kicked his feet in a tantrum that may or may not have been in mimicry of one of Gerdrut's bad days.

"I mean it this time," she said, scowling.

"Sure you do," said Anna with a robust laugh. She had stopped doing flips and was now testing the strength of a young linden tree by hanging from one of the lower branches, her legs kicking back and forth. "Just like the last time. And the time before that."

"But now I'm serious."

They stared at her, unconvinced.

Which she supposed was fair. How many times had she told them that she was done telling stories? She was going to become a model teacher. A fine, honest lady once and for all.

It never lasted.

Just one more lie, as Madam Sauer had said.

"But, Serilda," said Fricz, shuffling toward her on his knees and peering up at her with wide, charmed eyes, "winter in Märchenfeld is so awfully boring. Without your stories, what will we have to look forward to?"

"A life of hard labor," muttered Hans. "Mending fences and plowing fields."

"And spinning," said Anna with a distraught sigh, before she curled her legs up and draped her knees over the branch, letting her hands and braids dangle. The tree groaned threateningly, but she ignored it. "So much spinning."

Of all the children, Serilda thought that Anna looked the most like her, especially since Anna had started wearing her long brown hair in twin braids, as Serilda had worn hers for most of her life. But Anna's tan skin was a few shades darker than Serilda's, and her hair wasn't quite as long yet. Plus, there were all the missing milk teeth . . . only some of which had fallen out naturally.

They also shared a mutual hatred for the laborious work of spinning wool. At eight years old, Anna had recently been taught the fine art on her family's wheel. Serilda had looked upon her with appropriate sympathy when she heard the news, referring to the work as *tedium incarnate.* The description had been repeated among the children all the following week, amusing Serilda and infuriating the witch, who had spent an entire hour lecturing on the importance of honest work.

"Please, Serilda," continued Gerdrut. "Your stories, I think they're sort of like spinning, too. Because it's like you're making something beautiful out of nothing."

"Why, Gerdrut! What an astute metaphor," said Serilda, impressed that Gerdrut had thought of such a comparison, but that was one thing she loved about children. They were always surprising her.

"And you're right, Gerdy," said Hans. "Serilda's stories take our dull existence and transform it into something special. It's like . . . like spinning straw into gold."

"Oh, now you're just smearing honey on my mouth," Serilda scoffed, even as she cast her eyes toward the sky, quickly darkening overhead. "Would that I could spin straw into gold. It'd be far more useful than this . . . spinning nothing but silly stories. Rotting your minds, as Madam Sauer would say."

"Curse Madam Sauer!" said Fricz. His brother shot him a warning look for the harsh language.

"Fricz, mind your tongue," said Serilda, feeling like a little chastisement was warranted, even if she appreciated his coming to her defense.

"I mean it. There's no harm in a few stories. She's just jealous, 'cause the only stories she can tell us are about old dead kings and their grubby descendants. She wouldn't know a good tale if it rose up and bit her."

The children laughed, until the branch that Anna was hanging from gave a sudden crack and she fell into a heap in the snow.

Serilda gasped and rushed toward her. "Anna!"

"Still alive!" said Anna. It was her favorite phrase, and one she had cause to use frequently. Untangling herself from the branch, she sat up and beamed at them all. "Good thing Solvilde put all this snow here to break my fall." With a giggle, she gave her head a shake, sending a tiny flurry of snowflakes cascading onto her shoulders. When she was done, she blinked up at Serilda. "So. You are going to finish the story, aren't you?"

Serilda tried to frown disapprovingly, but she knew she wasn't doing a very good job at being the mature adult among them. "You're relentless. And, I must admit, quite persuasive." She heaved a drawn-out sigh. "Fine. Fine! A quick story, because the hunt will be riding tonight and we all should be getting home. Come here."

She forged a path through the snow to a small copse of trees, where there was a bed of dry pine needles and the drooping branches offered some protection from the chill. The children eagerly gathered around her, claiming spots amid the roots, shoulder to shoulder for what warmth they could share.

"Tell us more about the god of lies!" said Gerdrut, sliding beside Hans in case she got scared.

Serilda shook her head. "I have another story I want to tell you now. The sort of story that belongs under a full moon." She gestured toward the horizon, where the new-risen moon was stained the color of summer straw. "This is a different story about the wild hunt, which only rides beneath a full moon, storming over the landscape with their night horses and hellhounds. Today, the hunt has but one leader at their helm—the wicked Erlking. But hundreds of years ago, the hunt was led not by the Erlking, but by his paramour, Perchta, the great huntress."

She was met with eager curiosity, the children leaning closer with bright eyes and growing smiles. Despite the cold, Serilda flushed with her own excitement. There was a shiver of anticipation, for even she rarely knew what twists and turns her stories would take before the words slipped from her tongue. Half the time, she was as surprised by the revelations as her listeners. It was part of what drew her to storytelling—not knowing the end, not knowing what would happen next. She was on the adventure every bit as much as the children were.

"The two were wildly in love," she continued. "Their passion could bring lightning crashing down from the heavens. When the Erlking looked at his fierce mistress, his black heart was so moved that storms would surge over the oceans and earthquakes would tremble the moun-taintops."

The children made faces. They tended to bemoan any mention of romance—even shy Nickel and dreamy Gerdrut, who Serilda sus-pected secretly enjoyed it.

"But there was one problem with their love. Perchta desperately yearned for a child. But the dark ones have more death than life in their blood, and thus cannot bring children into the world. Therefore, such a wish was impossible . . . or so Perchta thought." Her eyes glinted as the story began to unfold in front of her.

"Still, it tore at the Erlking's rotten heart to see his love pining away, year after year, for a child to call her own. How she wept, her tears becom-ing torrents of rain that soaked the fields. How she moaned, her cries rolling like thunder over the hills. Unable to stand seeing her thus, the Erlking traveled to the end of the world to plead to Eostrig, the god of fertility, begging them to place a child into Perchta's womb. But Eostrig, who watches over all new life, could tell that Perchta was made of more cruelty than motherly affection and they dared not subject a child to such a parent. No amount of pleading from the Erlking could sway them.

"And so the Erlking made his way back through the wilderness, loathe to think how this news would disappoint his love. But—as he was riding through the Aschen Wood . . ." Serilda paused, meeting each of the children's gazes in turn, for these words had sent a new energy thrilling through them. The Aschen Wood was the setting of so many stories, not just her own. It was the source of more folktales, more night terrors, more superstitions than she could count, especially here in Märchenfeld. The Aschen Wood lay just to the north of their small town, a short ride through the fields, and its haunting presence was felt by all the villagers from the time they were toddling babes, raised on warnings of all the creatures that lived in that forest, from those who were silly and mischievous, to others foul and cruel.

The name cast a new spell over the children. No longer was Serilda's story of Perchta and her Erlking a distant tale. Now it was at their very doorstep.

"As he traveled through the Aschen Wood, the Erlking heard a most unpleasant sound. Sniffling. Sobbing. Wet, blubbery, disgusting noises most often associated with wet, blubbery, disgusting . . . *children*. He saw the mongrel then, a pathetic little thing, barely big enough to walk about on its pudgy legs. It was a human baby boy, covered head to foot in scratches and mud, wailing for his mother. Which was when the Erlking had a most devious idea."

She smiled, and the children smiled back, for they, too, could see where the story was headed.

Or so they thought.

"And so, the Erlking picked up the child by his filthy nightgown and deposited him into one of the large sacks on the side of his horse. And off he went, racing back to Gravenstone Castle, where Perchta waited to greet him.

"He presented the child to his love, and her joy made the sun itself burn brighter. Months went by, and Perchta doted on that child as only a queen can. She took him on tours of the dead swamps that lie deep in the woods. She bathed him in sulfur springs and dressed him in the skins of the finest beasts she had ever hunted—the fur of a rasselbock and the feathers of a stoppelhahn. She rocked him in the branches of willow trees and sang lullabies to lull him to sleep. He was even gifted his own hellhound to ride, so that he might join his huntress mother on her monthly outings. She was content, then, for some years.

"However, as time passed, the Erlking began to notice a new melancholy overtaking his love. One night he asked her what was the matter, and with a sorrowful cry, Perchta gestured at her baby boy—who was no longer a baby, but had become a wiry, strong-willed child—and said, 'I have never wanted anything more than to have a babe of my own. But alas—this creature before me is no baby. He is a child now, and soon he will be a man. I no longer want him.'"

Nickel gasped, horrified to think that a mother, apparently so devoted, could say such a thing. He was a sensitive boy, and perhaps Serilda had not yet told him enough of the old tales, which so often began with parents or stepparents finding themselves utterly disenchanted with their offspring.

"And so, the Erlking lured the boy back out into the forest, telling him that they were going to practice his archery and bring home a game bird for a feast. But when they were deep enough in the woods, the Erlking took his long hunting blade from his belt, crept up behind the boy…"

The children sank away from her, aghast. Gerdrut buried her face in Hans's arm.

"… and slit his throat, leaving him in a cold creek to die."

Serilda waited a moment for their shock and disgust to ease before she continued. "Then the Erlking went off in search of new prey. Not wild beasts this time, but another human child to give to his love. And the Erlking has been taking lost little children back to his castle ever since."

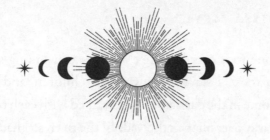

Chapter 3

Serilda was half icicle by the time she spotted the cabin's light across the field, illuminating the snow in a halo of gold. The night was well-lit by the full moon, and she could clearly make out her small house, the gristmill behind it, the waterwheel on the edge of the Sorge River. She could smell the wood smoke, and this gave her a new spark of energy as she cut across the field.

Safety.

Warmth.

Home.

She yanked open the front door and stumbled inside with a dramatic sigh of relief. She fell back against the wood frame and began tearing off her soaked boots and stockings. She tossed them halfway across the room, where they landed with wet plops beside the hearth.

"I . . . am so . . . c-cold."

Her father jumped up from his seat beside the fireplace, where he'd been darning a pair of socks. "Where have you been? The sun set more than an hour ago!"

"S-sorry, Papa," she stammered, hanging her cloak on a peg by the door and peeling off her scarf to join it.

"And where are your mittens? Don't tell me you lost them again."

"Not lost," she breathed, pulling the second chair closer to the fire.

She crossed one foot over her knee and began working some feeling back into her toes. "I stayed late with the children, and didn't want them going home in the dark alone, so I walked with each of them. And the twins live way over on the other side of the river, so I had to go all the way back, and then—oh, it does feel good to be home."

Her father frowned. He was not an old man, but anxious wrinkles had become permanent fixtures on his face long ago. Maybe it was due to raising a child on his own, or fending off gossip from the rest of the town, or maybe he'd always been the sort to worry, whether it was warranted or not. When she was little, she'd made a game of telling him stories about the dangerous mischief she'd gotten herself into and delighted in his utter horror, before laughing and telling him she had made it all up.

Now she could see how that maybe wasn't the kindest way to treat the person she loved most in this world.

"And the mittens?" he asked.

"Traded them for some magic dandelion seeds," she said.

He glared at her.

She smiled sheepishly. "I gave them to Gerdrut. Water, please? I'm so thirsty."

He shook his head, grumbling to himself as he stepped over to the pail in the corner where they gathered snow to be melted nightly by the hearth. Taking a ladle from above the fireplace, he scooped out some water and held it out to her. It was still cold, and tasted of winter going down her throat.

Her father returned to the fire and stirred the hanging pot. "I hate for you to be out all alone, on a full moon at that. Things happen, you know. Children go missing."

She couldn't help smiling at this. Her story today had been inspired by years and years of her father's doom-filled warnings.

"I'm not a child anymore."

"It isn't just children. Full-grown men have been found the next day, dazed and muttering about goblins and nixes. Don't be thinking it isn't dangerous on nights like this. Thought I raised you with more sense."

Serilda beamed at him, because they both knew that the way he'd raised her was on a steady stream of warnings and superstitions that had done more to ignite her imagination than they had to inspire the sense of self-preservation he'd been striving for.

"I'm fine, Papa. Not kidnapped, not ferried away by some ghoul. After all, who would want me, really?"

He fixed her with an irritated look. "Any ghoul would be blasted lucky to have you."

Reaching over, Serilda pressed her frigid-cold fingers against his cheeks. He flinched, but didn't pull away, allowing her to tilt his head down so she could press a kiss against his brow.

"If any come looking," she said, releasing him, "I'll tell them you said that."

"It is not a joking matter, Serilda. Next time you think you'll be late on a full moon, best you take the horse."

She refrained from pointing out that Zelig, their old horse who was more vintage decor now than useful farm stud, had no chance whatsoever of outrunning the wild hunt.

Instead, she said, "Gladly, Papa, if it will ease your heart. Now, let's eat. It smells scrumptious."

He pulled two wooden bowls down from a shelf. "Wise girl. Best to be asleep well before the witching hour."

(

The witching hour had come and the hunt surged across the countryside . . .

These were the words shimmering in Serilda's mind when her eyes snapped open. The fire in the hearth had burned down to embers, emanating only the faintest glow over the room. Her cot had been in the corner of this front room since she could remember, with her father taking the only other room, at the back of the house, its rear wall shared with the gristmill behind them. She could hear his heavy snores through the doorway and for a moment she wondered if that was what had startled her awake.

A log in the fire broke suddenly and collapsed, emitting a spray of sparks that singed the masonry before blackening, dying.

Then—a sound so distant it might have been her imagination if not for the ice-cold finger it sent skimming down her spine.

Howls.

Almost wolflike, which was not uncommon. Their neighbors took great care to protect their flocks from the predators that regularly came prowling.

But there was something different about this cry. Something unholy. Something savage.

"Hellhounds," she whispered to herself. "The hunt."

She sat wide-eyed in shaken silence for a long while, listening to see if she could discern whether they were coming closer or moving farther away, but there was only the crackling of the fire and the rowdy snores in the next room. She began to wonder whether it had been a dream. Her wandering mind getting her into trouble yet again.

Serilda sank back into the cot and pulled the blankets to her chin, but her eyes would not close. She stared at the door, where moonlight seeped through the gaps.

Another howl, then another, in rapid succession, sent her jerking upward again, her heart rattling in her chest. These had been loud. Much louder than before.

The hunt was coming closer.

Serilda once again forced herself to lie down, and this time she screwed her eyes shut so tight her whole face was pinched up. She knew that sleep was impossible now, but she had to pretend. She had heard too many stories of villagers being lured from their beds by the seduction of the hunt, only to be found shivering in their nightgowns at the edge of the forest the next dawn.

Or, for the unlucky ones, never seen again at all. And historically, she and luck didn't get along well. Best not to take her chances.

She vowed to stay right where she was, motionless, barely breathing, until the ghostly parade had passed. Let them find some other hapless peasant to prey on. Her need for excitement was not yet *that* desperate.

She curled herself into a ball, clutching the blanket in her fingertips, waiting for the night to be over. What a great story she would tell the children after this. *Of course the hunt is real, for I've heard it with my own—*

"No—Meadowsweet! This way!"

A girl's voice, trembling and shrill.

Serilda's eyes snapped open again.

The voice had been so clear. It had sounded as if it had come from right outside the window above her bed, which her father had nailed a board over at the start of winter to help keep out the cold.

The voice came again, more frightened still: "Quick! They're coming!"

Something banged against the wall.

"I'm trying," another feminine voice whined. "It's locked!"

They were so close, as if Serilda could reach her hand through the wall and touch them.

She realized with a start that whoever it was, they were trying to get into the cellar beneath the house.

They were trying to hide.

Whoever they were, they were being hunted.

Serilda gave herself no time to think, or to wonder whether it might be a trick of the hunters to lure out fresh prey. To lure *her* from the safety of her bed.

She tossed her feet out from the blankets and rushed to the door. In a blink, she had thrown her cloak on over her nightgown and stuffed her feet into her still-damp boots. She grabbed the lantern off its shelf and fumbled briefly with a matchstick before the wick flared to life.

Serilda yanked open the door and was struck with a gust of wind, a flurry of snowflakes—and a squeal of surprise. She swiveled the lantern toward the cellar door. Two figures were crouched against the wall, their long arms entwined around each other, their immense eyes blinking at her.

Serilda blinked back, equally stunned. For though she had known *someone* was out here, she had not expected to discover that they were actually *something*.

These creatures were not human. At least, not entirely. Their eyes were enormous black pools, their faces as delicate as spindle flowers, their ears tall and pointed and a little fuzzy, like those of a fox. Their limbs were long and willowy branches and their skin shone tawny gold in the glow of the lantern—and there was a lot of skin to be seen. Despite being in the middle of winter, the collection of fur pelts they wore covered little more than what was necessary for the barest sense of modesty. Their hair was cut short and wild and, Serilda realized with a heady sense of awe, was not hair at all, but tufts of lichen and moss.

"Moss maidens," she breathed. For of all her many tales of the dark ones and the nature spirits and all manner of ghosts and ghouls, in all her eighteen years Serilda had only ever met plain, boring humans.

One of the girls sprang to her feet, using her body to block the other from Serilda's view.

"We are not thieves," she said, her tone sharp. "We ask for nothing but shelter."

Serilda flinched. She knew that humans bore a deep distrust for the forest folk. They were regarded as strange. Occasionally helpful at best, thieves and murderers at worst. To this day, the baker's wife insisted that her oldest child was a changeling. (Changeling or not, that child was now a full-grown man, happily married with four offspring of his own.)

Another howl echoed across the fields, sounding as if it came from every direction at once.

Serilda shivered and looked around, but though the fields stretching away from the mill were brightly illuminated under the full moon, she could see no sign of the hunt.

"Parsley, we must go," said the smaller of the two, jumping to her feet and grasping the other's arm. "They are near."

The other, Parsley, nodded fiercely, not taking her gaze from Serilda. "Into the river, then. Disguising our scent is our only hope."

They grasped hands and started to turn away.

"Wait!" Serilda cried. "Wait."

Setting the lantern down beside the cellar door, she reached beneath the wooden plank where her father kept the key. Though her hands were growing numb from the cold, it took her only a moment to undo the lock and throw open the wide flat door. The maidens eyed her warily.

"The river runs slow this time of year, the surface half frozen already. It won't offer much protection. Get in here and pass me up an onion. I'll rub it on the door, and hopefully it will disguise your scent well enough."

They stared at her, and for a long moment Serilda thought they would laugh at her ridiculous attempts to help them. They were forest folk. What need did they have for the pathetic efforts of humans?

But then Parsley nodded. The smaller maiden—Meadowsweet, if she had heard right—climbed down into the pitch-black of the cellar and handed up an onion from one of the crates below. There was no word of gratitude—no word of anything.

As soon as they were both inside, Serilda shut the door and fitted the lock back onto the bolt.

Tearing the skin from the onion, she rubbed its flesh against the edges of the hatch. Her eyes began to sting and she tried not to worry about small details, like the pile of snow that had fallen from the cellar door when she'd thrown it open, or how the trail of the maidens would lead the hellhounds directly to her home.

Trail . . . *footsteps.*

Spinning around, she searched the field, afraid to see two paths of footprints in the snow, leading straight to her.

But she couldn't see anything.

It all felt so surreal that if her eyes hadn't been watering from the onion, she would have been sure she was in the middle of a vivid dream.

She threw the onion away, as hard as she could. It landed in the river with a splash.

Not a moment later, she heard the growls.

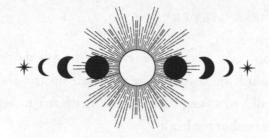

Chapter 4

They came upon her like death itself—yapping and snarling as they charged across the fields. They were twice as big as any hunting dog she'd ever seen, the tops of their ears nearly as high as her shoulders. But their bodies were skinny, with ribs threatening to burst through their bristled fur. Strings of thick saliva clung to pronounced fangs. Most disturbing of all was the burning glow that could be seen through their throats, nostrils, eyes—even areas where their mangy skin was stretched too thin across their bones. As if they did not have blood coursing through their bodies, but the very fires of Verloren.

Serilda barely had time to scream before one of the beasts launched at her, its jaws snapping at her face. Humongous paws knocked into her shoulders. She fell into the snow, instinctively covering her face with her arms. The hound landed on all fours astride her, smelling of sulfur and rot.

To her surprise, it did not clamp its teeth into her, but waited. Trembling, Serilda dared to peer up through the gap in her arms. The hound's eyes blazed as it drew in a long sniff, the air kindling the glow behind its leathery nostrils. Something wet dripped onto her chin. Serilda gasped and tried to scrub it away, unable to stifle a whimper.

"Leave it," demanded a voice—quiet, yet sharp.

The hound pulled away, leaving Serilda shaking and gasping for breath. As soon as she was sure she was free, she rolled over and scrambled back toward the cottage. She snatched up the shovel that lay against the wall and swung back around, her heart racing as she prepared to strike back at the beast.

But she was no longer facing the hounds.

She blinked up at the horse who had come to a halt mere steps from where she had just lain. A black warhorse, its muscles undulating, nostrils blowing great clouds of steam.

Its rider was cast in moonlight, beautiful and terrible at once, with silver-tinted skin and eyes the color of thin ice over a deep lake and long black hair that hung loose around his shoulders. He wore fine leather armor, with two thin belts at his hips holding an assortment of knives and a curved horn. A quiver of arrows jutted over one shoulder. He had the air of a king, confident in his control of the beast beneath him. Sure in the respect he commanded from anyone who crossed his path.

He was dangerous.

He was glorious.

He was not alone. There were at least two dozen other horses, each one black as coal, but for their lightning-white manes and tails. Each bore a rider—men and women, young and old, some dressed in fine robes, others in tattered rags.

Some were ghosts. She could tell from the way their silhouettes blurred against the night sky.

Others were dark ones, recognized by their unearthly beauty. Immortal demons who had long ago escaped from Verloren and their once master, the god of death.

And they were all watching her. The hounds, too. They had heeled to the leader's command and were now pacing hungrily at the back of the hunt, awaiting their next order.

Serilda looked back up at the leader. She knew who he was, but she dared not think the name aloud in her thoughts, for fear she might be right.

He peered into her, through her, with the exact same look one gives a flea-ridden mutt who has just stolen one's supper. "In which direction have they gone?"

Serilda shivered. *His voice.* Serene. Cutting. If he'd bothered to speak poetry to her, rather than a simple question, she would have been ensorcelled already.

As it was, she found herself managing to shake away some of the spell his presence had cast, remembering the moss maidens who were, even now, mere feet away from her, hidden beneath the cellar door, and her father, hopefully still fast asleep inside the house.

She was alone, trapped in the attention of this being who was more demon than man.

Serilda tentatively set the shovel back down and asked, "In which direction have *who* gone, my lord?"

For surely he was nobility, in whatever hierarchy the dark ones claimed.

A king, her mind whispered, and she shushed it. It was simply too unthinkable.

His pale eyes narrowed. The question hung in the bitter air between them for a long time, while Serilda's shivers overtook her body. She *was* still in her nightgown beneath the cloak, and her toes were quickly going numb.

The Erl—no, the hunter, she would call him. The hunter did not respond to her question, to her disappointment. For if he'd answered *the moss maidens,* she would have been able to lob a question back at him. What was he doing hunting the forest folk? What did he want with them? They were not beasts to be slain and beheaded, their skins to decorate a castle hall.

At least, she certainly hoped that wasn't his intention. The mere thought of it curdled her stomach.

But the hunter said nothing, just held her gaze while his steed held perfectly, unnaturally still.

Unable to stand any amount of silence for too long, and especially a silence while surrounded by phantoms and wraiths, Serilda let out a startled cry. "Oh, forgive me! Am I in your way? Please . . ." She stepped back and curtsied, waving them on. "Don't mind me. I was only about to do my midnight harvesting, but I'll wait for you to pass."

The hunter did not move. A few of the other steeds that had formed a crescent around them stamped their hoofs into the snow and let out impatient snorts.

After another long silence, the hunter said, "You do not intend to join us?"

Serilda swallowed. She could not tell if it was an invitation or a threat, but the thought of *joining* this ghastly troupe, of going along on the hunt, left a hollow terror in her chest.

She tried to keep from stammering as she said, "I'll be useless to you, my lord. Never learned any hunting skills, and can barely stay upright in a saddle. Best you go on and leave me to my work."

The hunter inclined his head, and for the first time, she sensed something new in his cold expression. Something like curiosity.

To her surprise, he swung his leg over the horse and before Serilda could gasp, he had landed on the ground before her.

Serilda was tall compared with most girls in the village, but the Erlki—the hunter dwarfed her by nearly a full head. His proportions were uncanny, long and slender as a water reed.

Or a sword, perhaps, was a more appropriate comparison.

She gulped hard as he took a step toward her.

"Pray tell," he said lowly, "what *is* your work, at such an hour, on such a night?"

She blinked rapidly, and for a terrifying moment, no words would come. Not only could she not speak, but her mind was desolate. Where normally there were stories and tales and lies, now there was a void. A nothingness like she'd never experienced.

So much for spinning straw into gold.

The hunter craned his head toward her, taunting. Knowing he had caught her. And next he would ask her again where the moss maidens were. What could she do but tell him? What option did she have?

Think. *Think.*

"I believe you said you were . . . harvesting?" he prompted, with a hint of lightness to his tone that was deceptive in its gentle curiosity. This was a trick—a trap.

Serilda managed to tear her gaze away from his, to a spot in the field where her own feet had trampled the snow when she'd rushed home earlier that evening. A few broken pieces of yellowed rye were poking up from the slush.

"Straw!" she said—practically shouted, so that the hunter actually looked startled. "I'm harvesting straw, of course. What else, my lord?"

His brows dipped in toward each other. "On New Year's night? Under a Snow Moon?"

"Why—surely. It's the best time to do it. I mean . . . not that it's the new year, exactly, but . . . the full moon. Otherwise it won't have quite the right properties for the . . . the spinning." She gulped, before adding, somewhat nervously, "Into . . . gold?"

She finished this absurd statement with a cheeky smile that the hunter did not reciprocate. He kept his attention fixed on her, suspicious, yet still . . . interested, somehow.

Serilda wrapped her arms around herself, as much as a shield against his shrewd gaze as the cold. She was starting to shiver in earnest now, her teeth newly chattering.

Finally, the hunter spoke again, but whatever she had hoped or expected him to say, it was certainly not—

"You bear the mark of Hulda."

Her heart skipped. "Hulda?"

"God of labor."

She gaped at him. Of course she knew who Hulda was. There were only seven gods, after all—they weren't difficult to keep track of. Hulda was the god mostly associated with good, honest work, as Madam Sauer would say. From farming to carpentry to, perhaps most of all, spinning.

She had hoped that the darkness of the night would have hidden her strange eyes with their embedded golden wheels, but perhaps the hunter had the keen sight of an owl, a nocturnal hunter through and through.

He had interpreted the mark as a spinning wheel. She opened her mouth, prepared, for once, to tell the truth. That she was not marked by the god of spinning, but rather, the god of lies. The mark he saw was the wheel of fate and fortune—or misfortune, as seemed to be the case more often than not.

It was an easy mistake to make.

But then she realized that being thus marked added some credibility to her lie of harvesting straw, so she forced herself to shrug, a little bashful at this supposed sorcery she contained.

"Yes," she said, her voice suddenly faint. "Hulda gave their blessing before I was born."

"For what purpose?"

"My mother was a talented seamstress," she lied. "She gifted a fine cloak to Hulda, and the god was so impressed that they told my mother her firstborn child would be gifted with the most miraculous of skills."

"Spinning straw into gold," the hunter drawled, his voice thick with disbelief.

Serilda nodded. "I try not to tell many people. Might make the other maidens jealous, or the men greedy. I trust you'll keep the secret?"

For the briefest moment, the hunter looked amused at this statement. Then he took a step closer, and the air around Serilda became still and so very, very cold. She felt touched by frost and realized for the first time that there was no cloud steaming the space before him when he breathed.

Something sharp pressed into the base of her chin. Serilda gasped. Surely she should have sensed him drawing the weapon, but she had neither seen nor felt him move. Yet here he was, holding a hunting knife at her throat.

"I will ask again," he said, in a tone almost sweet, "where are the forest creatures?"

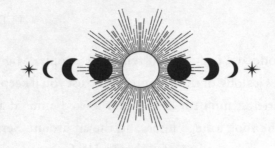

Chapter 5

Serilda held the hunter's soulless gaze, feeling too brittle, too vulnerable.

And yet her tongue—that idiotic, lying tongue—went right on talking. "My lord," she said, with a tinge of sympathy, as if embarrassed to have to say this, for surely such a skilled hunter would not like appearing the simpleton, "the forest creatures live in the Aschen Wood, to the west of the Great Oak. And . . . a little to the north, I think. At least, that's what the stories say."

For the first time, a flicker of anger passed over the hunter's face. Anger—but also uncertainty. He couldn't quite tell whether she was playing games with him or not.

Even a great tyrant such as he couldn't tell if she was lying.

She lifted a hand and laid her fingers ever so delicately on his wrist.

He twitched at the unexpected touch.

She started at the feel of his skin.

Her fingers might have been cold, but at least they still had warm blood coursing through them.

Whereas the hunter's skin had quite frosted over.

Without warning, he jerked away, freeing her from the imminent threat of his blade.

"I mean no disrespect," Serilda said, "but I really must tend to my work. The moon will be gone soon and the straw will not be so compliant. I like to work with the best materials, when I can."

Without waiting for a response, Serilda picked up the shovel again, along with a bucket overflowing with snow, which she promptly dumped out. Head lifted high, she dared to walk past the hunter, past his horse, into the field. The rest of the hunting party backed away, giving her space, as Serilda began scooping away the top layer of snow to reveal the crushed grain underneath; the sad little stalks that had been left behind from the fall harvest.

It looked nothing like gold.

What a ridiculous lie this was turning into.

But Serilda knew that full-hearted commitment was the only way to persuade someone of an untruth. So she kept her face placid as she began to pull the stalks up with her bare, freezing hands and toss them into the bucket.

For a long while, there were only the sounds of her working, and the occasional shuffle of horse hooves, and the low growl of the hounds.

Then a light, raspy voice said, "I have heard tales of gold-spinners, blessed by Hulda."

Serilda looked up at the nearest rider. A pale-skinned woman, hazy around the edges, hair in a braided crown atop her head. She wore riding breeches and leather armor accented by a deep red stain all down the front of the tunic. It was a sickening amount of blood—all, no doubt, from the deep gash across her throat.

She held Serilda's gaze a moment—emotionless—before glancing at their leader. "I believe she speaks true."

The hunter did not acknowledge her statement. Instead, Serilda heard his boots crunching lightly through the snow until he was standing behind her. She lowered her gaze, focused on her task, though the grain stalks were cutting her palms and mud was already caked beneath her fingernails. Why hadn't she grabbed her mittens? As soon as she thought it, she remembered that she'd given them to Gerdrut. She must look like such a fool.

Gathering straw to spin into gold. Honestly, Serilda. Of all the thoughtless, absurd things you might have said—

"How pleasant to know that Hulda's gift has not gone wasted," drawled the hunter. "It is a rare treasure indeed."

She glanced over her shoulder, but he was already turning away. Lithe as a spotted lynx, he mounted his steed. His horse snorted.

The hunter did not look at Serilda as he signaled to the other riders.

As fast as they had arrived, they were gone again. Thundering hooves, a flurry of snow and ice, the renewed howls of the hellhounds. A storm cloud, ominous and crackling, racing across the field.

Then, nothing but glistening snow and the round moon kissing the horizon.

Serilda let out a shaken breath, hardly able to believe her good fortune.

She had survived an encounter with the wild hunt.

She had lied to the face of the Erlking himself.

What a tragedy, she thought, that no one would ever believe her.

She waited until the usual sounds of the night had begun to return. Frozen branches creaking. The river's soothing burble. A distant hoot of an owl.

Finally, she retrieved the lantern and dared to throw open the cellar door.

The moss maidens emerged, staring at Serilda as if she had turned blue in the time since they'd last seen her.

She was so cold, she wouldn't have doubted it.

She tried to smile, but it was difficult to do when her teeth were chattering. "Will you be all right now? Can you find your way back to the forest?"

The taller maiden, Parsley, sneered, as if insulted by such a question. "It is you humans who regularly lose yourselves, not us."

"I didn't mean to offend." She glanced down at their immodest furs. "You must be so cold."

The maiden didn't respond, just stared intently at Serilda, both curious and irritated. "You have saved our lives, and risked your own to do it. What for?"

Serilda's heart fluttered gleefully. It sounded so heroic, when put that way.

But heroes were supposed to be humble, so she merely shrugged. "It hardly seemed right, chasing you down like that, as if you were wild animals. What did the hunt want with you, anyway?"

It was Meadowsweet who spoke, seeming to overcome her shyness. "The Erlking has long hunted the forest folk, and all manner of magical kin besides."

"He sees it as sport," said Parsley. "Suppose, when you've been hunting so long as he has, taking home the head of a common stag must not seem like much of a prize."

Serilda's lips parted in shock. "He meant to *kill* you?"

They both looked at her as if she were dense. But Serilda had assumed the hunt was chasing them to capture them. Which, perhaps, was worse in some ways. But to murder such graceful beings for the fun of it? The idea sickened her.

"We typically have means of protecting ourselves from the hunt, and evading those hounds," said Parsley. "They cannot find us when we stay under the protection of our Shrub Grandmother. But my sister and I were not able to make it back before nightfall."

"I am glad I could help," said Serilda. "You are welcome to hide in my root cellar anytime you'd like."

"We owe you a debt," said Meadowsweet.

Serilda shook her head. "I won't hear of it. Believe me. The adventure was well worth the risk."

The maidens exchanged a look, and whatever passed between them, Serilda could see they didn't like it. But there was resignation in Parsley's scowl as she stepped closer to Serilda and fidgeted with something on her finger.

"All magic requires payment, to keep our worlds in balance. Will you accept this token in return for the aid you've given me this night?"

Struck speechless, Serilda opened her palm. The maiden dropped a ring onto it. "This isn't necessary . . . and I certainly didn't do any *magic.*"

Parsley tilted her head, a rather birdlike gesture. "Are you certain?"

Before Serilda could respond, Meadowsweet had stepped closer and removed a thin chain from her neck.

"And will you accept this token," she said, "in return for the aid you've given me?"

She looped the necklace around Serilda's outstretched palm. It bore a small oval locket.

Both pieces of jewelry shone gold in the moonlight.

Actual gold.

They must be worth a great deal.

But what were forest folk doing with them? She had always believed that they had no use for material riches. That they saw humankind's obsession with gold and gems as something unsavory, even repulsive.

Perhaps that was why it was so easy for them to give these gifts to Serilda. Whereas, for her and her father, these were a treasure like nothing she'd ever held.

And yet—

She shook her head and held her hand out toward them. "I can't take these. Thank you, but . . . anyone would have helped you. You don't need to pay me."

Parsley chuckled mildly. "You must not know much of humans, to believe that," she said sourly. She tilted her chin toward the gifts. "If you do not accept these tokens, then our debt has not been paid and we must be in your service until it is." Her gaze darkened warningly. "We would much prefer that you take the gifts."

Pressing her lips together, Serilda nodded and closed her hand around the jewelry. "Thank you, then," she said. "Consider the debt paid."

They nodded, and it felt as if a bargain had been struck and signed in blood for all the loftiness the moment carried.

Desperate to break the tension, Serilda held her arms out toward them. "I feel so close to you both. Shall we embrace?"

Meadowsweet gaped at her. Parsley outright *snarled*.

The tension did not break.

Serilda drew her arms quickly back. "No. That would be odd."

"Come," said Parsley. "Grandmother will be worried."

And just like skittish deer, they ran off, disappearing down the river-bank.

"By the old gods," muttered Serilda. "What a night."

She banged her boots on the side of the house to rid them of snow before going inside. Snores greeted her. Her father was still sleeping like a groundhog, utterly oblivious.

Serilda slipped off her cloak and sat with a sigh before the hearth. She added a block of bog peat to keep the fire smoldering. In the light of the embers, she tilted forward and peered down at her rewards.

One golden ring.

One golden locket.

When they caught the light, she saw that the ring bore a mark. A crest, like something a noble family might put on their fancy wax seals.

Serilda had to squint to make it out. The design appeared to be of a tatzelwurm, a great mythical beast that was mostly serpentine with a feline head. Its body was wrapped elegantly around the letter *R*. Serilda had never seen anything quite like it before.

Digging her thumbnails into the locket's clasp, she pried it open with a snap.

Her breath caught with delight.

She'd expected the locket to be empty, but inside there was a portrait—the tiniest, most delicate painting she'd ever seen—showing the resemblance of a most lovely little girl. She was but a child, Anna's age if not a little younger, but clearly a princess or duchess or someone of much importance. Strings of pearls decorated her golden curls and a collar of lace framed her porcelain cheeks.

The regal lift of her chin was somehow completely at odds with the impish glint in her eyes.

Serilda shut the locket and slipped the chain over her head. She slid the ring onto her finger. With a sigh, she crawled back beneath her covers.

It was little comfort that she now had proof about what had transpired this night. Probably, if she showed anyone, they would think these things were stolen. Bad enough to be a liar. Becoming a thief was the logical progression.

Serilda lay sleepless, staring up at the golden patterns and creeping shadows on the ceiling rafters, gripping the locket in her fist.

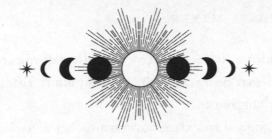

Chapter 6

Sometimes Serilda would spend hours thinking about evidence. Those little clues left behind in a story that bridged the gap between fantasy and reality.

What evidence did she have that she'd been cursed by Wyrdith, the god of stories and fortune? The bedtime tales her father had told her, though she'd never dared to ask if they were real or not. The golden wheels over her black irises. Her uncontrollable tongue. A mother who had no interest in watching her grow up, who left without so much as a goodbye.

What evidence was there that the Erlking murdered the children who got lost in the woods? Not much. Mostly hearsay. Rumors of a haunting figure that stalked through the trees, listening for a child's frightened cries. And long ago, once every generation or so, a small body discovered at the forest's edge. Barely familiar, oft picked clean by the crows. But parents always recognized their own missing child, even a decade later. Even when all that was left was a corpse.

But that had not happened in recent memory, and it was hardly proof.

Superstitious nonsense.

This, however, was different.

Quite different.

What evidence did Serilda have that she had rescued two moss maidens who were being chased by the wild hunt? That she had out-witted the Erlking himself?

A golden ring and a necklace, warm against her skin when she awoke.

Outside—a square of dead grass revealed where she had shoveled away the snow.

An open cellar door, left unlocked, the wood still smelling of raw onion.

But not, she noted with bewilderment, hoofprints or tracks left in the fields. The snow was as pristine as it had been when she'd come trekking home the night before. The only footprints she saw were her own. There had been no mark left behind of her midnight visitors, not the delicate feet of the moss maidens nor the clomping hooves of the horses nor the lupine tracks of the hounds.

Just a delicate field of white, glittering almost cheerfully in the morning sun.

As it soon turned out, the evidence she *did* have would do her no good.

She told her father the story—every word a singular truth. And he listened, rapt, even horrified. He studied the seal on the ring and the locket's portrait with speechless awe. He went out to inspect the cellar door. He stood a long time, staring out at the empty horizon, beyond which lay the Aschen Wood.

Then, when Serilda thought she could stand the silence no longer, he began to laugh. A full belly laugh tinged with something dark that she couldn't quite place.

Panic? Fear?

"You'd think by now," he said, turning back to face her, "I'd have learned not to be so gullible. Oh, Serilda." He took her face into his rough palms. "How can you speak these things without so much as a hint of a smile? You very nearly had me fooled, yet again. Where did you get these, truthfully, now?" He lifted the locket from her collar-bone, shaking his head. He'd gone pale while she recounted the events of the night before, but color was now rushing back into his cheeks. "Were they a gift from some young lad in town? I've been wondering if you might be sweet on someone and too shy to tell me."

Serilda stepped back, tucking the locket beneath her dress. She hesitated, tempted to try again. To *insist*. He had to believe her. For once, it was real. It had happened. She wasn't lying. And she might have tried again, if it hadn't been for the haunted look lurking behind his gaze, not entirely covered up by his denial. He was worried about her. Despite his strained laughter, he was terrified that this one could be true.

She didn't want that. He already worried enough.

"Of course not, Papa. I'm not sweet on anyone, and when have you ever known me to be shy?" She shrugged. "If you must know the truth of it, I found the ring stuck around a fairy's toadstool, and I stole the necklace from the schellenrock who lives in the river."

He guffawed. "Now *that* I'd be closer to believing."

He went back inside and Serilda knew in that moment, in the deepest corner of her heart, that if he wouldn't believe her, no one would.

They had heard far too many tales before.

She told herself it was better this way. If she wasn't beholden to the truth of what had happened under the full moon, then she would have no qualms about embellishing it.

And she did dearly love to embellish.

"Speaking of young village lads," Papa called through the open door, "I thought I should tell you. Thomas Lindbeck has agreed to help around the mill this spring."

The name was a kick to her chest. "Thomas Lindbeck?" she said, darting back into the house. "Hans's brother? What for? You've never hired help before."

"I'm getting older. Thought it'd be nice to have a strapping young man to do some of the heavy lifting."

She scowled. "You're barely forty."

Her father glanced up from stoking the fire, chagrined. Sighing, he set down the poker and stood to face her, brushing off his hands. "All right. He came and asked for the work. He's hoping to earn some extra coin, so that . . ."

"So that what?" she prompted, his hesitation making her tense.

His look was pitying in a way that turned her stomach.

"So he can be making a proposal to Bluma Rask, is my understanding."

A proposal.

Of marriage.

"I see," said Serilda, forcing a tight smile. "I didn't realize they were so . . . well. Good. They're a charming match." She glanced at the fireplace. "I'll get some apples for our breakfast. Do you want anything else from the cellar?"

He shook his head, watching her carefully. Her nerves hummed with irritation. She was careful not to stomp or grind her teeth as she headed back outside.

What did she care if Thomas Lindbeck wanted to marry Bluma Rask, or anyone else for that matter? She had no claim to him, not anymore. It had been nearly two years since he'd stopped looking at Serilda like she was the sun itself, and started looking at her like she was a storm cloud brewing ominously on the horizon.

When he bothered to look at her at all, that is.

She wished a happy, long life on him and Bluma. A little farmhouse. A yard full of children. Endless conversations about the price of livestock and unfavorable weather.

A life without curses.

A life without stories.

Serilda paused as she threw open the cellar door, where just last night she had hidden two magical creatures. She stood in this very spot and faced down an otherworldly beast and a wicked king and a whole legion of undead hunters.

She was not the sort to pine for a simple life, and she would not pine for the likes of Thomas Lindbeck.

Stories change with repeated tellings, and hers was no different. The night of the Snow Moon became increasingly adventurous, and more and more surreal. When she told the tale to the children, it was not moss maidens she had rescued, but a vicious little water nix who had thanked her only by trying to bite off her fingers before it jumped into the river and disappeared.

When Farmer Baumann brought extra firewood for the schoolhouse and Gerdrut encouraged Serilda to repeat the story, she insisted that the Erlking had not ridden upon a black steed, but rather a massive wyvern who blew acrid smoke from its nostrils and oozed molten rock from between its scales.

When Serilda went to barter for some of Mother Weber's raw wool and was asked by Anna to again repeat the fantastical tale, she dared not explain how she had fooled the Erlking with a lie about her magical spinning abilities. Mother Weber had been the one to teach Serilda the technique when she was young, and she had never stopped criticizing Serilda for her lack of skill. To this day she liked to gripe about how the local sheep deserved to have their coats turned into something finer than the lumpy, uneven threads that would come off Serilda's bobbins. She probably would have laughed Serilda right out of their cottage if she heard how Serilda had lied to the Erlking about her spinning talent, of all things.

Instead, Serilda turned her story-self into a bold warrior. She regaled her small audience with a feat of daring and bravery. How she had brandished a lethal fire iron (no mere shovel for her!), threatening the Erlking and driving away his demon attendants. She mimicked precisely how she had swung, stabbed, and clobbered her enemies. How she had driven the poker into the heart of a hellhound, then flung it off into one of the buckets on the waterwheel.

The children were in stitches, and by the time Serilda's story ended with the Erlking fleeing from her with girlish squeals and a lump the size of a goose egg on his head, Anna and her toddler brother ran off to begin their own playacting, deciding who would be Serilda and who would be the terrible king. Mother Weber shook her head, but Serilda was sure she saw the hint of a smile disguised behind her knitting needles.

She tried to enjoy their reactions. The open mouths, the intent gazes, the giddy laughter. Usually, this was all she craved.

But with every telling, Serilda felt that the reality of the story was slipping away from her. Becoming fogged over by time and alterations.

She wondered how long it would be before she, too, began to doubt what had transpired that night.

Such thoughts filled her with unexpected regret. Sometimes, when she was alone, she would pull out the chain from beneath the collar of her dress and stare at the portrait of the young girl, who she'd declared a princess in her imagination. Then she would rub her thumb over the engraving on the ring. The tatzelwurm twisted around an ornate *R*.

She promised herself that she would never forget. Not a single detail.

A loud *caw* startled Serilda from her melancholy. She looked up to see a bird watching her through the cottage doorway, which she'd left open to air out the little home while the sun was shining, knowing another winter storm would be upon them any day.

And here she was, distracted once again from her task. She was supposed to be spinning all this wool she'd gotten from Mother Weber, turning it into usable yarn for their mending and knitting.

The worst sort of work. *Tedium incarnate.* She would have rather been skating on the newly frozen pond or freezing caramel drops in the snow for an evening treat.

Instead, she'd been lost in thought again, staring at the small portrait.

She shut the locket and tucked it into her dress. Pushing back the three-legged stool, she walked around the spinning wheel to the door. She hadn't realized how cold it had gotten. She rubbed her hands together to try and return some warmth to her fingers.

She paused, one hand on the door, noticing the bird who had startled her from her reverie. It was perched on one of the barren branches of the hazelnut tree that stood just beyond their garden. It was the biggest raven she'd ever seen. A monstrous shadow of a creature silhouetted against the dusky sky.

Sometimes she would toss out bread crumbs for the birds. Probably this one had heard about the feast.

"Sincerest apologies," she said, preparing to shut the door. "I have nothing for you today."

The bird cocked its head to the side, which is when Serilda saw it. *Really* saw it. She went still.

It had seemed to be watching her before, but now—

With a ruffle of its feathers, the bird leaped from the branch. The tree branches swayed and released drifts of powdery snow as the bird soared off into the sky, growing smaller as it beat its heavy wings. Heading north, in the direction of the Aschen Wood.

Serilda would have thought nothing of it, except the creature had been missing its eyes. There had been nothing to watch her but empty sockets. And when it had taken to the air, bits of violet-gray sky had been visible through the threadbare holes in its wings.

"Nachtkrapp," she whispered, bracing herself against the door.

A night raven. Who could kill with one look of its empty eyes if it chose to. Who was said to devour the hearts of children.

She watched until the fiend was out of sight, and her gaze caught on the white moon beginning to rise in the distance. The Hunger Moon, rising when the world was at its most desolate, when humans and creatures alike began to wonder if they had stored away enough food to last them through the rest of the dreary winter.

Four weeks had passed.

Tonight, the hunt would ride again.

With a shaky breath, Serilda slammed the door shut.

The
Hunger
Moon

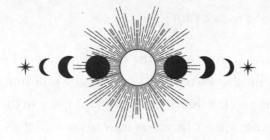

Chapter 7

She had been trying not to think of the night raven as dusk slid away to darkness, but the chilling visitor maintained a hold over her thoughts. Serilda shivered each time she pictured those empty sockets where glossy black eyes should have been. The missing patches of feathers on its wings when it had taken to the air. Like a dead thing. A forsaken thing.

It felt like a bad omen.

Despite her efforts to appear jolly as she prepared the evening bread for her and Papa, she could feel his suspicions frosting the air of their small cabin. He could surely tell that something was bothering her, but he hadn't asked. Probably he knew he wouldn't get an honest answer if he did.

Serilda considered telling him about the bird, but what was the point? He would only shake his head at her wild imagination again. Or worse—get that distant, shadowed look, like his worst nightmare had come to call.

Instead, their talk was empty as they each sipped at their parsnip stew flavored with marjoram and veal sausage. He told her that he had been given a job laying bricks on the new town hall that was being built in Mondbrück, a small city to the south, which would pay enough to last them until the spring. Work was always slow in the winter, when parts of the river froze over and the water flowed too slowly to create enough force for the waterwheel to power the millstones. Papa used the time to sharpen the stones and make any repairs to the equipment, but this late in the season, there was little to do until the snow thawed, and he was usually forced to find work elsewhere.

At least Zelig would appreciate the exercise, she said. Traveling to and from Mondbrück every day was sure to help keep the old horse agile for a little longer.

Then Serilda told him how excited little Gerdrut was over a wiggly milk tooth—her first. She'd already picked out a space in the garden where she would plant it, but was worried that the soil would be too hard in the winter and it wouldn't allow her new tooth to grow in nice and strong. Papa snickered and told Serilda that when she'd lost *her* first milk tooth, she'd refused to plant it in the garden, instead leaving it out on the front step alongside a plate of biscuits, in hopes that a tooth witch would come and steal both the tooth and Serilda away on a night of adventure.

"I must have been so disappointed when she didn't come."

Her father shrugged. "I wouldn't know. The next morning, you told me the wildest tale of your journeys with the witch. Took you all the way to the great palaces of Ottelien, if I remember right."

And on and on, each of them saying nothing at all, and her father's gaze becoming more speculative as he watched her over the rim of his bowl.

He had just opened his mouth, and Serilda was certain he was preparing to ask her what was the matter, when a knock sounded at the door.

Serilda jumped. Her stew would have sloshed over the sides of her bowl if she hadn't been nearly finished. She and her father both glanced at the closed door, then at each other, bewildered. Out here, in the dead of winter, when the world was quiet and still, one always heard when a visitor was approaching. But they had heard no footsteps, no galloping horses, no carriage wheels in the snow.

They both stood, but Serilda was quicker on her feet.

"Serilda—"

"I'll get it, Papa," she said. "You finish your meal."

She tipped up the bowl, slurping at the last dregs of stew, then dropped it onto her chair as she crossed the room.

She opened the door, and promptly drew in an icy breath.

The man was broad-shouldered and smartly dressed, and he had an iron chisel jutting from his left eye socket.

Serilda had barely registered the sight when a hand grabbed her shoulder, pulling her back. The door slammed shut. She was swung around to face her father, his eyes wild.

"That was—what—tell me that man wasn't a . . . a . . ." Papa had gone ghostly white. Whiter, actually, than the ghost on their doorstep, who had been rather dark-skinned.

"Father," Serilda whispered. "Calm yourself. We must see what he wants."

She started to pull away, but he held tight to her arms. "What he wants?" he hissed, as if the idea were ludicrous. "He is a dead man! Standing at our door! What if he is . . . is one of *his*?"

One of his. The Erlking's.

Serilda swallowed, knowing, without being able to explain how she knew, that the ghost was indeed a servant of the Erlking's. Or, a confidant of sorts, if not a servant. She knew little about the inner workings of the dark ones' court.

"We must be civil," she said firmly, proud when her voice sounded not only brave, but practical. "Even to the dead. Especially to the dead."

Prying away his fingers, she squared her shoulders and turned back to the door. When she opened it, the man had not moved and his expression was unchanged from its calm indifference. It was difficult not to stare at the chisel or the line of dark blood that soaked into his gray-streaked beard, but Serilda forced herself to meet his good eye, which did not catch the light of the fire as one would expect. She did not think he was an old man, despite the flecks of gray. Perhaps only a few years older than her father. Again she couldn't help but notice his clothing, which, though fine, was also a century or two outdated. A flat black cap ornamented with golden plumes perfectly coordinated with a velvet cape over an ivory jerkin. If he weren't dead, he might have been a nobleman—but what would a nobleman be doing with a woodcarver's tool lodged in his eye?

Serilda desperately wanted to ask.

Instead, she curtsied as well as she could. "Good evening, sir. How may we be of service?"

"The honor of your presence has been requested by His Grim, Erlkönig, the Alder King."

"No!" said her father, once again taking her arm, but this time Serilda refused to be pulled back into the house. "Serilda, the Erlking!"

She glanced at him, and watched his disbelief turn swiftly to understanding.

He knew.

He knew her story had been the truth.

Serilda puffed up her chest, vindicated. "Yes, Papa. I truly did meet the Erlking on New Year's night. But I cannot imagine . . ." She turned back to the ghost. "What can he possibly want with me now?"

"At the moment?" drawled the apparition. "Obedience." He stepped back, gesturing into the night, and Serilda saw that he had brought a carriage.

Or—a cage.

It was difficult to tell for sure, as the rounded transport appeared to be made of curved bars that were as pale as the surrounding snow.

Inside the bars, heavy black curtains shimmered with a touch of silver underneath the bulbous moon. She could not see what might be inside.

The carriage-cage was being drawn by two bahkauv. They were miserable-looking beasts, bull-like, with horns that twisted in corkscrews from their ears and massive hunched backs that forced their heads to hang awkwardly toward the ground. Their tails were long and serpentine, their mouths wrapped around ill-fitting teeth. They waited motionless for the coachman, for as there was no one atop the driver's seat, she thought this ghost must be the one who would be driving them.

Back to Gravenstone, the Erlking's castle.

"No," said her father. "You can't take her. Please. Serilda."

She turned again to face him, startled by the look of anguish that greeted her. For though everyone held suspicions and fears of the Erlking and his ghostly courtiers, she thought she saw something else hidden behind her father's eyes. Not just fear sparked by a hundred haunting tales, but . . . knowledge, accompanied by despair. A certainty of the terrible things that might await her if she went with this man.

"Perhaps it would be useful if I were to tell you," said the ghost, "that this summoning is not by mere request. Should you decline, there will be unfortunate consequences."

Serilda's pulse stirred and she grabbed her father's hands, squeezing them tight. "He's right, Father. One cannot say no to a summons from the Erlking. Not unless they wish to bring some catastrophe upon themselves . . . or their family."

"Or their entire town, or everyone they've ever loved . . . ," added the ghost in a bored tone. She expected him to yawn as a conclusion to the statement, but he managed to preserve his integrity with a sharp, warning glare instead.

"Serilda," said Papa, his voice lowered, though there was no hope of speaking in secrecy. "What did you say when you met him before? What could he possibly want now?"

She shook her head. "Exactly what I told you, Papa. Just a story." She shrugged, as nonchalantly as she could. "Perhaps he wants to hear another."

Her father's eyes clouded over with doubt, and yet . . . also a slim bit of hope. As though this seemed plausible.

She guessed that he had forgotten what sort of story she had told that night.

The Erlking believed that she could spin straw into gold.

But—surely, *that* wasn't what this was about. What would the Erlking want with spun gold?

"I have to go, Papa. We both know it." She nodded at the coachman. "I need a moment."

Shutting the door, she quickly set about the room, changing into her warmest stockings, her riding cloak, her boots.

"Will you prepare a pack of food?" she asked her father when he did not move from the door, but stood sullen, wringing his hands in distress. Her request was as much a means of pulling him from his stupor as it was an acknowledgment that she'd need food. At the moment, she was still full from their evening bread and with the sudden nerves overtaking her insides, she doubted she would have an appetite anytime soon.

When she was ready and could think of nothing else she might need, her father had a yellow apple, a slice of buttered rye, and a square of hard cheese wrapped in a handkerchief. She took it from him in exchange for a kiss on his cheek.

"I will be all right," she whispered, hoping that her expression conveyed more certainty than she actually felt.

From Papa's furrowed brow, she didn't think it mattered. She knew he would not sleep tonight, not until she was safely returned.

"Be careful, my girl," he said, pulling her into a tight embrace. "They say he is most charming, but never forget that such charm hides a cruel and wicked heart."

She laughed. "Papa, I assure you, the Erlking has no interest in charming me. Whatever he has summoned me for, it is not *that*."

He grunted, unwilling to agree, but said nothing more.

With one last squeeze of his hand, Serilda pulled open the door.

The ghost stood waiting beside the carriage. He watched her coolly as Serilda made her way along the garden's snowy path.

Only once she got close did she see that what had appeared as the bars of a cage were, in fact, the rib cage of some enormous beast. Her feet halted as she stared at the whitened bones, each one intricately carved with barbed vines and budding moonflowers and creatures great and small. Bats and mice and owls. Tatzelwurm and nachtkrapp.

The coachman cleared his throat impatiently, and Serilda yanked her hand away from where she had been tracing a nachtkrapp's bedraggled wing.

She accepted his hand, letting him assist her into the carriage. The ghost's fingers were solid enough, but they felt like touching . . . well, a dead man. His skin was brittle, as if his hand would crumble to dust if she squeezed too tight, and there was no warmth to his touch. He was not *ice*-cold like the Erlking had been—the difference, she supposed, between a creature from the underworld whose blood likely ran cold in his veins and a specter who had no blood left at all.

She tried to stifle a shudder as she pulled back the curtain and stepped into the carriage, then wrapped her cloak around her arms and tried to pretend it was only the winter air making her shiver.

Inside, a cushioned bench awaited her. The carriage was small and would hardly have fit a second passenger, but as she was alone, she found it quite cozy, and surprisingly warm as the heavy drapes blocked out the frigid night air. A small lantern was attached to the ceiling, crafted from the skull and jagged-toothed jaws of yet another creature. A candle made of dark green wax burned inside the skull, its warm flame not only making the space quite comfortable with its gentle heat, but also sending a golden light through the eye sockets, the nostrils, the spaces in between sharp, grinning teeth.

Serilda settled onto the bench, a little overwhelmed to be given traveling accommodations that were so eerily luxurious.

On a whim, she stretched up a finger and traced the lantern's jawbone. She whispered a quiet thank-you that it had given its life so she might ride in such comfort.

The jaws snapped shut.

Yelping, Serilda yanked her hand back.

A moment passed. The lantern opened its maw again. As if nothing had happened.

Outside, she heard the crack of a whip, and the carriage lurched into the night.

Chapter 8

Parting the heavy drapes, Serilda watched the passing landscape. Having only ever traveled to the neighboring towns of Mondbrück and Fleck, and once when she was a child to the city of Nordenburg, Serilda had little experience of the world beyond Märchenfeld, and a heart that yearned to see more. To know more. To capture every tiny detail and store it away in her memory for future musings.

They passed quickly over the rolling farmlands and then onto the road that ran parallel to the Sorge River. For a while, they were trapped between the winding black river to her right and the Aschen Wood, a dark threat to her left.

Until, finally, the carriage veered off the commonly traveled road onto a bumpier path heading straight into the forest.

Serilda braced herself as the tree cover loomed ahead of them, half expecting to feel a change in the air as they passed into the shadows of the boughs. A chill trickled down her spine. But she felt nothing out of the ordinary, except perhaps that the air grew a tinge warmer, with the trees offering shelter from the wind.

It was also much darker, and though she squinted for any glimpses afforded by the full moon, its light barely filtered through the tight-knit branches. Occasionally there were faint silver glimmers alighting on a gnarled tree trunk. Illuminating a pool of standing water. Catching the beat of wings as some nocturnal bird flitted between the boughs.

It was a wonder the bahkauv could find their way, or that the coachman knew where to go in such darkness. But their pace never slowed. The thud of their hooves was louder here, echoing back to her from the forest.

Travelers rarely ventured into the Aschen Wood unless they had no other choice, and with good reason. Mortals did not belong here.

For the first time, she began to feel afraid.

"Stop it, Serilda," she muttered, letting the curtain close. There wasn't much point in looking out at the scenery, anyhow, with the darkness growing thicker by the moment. She glanced at the skull lantern and imagined that it was watching her.

She smiled at it.

It did not smile back.

"You look hungry," she said, opening the pack her father had sent. "Just skin and bones ... without even the skin." She pulled out the cheese and broke it in half, then held one portion out to the lantern.

The nostrils flared, and she imagined she could hear a long, airy sniff. Before the teeth pulled back in disgust.

"Suit yourself." Leaning against the bench, she took a bite, reveling in the comfort of something as simple as salty, crumbly cheese. "With teeth like that, you're probably used to hunting for your food. I wonder what type of beast you were. Not a wolf. At least, not a normal one. A dire wolf perhaps, but no—even bigger." She pondered a long time, while the candle flame wavered unhelpfully. "I suppose I could ask the coachman, but he doesn't seem the chatty sort. You two must get along well."

She had just finished the hunk of cheese when she felt a change in the path under the carriage wheels. From the vibration and bounce of a rough, rarely traversed forest road to something smooth and straight.

Serilda peeled back the curtain again.

To her surprise, they had passed outside of the woods and were heading toward an enormous lake that shimmered with moonlight. It was surrounded by more forests to the east and, though she couldn't see them in the darkness, no doubt the foothills of the Rückgrat Mountains to the north. The western edge of the lake disappeared in a shroud of thick mist. Otherwise, the world glittered in white diamond snow.

Most surprising was that they were nearing a city. It was surrounded by a thick stone wall with a wrought-iron gate, with thatched roofs on the outer buildings, tall spires and clock towers farther in. Beyond the rows of houses and shops, barely visible on the edge of the lake, stood a castle.

The carriage turned, and the castle was no longer in Serilda's view as they drove through the massive entry gate. It had not been shut, which surprised her. For a town so close to the Aschen Wood, she would have thought for sure they would keep their gate locked at night, especially during a full moon. She watched the buildings pass by, their facades a patchwork of half-timbered framing and ornamental designs carved into gables and overhangs. The city seemed huge and dense compared with their little town of Märchenfeld, but she knew, logically, that it was probably still quite small compared with the larger trade cities to the south, or the port cities to the far west.

At first, she thought the city might be abandoned; but no, it felt too tidy, too well-maintained. Upon closer inspection, there were signs of life. Though she saw no one, and no window glowed with candlelight (not surprising, for they must be near the witching hour by now), there were neat, snow-dusted garden patches and the smell of recent chimney smoke. From the distance, she heard the unmistakable bleat of a goat and the answering yowl of a cat.

The people were simply asleep, she thought. As they should be. As *she* would have been, if she hadn't been summoned for this strange escapade.

Which brought her thoughts circling back to the more pressing mystery.

Where was she?

The Aschen Wood was the territory of the dark ones and the forest folk. She had always pictured Gravenstone Castle standing dark and ominous somewhere deep in the forest, a fortress of slim towers taller than the most ancient trees. No stories had ever mentioned a lake . . . or a city, for that matter.

As the carriage passed along the main thoroughfare of the town, the castle loomed back into view. It was a handsome building, stalwart and commanding, with a bevy of turrets and towers surrounding a large central keep.

It wasn't until the carriage turned away from the last row of houses and began crossing over a long, narrow bridge that Serilda realized the castle was not built at the edge of the town, but on an island out in the lake itself. The ink-black water reflected its moonlit stonework. The wheels of the carriage clattered loudly on the cobblestone bridge, and a chill enveloped Serilda as she craned her neck to see the imposing watchtowers flanking the barbican.

They passed over a wooden drawbridge, under the arched gateway, and into the courtyard. The mist hung cloyingly to the surrounding buildings, so that the castle was never revealed in its entirety, but shown only in glimpses before being shrouded once more. The carriage stopped and a figure darted out from a stable. A boy, perhaps a few years her junior, in a simple tunic and shaggy haircut.

A moment passed before the carriage door was opened, revealing the coachman. He stepped aside, gesturing for Serilda to follow. She bid farewell to the lantern, earning her a peculiar look from the ghostly driver, and stepped down onto the cobblestones, grateful when the coachman did not offer his hand again. The stable boy already had the huge beasts untethered and was ushering them back toward the stable.

Serilda wondered if the massive steeds she'd seen during the hunt were stabled there, as well, and what other creatures might be kept by the Erlking. She wanted to ask, but the coachman was already gliding toward the central keep. Serilda skipped after him, flashing a grateful smile at the stable boy as she passed.

He flinched away from the look, ducking his head, showing a mottle of bruises along the back of his neck that disappeared down the collar of his shirt.

Serilda's feet stumbled. Her heart squeezed. Were these bruises from his ghostly life here among the dark ones? Or were they from before? Possibly even the cause of his death? Otherwise, she couldn't see what might have killed him.

A startled cry drew Serilda's attention toward the other side of the courtyard.

Her eyes widened—first, to see an iron-barred kennel and the pack of burning hellhounds tied to a post at its center.

Second, to see the one hound that had broken loose. The one charging right at her. Eyes aflame. Searing lips pulled back against brazen fangs.

Serilda screamed and turned, sprinting back toward the open portcullis and lowered drawbridge. But she had no hope of outrunning the beast.

As she raced past the carriage, she changed course, hoisting herself up on a wheel and grabbing the bars of the rib cage and what might have been a piece of spine to scramble up onto the carriage roof. She had just pulled up her leg when she heard the snap and felt the surge of hot air blowing off the beast.

She scrambled around on her hands and knees. Below, the hound was pacing back and forth, its glowing eyes watching her, its nostrils flared with hunger. The chain that should have had it leashed to the post dragged loudly across the cobblestones.

Distantly, she heard shouts and orders. *Heel. Come. Leave it.*

Ignoring them all, the hound reared back on its hind legs, paws thrashing at the carriage door.

She shrank back. The creature was huge. If it tried to jump—

A loud *thwack* interrupted the thought.

The hound yelped and jerked, going stiff.

It took Serilda a gasping moment to notice the long arrow shaft fletched with shining black feathers. It had gone into one of the hound's eyes and out through the side of its jaw. Black smoke oozed from the wound, as the flames slowly dimmed behind its ragged fur.

The hound fell to the side, its legs twitching as it wheezed its last breaths.

Dizzy with the rush of blood, Serilda tore her gaze away. The Erlking stood on the steps of the castle's keep, dressed in the same fine leather, his black hair draped loosely across his shoulders. A massive crossbow hung at his side.

Ignoring Serilda, he turned his falcon's gaze on the woman who stood between the kennel and the carriage. She had the striking elegance of a dark one, but her clothing was utilitarian, her arms and legs covered in leather braces.

"What happened?" he asked, his tone suggesting a calm that Serilda didn't believe for a moment.

The woman dropped into a hasty bow. "I was preparing the hounds for the hunt, Your Grim. The kennel gate was open and I believe the chain had been cut. My back was turned. I didn't realize what was happening until the beast was free and . . ." Her gaze turned swiftly up to Serilda, still perched on top of the carriage, then down to the body of the hound. "I take full responsibility, my lord."

"Why?" drawled the Erlking. "Did you cut the chain?"

"Of course not, my lord. But they are in my care."

The king grunted. "Why didn't it respond to my commands?"

"That one was a pup, not yet fully trained. But no one gets fed until after the hunt, and so . . . it was hungry."

Serilda's eyes bugged as she looked again at the beast, whose body stretched out would have been nearly as long as she was tall. Its fires had been extinguished, leaving it a mound of black fur tight against its ribs, and teeth that looked strong enough to crush a human skull. She could see now that it *was* smaller than those she had seen during the hunt, but still. It was only a *pup*?

The thought was not comforting.

"Finish your work," said the king. "And clean up the body." He swung the crossbow up onto his back as he descended the steps, pausing before the woman, who Serilda guessed was the master of the hounds. "You are not responsible for this incident," he said to the top of her bowed head. "This could only have been the poltergeist."

His lip curled, just slightly, as if the word had a bitter taste.

"Thank you, Your Grim," murmured the woman. "I will ensure it does not happen again."

The Erlking crossed the courtyard and stood at the wheel of the carriage, peering up at Serilda. Knowing that it would be foolish to try to bow or curtsy while in such a predicament, Serilda merely smiled. "Are things always so exhilarating around here?"

"Not always," responded the Erlking in his measured tone. He moved closer, bringing the shadows along with him. Serilda's instincts told her to cower, despite how she towered above him on the carriage roof. "The hounds are rarely treated to the flesh of humans. One can understand why it was so easily excited."

Her eyebrows shot upward. She wanted to think it was a joke, but she wasn't convinced the dark ones knew what a joke was.

"Your Ma—Your Grim," she said, with only a bit of a waver. "What a great honor it is to be once again in your presence. I hardly could have expected to be summoned to Gravenstone Castle by the Alder King himself."

The corner of his luscious mouth twitched. In the moonlight, his lips were purple, like a fresh bruise or a squashed blackberry. Strangely, Serilda's mouth watered at the thought.

"So you do know who I am," he said almost mockingly. "I had wondered." His gaze skittered quickly around the courtyard. The stables, the kennels, the ominous walls. "You are mistaken. This is not Gravenstone Castle. My home is haunted with memories I have no wish to relive, so I spend little time there. Instead, I have claimed Adalheid as my home and sanctuary." He was smiling at some unknown pleasure when he met Serilda's gaze again. "The royal family was not using it."

Adalheid. The name seemed familiar, but Serilda could not place where, exactly, it was.

Just as she wasn't sure what royal family he was talking about. Märchenfeld and the Aschen Wood were situated in the northernmost region of the Kingdom of Tulvask, currently under the rule of Queen Agnette II and the House of Rosenstadt. But as Serilda understood, it was a relationship based on arbitrary lines drawn on a map, a few taxes, the occasional trade road built or maintained, and the promise of military aid if required—which it never was, given that they were well-protected by the towering basalt cliffs that dropped off into a treacherous sea on one side, and the foreboding Rückgrat Mountains on the other. The capital city of Verene was so far to the south that she didn't know a single person who had ever actually been there, nor could she recall a member of the royal family ever having come to their corner of the realm. People talked about the royal family and their laws like someone else's problem—nothing that held direct consequence for them. Some people in town even thought that the government was content to leave them alone for fear of annoying the true rulers of the north.

The Erlking and his dark ones, who answered to no one when they stormed out from behind the veil.

And Shrub Grandmother and the forest folk, who would never succumb to the rule of humans.

"I suspect," said Serilda, "that few would argue with your laying claim to such a castle. Or . . . anything at all that you wanted."

"Indeed," said the Erlking, as he gestured at the coachman's bench. "You may come down now."

She glanced toward the kennel. The rest of the hounds were watching her eagerly, straining against their chains. But the chains did seem to be holding them, and the kennel door seemed securely latched.

She also noticed for the first time that they had gained an audience. More ghosts, with those wispy edges, as if they might fade away to nothing as soon as they passed out of the moonlight.

The dark ones frightened her more. Unlike the ghosts, they were as solid as she was. Almost elflike in appearance, with skin that shimmered in tones of silver and bronze and gold. Everything about them was sharp. Their cheekbones, the jut of their shoulders, their fingernails. They were the king's original court, had been at his side since the beforetimes, when they had first escaped from Verloren. They watched her now with keen, malicious eyes.

There were creatures, too. Some the size of cats, with black-taloned fingers and small pointed horns. Others the size of Serilda's hand, with batlike wings and sapphire-blue skin. Some might have been human, if it weren't for the scales on their skin or the mop of dripping seaweed that clung to their scalps. Goblins, kobolds, fairies, nixes. She could not begin to guess at them all.

The king cleared his throat. "By all means, take your time. I am quite fond of being looked down upon by human children."

She frowned. "I'm eighteen."

"Precisely so."

She made a face, which he ignored.

Serilda climbed down onto the bench as gracefully as she could, accepting the king's hand as she descended to the ground. She tried to focus more on keeping her trembling legs strong beneath her than the feeling of cold dread that slithered up her arm at his touch.

"Ready the hunt!" the king bellowed as he led her toward the keep. "The mortal and I have business to attend to. I want the hounds and steeds ready as soon as we are finished."

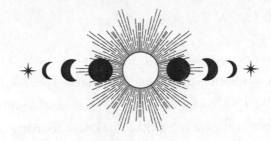

Chapter 9

The entrance to the keep was flanked by two enormous bronze statues of hunting hounds—so lifelike Serilda shied away as she passed them. Ducking into the keep's shadow, she had to jog to catch up with the king's long strides. She wanted to pause and marvel at everything—the enormous and ancient wooden doors with their black metal hinges and raw chiseled bolts. The chandeliers crafted of iron and antlers and bone. Stone pillars carved with intricate designs of brambles and rosebuds.

They had entered into an entry hall, with two wide staircases curving upward and a set of doors leading into opposing corridors to Serilda's left and right, but the king led them straight ahead. Through an arched doorway, into what must be the great hall, lit with candlelight at every turn. Sconces on the walls, tall candelabras in the corners, while more chandeliers, some as big as the carriage she'd ridden in, hung from the raftered ceiling. Thick carpets and animal pelts covered the floors. Tapestries decorated the walls, but they did little to add vibrancy to a space that was as eerie as it was majestic.

The decor was all reminiscent of a hunting lodge, with an impressive collection of taxidermied beasts. Disembodied heads on the walls and whole stuffed bodies ready to pounce from the corners. From a small basilisk to an enormous boar, a wingless dragon to a gem-eyed serpent.

There were beasts with crooked horns, mighty shells, and too many heads. Serilda was both horrified and fascinated. They were nightmares come to life. Well—not life. Clearly these were dead. But to think they might have been real gave her a thrill, to know so many of the stories she'd crafted over the years had some basis in reality.

At the same time, seeing such glorious creatures, lifeless and used as impressive props, made her feel a little sick to her stomach.

Even the fire crackling in the central hearth, inside a fireplace so tall that Serilda could have stood up inside without touching the flue, did little to chase away the chill that permeated the air. She was tempted to go and stand by that fire, if only for a moment—her instincts craving its homey warmth—until her eye caught on the massive creature mounted above the mantel.

She froze, unable to look away.

It was serpentine, with two crests of small pointed thorns curving across its brow, and needlelike teeth set into rows along its protruding mouth. Slitted green eyes were ringed with what appeared to be gray pearls embedded in its skin, and a single red stone sparkled in the center of its brow, a cross between a pretty bauble and a watchful third eye. An arrow with black fletching still protruded from beneath one of its bat-like wings, so small it seemed impossible that it could have been a killing strike. In fact, the beast hardly looked dead at all. The way it had been preserved and mounted, it looked ready to jump off the fireplace and snatch Serilda up in its jaws. As she drew closer, she wondered if she was only imagining the warm breath, the throaty purr, leaking out from the creature's mouth.

"Is that a . . . ?" she started, but words failed her. "What *is* that?"

"A rubinrot wyvern," came the answer from behind her. She jumped and spun around. She hadn't realized the coachman had followed them. He stood serenely a few feet away, his hands clasped behind his back, seemingly unbothered by the blood that was even now dripping from his impaled eye socket. "Very rare. His Grim traveled to Lysreich to hunt it."

"Lysreich?" said Serilda, stunned. She pictured the map on the wall of the schoolhouse. Lysreich was across the sea, far to the west. "Does he often travel far to . . . hunt?"

"When there is a worthy prize," came the vague answer. He glanced toward the door where the king had gone. "I suggest you keep up. His mild temper can be deceiving."

"Right. Sorry." Serilda hurried after the king. The next room might have been a parlor or game room, the massive fireplace that it shared with the great hall casting orange light across an assortment of richly upholstered chairs and lounges. But the king was not there.

She moved ahead. Through another door—into a dining hall. And there was the king, standing at the head of the ridiculous table, his arms crossed and a glower in his cool eyes.

"My goodness," said Serilda, estimating that the table could likely seat a hundred guests along its never-ending length. "How old was the tree that gave its life to make that?"

"Not as old as I am, I assure you." The king sounded displeased, and Serilda felt chastised and, briefly, afraid. Not that she hadn't felt a little concerned from the moment a ghost appeared on her doorstep, but there was a thinly veiled warning in the king's voice that made her stand taller. She was forced to acknowledge a fact she'd been trying hard to ignore all night.

The Erlking did not have a reputation for kindness.

"Come closer," he said.

Trying to hide her nervousness, Serilda paced toward him. She glanced at the walls as she passed, which were hung with bright-colored tapestries. They continued the theme of the hunt, depicting images of hellhounds snarling around a frightened unicorn or a storm of hunters surging upon a winged lion.

As she walked, the images grew in brutality. Death. Blood. Anguished pain on the faces of the prey—in stark contrast to the glee in the eyes of the hunters.

Serilda shuddered and faced the king.

He was watching her closely, though she could read no emotion from him. "I trust you understand why I sent for you."

Her heart skipped. "I imagine it's because you found me so very charming."

"Do humans find you charming?"

He spoke with honest curiosity, but Serilda couldn't help feeling like it was an insult. "Some do. Children, mostly."

"Children have odious taste."

Serilda bit the inside of her cheek. "In some things, perhaps. But I've always appreciated their utter lack of bias."

The king stepped forward and, without warning, reached up to grasp her chin. He tilted her face upward. Her breath caught, staring into eyes the color of a clouded sky before a blizzard, with lashes as thick as pine needles. But while she might have been temporarily dazzled by his unnatural beauty, he was appraising her without any warmth in his expression. Only calculations, and the slightest shade of curiosity.

He studied her long enough for her breaths to quicken in discomfort and a cold sweat to prickle at the back of her neck. His attention lingered on her eyes, intrigued, if hardly entranced. Most people tried to study her face in secretive glances, as much curious as horrified, but the king stared openly.

Not disgusted, exactly, but . . .

Well. She couldn't tell *what* he felt.

Finally, he released her and nodded toward the dining table. "My court often dines here after a long hunt," he said. "I think of the dining hall as a sacred space, where bread is broken, wine is savored, toasts are made. It is for celebration and sustenance." He paused, sweeping a hand toward the tapestries. "As such, it is one of my preferred rooms in which to display our greatest victories. Each is a treasure. A reminder that though the weeks are long, there is always a full moon to prepare for. Soon, we will ride again. I like to think that it keeps up morale."

He turned his back on Serilda and moved toward a long buffet against the wall. Pewter goblets were stacked on one end, plates and bowls on the other, ready for the next meal. On the wall, a plaque held a taxidermy bird, with long legs and a narrow beak. It reminded Serilda of a water crane or heron, except that its wings, spread wide as if preparing to take flight, were cast in shades of luminescent yellow and orange, each feather tipped with cobalt blue. At first, Serilda thought it might be a trick of the candlelight, but the more she stared, the more she became convinced that the feathers were glowing.

"This is a hercinia," said the king. "They live in the westernmost part of the Aschen Wood. It is one of the many forest creatures that is said to be under the protection of Pusch-Grohla and her maidens."

Serilda stilled at the mention of the moss maidens and their Shrub Grandmother.

"I'm rather fond of this acquisition. Quite pretty, don't you agree?"

"Lovely," said Serilda around a heavy tongue.

"And yet, you see how it does not quite fit this wall." He stepped back, eyeing the space with displeasure. "For some time now I have been waiting to find something just right to act as an ornament on either side of the bird. Imagine my delight when last full moon, my hounds picked up the scent of not one, but *two* moss maidens. Can you picture it? Their pretty faces, those foxlike ears, the crown of greenery. Here and here." He gestured to the left and right of the bird's wings. "Forever watching us feast upon the animals they strive so very hard to protect." He glanced at Serilda. "I rather enjoy a bit of irony."

Her stomach was roiling, and it was all she could do not to show how such an idea disgusted her. The moss maidens were not animals. They were not beasts to be hunted, to be murdered. They were not *decor*.

"Part of the brilliance of irony, I feel," continued the king, "is that it so often makes fools of others, without them being any the wiser." His tone sharpened. "I have had much time to think on our last meeting, and what a fool you must think I am."

Serilda's eyes widened. "No. Never."

"You were so very convincing, with your tale of gold, of having been god-blessed. It was only when the moon had set that I thought— why would a human girl, who can succumb so easily to the frost, be gathering straw in the snow without so much as a pair of gloves with which to protect her fragile hands?" He took Serilda's hands into his and her heart leaped into her throat. His voice froze over. "I don't know what magic you wove that night, but I am not one to forgive mockery." His grip tightened. She bit back a frightened whimper. One elegant eyebrow lifted, and she could tell the Erlking took some enjoyment in this. Watching her squirm. His prey, cornered. For a moment it looked like he might even smile. But it was not a smile, rather something cruel and victorious that curled back his lips. "But I believe in fair chances. And so—a test. You have until one hour before sunrise to complete it."

"A test?" she whispered. "What sort of test?"

"Nothing you aren't perfectly capable of," he said. "That is . . . unless you were lying."

Her stomach dropped.

"And if you were lying," he continued, bending his head toward her, "then you also kept me from my prey that night, an offense that I find unforgivable. If such is the case, it will be *your* head that takes a place on my wall. Manfred"—he glanced at the coachman—"did she have family?"

"A father, I presume," he answered.

"Good. I will take his head, too. I appreciate symmetry."

"Wait," cried Serilda. "My lord—please, I—"

"For your sake and his," interrupted the Erlking, "I do hope you were telling the truth." He lifted her hand and kissed the inside of her wrist. The iciness of his touch seared her skin. "If you'll excuse me, I must see to the hunt." He glanced at the coachman. "Take her to the dungeons."

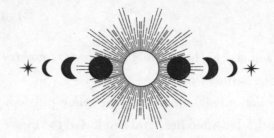

Chapter 10

Serilda had barely grasped the meaning of the king's words before the coachman had taken hold of her elbow and was dragging her from the dining hall.

"Wait! The dungeons?" she cried. "He can't mean that!"

"Can't he? His Darkness does not favor mercy," said the ghost, his grip never loosening. He dragged her down a narrow corridor, then paused at a doorway to a steep staircase. He peered at her. "Will you walk on your own, or must I drag you the entire way? I warn you, these stairs can be treacherous."

Serilda sagged, staring down the stairwell that spiraled fast from view. Her mind was spinning from everything the Erlking had said. Her head. Her father's. A test. The dungeons.

She swayed, and might have fallen if the ghost's grip hadn't tightened on her arm.

"I can walk," she whispered.

"Very convincing," said the coachman, though he did release her. Taking a torch from a bracket beside the door, he headed into the stairwell.

Serilda hesitated, glancing back down the corridor. She felt confident she could retrace her steps back through the keep, and there was no one else in sight. Was there any hope of escaping?

"Do not forget who this castle belongs to," said the ghost. "If you run, he will only further relish the chase."

Swallowing hard, Serilda turned back. Dread settled like a stone in her stomach, but when the ghost started down the steps, she followed. She kept one hand on the wall for balance on the steep, narrow stairs, feeling dizzy as they descended.

Down some more.

And down again.

They must be underground now, somewhere amid the ancient foundations of the castle. Perhaps even beneath the surface of the lake.

They reached the bottom level and tromped through an open set of barred gates. Serilda shuddered to see a row of heavy wooden doors lining the wall to her right, each one reinforced with iron.

Cell doors. Serilda craned her neck to peer through the slitted windows, catching glimpses of manacles and chains hung from the ceiling, though she could not see enough to know whether any prisoners were dangling from them. She tried not to wonder if that would be her fate. She heard no moans, no crying, not the sounds she would expect to hear from tortured and starving prisoners. Perhaps these cells were empty. Or perhaps the prisoners were long dead. The only "prisoners" she'd ever heard of the Erlking taking were the children he'd once gifted to Perchta, though they wouldn't have been kept in the dungeons. Oh, and the lost souls that followed the hunt on its chaotic rides, though they were more often left for dead by the roadside, not spirited away to his castle.

Never had she heard rumors of the Erlking keeping humans locked up in a dungeon.

But then, perhaps there were no rumors because no one ever lived to tell them.

"Stop it," she whispered harshly to herself.

The coachman glanced back at her.

"Sorry," she muttered. "Not you."

A small critter caught her eye then, darting along the corridor wall before scurrying into a small hole in the mortar. A rat.

Lovely.

Then—something strange. A new scent collecting around her. Something sweet and familiar and entirely unexpected in the musty air.

"Here." The ghost paused and gestured to a cell door that had been left open.

Serilda hesitated. This was it, then. She was to be a prisoner of the Erlking, locked in a dank, horrible cell. Left to starve and rot away into nothing. Or at least, trapped until morning, when she would have her head lopped off and hung up in the dining hall. She wondered if she would become a ghost herself, haunting these cold, dim corridors. Perhaps that was what the king wanted. Another servant for his dead retinue.

She looked at the phantom with the chisel in his eye. Could she fight him? Push him into the cell and lock the door, then hide somewhere until she found a chance to escape?

Returning her look, the ghost slowly smiled. "I'm already dead."

"I wasn't thinking about killing you."

"You are a terrible liar."

She wrinkled her nose.

"Go on. You're wasting time."

"You're all so impatient," she grumbled, ducking past him. "Don't you have an eternity ahead of you?"

"Yes," he said. "And you have until one hour to dawn."

Serilda stepped through the cell door, bracing herself for the inevitable slam and locking of the grate. She'd pictured bloodstains on the walls and shackles on the ceiling and rats darting into the corners.

Instead, she saw . . . straw.

Not a tidy bale of it, but a messy pile, a full cartload's worth. It was the source of the sweet aroma she'd noticed before, carrying the faint familiarity of harvest work in the fall, when all the town pitched in.

In the back corner of the cell there stood a spinning wheel, surrounded by piles of empty wooden bobbins.

It made sense, and yet—it didn't.

The Erlking had brought her here to spin straw into gold, because once again her tongue had created a ridiculous story, meant to do nothing more than entertain. Well, in this case, to distract.

He was just giving her a chance to prove herself.

A chance.

A chance she would fail at.

Hopelessness had just begun to needle at her when the cell door slammed shut. She spun around, jumping as the lock thundered into place.

Through the grated window, the ghost peered at her with his good eye. "If it matters at all to you," he said thoughtfully, "I actually hope you succeed."

Then he yanked shut the wooden sash over the grate, cutting her off from everything.

Serilda stared at the door, listening to the retreat of his footsteps, dizzy with how quickly and completely her life had crumbled.

She had told her father it would be all right.

Kissed him goodbye, like it was nothing.

"I should have held him longer," she whispered to the solitude.

Turning, she surveyed the cell. Her sleeping cot at home might have fit inside, twice side by side, and she could easily have touched the ceiling without standing on tiptoes. It was all made more cramped by the spinning wheel and bobbins stacked against the far wall.

A single pewter candlestick had been left in the corner near the door, far enough from the straw that it wouldn't pose a hazard. Far enough to make the spinning wheel's shadow dance monstrously against the stone wall, which still showed chisel marks from when this cell had been cut into the island's rock. Serilda thought of the wastefulness—an entire candle left to burn only for her, so she might complete this absurd task. Candles were a valuable commodity, to be hoarded and preserved, to be used only when absolutely necessary.

Her stomach gurgled, and only then did she realize she'd forgotten the apple her father had packed inside the carriage.

At that thought, a stunted, panicky laugh fell from her lips. She was going to die here.

She studied the straw, toeing a few pieces that had drifted from the pile. It was clean straw. Sweet-smelling and dry. She wondered if the Erlking had ordered it harvested earlier that night, under the Hunger Moon, because she'd told him that gathering straw touched by the full moon made it better for her work. It seemed unlikely. Any straw gathered recently would still be wet from the snow.

Because, of course, the king did not believe her lies, and he was right. What he asked for could not be done. Or, at least, not by her. She had heard tales of magical ones who could do marvelous things. Of people who really had been blessed by Hulda. Who could spin not only gold, but also silver and silk and strands of perfect white pearls.

But the only blessing she carried was from the god of lies, and now her cursed tongue had ruined her.

How foolish she'd been to think for a moment that she had tricked the Erlking and gotten away with it. Of course he would realize that a simple village maiden could not possess such a gift. If she could spin straw into gold, her father would hardly still be toiling away at the gristmill. The schoolhouse would not need new thatching, and the fountain that stood crumbling in the middle of Märchenfeld's square would have been repaired ages ago. If she could spin straw into gold, she would have ensured by now that her whole village prospered.

But she did not have such magic. And the king knew it.

A hand went to her throat as she worried over how he would do it—with a sword? An ax?—when her fingers brushed the slender chain of the necklace. She pulled it from beneath her dress collar and opened the locket, turning it so she could see the face of the girl inside. The child peered out at Serilda with her teasing eyes, as if there were a secret near to bursting inside of her.

"There's no hurt in trying, is there?" she whispered.

The king had given her until one hour to sunrise. It was already after midnight. Here in the bowels of the castle, the only way to track the passing of time was by the candle burning in the corner. The persistent melting of wax.

Too slow.

Far too fast.

No matter. She was hardly one to sit still for hours, suffocating in her own self-pity.

"If Hulda can do it, why can't I?" she said, grabbing a handful of straw from the pile. She approached the spinning wheel as if she were approaching a sleeping wyvern. Unclasping her traveling cloak, she folded it neatly and settled it in the corner. Then she hooked one ankle around the leg of the stool that had been provided and sat down.

The strands of straw were tough, the ends scratchy against her fore-arms. She stared at them and tried to picture tufts of wool like those Mother Weber had sold her countless times.

The straw was nothing like the thick, fuzzy wool she was used to, but she inhaled a deep breath anyway and loaded the first empty bob-bin onto the flyer. She spent a long time looking from the bobbin to the fistful of straw. Usually she started with a leader yarn, to make it easier for the wool to wrap around the bobbin, but she had no yarn. Shrug-ging, she tied on a piece of straw. The first one broke, but the second held. Now what? She couldn't just twist the ends together to form one long strand.

Could she?

She twisted and twisted.

It held . . . sort of.

"Good enough," she muttered, running the leader yarn through the hooks, then out through the maiden hole. The entire setup was beyond precarious, ready to fall apart as soon as she pulled too tight or released those weakly connected strands.

Afraid to let go, she leaned over and used her nose to push down on one of the wheel's spokes, so that it gradually started to turn. "Here we go," she said, pressing her foot onto the treadle.

The straw pulled from her fingers.

The tenuous connections disintegrated.

Serilda paused. Growled to herself.

Then she tried again.

This time, she started the wheel sooner.

No luck.

Next, she tried knotting a few ends of straw together.

"Please work," she whispered as her foot started to pedal. The wheel turned. The straw wound around the bobbin. "Gold. Please. Please turn into gold."

But the plain, dry straw continued to be plain, dry straw, no matter how many times it slipped through the maiden hole or wound around the bobbin.

Before long, she had run out of knotted strands, and what had been successfully looped around the bobbin started to splinter as soon as she took it off the flyer.

"No, no, no . . ."

She grabbed a fresh bobbin and started over.

Pushing, forcing the straw through.

Her foot mashing against the treadle.

"Please," she said again, pushing another strand in. Then another.

"Please." Her voice broke, and the tears started. Tears she'd hardly known were waiting to be released until they all flooded forward at once. She hunched forward, clutching the useless straw in her fists, and sobbed. That one word stuck on her tongue, whispered to no one but the cell walls and the locked door and this awful castle full of awful ghosts and demons and monsters. "*Please.*"

"What are you doing to that poor spinning wheel?"

Serilda screamed and tumbled off the stool. She landed on the ground with a bewildered grunt, one shoulder smacking the stone wall. She looked up, pushing away the strands of hair that had fallen into her face and stuck to her damp cheek.

There was a figure sitting on top of the pile of straw, cross-legged, peering at her with mild curiosity.

A man.

Or . . . a boy. A boy about her age, she guessed, with copper hair that hung in wild tangles to his shoulders and a face that was covered in both freckles and dirt. He wore a simple linen shirt, slightly old-fashioned with its generous sleeves, which he'd left untucked over emerald-green hose. No shoes, no tunic, no overcoat, no hat. He might have been getting ready for bed, except he looked wide-awake.

She looked past him to the door, still shut tight.

"H-how did you get in here?" she stammered, pushing herself upright.

The boy cocked his head and said, as if it were the most natural thing in the world, "Magic."

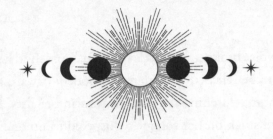

Chapter 11

he blinked.

He blinked back, then added, "I am *extremely* powerful."

Serilda's brow furrowed, unable to tell if he meant it. "Is that so?"

In response, the boy grinned. It was the sort of look that was meant to hide secrets—lopsided and laughing, with flecks of gold sparking in his eyes. Standing, he brushed away the bits of straw that clung to his hose and glanced around, taking in the spinning wheel, the cramped room, the barred window in the door. "Not the most pleasant of accommodations. Lighting could be improved. That stench, too. Is this meant to be a bed?" He toed at the pile of straw.

"We're in a dungeon," Serilda said helpfully.

The boy cast her a wry look. *Obviously* they were in a dungeon.

Serilda flushed. "In Adalheid Castle, to be precise."

"Never been summoned to a dungeon before. Wouldn't have been my first choice."

"Summoned?"

"Must have been. You are a witch, aren't you?"

She gawked at him, wondering if she should be offended. Unlike all the times she'd called Madam Sauer a witch, this boy did not cast around the word like an insult. "No, I'm not a witch. And I didn't summon you. I was just sitting here, crying, contemplating my own demise, thank you muchly."

His eyebrows rose. "Sounds like something a witch would say."

With a snort, Serilda rubbed a palm into her eye. It had been a long night, full of novelty and surprise, terror and uncertainty, and now a most unwelcome threat against her life. Her brain was foggy with exhaustion.

"I don't know. Perhaps I did summon you," she conceded. "Wouldn't be the strangest thing that's happened tonight. But if I did, you have my apologies. I didn't mean to."

He crouched down so that they were eye level with each other and studied her, his expression dark with suspicion. But a moment later, the shadow vanished. His face split into that wide, teasing grin again. "Are all mortals as gullible as you are?"

She frowned. "Pardon?"

"I was only joking. You didn't summon me. Did you really think you might have?" He clicked his tongue. "You did. I can tell. That suggests a fair bit of egotism, don't you think?"

Her mouth worked, but she was flustered by the swift changes in his mood. "You're toying with me," she finally stammered, launching to her feet. "I have only hours left to live, and you've come here to mock me."

"Ah, don't look at me like that," he said, peering up at her. "It was only a bit of fun. You seemed like you could use a laugh."

"Am I laughing?" Serilda asked, suddenly angry, perhaps even a little embarrassed.

"No," admitted the boy. "But I think you would be. If you weren't locked inside a dungeon and, as you say, probably going to die in the morning." He trailed his hand through the straw. Picking up one strand, he stood and appraised Serilda. Really looked at her this time. She could see him taking in her plain dress, her muddied boots, the twin braids of dark brown hair that hung to her waist. She knew she must be a wreck from crying, with a red nose and blotchy cheeks, just as she knew it was not these things but the golden wheels in her eyes that garnered that flash of curiosity.

In the past, when Serilda would meet an unfamiliar boy in the village or the market, she would shy away from his roving attention. Turn her head, lower her lashes, so that her gaze could not be seen. Try to stretch out those brief moments when a boy might look at her and wonder if she had a suitor, or if her heart was free to be captured . . . before they saw the truth of her face and flinched away, dismissing that momentary interest as quickly as it had come.

But Serilda cared nothing for this boy or whatever he might think of her. For him to treat her desperation like a game made him almost as cruel as the king who had locked her in here. She swiped her sleeve across her nose, sniffling, then straightened beneath his scrutiny.

"I'm beginning to reconsider," he said. "Maybe you really are a witch."

She lifted an eyebrow. "Let's find out. Shall I turn you into a toad or a cat?"

"Oh—a toad, most definitely," he said, not missing a beat. "Cats don't get much notice. But a toad? Could cause all sorts of trouble at the next feast." He cocked his head to one side. "But no. You're not a witch."

"Met many witches, have you?"

"Just can't imagine a witch ever looking as pitiful and helpless as you did just now."

"I'm not pitiful," she said through her teeth. "Or helpless. Who are you, anyway? If I didn't summon you, then why are you here?"

"I make it my business to know everything of note that happens in this castle. Congratulations. I've deemed you noteworthy." He flourished the piece of straw toward her, as if he was bestowing her with a knighthood.

"I'm flattered," she deadpanned.

The boy laughed and lifted his hands in what might have been a show of peace. "All right. You're neither pitiful nor helpless. I must have misunderstood all the weeping and moaning and so on and so forth.

Forgive me." His tone was far too light for it to sound like a *real* apology, but Serilda felt her anger beginning to cool nevertheless. The boy turned around, examining the room. "So. The Erlking brought a mortal to the castle and locked her up. A bunch of straw, a spinning wheel. Easy enough to guess what he wants."

"Indeed. He wants some straw baskets for storing all the yarn that's going to be spun on this wheel. I think he means to take up knitting."

"He does need a hobby," said the boy. "One can only go around kidnapping people and butchering magical creatures for so many centuries before it gets tiresome."

She didn't want to, but she couldn't help the way her mouth twitched into an almost-smile.

The boy caught it and his grin widened further. She noticed that one of his canine teeth was a bit sharper than the other. "He wants you to spin this straw into gold."

She sighed, the momentary humor evaporating. "He does."

"Why does he believe you can do it?"

Serilda hesitated, before answering, "Because I told him that I could."

Surprise flashed across his face—genuine, this time. "Can you?"

"No. It was a story I made up to . . . it's complicated."

"You lied to Erlkönig?"

She nodded.

"Direct to his face?"

She nodded again, and was rewarded with something more than mere curiosity. For a moment, the boy looked impressed.

"Except," Serilda hastened to add, "he doesn't really believe me. He might have at the time, but not anymore. This is a test. And when I fail, he will have me killed."

"Yes, I heard about that. Might have been eavesdropping upstairs. To be honest, I thought I'd come down here and find you wallowing in self-misery. Which you were, clearly."

"I wasn't wallowing!"

"I have my opinion, you have yours. What I find more interesting is how you were also . . . *trying*." He gestured to the spinning wheel, and the bobbin wrapped with broken and knotted bits of straw. "I didn't expect that. At least, not from a girl who is decidedly *un*witchy."

Serilda rolled her eyes. "Not that it did me any good. I'm not a gold-spinner. I can't do this." A thought occurred to her then. "But . . . *you* have magic. You got in here, somehow. Can you get me out of here?"

It was only a temporary solution, she knew. The Erlking would come for her again, and next time, she knew he would follow through on his threats. He might not just come for her, but for her father, perhaps for the entire village of Märchenfeld.

Could she risk that?

From the boy's crossed arms and shaking head, though, it seemed that she wouldn't need to make the choice. "I said I'm extremely powerful, not a miracle worker. I can go anywhere in the castle, but I can't pull *you* through a solid door, and I have no key with which to unlock it."

Her shoulders sank.

"Don't look so discouraged," said the boy. "You aren't dead yet. That's a distinct advantage over just about everyone else in this castle."

"I find that only mildly comforting."

"I live to serve."

"I doubt that."

His eyes danced briefly, but then became unexpectedly serious. He appeared to be considering something for a long moment, before his gaze turned intense, almost cunning.

"All right," he said slowly, as if he'd only just made up his mind about something. "You win. I've decided to help you."

Serilda's heart lifted, filling fast with untethered hope.

"In exchange," he continued, "for *this*."

He pointed a finger at her. His sleeve slipped back toward his elbow, revealing a ghastly knot of scar tissue above his wrist.

Serilda gaped at his extended arm, momentarily speechless.

He was pointing at her heart.

She stepped back and placed a protective hand to her chest, where she could feel her heartbeat thudding underneath. Her gaze lingered on his hand, as if he might reach into her chest and tear out the beating organ at any moment. He didn't exactly look like one of the dark ones, with their majestic figures and flawless beauty, but he didn't look half-faded like a ghost, either. He seemed harmless enough, but she couldn't trust that. She couldn't trust anyone in this castle.

The boy frowned, confused at her reaction. Then understanding hit him and he dropped his hand with a roll of his eyes. "Not your *heart*," he said, exasperated. "That locket."

Oh. That.

Her hand shifted to the chain around her neck. She gripped the locket, still hanging open, in her fist. "It will hardly suit you."

"Strongly disagree. Besides, there's something familiar about her," said the boy.

"Who?"

"The girl in the—!" He paused, his expression darkening. "It would appear that you're trying to be aggravating, but that is *my* talent, I'll have you know."

"I just don't understand why you would want it. It's a painting of a child, not some great beauty."

"I can see that. Who is she? Do you know her?"

Serilda looked down, tilting the portrait toward the candlelight. "You're the one who just claimed to know her."

"I didn't say I *know* her. Just that there's something familiar. Something . . . " He seemed to be struggling to find the right words, but all that came out was a disgruntled growl. "You wouldn't understand."

"That's what people say when they can't be bothered to explain."

"It's also what people say when someone else truly won't understand."

She shrugged. "Fine. The girl is a princess. Obviously." The words were out before she had thought to say them. In the next moment she considered taking them back, confessing that she had no idea who the girl was. But what did it matter? Maybe she *was* a princess. She certainly looked like she could be. "But one with a very tragic story, I'm afraid."

With that mysterious statement hanging between them, she snapped the locket shut.

"Well then, it must not be a family heirloom," he said.

She bristled. "I could have distant royalty in my blood."

"That's about as likely as me being the son of a duke, don't you think?" He swept an arm down his plain clothes, practically undergarments, to prove his point. "And if it isn't a family heirloom, then it must not be all that precious. Surely not as precious as your life. This is a bargain I'm offering you. My help for an apple and an egg."

"A bit pricier than that," she muttered. But her heart was sinking. She knew he had already won the argument.

He must have known, too, as a smug smile crossed his mouth. He rocked back on his heels. "What'll it be? Do you want my help or not?"

She looked down at the locket, lightly tracing the golden clasp with the pad of her finger. It was almost heartbreaking to part with it, but she knew that was silly. This boy seemed convinced that he could help her. She didn't know what he could do, but clearly he had some bit of magic, and besides—she didn't exactly have a lot of options. His appearance was miraculous enough for one night.

Scowling, she lifted the chain from around her throat. She held it out to him, hoping he wasn't about to laugh at her gullibility, *again*. He could easily grab the offering, cackle, and disappear as fast as he'd come.

But he did not.

In fact, he took the chain with the utmost care, a hint of deference on his face. And in that moment, it was as if the air around them pulsed. Pressing in against Serilda, muffling her ears, squeezing her chest.

Magic.

Then the moment passed, the magic evaporating.

Serilda inhaled deeply, as if it were the first real breath she'd taken all night.

The boy slipped the necklace over his head and jutted his chin toward her. "Move."

Serilda tensed, startled by his abruptness. "I beg your pardon?"

"You're in the way," he said, gesturing at the spinning wheel. "I need space to work."

"Would it hurt to ask politely?"

He fixed her with a look so openly annoyed, she wondered if his irritation might rival her own. "I'm helping you."

"And I've paid you for the honor," she said, indicating the necklace at his throat. "I don't think a shred of civility is unwarranted."

He opened his mouth, but hesitated. His brow furrowed. "Would you like me to give the necklace back and leave you to your fate?"

"Of course not. But you still haven't told me how, exactly, you plan to help me."

He sighed, a bit dramatically. "Suit yourself. After all, why be accommodating when one can be difficult?"

He stepped toward her—and kept coming, as if he might trample her like an errant mule cart if she didn't get out of the way. Teeth gritted, Serilda planted her feet.

She did not move.

He did not stop.

He collided into her, his chin smacking her forehead, his chest knocking Serilda back with such force she stumbled and fell onto the straw with a surprised *oof*.

"Ow!" she yelped, resisting the urge to rub the sore spot on her rump where the straw had only barely softened her fall. "What is wrong with you?" She glared up at him, both infuriated and baffled. If he thought she was going to let him intimidate her—!

But something in his expression stopped her tirade before it had really gotten started.

He was staring at her, but this was different from when he'd studied her before. His lips hung open. Eyes full of blatant disbelief, while one hand idly rubbed his shoulder where it had hit the wall when he, too, had stumbled back from their collision.

"Well?" shouted Serilda, climbing to her feet and picking stray bits of straw from her skirt. "What did you do that for?"

Planting her hands on her hips, she waited.

After a moment, he did approach her again, but with more hesitation. His expression was not as chagrined as it should have been, but more—curious. Something about the way he was studying her clouded Serilda's ire. She was tempted to back away from him, not that there was anywhere for her to go. And if she hadn't budged before, she most certainly wasn't going to now. So she held her ground, tilting her chin up with a lifetime's worth of stubbornness.

No apology came.

Instead, when he was an arm's distance from her, the boy raised his hands between them. She looked down. His fingers, pale and rough with calluses, were *trembling*.

Serilda followed the movement of his hands as they came closer, nearing her shoulders. Inch by tentative inch.

"What are you doing?"

In answer, he settled his fingers onto her upper arms. The touch was impossibly delicate at first, then he let the weight of his hands settle along her arms, pressing gently against the thin muslin sleeves of her dress. It was not a threatening touch, and yet, Serilda's pulse jolted with something like fear.

No—not fear.

Nerves.

The boy exhaled sharply, drawing her attention back to his face.

Oh wicked gods, the *look* he was giving her. Serilda had never been looked at like that before. She didn't know what to make of it. The intensity. The heat. The raw astonishment.

He was going to kiss her.

Wait.

Why?

Nobody ever wanted to kiss her. There might have been a time once, with Thomas Lindbeck, but . . . that was short-lived and ended in catastrophe.

She was unlucky. Strange. Cursed.

And . . . and besides. She didn't want him to kiss her. She didn't know this boy. She certainly didn't *like* him.

She didn't even know his name.

So why had she just licked her lips?

That small movement brought the boy's attention to her mouth, and suddenly, his expression cleared. He yanked his hands away and took the biggest step back that he could without once again crashing into the wall.

"I'm sorry," he said, his voice rougher than before.

She couldn't remember what he was supposed to be apologizing for.

He tucked his hands behind his back, as though he was afraid they would reach out for her again if left to their own devices.

"All right," she breathed.

"You're really alive," he said. He said it as a statement of fact, but one he wasn't sure he believed.

"Well . . . yes," she said. "I thought that had been well established, what with the Erlking hoping to kill me at dawn and all that."

"No. Yes. I mean, I knew that, of course. I just . . . " He rubbed the palms of his hands against his shirt, as if testing his own tangibility. Then he roughly shook his head. "I suppose I hadn't fully considered what all it meant. Been a long time since I met a real mortal. Didn't realize you'd be so . . . so . . ."

She waited, unable to guess at what word he was searching for.

Until finally, he settled on, "*Warm.*"

Her eyebrows rose, even as heat rushed unbidden into her cheeks. She tried to ignore it. "How long has it been since you met someone who wasn't a ghost?"

His lips twisted to one side. "Not exactly sure. A few centuries, probably."

Her jaw fell. "Centuries?"

He held her gaze a moment longer, before sighing. "Actually, no. The truth is, I don't think I've ever met a living girl before." He cleared his throat, distracted. "I can pass through ghosts when I want to. Just sort of assumed it'd be the same with . . . well, with anyone. Not that I do it a whole lot. Seems like poor etiquette, doesn't it? Walking right through somebody. But I try to avoid touching them when I can. Not that I . . . I don't dislike the other ghosts. Some make for fine company, surprisingly enough. But . . . to feel them can be . . ."

"Disagreeable?" Serilda suggested, her fingers curling at the memory of the coachman's cool, fragile skin.

The boy chuckled. "Yes. Precisely."

"You didn't seem to have any qualms about trying to walk through *me*."

"You wouldn't move!"

"I would have moved. You only needed to say *please*. If you're concerned with etiquette, that might be a good place to start."

He huffed, but there was little heat behind his look. If anything, he seemed a little shaken. "Fine, fine," he muttered absently. "I'll keep that in mind the next time I'm saving your life." Swallowing hard, he glanced at the candle in the corner. "We need to get started. We haven't much time left."

He dared to meet her eye again.

Serilda held the look, more bewildered with every passing moment.

Arriving at some internal decision, the boy gave a firm nod. "Right, then."

He reached for her again. This time, when he took hold of Serilda's arms, it was determined and quick as he forcefully shifted her body two steps to the side. She squeaked, in danger of losing her balance when he released her.

"What—"

"I told you," he interrupted. "You're in my way. Please and thank you."

"That isn't how those words work."

He shrugged, but Serilda noticed how he squeezed his hands into fists as he faced the spinning wheel. And if she were telling this moment as a part of a story, she would say that the gesture, subtle as it was, carried a deeper meaning. As though he were trying to prolong that sensation, the feeling of his hands in contact with her shoulders, just a moment longer.

She shook her head, reminding herself that this was not one of her tales. As unbelievable as it might be, she was truly trapped in a dungeon, held prisoner by the Erlking, tasked with this impossible request. And now there was this boy, righting the stool and sitting down at the spinning wheel.

She blinked, looking from him to the spinning wheel to the pile of straw at her feet. "You can't mean to . . . ?"

"How did you think I was planning to help you?" He grabbed a handful of straw near his toe. "I already told you I can't help you escape. So instead . . ." He heaved a sigh, fraught with dread. "I suppose we shall spin straw into gold."

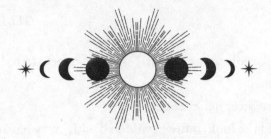

Chapter 12

He pressed his foot against the treadle. The wheel began to spin, filling the room with a steady whirring sound. He took the straw and, just as Serilda had, looped one strand around the bobbin as a leader yarn. Except it actually stayed for him.

Next, he started to feed the small bundle of straw through the hole, bit by bit, piece by piece. The wheel turned.

And Serilda gasped.

The straw emerged—no longer pale and inflexible and rough. At some point between entering the maiden hole and winding around the bobbin, in a blur too quick for her eyes to catch, the straw had been transformed into a malleable thread of glistening gold.

The boy's hands were quick and confident. Soon, he had a second handful gathered from the floor beside him and was feeding it through. His foot tapped a steady pace. His eyes were focused, but calm, as if he'd done this a thousand times.

Serilda's mouth hung agape as the bobbin filled with delicate, shimmering strands.

Gold.

Could it be?

Suddenly, the boy paused.

Serilda looked at him, disappointed. "Why did you stop?"

"I'm just wondering if you plan to stand there gawking at me all night?"

"If you're suggesting I take a nap instead, I'll gladly comply."

"Or perhaps you could . . . help?"

"How?"

He circled his fingers around his temple, like her presence was giving him a headache. Then he whirled his hand in her direction and proclaimed, in a ridiculously staunch voice, "I do beseech you, oh fair one, would you *please* assist me with this most tedious of tasks by gathering the straw and bringing it within my reach, so that our progress might be hastened and you don't get your head chopped off at dawn?"

Serilda pressed her lips. He was mocking her, but . . . at least this time he *did* say please.

"With pleasure," she snapped.

He grumbled something she couldn't make out.

Serilda bent down and started using her arms to sweep the pile of straw closer to him. It wasn't long before they fell into a rhythm of sorts. Serilda gathered up the straw, handing it to the boy in great bunches, which he worked seamlessly through the maiden hole, piece by piece. When a bobbin was full, he paused only long enough to swap it for the next; the Erlking, or more likely his undead servants, had provided plenty of bobbins in expectation of Serilda's abilities. Odd, she thought, as the king had clearly held such little confidence that she would succeed.

Perhaps he was an optimist.

She giggled at the thought, earning a suspicious glance from the stranger.

"What's your name?" she asked. She thought nothing much of the question—merely a nicety—but the boy's foot immediately stopped pedaling.

"Why do you want to know?"

She glanced up from gathering another armful of straw. He was looking at her suspiciously, a long piece of straw gripped between his fingers. The wheel's turning gradually slowed.

She furrowed her brow. "It's hardly an odd thing to ask a person." Then, with a bit more truthfulness, she added, "And I want to know what I should call you when I'm telling everyone back home about my harrowing journey to the Erlking's castle and the chivalrous stranger who came to my aid."

His suspicion faded into a haughty grin. "Chivalrous?"

"Except for the part where you refused to help me unless I gave up my necklace."

He gave her a one-shouldered shrug. "Not my fault. Magic doesn't work without payment. By the way"—he removed a full bobbin from the flyer, replacing it with an empty one to begin the process again—"this isn't his castle."

"Right, I know," said Serilda. Although, she didn't know that. Not really. This may not be Gravenstone, but it seemed clear that the Erlking had claimed it for himself regardless.

Posture stiff, the boy stepped on the treadle again.

"My name is Serilda," she said, irritated that he hadn't answered her question. "A right pleasure it's been to make your acquaintance."

His gaze flickered to her before he said begrudgingly, "You may call me Gild."

"Gild? I've never heard that name before. Is it short for something?"

The only answer was a quiet grunt.

She wanted to ask about what he'd said before, about the girl in the locket seeming familiar, about how she wouldn't understand. But somehow she knew it would only make him more cross, and she wasn't even sure what she'd said to make him so grumpy in the first place.

"Forgive me for attempting to make idle chatter. I can tell it isn't a pastime you cherish."

She went to drop another batch of straw at his feet, but he surprised her by reaching out to take it directly from her grip. His fingers brushed hers. A whisper of a touch, almost unnoticeable before it was gone and his hands were busy at their work again.

Almost unnoticeable.

If it hadn't seemed entirely too purposeful.

If it hadn't set all her nerves aflame.

If Gild's gaze hadn't become extra intense on the straw, as he actively avoided looking at her.

"I don't mind idle chatter," he said, barely heard above the spinning of the wheel. "But I might be out of practice."

Serilda turned away to examine their progress. Though time seemed to pass in staggers and blinks, she was pleased to see that they were more than a third of the way through their task, and the bobbins full of golden thread were beginning to pile up beside him. At least Gild was efficient.

For that alone, Mother Weber would have liked him.

Serilda picked up one of the spools of thread to study it. The golden thread was thick, like yarn, but hard and pliant, like a chain. She wondered how much one of these gold-covered bobbins would be worth. Probably more than her father made from his miller's toll in an entire season.

"You had to say straw?" Gild asked, breaking the silence. He shook his head, even as he gathered the next bundle of stalks. "You couldn't have told him you could spin gold from silk, or even wool?" He opened his palms and Serilda could see that they were covered in scratches from the brittle material.

She grinned apologetically. "I may not have fully considered the repercussions."

He grunted.

"Do you mean to tell me that you can spin gold from anything?"

"Anything that can be spun. My favorite material to work with is the fur of a dahut."

"A dahut? What is that?"

"Similar to a mountain goat," he said. "Except the legs on one side of their body are shorter than the other. Helpful for climbing steep mountainsides. Trouble is, it means they can only go around the mountain in one direction."

Serilda stared at him. He seemed serious, and yet . . .

It was awfully like something that she would have made up. She would sooner believe in a tatzelwurm.

Of course, given the creatures she'd seen hung up on the Erlking's walls, she could no longer be sure that anything was mere myth.

Still.

A dahut?

A bark of laughter escaped her. "Now I know you're teasing."

His eyes glimmered, but he did not respond either way.

Serilda lit up, struck with sudden inspiration. "Would you care to hear a story?"

He frowned, surprised. "Like a fairy tale?"

"Exactly. I always like hearing a story when I work. Or . . . in my case, making one up. Time slips away and before you know it, you're finished. And all the while, you've been transported somewhere vibrant and exciting and wonderful."

He didn't say *no*, exactly, but his expression made it clear he thought this was a bizarre suggestion.

But Serilda had created stories at far less passionate invitations.

She paused in her work just long enough to think, to let the first threads of a tale begin to wind themselves through her imagination.

Then she began.

It has long been known that when the wild hunt rides beneath a full moon, they often claim for themselves lost and unhappy souls, coaxing them along on their destructive path. Oftentimes, those poor souls are never seen again. Drunkards get lost on their way home from the tavern. Sailors docked for the week will wander off, unnoticed by their peers. It is said that anyone who dares step into the moonlight during the witching hour could find themselves the next morning alone and shivering, covered in blood and gristle from whatever beast the hunt captured in the night, though they have no memory of the events that transpired. It's a seduction of sorts, the call of the hunt. Some men and women long for the chance to be feral themselves. Vicious and brutal. Where bloodlust sings a raucous ballad in their veins. There was a time, even, when it was thought to be a gift, to be taken for one night by the hunt, so long as you lived through to see the sun rise and did not lose yourself in the night. If you did not become one of the phantoms destined for eternal servitude to the Erlking's court.

But even those who once believed that to join the hunt was its own sort of dark honor knew that there was one type of soul who had no business being among the ghouls and hounds.

The innocent souls of children.

But every decade or so, it was this very prize that the hunt sought. For the Erlking had made it his duty to bring a new child to his love, the cruel huntress Perchta, whenever she should grow bored of the last gift he'd presented. Which was, of course, when that child should grow to be too old for her liking.

At first, the Erlking claimed whatever lost babe might be wandering in the Aschen Wood. But over time he prided himself on securing for his love not just any child—but the best child. The most beautiful. The most clever. The most amusing, if you will.

It once so happened that the Erlking heard rumors of a young princess who was proclaimed far and wide to be the most lovely girl the world had ever known. She had golden, bouncy curls and laughing sky-blue eyes, and all who met her were charmed by her exuberance. As soon as he heard tell of the child, the Erlking was determined to claim her and bring her to his mistress.

And so, on the night of a cold Hunger Moon, the Erlking and his hunters rode to the gate of a castle, and with their magical wiles, lured the child from her bed. She walked down the candlelit corridors as if in a dream, and out across the drawbridge, where she was met by the wild hunt. The Erlking promptly swept her onto his horse and carried her off into the woods.

He had invited Perchta to meet him in a forest clearing to receive her gift, and when he showed her the child, so bright-eyed and rosy-cheeked beneath the full moon, the huntress immediately fell in love and vowed to dote on her with all the affection a mother might bestow on a most beloved daughter.

But Perchta and the Erlking were not alone in the woods that night.

For a prince—the very brother to the stolen child—had also awoken, a feeling of dread thumping in his chest. Upon finding his sister's bed empty and all her attendants in an enchanted sleep, he ran to the stables. He grabbed his hunting weapons and mounted his steed and raced off into the forest, alone but unafraid, following the haunting cries of hellhounds. He rode faster than he had ever ridden before, all but flying along the path through the trees, for he knew that if the sun were to rise with his sister trapped inside the Erlking's castle, she would be trapped on the other side of the veil, and lost to him forever.

He knew he was getting closer. He could see the towers of Gravenstone over the boughs of the trees, highlighted beneath a brightening winter sky. He reached a clearing outside the swampy moat. The drawbridge was down. Ahead of him, Perchta had the princess on her steed, racing toward the castle gate.

The prince knew he would not make it to her in time.

And so he readied his bow. Nocked an arrow. And prayed to any god who would hear him that his arrow would fly true.

He shot.

The arrow crested over the moat, as if guided by the hand of Tyrr, the god of archery and war. It buried itself into Perchta's back—straight through to her heart.

Perchta slipped from her mount.

The Erlking leaped from his steed, barely managing to catch her in his arms. As the stars began to fade from his lover's eyes, he looked up and saw the prince bearing down on his castle, desperate to reach his sister.

The Erlking was overcome with fury.

In that moment, he made a choice. One that haunts him to this day.

It is impossible to say if he might have saved the huntress's life. He might yet have carried her into his castle. They say the dark ones know boundless ways to tether a life to the veil, to keep one from slipping beyond the gates into Verloren. Perhaps he could have kept her with him.

But he chose different.

Leaving Perchta to die on that bridge, the Erlking stood and snatched the princess from the abandoned horse. He pulled a gold-tipped arrow from his quiver and, gripping it tight in his fist, raised it above the child. It was naught but an act of coldhearted revenge against the prince, who had dared strike down the great huntress.

Seeing what the Erlking meant to do, the prince ran at him, trying to reach his sister.

But he was driven back by the hounds. Their teeth. Their claws. Their burning eyes. They surrounded the prince, snapping, biting, tearing at his flesh. He screamed, unable to fight them off. Fully awake now, the princess cried her brother's name and reached out to him as she fought against the king's hold.

Too late. The king drove the arrow into her flesh just as the sky was set aflame by the first rays of morning light.

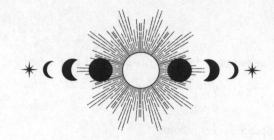

Chapter 13

Serilda wasn't sure how long it had been since she'd sat down. How long she'd had her back pressed to the cold cell wall, eyes shut, wrapped up in the story as if she were watching it happen right in front of her. But as the tale came to a tremulous close, she inhaled a deep breath, and slowly peeled her eyes open.

Gild, still seated on the stool on the far side of the cell, was openly gawking at her.

He looked positively aghast.

She stiffened. "What? Why are you looking at me like that?"

He shook his head. "You said stories are supposed to be vibrant and exciting and . . . and wonderful. Those were the words you used. But that story was"—he searched for the right word, finally landing on—"awful!"

"Awful?" she barked. "How dare you."

"How dare I?" he said, standing. "Fairy tales have happy endings! The prince is supposed to save the princess. Kill the Erlking *and* the huntress, then they both ride on home to their awaiting family and are celebrated by all the land. Happily. Forever! What is this . . . this rubbish, what with the king stabbing his sister, the prince getting mauled by his hounds . . . I can't remember all too many stories, but I'm certain that is the absolute worst I've ever heard."

Trying to temper her anger, Serilda stood and crossed her arms over her chest. "You're saying the story made you feel something then?"

"Of course it made me feel something. And that something is awful!"

A delighted smile broke across her face. "Ha! I will gladly take *awful* over *indifferent*. Not every story has a happy ending. Life isn't like that, you know."

"Which is why we listen to stories!" he shouted, throwing his hands into the air. "You can't end it there. Tell me the prince gets revenge, at least?"

Serilda pressed a finger to her lips, considering.

But then her gaze fell on the bobbins stacked neatly against the wall. Each one glimmered like the vein of a lost gold mine.

She gasped. "You finished!" She stepped forward, about to grab a bobbin off the nearest stack, when Gild stepped in front of her, blocking her path.

"Oh no. Not until you tell me what happens next."

She huffed. "I don't know what happens next."

His expression was priceless. A little dismayed, a little horrified. "How can you not know? It's your story."

"Not every story is willing to reveal itself right away. Some of them are bashful."

As he tried to ponder this, Serilda ducked around him and snatched up one of the bobbins, holding it toward the candlelight. "This is stunning. Is it all real gold?"

"Of course it's real gold," he grumbled. "You think I would try to trick you?"

She smirked. "I certainly think you're capable of it."

His sullen face broke into a proud grin. "Suppose I am."

Serilda inspected the thread. Strong and pliant. "I wonder if I would enjoy spinning if I could create something so beautiful."

"You don't like spinning?"

She made a face. "*No.* Why? Do you?"

"Sometimes. I've always found it to be"—again, he searched for the right word—"satisfying, I suppose. It calms me some."

She scoffed. "I've heard other people say that. But for me, it just . . . makes me impatient to be done with it."

He chuckled. "You like to tell stories, though."

"I love to," she said. "But that's what got me into this mess. I help teach at the school and one of the kids mentioned that spinning stories is a bit like spinning straw into gold. Like creating something that sparkles from nothing at all."

"*That* tale did not sparkle," said Gild, rocking back on his heels. "It was mostly gloom and death and darkness."

"You say those words like they're bad things. But when it comes to the age-old art of storytelling," she said sagely, "you need darkness to appreciate the light."

His mouth quirked to one side, like he wasn't willing to give this a complete smile. Then he seemed to steel himself, before reaching for Serilda's hands.

She tensed, but all he did was steal the bobbin gently from her fingertips. Still—she didn't think she was imagining how his touch lingered a second longer than it had to, or how his throat bobbed as he set the gold back down on the pile.

He cleared his throat gently. "The king's meticulous for details. He'll notice if one is missing."

"Of course," she murmured, still feeling the tingle on her knuckles. "I wasn't planning to take it. I'm not a thief."

He chuckled. "You say *that* word like it's a bad thing."

Before she could think up a clever response, they heard the thump of footsteps outside the cell.

They both went still.

Then, to her astonishment, Gild closed the distance to her in a stride and this time, he did grab her hands, taking them both into his. "Serilda?"

She gasped, not sure if she was more startled by his touch or the sound of her name uttered with such urgency.

"Have I completed the task to your satisfaction?"

"What?"

"You must say it, to conclude our bargain. Magical agreements are not to be lightly dismissed."

"Oh. O-of course." She glanced at the locket, shining brightly against his dreary tunic, hiding the portrait of a girl who was every bit as much an enigma now, even if she had inspired Serilda's tragic tale.

"Yes, the task is complete," she said. "I cannot have a complaint."

It was true, despite her resentment at giving up the locket. This boy had promised her the blue of the sky. What he had done should have been impossible, but he'd done it.

He smiled, just slightly, but it was enough to make her breath catch. There was something hopelessly genuine about it.

Then, surprise upon surprise, Gild lifted her hand. She thought he might kiss it, which would have been the pinnacle of odd occurrences for the night.

But he did not kiss her hand.

He did something even stranger.

Closing his eyes, Gild held her fist lightly against his cheek, taking from her the most delicate of caresses.

"Thank you," he murmured.

"What for?"

Gild opened his mouth to say something more, but hesitated. His thumb had brushed the band of the golden ring given to her by the moss maidens. He peered down at it, taking in the seal with its engraved *R*.

His eyebrows pinched with curiosity.

A key creaked inside the lock.

Serilda pulled away and spun to face the door.

"Good luck," Gild whispered.

She glanced over her shoulder, but froze.

He was gone. She was alone.

The cell door groaned as it opened.

Serilda stood straighter, trying to smother the odd fluttering in the pit of her stomach, as the Erlking sauntered into the cell. His servant, the same ghost with the missing eye, waited in the corridor with a torch held aloft.

The king paused a few steps past the door, and in that moment, the candle, now nothing more than a puddle of wax on the pewter candlestick, finally gave up. The flame expired with a quiet hiss and a curl of black smoke.

The king seemed unperturbed by the shadows. His gaze swept over the empty floor, not a piece of straw to be seen. Then to the spinning wheel, and finally to the stacks of bobbins and their glittering gold thread.

Serilda managed something akin to a curtsy. "Your Darkness. I hope you had a nice hunt."

He did not look at her as he stepped forward and picked up one of the bobbins.

"Light," he ordered.

The coachman glanced at Serilda as he stepped forward, raising the torch. He looked astonished.

But he was smiling.

Serilda held her breath as the king studied the thread. She nervously rubbed her thumb across the ring on her finger.

Ages passed before the Erlking's fingers clenched around the bobbin, encircling it in a tight fist. "Tell me your name."

"Serilda, my lord."

He considered her a long while. Another age passed before he said, "It would seem that I owe you an apology, Lady Serilda. I doubted you most severely. In fact, I was convinced that you had taken me for a fool. Told me grand lies and stolen from me my rightful prey. But"—he glanced down at his closed fist—"it would seem that you have been given the blessing of Hulda after all."

She lifted her chin. "I hope you are pleased."

"Quite," he said, though his tone remained sullen. "You said before that the blessing was in favor to your mother, a talented seamstress, if I do recall."

This. This was the worst part of Serilda's terrible habit. It was so easy to forget what lies one had told, and in what detail. She tried to dredge up the memory of that night and what she had said to the king, but it was all a blur. So she merely shrugged. "That is the story I've been told. But I never knew my mother."

"Dead?"

"Gone," she answered. "The moment I was weaned from her milk."

"A mother knew that her child was god-blessed, yet she did not stay to teach her how to use such a gift?"

"I do not think she saw it as a gift. The town . . . all the villagers see my mark as a sign of misfortune. They believe I bring bad luck, and I'm not sure they're wrong. After all, tonight my so-called gift has brought me into the dungeon of the great and horrible Alder King himself."

His expression showed a hint of thawing at that. "So it has," he muttered. "But the superstitions of humans are so often the result of ignorance and ill-placed blame. I would pay them little heed."

"Begging your pardon, but that seems like an easy thing for the king of the dark ones to say, who surely carries no concerns over long winters or failed crops. Sometimes superstitions are all that we have been given by the gods in order to make sense of our world. Superstitions . . . and stories."

"You expect me to believe that the ability to do this"—he held up the bobbin of gold thread—"portends ill fortune?"

She glanced at the bobbin. She'd almost forgotten that *this* was the blessing the Erlking believed she had been given.

It made her wonder whether Gild saw his talent as a gift or a curse.

"As I understand," she said, "gold has caused as many problems as it has ever solved."

A silence settled over them, cloaking the room.

Serilda hesitated to meet his eye again. When she did, she was startled to see a grin stealing across his lips.

And then, horror of horrors, he *laughed*.

Serilda's stomach swooped.

"Serilda," he said, his voice newly warmed. "I have met many humans, but there is an oddity about you. It is . . . refreshing."

The Erlking stepped closer, blocking the torchlight from her view. The hand that did not hold the thread lifted and grasped a strand of hair that had come loose from one of her braids. Serilda had been given little occasion to peer at her reflection, but if she had any vanity, it was for her hair, which fell past her waist in thick waves. Fricz had once told her that it was the exact color of his father's favorite aged ale—a dark, rich brown, just without all the foamy white stuff on top. At the time Serilda had wondered if she should be offended, but now she was sure it had been meant as a compliment.

The Erlking tucked the loose strand behind her ear—the touch excruciatingly tender. She averted her gaze as the tips of his fingers barely traced the edge of her cheek, faint as cobwebs against her skin.

Strange, she thought, to experience two such gentle touches in such short order, and yet to feel so very differently about them. Gild's caress of her hand had struck her as bizarre and unexpected, yes, but it had also brought a tingly warmth to the surface of her skin.

Whereas everything the Erlking did felt calculated. He must know how his unearthly beauty could make any human heart pound faster, yet his touch left Serilda feeling as though she had suffered the caress of a viper.

"It is a shame," he said quietly. "You might have been beautiful."

Her stomach curdled, though less from the insult than from his nearness.

Pulling away, the king tossed the bobbin of thread at the ghost, who snatched it easily from the air.

"Have it all taken to the undercroft."

"Yes, Your Grim. And the girl?"

Serilda tensed.

The Erlking gave her a dismissive look, before his teeth, faintly sharpened, glinted in the torchlight. "She may rest in the north tower until sunrise. I'm sure she is quite exhausted from her toils."

The king departed, once again leaving her alone with the coachman.

He met her gaze, that smile returning. "Well, I'll eat a broom. I thought there might be more to you than meets the eye."

Serilda returned the smile, unable to tell if he was making light of his own missing eyeball. "I like to surprise people when I can."

Serilda gathered up her cloak and followed him from the dungeons. Up spiraling steps and along narrow halls. Past tapestries, antlers, disembodied animal heads. Swords and axes and enormous chandeliers dripping with dark wax. The overall effect was one of mixed gloom and violence, which must have suited the Erlking fine. When they passed a narrow window inlaid with leaded diamonds of glass, Serilda saw an indigo sky.

Dawn was approaching.

Never had she gone an entire night without sleep, and her exhaustion was overwhelming. Her lids felt almost impossible to keep open as she trudged behind the apparition.

"Am I still a prisoner?" she asked.

It took the ghost a long time to answer.

An unnervingly long time.

Until, at some point, she realized that he did not intend to answer at all.

She frowned. "I suppose a tower will be better than a dungeon," she said through a thick yawn. Her body felt cumbersome as the ghost led her up another stairwell and through a low arched door, into a sitting area connected to a bedchamber.

Serilda stepped inside. Even with her bleary-eyed weariness, she felt a twinge of awe. The room was not *cozy,* but there was a dark elegance that stole her breath. The windows were hung with lace curtains, black and delicate. An ebony washstand held a porcelain water pitcher and bowl, both painted with wine-red roses and large, lifelike moths. A small side table sat beside the bed, holding a burning green candle and a vase with a tiny bouquet of snowdrops, nival flowers with pretty, bowed heads. A fire roared in the hearth, and over the mantel hung an ornately framed painting of a brutal winter landscape, dark and desolate beneath a glowing moon.

Capturing her attention most, though, was the four-poster bed, wrapped on all sides by emerald-green drapes.

"Thank you," she breathed, as the ghost lit the candle beside the bed.

He bowed and started to leave the room.

But he paused at the door. His expression was wary as he glanced back at her. "Have you ever watched a cat hunting a mouse?"

She blinked at him, startled that he would encourage conversation.

"Yes. My father used to keep a mousing cat for the mill."

"Then you know how they like to play. They will let the mouse go, allow it to think, however briefly, that it is free. Then they will pounce again, and again, until they eventually grow bored and devour their prey bit by bit."

Her chest tightened.

The ghost's voice carried little emotion, even as his eye clouded with sorrow. "You asked if you were still a prisoner," he said. "But we are *all* prisoners. Once His Darkness has you, he does not like to let you go."

With these eerie words hanging in the air, he respectfully inclined his head again and departed.

He left the door open.

Unlocked.

Serilda had only enough presence of mind to know that she might be able to escape. This might be her only chance.

But her slowing pulse told her it was as impossible as spinning straw into gold.

She was desperate for sleep.

Serilda shut the bedroom door. There was no lock, not on the outside to keep her in. Not on the inside to keep others out.

She spun around and allowed herself to forget about ghosts and prisons and kings. Of cats and mice. Of hunters and the hunted.

She kicked off her shoes as she pulled back one of the velvet curtains. An actual gasp escaped her lips to see the luscious bedding that awaited her. An embroidered coverlet, a sheepskin throw—*pillows*. Real pillows, stuffed with feathers.

She slipped out of her filthy dress, finding a piece of straw caught in the fabric of her skirt as she dropped the cloth into a puddle on the floor beside her cloak. She didn't bother with her chemise before climbing under the coverlet. The mattress sank invitingly beneath her weight. Engulfing her. Embracing her. It was the most miraculous thing she'd ever felt.

As the sky lightened beyond the window, Serilda allowed herself to enjoy this moment of comfort, such a perfect complement to the all-consuming weariness that clung to her bones, weighed down her eyelids, deepened her breaths.

Dragged her down into sleep.

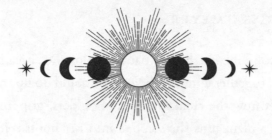

Chapter 14

She awoke shivering.

Serilda curled in on herself, grasping for heavy blankets, feathered pillows. Her fingers found only her own thin muslin chemise and gooseflesh-covered arms. With a groan, she rolled onto her other side, thrashing her feet around, searching for the coverlet she must have kicked off. For the sheepskin throw that had so delectably weighed down her legs.

Her limbs met only crisp wintry air.

Shaking, she rubbed freezing fingers into her eyes and forced them open.

Sunlight spilled through the windows, shockingly bright.

She sat up, blinking to clear her vision.

The velvet drapes around the postered bed were gone, explaining that wicked draft. So, too, the blankets. The pillows. The hearth lay empty of everything but soot and dust. The furniture remained, though the side table was toppled onto its side. No sign of the porcelain bowl, the pitcher, the candle, or the little vase of flowers. The glass on one window was shattered. The gossamer window drapes, vanished. Cobwebs clung to the chandelier and bedposts, some so thick with dust they looked like black yarn.

Scrambling from the bed, Serilda hurried to pull on her dress. Her fingers were so numb she had to pause to blow hot breath over them and rub them together a minute before she could do up the last of the buttons. She threw the cloak over her shoulders, gripping it around her arms like a blanket as she stepped into her boots. Her heart was thudding as she peered around at the barrenness of the room, so stark against the memories of the night before.

Or—the early morning.

How long had she slept?

Certainly not more than a few hours, and yet the room felt as though it had sat abandoned and untouched for a hundred years.

She peeked out into the sitting room. There were the same uphol-stered chairs, now smelling of mildew and rot, the fabric chewed through in spots by rodents.

Her footsteps echoed hollowly as she made her way down the stair-well, rubbing sleep from her eyes. Water dripped down the stones, leak-ing in from the occasional narrow window, many of which had broken or missing panes. A few tiny sprigs of bristle-leafed weeds had sprouted up between the mortar on the steps, coaxed to life by the shard of morning light that struck them and the cold moisture in the air.

Serilda shivered again as she reached the main floor of the castle.

She might have been transported to a different world, a different time. This could not be the same castle she'd fallen asleep in. The wide hall might have the same stonework, the same enormous chandeliers, but nature had laid claim to these walls. Sparse vines of ivy trailed along the floor, climbing up the doorframes. The candles were gone from the chandeliers and the sconces. The carpets, disappeared. All the taxi-dermy beasts, the stuffed victims of the hunt, vanished.

There was a tapestry hanging in tatters against the far wall. Serilda approached it hesitantly, her boots crunching on chipped stone and dry leaves. She recognized the tapestry with its image of an enormous black stag in a forest clearing. But last night, the image had depicted the animal being shot through with a dozen arrows, the blood leaking from its wounds making it clear that it would not survive the night. But now that same beast stood exalted among the sun-dappled trees, graceful and strong, its massive antlers stretching toward the moon.

Last night, the macabre depiction had been pristine and vibrant.

Whereas this tapestry was marred by moth holes and mildew, the dye of the fabric long faded from time.

Serilda swallowed hard. She had once entertained the children with a tale of a king who was invited to partake in the wedding of an ogre. Sensing that to decline would be to offer great insult, the king attended the wedding, and relished in the ogre's hospitality. He enjoyed the drink, feasted on the foods, danced until his shoes were worn through, then fell happily asleep. But when he awoke, everyone had gone. The king returned home only to find that a hundred years had passed. All his family were dead and his kingdom had fallen into the hands of another, and no one alive could remember who he was.

Staring at the tapestry now, her breath steaming the air, Serilda felt a bewildering fear that this was what had happened to her.

How many years had passed while she slept?

Where was the Erlking and his ghostly court?

Where was Gild?

She frowned at this question. Gild might have helped her, even saved her life, but he'd also taken her locket, and she wasn't happy about it.

"Hello?" Serilda called. Her voice echoed back to her through the empty hall. "Where did everyone go?"

She picked her way over the vines into the great hall. Debris littered the floor. The remains of birds' nests clung to the ceiling beams. The massive central fireplace still bore marks of black soot, but otherwise appeared to have sat cold and empty for ages. A pile of fabric shreds and twigs in the hearth's corner might have been the home for a dormouse or ground squirrel.

A shrill *caw* split the air.

Serilda spun around.

The bird was perched on the leg of a toppled chair. It fluffed its black feathers, irritated, as if Serilda had disturbed its rest.

"Don't you give me that look," she spat. "*You* startled *me.*"

The bird cocked its head, and through the dust motes hanging in the air, Serilda saw that it was not a crow, but another nachtkrapp.

She stood taller, holding its hollow-eyed gaze. "Oh, hello," she said warily. "Are you the same bird who visited me before? Or are you a descendant from the future?"

It said nothing. Beastly creature or not, it was still just a bird.

The loud creak of wood echoed distantly in the castle. A door opening, or timber rafters shifting under the weight of stone and time. She listened for footsteps, but there were no sounds but the quiet, soothing crash of waves on the lake. The flutter of wild birds in the corners of lofted ceilings. The scuttle of rodents along the walls.

With another glance at the nachtkrapp, Serilda moved toward the creaking sound, or what direction she thought it had come from. She crept through a long, narrow corridor and had just passed an open doorway when she heard it again. The slow groaning of heavy wood and unoiled hinges.

She paused and looked through the doorway, to a straight staircase. Two unlit torches hung on the walls, and at the top, barely discernible in the darkness, a closed arched door.

Serilda made her way up the stairs, where centuries of footsteps had left subtle grooves in the stone. The door opened easily. Shimmering, rosy light spilled into the stairwell.

Serilda emerged into a vast hallway with seven narrow stained-glass windows lined up along the exterior wall. Their once vibrant colors were dulled beneath a layer of grime, but it was still easy to recognize the depictions of the old gods. Freydon harvesting golden stalks of wheat. Solvilde puffing air into a ship's sails. Hulda seated at a spinning wheel. Tyrr preparing to shoot an arrow from a bow. Eostrig sowing seeds. Velos holding aloft a lantern to guide souls to Verloren. Of the seven windows, Velos's was the only one that was broken, a few pieces of the god's robes left shattered and barely clinging to the leading.

The seventh god waited at the end of the line. Serilda's own patron deity—Wyrdith, the god of stories and fortune, lies and fate. Though they were often depicted with the wheel of fortune, here the artist had chosen to show them as the storyteller, holding a golden plume in one hand and a scroll of parchment in the other.

Serilda stared at the god, trying to feel some sort of affinity for the being who had supposedly granted her golden-wheeled eyes and a talent for deception. But she felt nothing for the god before her, surrounded in hues of emerald and rose, looking regal and wise as they peered up toward the sky, as if even a god might wait for divine inspiration.

It was not at all how she'd imagined her trickster godparent to look, and she couldn't help feeling like the artist had gotten them all wrong.

She turned away. At the end of the procession of windows, the hall took a sharp turn. Plain leaded windows to one side, looking out over the misty lake. On the other, a row of standing iron candelabras, devoid of candles.

Between the candelabras stood a series of polished oak doors. All closed, except the last.

Serilda paused, staring at the pool of light spilling across the worn, tattered carpet. It was not rich daylight she was seeing, tinted cool gray from the overcast skies. It was not like the light coming in from the windows.

It was warm and flickering like candlelight, cut through with dancing shadows.

Serilda swiped away a cobweb that hung across the passage and moved toward the doorway. Her footsteps landed quietly on the carpet. She barely breathed.

When she was not ten steps from the room, she spied the edge of a tapestry. She couldn't make out the design, but its saturated colors surprised her. Vivid, apparently unfaded, when everything around her was dim and cold and rotting away under time.

The light in the room darkened, but she was so focused on the tapestry, she barely noticed.

She took another step.

From somewhere below, deep in the heart of the castle, a scream.

Serilda froze. The noise was laced with agony.

The door to the room before her slammed shut.

She jumped back, just as a feral screech exploded through the hall. A blur of wings and talons flew at her. She screamed, one arm flailing. A claw slashed across her cheek. She threw her arm out, managing to strike one of the beast's wings. It hissed and lurched backward.

Serilda crashed against the wall, both arms raised in an effort to protect herself. She peered up, expecting an enormous nachtkrapp to be preparing for a second attack, but the creature before her was not a night raven.

It was far worse.

The size of a toddler, but with the face of a devil. Horns spiraled forward from the sides of its head. Black leathery wings sprouted from its back. Its proportions were all wrong. Arms too short; legs too long; fingers tipped with spindly, pointed claws. Its skin was gray and purple; its eyes slitted like a cat. When it hissed at her, she saw that it had no teeth, but a serpent's pointed tongue.

The creature was a nightmare, literally.

A drude.

Fear claimed her, crowding out any thoughts beyond horror, and some animalistic instinct to run. To get away.

Except her feet wouldn't move. Her heart felt like it was the size of a melon, pressing against her ribs, squeezing the air from her lungs.

Her hand reached for her stinging cheek, wet with blood.

The drude shrieked and lunged for her, wings spread wide.

Serilda tried to strike out at it, but its talons latched on to her wrists, their sharp points puncturing like needles. Its wail invaded her, a scream so unearthly it felt as though it were piercing her soul. Her mind crystallized into nothing but fury and pain—then shattered.

Serilda was back in the castle's dining hall, surrounded by disgusting tapestries. The Erlking was looming over her, his smile easy and proud. He gestured to the wall. She turned, her stomach in knots.

The hercinia bird was above the buffet, its glowing wings stretched out. But this time, it was alive. Screeching in pain. Its wings kept fluttering, trying to fly away, but they were mounted to a board, stuck through with thick iron nails.

And on the wall to either side, two disembodied heads had been placed on stone plaques. To the right—Gild, glowering at her with hate, his eyes flashing. This was her fault. He had tried to help her, and this was what had become of him.

And to the left—her father, his eyes open wide, his mouth twisting, trying desperately to form words.

She stepped closer to him, straining to hear him with tears on her cheeks.

Until a word finally came. A whisper as harsh as a scream.

Liar.

Distantly, a roar thundered through the dining hall.

No.

Not the dining hall.

From a corridor, upstairs.

Serilda's eyes snapped open. She had fallen against one of the corridor's windows, her shoulder cracking the glass, leaving a series of hairline fractures.

Her wrists were bleeding, but the drude had released her. It was standing a few feet away, its knees bent and wings lifted, preparing to take flight again. It was screeching, the sound shrill enough to make Serilda press her hands to her ears.

The drude jumped upward, but had barely left the ground when one of the candelabras tipped over. No—was *shoved* over. It crashed against the drude, momentarily pinning it to the ground.

The creature howled and crawled out from beneath the heavy iron. It might have been limping, but it took flight again with ease.

A wind like a sea storm rushed through the hall, smelling of ice, tossing Serilda's hair into her face and thrusting the drude against one of the doors with such force the chandeliers trembled overhead. The beast collapsed to the ground with a hiss of pain.

Seeing her chance, Serilda scrambled to her feet and ran.

Behind her, she heard something fall. Something crash. Another door slamming shut so hard the wall torches shuddered.

She whipped past the stained-glass windows with their watchful gods, down the staircase, her heart choking her.

She tried to remember where she was, but her eyes were blurred and her thoughts muddled. The halls were as unfamiliar as a labyrinth, and nothing looked the same as last night.

Another scream lifted the hairs on Serilda's neck.

She collapsed against a pillar, gasping for breath. It had sounded close this time, but she didn't know which direction it had come from. She didn't know if she wanted to find out the source of the scream or not. It sounded like someone needed help. It sounded like someone was dying.

She waited, struggling to listen over the mad thumping of her heart and her rapid, halting breaths.

The scream did not come again.

Legs shaking, Serilda headed toward what she thought was the great hall. But when she turned again, she found herself facing an alcove with a set of wide-open double doors. The room beyond was enormous and in as much disrepair as the rest of the castle. What little furniture remained was toppled and broken. Crackled ivy leaves littered the floor, along with chipped stone and twigs dragged in by whatever critters had tried to make this forsaken place their home.

A raised dais stood at the far end of one room, with two ornate chairs on top of it.

Not chairs, exactly. Thrones. Each one gilded and upholstered in cobalt blue.

They appeared pristine, untouched by the decay that had ruined the rest of the castle, preserved by what magic she couldn't begin to guess. It looked as if the castle's rulers might be returning any moment. If only the rest of their castle weren't being slowly eroded away. Claimed by nature, by death.

And this *was* a place of death. It was unmistakable. The smell of rot. The taste of ashes on her tongue. The way misery and suffering clung to the walls like invisible cobwebs, floating on the air like bits of ephemeral dust.

She was halfway across the throne room when she heard the low, squelching sound.

She paused, listening.

On her next step, she heard it again, and this time, she felt the sole of her boot sticking to the stone.

Her gaze dropped to the floor and the trail of bloody footprints that stretched out behind her to the corridor she had just left. A dark pool now swelled around the edges of the throne room, spilling out into the corridor.

Her insides spasmed.

She backed away, slowly at first—then turned and fled, toward the large double doors facing the thrones. The moment she crossed the threshold, the doors slammed shut.

She did not stop. She passed from one grand, decrepit parlor into another, until suddenly she recognized where she was. The enormous fireplace. The carved doors.

She'd found the great hall.

With a shuddering, hopeful cry, she launched herself toward the doors and yanked them open. Gray light spilled across the courtyard, which had fared little better with time. The hound statues at the base of the steps were now streaked with green decay, their surfaces pocked by corrosion. The stables were collapsing on one end, the thatched roof mottled with holes. The courtyard itself was being devoured by brambles and spiny musk thistles. A wayfaring tree had sprouted up in the southern corner, its roots tearing through the cobblestones, its barren winter branches like skeletal fingers reaching for the gray sky. The berries that had not been picked clean by the birds had fallen onto the stone and were rotting away into bloodlike splatters.

But the gate was open. The drawbridge was down.

She could have wept with relief.

As a freezing wind blew off the lake, tossing back her hair and cloak, Serilda ran as hard as she could. Behind her she could still hear the screaming, the cries, the cacophony of death.

Wood thundered underfoot as she crossed the drawbridge. On the other side, the narrow bridge that connected the castle to the town stood weathered from time. Its stones chipping away. One section of rail having collapsed down into the water below. It would have been frightfully treacherous in a carriage, but even the fragile, narrow middle of the bridge still afforded plenty of room for lone Serilda. She ran until all she could hear were the wind whistling in her ears and her own panting breaths.

She finally slowed and grabbed on to a pillar, which had just last night held a blazing torch, but was now nothing more than damp, worn stone. She leaned against it as she struggled to catch her breath.

Slowly, she dared to turn.

The castle reared up from the mist, as eerie and imposing as it had been the night before. But this was no grand fortress for Erlkönig, the Alder King.

Now Adalheid Castle was nothing more than ruins.

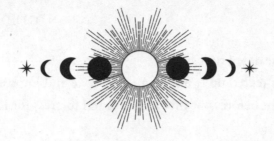

Chapter 15

When she had passed through the small city the night before, it had been quiet and solemn, as though all the villagers had sequestered themselves behind locked doors and shuttered windows, frightened of what might be prowling their streets beneath the Hunger Moon.

But as Serilda made her way over the bridge, she saw that during the night—or, the century, if she had indeed slept for a hundred years—life had returned to the town. No longer did it appear foreboding and half-abandoned in the shadow of the enormous castle. In the morning daylight, it actually looked rather lovely. Tall half-timbered houses lined the lakeshore, painted in tones of pale green and marigold and accented with dark wood trim. Bright morning sun alighted on snowy rooftops and gardens where more than one little snowman was slowly wasting away. A parade of small fishing boats was moored along a series of docks, and on the road that stretched along a pebbled beach there stood a row of thatched-roof shelters that Serilda didn't remember seeing the night before.

A market.

That was the greatest transformation of all, she noted, as the sounds of merry bustling greeted her. The villagers had emerged and reclaimed their city, as if the wild hunt had never ridden past. As if the castle on the water, just beyond their doorsteps, was not overrun with monsters and ghosts.

The sight that greeted Serilda as she neared the end of the bridge was lively, boisterous, and completely commonplace. People dressed in heavy cloaks and woolen hats meandered among the booths, examining animal furs and woven cloth, baskets of turnips and bundles of candied nuts, wooden clogs and metalwork. Shaggy mules pulled carts laden with apples and cabbages, pigs and geese, while chickens clucked and waddled freely among the streets. A group of children were lying on their stomachs on the end of one of the docks, playing a game with bright-painted stones.

Serilda was filled with relief to see them. All of them. They might be strangers, but they were human and they were alive. She'd feared that the town, like the castle, might have been lost to time, becoming an obsolete ghost town while she slumbered. She feared it might be just as haunted as the ruins she'd left behind.

But this city was not in ruins, and apparently, not haunted, either. If anything, her first impression was that the town was quite prosperous. There were no homes she could see that were in desperate need of repairs. Roofs were well-thatched or neatly tiled, gates were sturdy, and sunlight was glinting off glass windows. Real glass. No one in Märchenfeld had glass windows, not even the vintner, who owned more land than anyone. If a building had windows at all, they were narrow and open to the weather in the summer, boarded up in the winter.

As she crested the bridge, Serilda again wondered just how long she had slept. Had she really awoken in another time?

But then she spotted a copper pail left alongside a blue-painted fence, and it struck her as familiar. She was sure she'd seen it last night. But if decades had passed, wouldn't the fence have rotted away by now, or the pail been blown off by some terrible storm?

It was not exactly confirmation, but it gave her hope that she had not stepped into another time, but had merely returned from behind the veil that separated the world of mortals from the realm of the dark ones.

Besides, the clothing was no different from what someone might wear in Märchenfeld—if perhaps sporting fewer stains and holes and a bit more ornamentation. But wouldn't the styles have changed had many years gone by?

Serilda tried to appear nonchalant, even pleasant, as she reached the end of the bridge. Soon the townspeople would notice her peculiar eyes and her very nature would come under question. Best to charm them while she could.

It was not long before they started to notice her.

At least—one woman noticed her, and let out a shaken wail that immediately drew the attention of everyone else nearby.

People turned, startled.

And as soon as they saw the girl in the worn traveling cloak stepping off the bridge, they stiffened, their eyes going round. Gasps and suspicious whispers made their course through the crowd.

Some of the children hissed, and Serilda glanced toward the dock. They were staring at her openly, their game forgotten.

Serilda smiled.

No one smiled back.

So much for charming them.

Bracing herself against this less-than-encouraging reception, she paused at the edge of the street. A silence had fallen over the market, as thick as a blanket of fresh snow, interrupted only by the occasional bray of a donkey or crow of a rooster, or someone farther down the street asking what was going on, then pushing and shoving to get closer, to see what had caused the disturbance.

Serilda caught a whiff of warm roasting nuts from a vendor down the way, and her stomach clenched with hunger. The market was not so different from the ones every weekend in Märchenfeld. Baskets of root vegetables and scavenged winter berries. Bins full of unshelled hazelnuts. Hard cheeses wrapped in cloth and loaves of steaming bread. Loads of fish, salted and fresh. Serilda's mouth watered to see it all.

"Lovely morning, isn't it?" she said, to no one in particular.

The crowd continued to gape, speechless. There was a woman with a toddler grasping at her skirts. A fishmonger with his wares spread out inside a tin trough full of packed snow. An elderly couple, each carrying a basket for their purchases, though all they had so far were some speckled eggs.

Gripping her smile like a shield, Serilda refused to shy away from their dismayed stares, even when those closest to her began to frown, their brows bunching when they noticed her eyes for the first time. She knew those looks well. The ones where people wondered whether the glint of gold was merely a trick of the light.

"Might one of you kind souls direct me to the nearest public house?" she asked loudly, so they could not pretend not to have heard.

But still, no one spoke.

A few of the gazes did shift beyond Serilda, toward the castle. As if anticipating a ghost army to be close behind.

There *wasn't*, was there?

Serilda glanced over her shoulder.

No. Just a bridge, sad and deteriorating. Some of the fishermen out in their boats had rowed closer to the shore, either having seen the stranger crossing the bridge or having noticed the change of atmosphere in town.

"Did she just come out of the *castle*?" squeaked a small voice. The children had crept closer, huddled in a shy group and staring at Serilda.

Another asked, "Is she a ghost?"

"Or a hunter?" said another in a trembling voice.

"Oh, forgive me," said Serilda, loud enough to let her voice carry.

"How frightfully rude of me. My name is Serilda. I was . . ." She glanced back at the castle. She was tempted—oh, so tempted—to tell them the truth of the night before. She had been summoned in a carriage made of bones, attacked by a hellhound, locked in the dungeons. She had met a gold-spinner and fled from a drude. Her lips tingled, eager to recount the tale.

But something in the faces of the townspeople gave her pause.

They were already frightened. Terrified, even, of her unexpected appearance.

She cleared her throat. "I was sent to study the history of this fine city. I am an assistant to a prominent scholar in Verene who is compiling a . . . compendium . . . of abandoned castles in the north. As you might imagine, these ruins are of particular interest for our research, being so remarkably . . . well . . . preserved." She glanced up at the castle again. It was not at all well-preserved. "Most of the castles I've inspected thus far have consisted of little more than a tower and a few foundational walls," she added, by way of explanation.

The looks she received were confused and suspicious and continually darting to the structure behind her.

Brightening, Serilda asked, "I need to be making my way back to Verene today, but I hoped I might find a bite to eat before I go?"

Finally, the elderly woman lifted a hand and pointed down the line of painted houses that curved around the lake. "The Wild Swan is just down the way. Lorraine can add meat to your bones." She paused, looking past Serilda again, before adding, "You won't be joined by none others, will you?"

This comment stirred the crowd. Anxious shuffling of feet and tightening of hands.

"No," said Serilda. "It's just me. I thank you for the help."

"Are you *alive*?"

She faced the children again. They remained huddled in their group, shoulder to shoulder, except the girl who had asked the question. She took a daring step closer to Serilda, even as the boy at her side hissed a warning.

Serilda laughed, pretending the question was in jest. "Very much so. Unless . . ." She gasped, her eyes widening in horror. "Is this . . . Verloren?"

The girl broke into a grin. "Nonsense with sauce. This is Adalheid."

"Oh, what relief." Serilda placed a hand to her heart. "I daresay, you hardly looked like ghouls and goblins."

"It isn't a joking matter," snarled a man from behind a table lined with wooden clogs and leather boots. "Not around here. And surely not from someone who dared enter that forsaken place." He gestured angrily toward the castle.

A shadow passed over the crowd, shuttering the expressions that had started to warm to her.

Serilda bowed her head. "My apologies, I did not mean to upset anyone. Thank you again for the recommendation." She tipped a smile toward the children, then turned and made her way through the crowd. She felt their stares on her back, the silence that persisted in her wake, their curiosity following after her like a hungry cat.

She passed a row of businesses facing the lake's shore, each hung with a metal sign indicating the owner's profession. A tailor, an apothecary, a goldsmith. The Wild Swan stood out from them all. It was the prettiest building along the shore, the plaster between its dark timbers painted the exact shade of the sky in June, with windows trimmed in yellow and corbels cut to look like lace. A sign hung over the walkway with a silhouette of a graceful swan, beneath which were painted the most wonderful words Serilda had ever seen.

FOOD-LODGING-ALE

She could have wept when she smelled the telltale aroma of simmering onions and roasted meats wafting toward her.

The inside of the public house was cozy and simply decorated. Serilda's eyes were drawn to a proverb whittled into the wooden beam above the fireplace. *As one calls into the forest, so it echoes back.* Something about the familiar saying made her shiver as she glanced around. The room was mostly empty but for an older man sipping a pint by the fire, and a woman seated at a long bar, bent over a book. She looked to be in her thirties, with a curvy figure, dark brown skin, and hair tied into a bun. She glanced up when Serilda came in and quickly flipped her book over to hold her place as she slipped off the stool.

"Sit anywhere you like," she said, gesturing at the surplus of empty tables. "Ale? Hot cider?"

"Cider, please." She chose a table at the window and knocked twice on the wood before sitting down, because supposedly demons didn't like the feel of oak, a holy tree with ties to Freydon. Serilda couldn't picture the Erlking being squeamish about a pub table, but it was a way to let people know that she, herself, wasn't evil. She figured it couldn't hurt, especially after the morning she'd had. Her seat had a perfect view of the castle ruins, its broken walls and crumbling towers blanketed by snow. More fishing boats had moved out onto the lake—bright spots of red and green on the calm black water.

"Here you are," said the woman, setting down a pewter mug full of steaming apple cider. "Are you hungry? We're usually quite slow on market days, so I don't have a full spread prepared this morning, but can gladly bring you . . ."

She trailed off, noticing Serilda's eyes for the first time. Then her gaze skipped down to the cut in Serilda's cheek.

"Goodness. Have you been in a brawl?"

Serilda pressed a hand to her face. She'd forgotten about the gash from the drude. The blood had dried into a hard crust. No wonder the townsfolk had looked so frightened.

"A brawl with a thornbush," she said, smiling. "I'm so clumsy some-times. You must be Lorraine? I was told this is the finest dining in all of Adalheid."

The woman gave a distracted chuckle. She had a motherly face—plump cheeks and an easy smile, but also keen eyes that weren't easily swayed by flattery. "That's me," she said slowly, gathering her thoughts. "And this is. Where are you coming in from?"

The other side of the veil, she was tempted to say. But instead, she told her, "Verene. I'm visiting ruins all over the realm on behalf of a noted scholar who is interested in the history of this area. Later today I'm intending to visit an abandoned schoolhouse near Märchenfeld, but I'm afraid I'm in need of transportation. Do you happen to know of anyone heading in that direction?"

The woman bunched her lips to one side, still giving Serilda that contemplative look. "Märchenfeld? That'd be a quick enough walk through the wood, but I wouldn't recommend that." Her gaze turned suspicious. "But how did you get here without a horse or carriage of your own?"

"Oh. I was brought last night by my business associate, but he had to continue on to . . ." She tried to picture the surrounding area, but she still wasn't entirely sure where Adalheid *was.* "Nordenburg. I told him I'd be able to meet him there."

"You came last night?" said Lorraine. "Where did you stay?"

Serilda tried not to huff. So many questions, when all she wanted was breakfast.

She probably should have started with the truth. She forgot, some-times, that lies had short legs. They never got you very far. Plus, the truth was usually easier to keep track of.

And so, she answered. With the truth.

"I stayed in the castle."

"What?" said the woman, a shadow crossing her features. "No one ever goes in that castle. And last night was . . ." Her eyes rounded in horror, and she took a few hasty steps back. "What are you, really?"

Her reaction startled Serilda. "*What* am I?"

"A specter? A wight?" She frowned, inspecting Serilda from head to foot. "Don't much look like a salige . . ."

Serilda slumped, suddenly exhausted. "I'm a human girl, I swear it."

"Then why would you tell such a story! To stay in the castle? The monsters in that place would have torn you limb from limb." She cocked her head. "I don't care for falsehoods, young miss. What's your *actual* story?"

Serilda started to laugh. Her actual story was so far-fetched she was having trouble believing it herself. "All right," she said. "If you insist. I am no scholar, just a miller's daughter. I was summoned by the Erlking last night and ordered to spin straw into gold. He threatened to kill me if I failed, but after I fulfilled the task, he let me go."

There. It was the truth. Mostly.

Lorraine held her gaze a long time, and Serilda expected her to scoff and cast her out of her restaurant for mocking the local superstitions.

Instead, some of her irritation seemed to fade, replaced with . . . wonder. "You are a gold-spinner?"

Serilda's hesitation was short. "Yes," she said. This lie had been told often enough now that it no longer seemed outlandish. "Blessed by Hulda."

"And you mean to tell me," said the woman, lowering herself into the seat across from Serilda, "that you were inside that castle on the Hunger Moon, and when the sun rose and the veil returned, the Erlking just . . . let you go?"

"So it would seem."

She grunted, astonished. But not disbelieving. At least, Serilda didn't think so.

"And I truly would like to go home today," Serilda added, hoping to steer them back to more pressing concerns. *Her* pressing concerns.

"I imagine one would after such an ordeal," said Lorraine, still staring at Serilda like she didn't know what to make of her. But also like she *believed* her. Cocking her head, she peered out the window toward the castle, deep in thought. Finally, she nodded. She stood and wiped her hands down on her apron. "Well. I do believe that Roland Haas was planning to head down toward Mondbrück today. I'm sure he'd let you ride along in the back of his wagon. Though it wouldn't be kind not to warn you, it probably won't be the most pleasant ride you've ever enjoyed."

Serilda beamed. "Any help would be marvelously appreciated."

"I'll get word to him, make sure he's still planning on going over today. In which case, best get your breakfast. I suspect he'll be leaving soon. Supposed to be another cold one." She started to turn away, but paused. "You did say you were hungry, didn't you?"

"Yes, please. I'm happy with whatever you have," said Serilda. "Thank you."

Lorraine nodded, her gaze lingering a moment longer on Serilda's eyes. "And I'll bring some ointment for that cheek." She turned and headed behind the bar, disappearing into the kitchen.

Which was about the time that Serilda was hit by a quiet guilt.

She had no coin. Nothing with which to buy this heavenly warm cider or the food that her stomach was howling for.

Except . . .

She twisted the moss maiden's ring around her finger, then gave a quick shake of her head.

"I'll offer to wash dishes," she murmured, knowing she should strike the deal before taking advantage of the innkeeper's hospitality. But she felt like she hadn't eaten in days, and the idea of being turned away was unbearable.

A noise outside drew her attention back to the window. She recognized the group of children from the dock—three girls and a boy—giggling and whispering beneath the hanging iron sign of the tailor next door. As one, they all craned their heads, peering at Serilda through the window.

She waved.

In unison, they screamed and dashed into a nearby alley.

Serilda snorted in amusement. It seemed superstitions were bound to follow her everywhere. Of course, she couldn't just be the girl with the wheel of misfortune in her eyes. Now she also had to be the girl who had emerged from the ruins of a haunted castle the morning after the Hunger Moon.

She wondered what stories the children were making up about her already.

She wondered what stories she would tell them, if given the chance.

If she was going to be the odd stranger who had ventured behind the veil, she wanted to make sure the rumors were worthy of her.

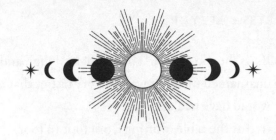

Chapter 16

The door to the public house swung open while Serilda was tending to the drude's scratch, and she was surprised to see one of the children strolling inside with feigned calm. The girl did not look at Serilda, but darted straight to the bar and climbed up on top of one of the stools. She leaned across the wood and hollered through the kitchen door. "Mama, I'm back!"

Lorraine appeared in the doorway with a bowl in her hand. "So early! Thought I wouldn't see you back here until nightfall."

The girl shrugged. "Wasn't much to do at the market, and I thought you could use some help."

Lorraine chuckled. "Well, I won't complain about that. Could you take this over to the young lady by the window?"

The girl hopped off the stool and took the bowl in both hands. As she approached, Serilda could see it was the same girl who had dared to ask if she was alive. And now that she was looking for it, the resemblance to the innkeeper was clear. Her skin was a shade lighter, but she had the same full cheeks and curious brown eyes.

"Your meal," said the girl, setting the bowl in front of Serilda.

Her mouth watered to see a fluffy golden bun marked with a buttery cross and a pastry filled with apples and cinnamon.

"This looks divine, thank you kindly." Serilda took the pastry and pulled it in half. As she took her first bite of flaky dough and soft apples, she let out an unashamed moan. It was a far cry tastier that the buttered rye bread she would have had at home.

The girl stayed at the table, shifting from foot to foot.

Serilda lifted an eyebrow at her and swallowed. "Go ahead. Ask your question."

The girl inhaled a quick breath before blurting, "How long were you in the castle? All night? No one remembers you coming to town. Did the hunt bring you? Did you see the ghosts? How did you get out?"

"Gods alive, I'm going to need sustenance before I can answer all those," said Serilda. Once she had gobbled down the first half of the pastry and washed it down with the cider, she glanced back out the window to see the other three children watching them.

"Your friends seem to be afraid of me," she said. "How did you get chosen to be the unlucky one to come in and gather all this information?"

The girl puffed up her chest. "I'm the bravest."

Serilda grinned. "I can tell."

"Henrietta thinks you're a nachzehrer," the girl added. "She thinks you probably died of some tragic accident and your spirit was drawn to Adalheid because of the dark ones, but you're not trapped behind the veil like the others, and you're probably going to kill everyone in town as soon as we go to sleep tonight, and eat our flesh, and then turn into a pig and run off to live in the woods."

"Henrietta sounds like a good storyteller."

"Is it true?"

"No," Serilda said with a laugh. "Though if it were, I probably wouldn't admit it." She took another bite of pastry, considering. "I'm not sure nachzehrer can talk. Their mouths are so busy eating their burial shrouds."

"And their own bodies," added the girl. "And everyone else."

"That, too."

The girl pondered. "I don't think nachzehrer like apple hand pies, either."

Serilda shook her head. "Strictly meat pies for the undead, I think. What's your name?"

"Leyna," said the girl. "Leyna De Ven."

"Tell me, Leyna De Ven. Did your friends by chance have a bet in place to determine whether or not you would be brave enough to come in and ask me all these questions?"

Her eyes lit with surprise. "How did you know?"

"I have some talent for mind-reading," said Serilda. In fact, she was very good at knowing what was in the minds of bored, mischievous children, having spent so much time with them.

Leyna looked properly impressed.

"How much was the bet for?"

"Two coppers," said Leyna.

"Then I will make you a deal. I will tell you the story of how I came to be in that castle this morning, in exchange for breakfast."

Beaming, the girl slid into the chair opposite Serilda. "Done!" She cast a winning smile out at her friends, who were bug-eyed to see that Leyna was not only talking to Serilda, but had even sat with her. "They thought I wouldn't do it," she said. "Even the adults down at the market are afraid of you. It's all anyone was talking about once you walked away. Said you had cursed eyes." She studied Serilda's face. "They *are* strange."

"All magical things are strange."

Leyna's eyes widened. "Is that how you read minds? Can you . . . *see* things?"

"Perhaps."

"Leyna! What are you doing, bothering our guest?"

Leyna stiffened. "Sorry, Mama. I was just—"

"I invited her to join me," said Serilda, with a sheepish smile. "I may not be a scholar's assistant, but I am truly curious about this city. I've never been to Adalheid before and I thought she could tell me more about it. I'm sorry if I'm keeping her from her work."

Lorraine tutted and set another plate of food in front of Serilda—pickled fish and boiled ham, dried plums, a tiny dish full of winter berries. "Not much work to be done today. She's all right." But she said this with a warning look at her daughter, and the meaning was clear. She was not to overstay her welcome at this table. "I've sent word off to Roland. I'll let you know as soon as I hear."

"Thank you. This town is lovely, I'm sad to not visit for longer. I hadn't heard much about Adalheid, but it seems so . . . prosperous."

"Oh," said Leyna. "That's because of the—"

"Fantastic leadership," interrupted Lorraine. "If I do say so myself."

Leyna rolled her eyes. "Ma's the mayor."

"For seven years now," said Lorraine proudly. "Ever since Burnard over there decided to retire." She nodded her head toward the man by the fireplace, who was lazily finishing his pint of ale.

"The mayor!" said Serilda. "You seem so young."

"Oh, I am," she said, with a bit of a preen. "But you won't find anyone who loves this town more than I do."

"Have you lived here long?"

"My whole life."

"Then you must know everything there is to know about this place."

"Of course I do," said Lorraine. Face growing serious, she lifted a finger. "But I'll tell you now, I'm no gossip."

Leyna laughed, but tried to cover it up with a cough.

Her mother glowered at her. "I won't suffer my daughter to gossip about the people around here, either. You understand me?"

Leyna quickly sobered under the intense look. "Of course, Mama."

Lorraine nodded. "You *did* say you were heading toward Märchen-feld, wasn't it?"

"Yes, thank you."

"Just making sure. I'll let you know what I hear." She bustled back toward the kitchen.

"No gossip," Leyna muttered as soon as her mother was gone. "The thing is, I think she might actually believe it." She leaned across the table, dropping her voice to a whisper. "But I guarantee she and my father started this inn *because* she loves to gossip, and everyone knows a public house is the best place for it."

The door opened, bringing with it a crisp breeze and the smell of fresh-baked bread. Leyna perked up, eyes brightening. "And look at that. Here comes the best gossip in town right now. Good morning, Madam Professor!"

A petite woman with fair skin and auburn hair paused a few feet past the door. "Oh, Leyna, when are you going to start calling me Frieda?" She hoisted a basket up higher on her hip. "Is your ma around?"

"She's just gone to the back," said Leyna. "She'll be right back."

As if on cue, Lorraine reappeared behind the bar, already beaming.

"Watch this," Leyna whispered, and it took Serilda a moment to realize she was talking to her.

"Frieda! What good timing," said Lorraine, strangely breathless, when she'd seemed fine a moment ago.

"Is it?" said Frieda, setting the basket down on the bar.

"We have a guest from out of town who is interested in the history of Adalheid and its castle," said Lorraine, gesturing toward Serilda.

"Oh! Well. Perhaps I can . . . um." Frieda glanced from Serilda to her basket. Back to Serilda. Back to the basket. Up to Lorraine. She seemed flustered, her cheeks pinkening, before she gave herself a little shake and lifted a napkin from the basket. "First, I . . . I brought some cinnamon-pear cakes for you and Leyna." She pulled out two small cakes wrapped in cloth. "I know they're your favorites this time of year. And I received a delivery from Vinter-Cort yesterday." She started pulling leather-bound books from the basket. "Two new volumes of poetry, a translation of folktales from Ottelien . . . the history of various trade routes, an updated bestiary, the theology of Freydon—oh! Look how lovely this is." She produced a codex with thick vellum pages. "*The Tales of Orlantha*, an epic adventure written in verse hundreds of years ago. I'm told there are sea monsters and battles and romance and"—she paused to visibly temper her enthusiasm—"I've been wanting to read it since I was a little girl. But . . . I thought I would let you choose first? If there's something you wanted to borrow?"

"I'm still reading the book you brought last week!" said Lorraine, though she did pick up one of the volumes of poetry and flip through it. "But I'll come to the library to choose something new as soon as I'm finished with it."

"Are you enjoying it?"

"Very much so."

Their eyes met, both filled with mutual smiles.

Leyna shot Serilda a knowing look.

"Good. Wonderful," said Frieda, starting to pack the books back into the basket. "I hope to see you at the library soon, then."

"You will. You're a gift to Adalheid, Frieda."

Frieda's cheeks went scarlet. "I'm sure you say that to everyone, Madam Mayor."

"No," piped up Leyna. "She really doesn't."

Lorraine shot her an annoyed look.

Clearing her throat, Frieda returned the napkin to the top of the basket and backed away from the bar. She turned to Serilda, a bit of a bounce in her step. "You're interested in learning more about Adalheid?"

"Before you get her to talking," interrupted Lorraine, "I'll warn you, I've heard that Roland will be waiting for you at the south gate in twenty minutes' time."

"Oh, thank you," said Serilda. She shot an apologetic look to Frieda. "You must be the town librarian?"

"That's me. Oh! I know just the thing. I'll be right back."

Without an explanation, Frieda bustled out of the public house.

Leyna settled her chin into her palms and waited for the door to shut to say, "Mama, I thought you didn't like poetry."

Lorraine stiffened. "That's not true! I have many varied interests, daughter of mine."

"Mm-hmm. Like . . . the history of ancient agriculture?"

With a glower, Lorraine picked up one of the cakes. "It was fascinating. And it doesn't hurt to read something other than fairy tales once in a while."

Leyna snorted. "It was four hundred pages long and you fell asleep every time you picked it up."

"That is not true."

"You know," said Leyna, drawing out the words, "you could just invite her over for evening bread. She's complimented your sauerkraut about a thousand times, and no one likes sauerkraut *that* much."

"Now, don't you get smart," said Lorraine. "Frieda is a friend, and the library provides a great service to this town."

Leyna shrugged. "I'm only saying, if you were to marry her, you'd eventually have to find something to talk about other than the latest shipment of library books."

"Marry!" said Lorraine. "Why—nonsense with sauce. Whatever makes you think . . . silly . . ." She let out a flustered huff, then turned and carried the cakes to the kitchen.

The man by the fireplace, the former mayor, clicked his tongue. "Funny how it can be so obvious to everyone else, innit?" He glanced up from his pint and sent a mischievous wink at Leyna, who laughed.

"They're hopeless, aren't they?"

The man shook his head. "Wouldn't say that. Some things just take time."

"I hope you don't mind my asking," Serilda said, "but . . . didn't you mention a father?"

Leyna nodded. "He died of consumption when I was four. I don't remember him much. Mama says he'll always be the first great love of her life, but the way she and Frieda have been flirting with each other the last few months, it's got me thinking it might be time for the second great love." She hesitated, becoming suddenly bashful. "Is that strange?"

"No," said Serilda. "I think it's very mature. My father is alone, too. I don't think he's found anyone yet to be that second love, but it would make me happy if he did."

"Your mother died?"

Serilda opened her mouth, but hesitated. Instead of an answer to the question, what came out was "I still owe you a story for the marvelous breakfast." They both looked down at her plate. Somehow, over the course of the librarian's visit, the food had magically disappeared.

Leyna sat up straighter, fidgeting excitedly in her seat. "Best be quick. Roland can be impatient."

"This is not a long tale. You see, my mother left when I was barely two years old." That part was true, or at least, it was what her father had told her. But he never gave many details, and Serilda—holding together the fragile heart of a little girl whose mother had not loved her enough to stay—never asked for them. Over the years, she had made up all sorts of tales to soften the blow of that truth.

Her mother was a moss maiden, who could not survive outside the woods for long, and though it pained her to leave her only child, she'd been forced to return to the wild.

Or her mother was a princess from a distant land, and she had to go back to assume responsibility for her kingdom, but she never wanted to subject her family to that life of politics and court drama.

Her mother was a military general, off fighting a distant war.

Her mother was the mistress of the god of death, and had been taken back to Verloren.

Her mother had loved her. She never would have left if she'd had a choice.

"In fact," Serilda said, her mind spinning a new tale, "that's why I really came here. For revenge."

Leyna's eyebrows shot upward.

"My mother was taken by the Erlking. Lured away by the wild hunt, all those years ago. I came here to face him. To find out whether she was left for dead somewhere or kept as a ghost in his retinue." She paused, before adding, "I came here to kill him."

Serilda didn't really mean it, yet as the words left her, a chill slipped down her spine. She reached for her cider, but like her plate, the mug was empty.

Leyna eyed her like she was seated across from the great huntress herself. "How does one kill the Erlking?"

Serilda stared back at the girl. Her mind turned and turned and gave her no help at all.

So she answered, entirely truthful, "I have no idea."

The door swung open and a breathless Frieda returned. Instead of her heavy basket, she now held only a single book, which she presented to Serilda as one would present the crown jewels.

"What's this?" asked Serilda, taking it gingerly into her hands. The book was delicate and old. The spine worn, the pages brittle and yellowed with time.

"A history of this region. It spans from the sea to the mountains and goes into depth on some of the earliest settlers, political designations, architectural styles . . . There are some truly beautiful maps. Adalheid isn't the focus of the book, but it is referenced on occasion. I thought you might find it useful?"

"Oh, thank you," said Serilda, simultaneously touched by her thoughtfulness and a little guilty that her interest in the history of Adalheid was really more about the undead presence in the castle ruins. "But I'm afraid I'm leaving today. I don't know when, or if, I'll be able to return this."

She tried to hand it back, but Frieda brushed it away. "Books are to be shared. Besides, this copy is a little outdated. I should order a new one for our collection."

"If you're sure . . . then, a thousand thank-yous."

Frieda beamed and clasped her hands together. "Speaking of your leaving, I passed Roland Haas on my way, heading toward the gate. If he's still giving you a ride, I think you'd best hurry."

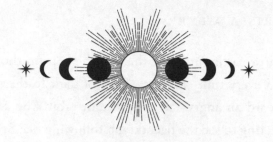

Chapter 17

Serilda had hoped that during the trip, she might be able to peruse some of the book the librarian had given her, but instead, she spent the ride in the back of Roland Haas's wagon sitting on a damp horse blanket and clinging as best she could to its high sides so the constant bumps in the road didn't launch her out. Simultaneously, she tried to fend off the curious pecks of the twenty-three chickens he was taking to the market in Mondbrück. The laces on her boots must have looked like the juiciest of worms, because the fowl hardly left her alone, no matter how many times she kicked to shoo them away.

She had suffered more than a few nips at her legs by the time Roland dropped her off at a crossroads a few miles east of Märchenfeld.

After profusely thanking the farmer, Serilda set off on foot. It wasn't long before the scenery became familiar. The Thorpe Farm, with its striking windmill turning over the snow-laden fields. Mother Garver's quaint cottage, whitewashed and surrounded by tidy boxwoods.

Rather than walking through town, she turned to the south, taking a shortcut through a series of pear and apple orchards, barren in the winter, their branches reaching scraggly fingers toward the sky. The cloud cover had burned off and the day was one of the warmest they'd had in months; but despite the sunshine and exercise, Serilda couldn't shake the chill that had settled into her bones from the moment she'd awoken in those castle ruins. Or the way the hair on the back of her neck prickled every time she saw a flash of dark feathers in the tree boughs or heard an angry caw of a distant crow. She kept glancing around, expecting to see the nachtkrapp following her. Spying on her. Eyeing her tasty eyes and fast-beating heart.

But all she saw were crows and jackdaws scavenging among the bare trees.

It was nearly dusk by the time the mill came into view, down in the valley carved out by the winding river. Smoke curled above the chimney. The hazelnut tree's snow-heavy branches bowed. Zelig, that beloved antique horse of theirs, poked his head curiously from the stable.

Her father had even shoveled a path from the road to their doorway. Serilda beamed and started to run.

"Papa!" she cried, when she thought she might be close enough for him to hear her.

A moment later, the door slammed open, revealing a frantic father. He puffed up when he saw her, overcome with relief. She rushed into his arms.

"You're back," he cried into her hair. "You came back."

Serilda laughed at him, pulling away so he could see her smile. "You sound as if you doubted it."

"I did," he said with a warm but tired laugh. "I didn't want to think it, but—but I thought—" His voice grew tight with emotion. "Well. You know what I thought. To be summoned by the Erlking—"

"Oh, Papa." She kissed his cheek. "The Erlking only keeps little children. What could he have wanted with an old spinster like me?"

He stepped away, his face pinched, and the lightness in Serilda's heart dampened. He was serious. He'd been terrified.

And she had been, too. There were moments during the night when she'd been sure she would never see his face again. But even in those moments, she'd given little thought to what he must be going through, not knowing where she'd been taken or what was to become of her.

Of course he'd thought she wouldn't come home.

"What did he do to your face?" he asked, brushing the hair away from her cheek.

She shook her head. "It wasn't the Erlking. It was . . ." Her hesitation was brief as she remembered the horror of the drude flying at her with its curved talons. But her father was already worried enough. "A branch. Caught me in the face, quite by surprise. But I'm all right now." She pressed her hands into his. "Everything is all right."

He nodded shakily, eyes shining with unshed tears. Then, clearing his throat, he seemed to brush off his burdensome feelings. "It will be."

The words were weighted with meaning, and Serilda frowned. "What do you mean?"

"Come inside. I haven't been able to eat all day, but we'll have a right feast now you're home."

Once they had seated themselves by the fire, two bowls of barley gruel topped with dried apricots in hand, Serilda told him all that had happened. She did her best not to embellish—a near-impossible feat. And perhaps, in her telling, the overnight journey had been fraught with a few more dangers (who was to say that a river nix hadn't been watching the carriage from the icy waters as they passed?). And perhaps, in this version of the truth, the stuffed creatures decorating the Erlking's castle had come to life, licking their lips and watching her with hungry eyes as she walked by. And perhaps the boy who had come to help her had been most chivalrous, and had not made her give up her necklace.

Perhaps she left out the part where he took her hand and pressed it, almost devotedly, to his cheek.

But as stories go, she recited the events of the night more or less as they had transpired, from the moment she had stepped inside the skeletal carriage to the long ride home being tormented by plump, feathered fiends.

By the time she finished, their bowls were long empty and the fire was craving a new log. Serilda stood, setting her dish aside as she went to the stack of firewood against the wall. Her father said nothing as she used the end of a log to rearrange some of the coals, before settling it neatly on top of the smoldering flames. As soon as the fire began to catch, she sat back down and dared to look over at him.

He was staring into the flames with distant, haunted eyes.

"Papa?" she said. "Are you all right?"

He pressed his lips tight together, and she saw his throat struggle with a hard gulp. "The Erlking believes you can do this incredible thing. Spin straw into gold," he said, his voice rough with emotion. "He will not be satisfied with one dungeon's worth. He will want more."

She lowered her gaze. This same thought had occurred to her—of course it had. But every time, she stuffed it back down into whatever dark place it had come from.

"He can hardly send for me every full moon until the end of time. I'm sure he will tire of me and move on to terrorizing someone else soon enough."

"Do not be flippant, Serilda. Time has no meaning to the dark ones. What if he does send for you again on the Crow Moon, and every full moon after that? And what if . . . what if this boy does not come to your aid the next time?"

Serilda looked away. She knew how narrowly she had escaped death, and that her father had, too. (Which was another small detail she might have left out of her telling.) She felt safe for now, but that security was an illusion. The veil kept their world divided from that of the dark ones *most* of the time, but not when there was a full moon. Not during an equinox or a solstice.

In four short weeks, the veil would once again release the wild hunt into their mortal realm.

What if he summoned her again?

"What I can't understand," she said slowly, "is what the Erlking could want with so much gold. He can steal anything he desires. I'm sure Queen Agnette herself would give him anything he asked for in return for merely being left alone. It doesn't seem like he would be concerned with material wealth, and there was no sign of . . . of pretentiousness in the castle. The furnishings were sumptuous in their own way, but I sense that he has no one to impress, that he cares only for his own comforts . . ." She trailed off, her mind circling on itself. "Why would he care about a plain village girl who can spin straw into gold?"

After a moment of pondering her own unanswerable questions, she glanced at her father.

He was still gazing into the hearth, but despite the cottage's comfortable heat, he looked strikingly pale.

Almost ghostlike.

"Papa!" Serilda launched herself from her chair and came to kneel beside him, taking his hands. He squeezed hers back, but could not look at her. "What's the matter? You look ill."

His eyes shut, his brow wrinkling with what emotions she couldn't name.

"I'm all right," he said—*lied,* Serilda was certain. His words were tense, his spirit subdued.

"No, you are not. Tell me what's wrong."

With a trembling breath, he opened his eyes again and met her gaze. A soft, worried smile touched his lips as he reached down to cup her face. "I won't let him take you again," he whispered. "I won't let him—" He clenched his teeth, but Serilda couldn't tell whether he was stifling a sob or a scream.

"Papa?" She took his hands into hers, tears brimming in her eyes to see the fear so plainly on his face. "I'm here now. I came back unharmed."

"This time, perhaps," he said. "But I could think of nothing but you being trapped by that monster, unable to come back to me. And I can't do it again. I can't spend another night like that, thinking I've lost you. Not you, too." The sob escaped this time as he hunched forward.

Not you, too.

It was as close as he ever came to mentioning her mother. She might have left when Serilda was just a baby, but her spirit had never gone completely. Shadows always clung to her father, especially as Serilda's birthday approached in the fall, around the time when her mother had vanished. She wondered if he even remembered telling her when she was little the story of how he'd made a wish to a god that he would marry the girl in the village he'd fallen in love with, and that they might have a healthy child together. Serilda may have been young when she'd heard the tale, but she remembered her father's eyes dancing with firelight at the memory. He'd glowed on the inside to mention her mother, but the moment had been brief, snatched away by the pain of her loss.

Serilda had known that he was probably making it up. After all, her father was many wonderful things. He was kind and generous. He thought always of others, putting everyone else's needs before his own. He was hardworking and patient and always kept a promise.

But he was not bold.

He was not the sort of man to approach a wounded beast. And if ever he met a god, he would be just as likely to prostrate himself and sob for mercy than to claim a wish.

And yet, Serilda had no other explanation for her peculiar eyes, and she'd always wondered if he'd made up the story as a means of comforting her. To show her that these strange wheels that marked her irises were not a sign of wickedness and misfortune, but of something special.

The story might have changed in her own tellings of it. To her, the wheel of fortune was a symbol of bad luck, no matter anyone else's interpretation. But she still warmed to remember her father's voice, laced with tenderness. *There was a girl in the village who I had fallen desperately in love with. And so, I made my wish. That we might be married. That we might have a child.*

As his hands trembled under Serilda's fingers, she steeled herself, and dared to ask the question that had so often been at the tip of her tongue. That had stayed elusive for her entire life, but now tugged at her, demanding to be heard.

Demanding to be asked.

"Papa," she whispered, as gently as she could. "What happened to my mother?"

He flinched.

"She didn't just leave us. Did she?"

He looked at Serilda. His face was flushed, his beard damp. He stared at her with haunted eyes.

"Papa . . . was she . . . did the hunt take her?" She tightened her grasp on her father's hands.

His face crumpled and he turned away.

It was enough of an answer.

Serilda inhaled shakily, thinking of the story she told Leyna in payment for breakfast just that morning.

My mother was taken by the Erlking. Lured away by the wild hunt.

"She always had an adventurous spirit," her father said, surprising her. He did not look at her. With a sniff, he pulled one hand from her grip and swiped at his nose. "She was like you in that way. Reckless. Not afraid of anything. She reminded me of a will-o'-the-wisp, glowing like starlight everywhere she went, always flitting about town, hardly ever stopping to catch a breath. At the festivals, she would dance and dance . . . and she never stopped laughing." He glanced at Serilda with his watery eyes, and for a moment, she could see the love that still lingered there. "She was so lovely. Dark hair, like yours. Dimples when she smiled in a special way. She had a chip on her front tooth." He chuckled, reminiscing. "Got it climbing trees when we were young. She was fearless. And I know she loved me, too. I never doubted it. But..."

Serilda waited for him to go on. For a long time, there was only the crackle of logs in the fire.

"Papa?" she nudged.

He swallowed. "She didn't want to stay here forever. She talked about traveling. She wanted to see Verene, she wanted to...to take a ship across the ocean. She wanted to see everything. And I think she knew—we both knew—that life wasn't for me." He sat back in the chair, his gaze lost in the flames. "I shouldn't have made the wish. To marry that wild, beautiful girl, start a family with her. We were in love, and at the time I thought she would want it, too. But looking back now, I can see how I was trapping her here."

The wish. Serilda's nerves tingled.

It was *true.* The Endless Moon, the old god, the wounded beast. It had been real.

She was well and truly cursed.

"She tried to be happy. I know she did. Almost three years we lived in this house. She grew a garden, planted that hazelnut tree." He gestured absently toward the front of the house. "She enjoyed working with me in the mill sometimes. Said anything was better than embroidery and"—a tentative smile touched his mouth as he glanced over at Serilda—"spinning. She loathed it as much as you do."

Serilda returned the smile, though her eyes were starting to water, too. It was a simple comment, but it felt like a special gift.

Her father's expression darkened then, though he didn't take his eyes off Serilda. "But she wasn't happy. She loved us—never doubt that, Serilda. She loved *you.* I know she would have done anything to stay, to watch you grow up. But when"—his voice grew hoarse and he squeezed her hands tighter—"when the hunt came calling . . ."

He shut his eyes.

He didn't have to finish. Serilda had heard enough stories. All her life she'd heard the stories.

Grown-ups and children alike leaving the safety of their homes in the middle of the night, dressed in nothing but their nightclothes, not bothering with shoes. Sometimes they were found. Sometimes they were still alive.

Sometimes.

Though their memories might be obscure, almost dreamlike, they were not usually the stuff of nightmares. They talked of a night racing after the hounds. Dancing in the woods. Drinking sweet nectar from a hunting horn beneath the moon's silver light.

"She went with them," Serilda whispered.

"I don't think she could resist."

"Papa? Did she . . . did they ever find her?"

She couldn't bring herself to say *her body,* but he knew that's what she meant. He shook his head. "Never."

She exhaled, not sure if this was the answer she'd wanted or not.

"I knew what had happened the moment I woke up. You were so little then, you used to snuggle in between us during the night. Every morning I would sit up and spend a moment smiling at you and your mother, fast asleep, wrapped up in the blankets, my two most precious things. I would think how lucky I was. But then, the day after the Mourning Moon, she was gone. And I knew. I just knew." He cleared his throat. "Maybe I should have told you all this a long time ago, but I didn't want you thinking that she'd left by choice. They say it's a siren song to those with restless souls, those who yearn for freedom. But if she'd been awake, if she'd been in her own mind, she would never have left you. You must believe that."

She nodded, but she wasn't sure how long it would be before she fully grasped everything her father was telling her.

"After that," he continued, "it was easier to tell people that she'd gone. Taken her few valuables and disappeared. I didn't want to tell the rest of town about the hunt, though with the timing, I'm sure there are those who guessed the truth. Still. With you and your . . . your eyes, there was enough suspicion already, and with all the stories of the hunt and the vile things the Erlking does, I didn't want you growing up thinking about what might have become of her. It was easier, I thought, to imagine her off on an adventure somewhere. Happy, wherever she was."

Serilda's thoughts churned with unanswered questions—one louder than them all.

She had been behind the veil. She had seen the hunters, the dark ones, the ghosts that the king kept as his servants. Her heart thundered as she dug her fingers into her father's wrist. "Papa. If she was never found . . . what if she's still there?"

His jaw tensed. "What?"

"What if the Erlking kept her? There are ghosts all over that castle. She could be one of them, trapped behind the veil."

"No," he said fiercely, rising to his feet. Serilda followed, her pulse rushing. "I know what you're thinking, and I won't allow it. I will not let that monster take you again. I won't lose you, too!"

She swallowed, torn. In the space of a few moments she felt an urge rise up in her. The need to return to that castle, to find out the truth of what had become of her mother.

But that desire was dampened by the horror in her father's eyes. His flushed face, his shaking fists.

"What choice do we have?" she said. "If he calls for me, I must go. Otherwise he will kill us both."

"Which is why we must leave."

She inhaled sharply. "Leave?"

"It's all I thought about since you left last night. When I could keep myself from imagining your body left dead by the road, that is."

She shuddered. "Papa—"

"We will go far away from the Aschen Wood," he said. "Somewhere you will be left alone. We can go south, all the way to Verene if we must. The hunt mostly keeps to rural roads. Maybe they won't venture into the city."

A humorless laugh escaped her. "And what would you do in the city, without the mill?"

"I would find work. We both would."

She gaped, bewildered to see that he meant this. He meant to leave the mill, their home.

"We have until the Crow Moon to make preparations," he continued. "We will sell what we can and travel light. Lose ourselves in the city. When enough time has passed, we can see about going farther, into Ottelien, perhaps. As we get farther away, we will ask what tales people tell about the Alder King and the wild hunt, then we will know once we are no longer in his domain. Even he can only travel so far."

"I'm not sure that's true," she said, thinking of the rubinrot wyvern mounted in the castle's great hall, which supposedly had been hunted all the way in Lysreich. "Besides, Father . . . I've seen nachtkrapp."

He tensed. "What?"

"I think they're watching me, for him. If they think I am trying to leave, I don't know what they'll do."

His brow furrowed. "We will have to be very careful, then. Make it seem like we're only leaving temporarily. Not draw any suspicion." He considered for a long moment. "We can go to Mondbrück. Pretend that we have business there. Stay at a nice inn for a few nights and then, when the full moon comes, we'll sneak away. Find refuge in a . . . barn or a stable. In some places, they put wax in their ears to block out the call of the horn. We will try that, so that even if the hunt passes near, you will not hear their call."

She nodded slowly. There were doubts crowding into her thoughts. Warnings from the coachman. Images of a cat toying with a mouse.

But she had so few options. If she continued to be called to the castle, eventually the Erlking would discover her lies, and he would kill her for them.

"All right," she breathed. "I will tell our neighbors about our upcoming trip to Mondbrück, and no doubt it will reach his spies as well. I will ensure that it is plenty convincing."

He took her into his arms, squeezing her tight. "This will work," he said, his voice thick with desperation. "After all, he cannot summon you if he cannot find you."

Chapter 18

The dream was a spectacle of gems and satin and honeyed wine. A gilded party, a grand celebration, sparkles in the air and lanterns hung from the trees and pathways scattered with daisies. Laughter tripping through a lush garden surrounded by tall castle walls that glittered with merry torches. A joyous occasion, brilliant and whimsical and bright.

A birthday party. A royal fete. The young princess stood on the steps adorned in silk and a beatific smile, clutching a gift in both arms.

And then—a shadow.

The gold melted away, flowing down into the cracks in the stone, out through the gate, until it filled the bottom of the lake.

No. It was not gold at all, but blood.

Serilda's eyes snapped open, a gasp filling her mouth. She sat up and reached for her chest, feeling a pressure there. Something pressing down on her, squeezing her life away.

Her fingers found only her nightgown, damp with sweat.

The dream tried to cling to her—its misty fingers sketching the nightmarish scene—but already the memory was fading. Serilda's eyes roved around the room, searching for the shadow, but she did not even know what she was looking for. A monster? A king? All she could remember was that feeling of dread, knowing that something horrible had happened and she could do nothing to stop it.

It took a long time for her to believe it hadn't been real. She sank back down onto the straw mattress with a shivering breath.

The door was edged in morning light, the nights growing shorter as spring approached. She could hear the steady drip of water off the rooftop as the snow melted. Soon it would be gone. Grasses would sprout vibrant green across the fields. Flowers would unfurl their heads toward the sky. Crows would gather in great flocks, eager to hunt for scurrying bugs in the dirt, hence why the last moon of winter was called the Crow Moon. It had nothing to do with eyeless, tattered beasts. But still, Serilda had been anxious all month, startling at every caw. Eyeing every dark-feathered bird with suspicion, as if every creature of the sky might be a spy for the Erlking.

But she had seen no more nachtkrapp.

She dared not hope that the king had forgotten her. Perhaps it had not been the gold he wanted, but revenge against the girl he'd believed had kept him from his prey. Now that he knew the supposed truth of her ability, maybe he had no use for her. Maybe he would leave her alone.

Or maybe he wouldn't.

He might yet return for her on every full moon until he was satisfied.

And he might never be satisfied. The uncertainty was the worst part. She and her father had made their plans, and she knew he would not reconsider, even if they might be running away for nothing. Uprooting their lives, seeking refuge in an unfamiliar city, for *nothing*.

With a sigh, she climbed out of bed and started to dress. Father was not in his room, having been gone early every morning this past week, he and Zelig making the trek to Mondbrück. He had hated leaving her so often, but Serilda had insisted it was the best way to make their ruse more believable. It only made sense that he would continue his work on the town hall until he was needed at the mill again. Soon the snow would melt in the mountains and the Sorge would surge with enough force to power the watermill, enough to turn the millstones and grind the winter wheat that would be harvested in the coming months.

It also gave him ample opportunity to bring home news of the upcoming spring market. All month long, Serilda had been telling anyone who would listen that she would be joining her father in Mondbrück for a few days so they could enjoy the opening festivities. They would return after the Crow Moon.

That was their story. If it was ever overheard by the Erlking's spies, she had no way of knowing.

No one around Märchenfeld seemed to care much, though the children expressed plenty of jealousy and demanded that she bring them each back a gift, or at least some candies. It crushed her heart as she promised them that she would, knowing it was not a promise she would keep.

Meanwhile, Papa took on the responsibility of quietly selling off many of their belongings during his travels to and from the larger town. Their house, which had been sparse before, was now downright barren. They would pack lightly, loading up a single cart that could be pulled by Zelig, and hope that the old horse had enough stamina left in his bones to get them to Verene once the full moon had passed. From there, Papa would hire a solicitor to handle the sale of the gristmill from afar, and with the proceeds, they would work toward establishing a new life.

That left a few small errands for Serilda, and one that she had been putting off all month.

She gathered up a stack of books, placing them neatly into a basket. Her hand skimmed over the volume that the librarian in Adalheid had given her, and she was met with another tug of guilt. She probably shouldn't have taken it to begin with, despite how eager Frieda had seemed to be giving it to her. She had no real intention of reading it. The history of industry and agriculture in this area was not nearly as interesting to her as the history of fairies and monsters, and a quick flip through the pages led her to believe that the author included little about the mysteries of the Aschen Wood.

Maybe she should donate it to the school?

After a long hesitation, she packed it into the basket and slipped out the door.

She had not passed beneath the branches of the still-barren hazelnut tree when she heard whistling. Glancing up the road, she saw a figure walking toward her. A mess of curly black hair and tan skin almost golden in the morning sun.

She went still.

She'd managed to avoid Thomas Lindbeck so far. He had only come into the mill a couple of times to clean the floors and oil the cogs, making sure everything was ready for the busier season, and she was normally teaching at the school on those days. With everything else happening, she had given him little thought, though her father mentioned a few times how lucky they were to have him working at the mill while they were gone. It would delay suspicions when they did not return after the Crow Moon, and farmers began arriving with grain to be milled.

Thomas was just about to turn off the road, heading toward the mill on the other side of the house, when he spotted her and his expression faltered. His whistling cut short.

The moment that passed between them was horrendously awkward, but blissfully brief.

Clearing his throat, he seemed to gather his courage before looking at Serilda again. Well, not *at* her, exactly. More . . . at the sky just above her head. Some people did this. Too uncomfortable to look her directly in the eye, they would find something else to focus on, as if she couldn't tell the difference.

"Good morning, Miss Serilda," he said, removing his cap.

"Thomas."

"Are you off to the school?"

"I am," she said, gripping the handle of the basket tighter. "I'm afraid you've missed my father. He's already gone to Mondbrück for the day."

"Won't be much longer before he's done over there, will it?" He nodded toward the river. "Water's picking up. Imagine this mill will be a flurry of activity soon enough."

"Yes, but the work on the town hall has been a boon for us, and I don't think he wishes to leave until it's finished." She cocked her head. "Are you worried about having to run the mill without him, should he not be back in time?"

"Naw, I think I can handle it," he said with a one-shouldered shrug. Finally meeting her eye for real. "He's taught me up pretty well. So long as nothing breaks, that is."

He flashed her a smile, showing the dimples that had once made her swoon.

Recognizing the peace offering, Serilda returned a weak grin. Thomas was the only boy in Märchenfeld that she had once upon a time thought . . . *maybe*. He was not the handsomest boy in town, but he was one of the few who didn't shy away from her gaze. At least, back then he hadn't. There had been a time when they were friends. He had even asked her to dance once at the Eostrig's Day festival, and Serilda had been sure she was falling deeply in love with him.

She'd been sure he felt the same way.

But the next morning it was discovered that one of the gates on the Lindbeck farm had been left unlocked. Wolves had gotten two of their goats, and a number of their chickens had either escaped or been carried off by the pack. It wasn't a difficult challenge for the Lindbecks to overcome—they had plenty of livestock. But still. Everyone in town had interpreted it as terrible ill fortune brought on by the cursed girl in their midst.

After that, he barely looked at her and made hasty excuses to leave whenever she was around.

She now regretted how many tears she'd wasted on him, but at the time, she had been devastated.

"I've heard that you're hoping to offer your hand to Bluma Rask."

She was surprised that the question had escaped.

Surprised more at the utter lack of spite it held.

Thomas's cheeks flushed as his hands brutally twisted and untwisted the cap. "I . . . yes. I hope to," he said cautiously. "This summer, I hope."

She was tempted to ask how long he planned to apprentice for her father, and if he hoped to one day take over the mill. The Lindbecks owned a fair amount of farmland, but he had three older brothers who would inherit before him. It was likely that he and Hans and their other siblings would have to find their own way in the world if they hoped to provide for a family of their own. If Thomas could get the coin for it, he might even be interested in buying the mill himself. She pictured him and his sweetheart living here, in the house she had grown up in.

Her stomach curdled at the thought. But not out of jealousy for Thomas's someday bride. Rather, she was jealous to think of the brood of children whose laughter might carry over these fields. They would splash in her river, climb her mother's hazelnut tree.

She had always been so happy here, even if it was only her and her father. It was a wonderful home for a family.

But what did it matter? She had to say goodbye. They would never be safe here. They could never come back.

She nodded, and her smile became a little less forced. "I'm very happy for you both."

"Thank you," he said with an uncomfortable chuckle. "But I haven't asked her yet."

"I won't say a word."

She bid him farewell and started down the road, wondering when, exactly, she had fallen out of love with Thomas Lindbeck. She did not remember her heart healing, and yet it seemed clear that it had.

As she walked she noticed that the town of Märchenfeld was beginning to awaken as if from a long nap. Snow was melting, flowers were blooming, and springtide would soon be heralded by Eostrig's Day, one of the biggest celebrations of the year. The festival took place on the equinox, which was still more than three weeks away, but there was much to do and everyone had a job—from preparing food and wine for the feast to sweeping the remnants of winter storms off the cobblestones in the city square. The equinox was a symbolic time, a reminder that winter had once again been bested by sunshine and rebirth, that life would return, that the harvest would be plentiful—unless it wasn't, but that would be a worry for another day. Spring was a time of hope.

But this year, Serilda's thoughts lingered on darker things. The conversation with her father had cast a shadow over everything she did this past month.

Her mother, who yearned for freedom, had been lured away by the hunt and never seen again.

Serilda had seen many ghosts in Adalheid Castle. Could her mother be among them? Was she dead? Had the Erlking kept her spirit?

Or—another thought, one that made her feel hollow inside.

What if her mother had not been killed? What if she had awoken the next day, abandoned somewhere in the wilds of the country . . . and simply chosen not to come back home?

The questions circled endlessly through her mind, darkening what otherwise would have been a most pleasant stroll. But at least she hadn't spotted a single hollow-eyed raven.

Anna and the twins were outside the schoolhouse, waiting for Hans and Gerdrut to arrive before they went in to begin their lessons.

"Miss Serilda!" cried Anna delightedly when she spotted her. "I've been practicing! Look!" Before Serilda could respond, Anna was upside down in a handstand. She even managed to take three walking steps on her hands before she dropped her feet back to the ground.

"Wonderfully done!" said Serilda. "I can tell you've been working hard on that."

"Don't you dare encourage that child," snapped Madam Sauer from the doorway. Her appearance was like the blowing out of a lantern—it extinguished all light from their small group. "If she spends any more time upside down, she's going to turn into a bat. And it isn't ladylike, Miss Anna. We can all see your bloomers when you do that."

"So?" said Anna, adjusting her dress. "Everyone sees Alvie's bloomers all the time." Alvie was her toddling baby brother.

"It is not the same," said the schoolmistress. "You must learn to act with propriety and grace." She lifted a finger. "You will sit still throughout today's lessons or I will have you tied to your seat, do you understand?"

Anna pouted. "Yes, Madam Sauer." But as soon as the old witch had gone back into the school, she made an ugly face that made Fricz cackle.

"I bet she's jealous," said Nickel with a small grin. "I think she'd rather like to be a bat, don't you?"

Anna flashed him an appreciative smile.

Madam Sauer was standing at the stove in the corner of the school-house, adding peat to the fire when Serilda entered. Despite the approaching spring, the world remained cold, and the students had difficulty focusing on their mathematics lessons even when their toes *weren't* numb inside their shoes.

"Good morning," Serilda chirped, hoping to start the conversation with brightness before it was tarnished by Madam Sauer's perpetually rotten mood.

The schoolteacher cast her a surly look, her eye darting to the basket on Serilda's elbow. "What is that?"

Serilda frowned. "Viper toenails," she deadpanned. "Swallow three at sunrise and they will help enliven an ill temper. I thought I'd bring you the whole lot of them."

She dropped the basket onto the teacher's desk with a heavy thud.

Madam Sauer glared at her, her cheeks reddening at the insult.

Serilda sighed, feeling a small twinge of guilt. She might feel terrible about leaving the children to her tedious lessons and strict expectations, but that didn't mean she had to spend her last days here trying to offend the witch. "I'm returning some books that I borrowed from the school," she said, pulling out the tomes—mostly compendiums of folktales and myths and stories of distant lands. They had received little appreciation in the schoolhouse, and Serilda didn't really want to give them back at all, but books were heavy and Zelig was old, and they didn't really belong to her.

It was time to disavow Madam Sauer of her suspicions that she was a thief.

Madam Sauer eyed the books with narrowed eyes. "Those have been missing for years."

She shrugged apologetically. "I hope you haven't missed them too much? The fairy tales in particular didn't seem to fit with the rest of your curriculum."

With a scoff, Madam Sauer stepped forward and picked up the book she'd gotten from the librarian in Adalheid. "This one is not mine."

"No," said Serilda. "It was given to me recently, but I thought you might enjoy it more."

"Did you steal it?"

Serilda's jaw tightened. "No," she said slowly. "Of course not. But if you don't want it, I'll happily take it back."

Madam Sauer grunted and gently turned a few of the brittle pages. "Fine," she finally spat, snapping the cover shut. "Put them on the shelf."

As she returned to the fire, Serilda couldn't resist copying Anna and making a face behind her back. Gathering up the books, she carried them to the small shelf.

"Not sure why I've even kept some of those," muttered the witch. "I know there are scholars who see value in the old tales, but if you ask me, they're poison to young minds."

"You can't mean that," said Serilda, even though she was fairly certain she did. "There's no harm in a fairy tale now and then. It prompts imagination and clever thinking, and good manners besides. It's never the nasty, greedy characters that live happily ever after. Only the good ones."

Madam Sauer straightened and fixed her with a dark look. "Oh, true, they might be bits of whimsy intended to frighten children into better behavior, but in my experience, they are most ineffective. Only real consequences can improve a child's moral aptitude."

Serilda's hands clenched, thinking of the willow branch that had struck the backs of her own hands so many times when Madam Sauer was trying to punish the lies right out of her.

"Far as I can tell," the witch continued, "the only thing those nonsense stories do is encourage innocent souls to want to run off and join the forest folk."

"Better than wanting to run off and join the dark ones," said Serilda.

A shadow eclipsed Madam Sauer's face, deepening the lines around her frowning mouth. "I've heard of your latest hoax. Carried off to the Erlking's castle, were you? Lived to tell the tale?" She loudly clicked her tongue, shaking her head. "You are inviting misfortune to your doorstep with such stories. I would advise you to take caution." She snorted. "Not that you've ever listened to me before."

Serilda bit her lip, wishing she could tell the old bat that it was far too late for caution. She glanced once more at the cover of the book the librarian had given her, before sliding it onto the shelf beside the other history tomes.

"I trust you've also heard that I will be gone to Mondbrück in a few days," she said. She was tempted to tell her that she would be going and never coming back. "My father and I are going to see the spring market."

Madam Sauer lifted an eyebrow. "You will be gone during the Crow Moon?"

"Yes," she answered, trying to keep the waver from her voice. "Is that a problem?"

The schoolteacher held her gaze for a long moment, studying her. Finally she turned away. "Not so long as you help the children with the Eostrig's Day preparations before you go. I haven't the time nor the patience for such frivolity."

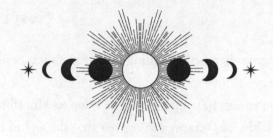

Chapter 19

er heart ached when she thought of how much she was going to miss the children. Serilda had every reason to believe that she would be even more of an outcast when they reached the big city—a stranger with unholy eyes—and she was dreading the inevitable loneliness. Yes, she would have her father, and she hoped to eventually find work and perhaps even make friends. She would certainly try to win over the people of Verene, or wherever they ended up. Maybe if she spun the story of her god-blessing just right, she could even persuade the people she met that it portended good fortune. She could be quite popular indeed if people believed her to be a good-luck charm.

But none of that eased her sadness.

She was going to miss these five children desperately, with their honesty, their laughter, their genuine adoration of one another.

She was going to miss telling them stories.

What if the people of Verene didn't like stories?

That would be dreadful.

"Serilda?"

She snapped her head up, startled from the maze of thoughts that she was so often lost in these days. "Pardon?"

"You stopped reading," said Hans, gripping a paintbrush.

"Oh. Oh, right. Sorry. I was . . . distracted."

She looked down at the book Madam Sauer had handed to her, insisting that the children hear the first five chapters before they were released for the afternoon. *Truths of Philosophy as Found in the Natural World.*

They had made it through twenty pages so far.

Twenty dense, dry, atrocious pages.

"Hans, why did you say anything?" said Fricz. "I'd rather suffer silence than another paragraph of that book."

"Fricz, preferring silence?" said Anna. "Now, that's saying something. Could you pass me that straw, please?"

Straw. Serilda watched as Nickel handed a few handfuls to Anna, who proceeded to stuff them into the large sackcloth doll laid out on the cobblestone road.

Serilda shut the book and leaned forward to inspect their work. For Eostrig's Day, the schoolchildren were traditionally tasked with making the effigies that would symbolize the seven gods at the festival. Over the past two days, they had completed the first three: Eostrig, god of spring and fertility; Tyrr, god of war and hunting; and Solvilde, god of the sky and sea. Now they were working on Velos, who was the god of death, but also of wisdom.

Though at this stage, it didn't look much like the god of anything. Just a series of grain sacks stuffed with leaves and straw and tied together to resemble a body. But it was beginning to take shape, with twigs for legs and buttons for eyes.

On the day of the festival, the seven figures would be paraded through town and adorned with dandelions and goose florets and whatever early blooms could be found along the way. Then they would be stood up all around the linden tree in the town square where they could watch over the feasting and dancing, while offerings of sweets and herbs were laid at their feet.

Supposedly, the ceremony was meant to ensure a good harvest, but

Serilda had lived through enough disappointing harvests to know that the gods probably weren't listening that closely. There were many superstitions associated with the equinox, and she placed little trust in any of them. She doubted that to touch Velos with one's left hand would bring a plague to the household in the following year, or that to give Eostrig a primrose, with its heart-shaped petals and sunshine-yellow middles, would later make for a fertile womb.

She already tried her best to ignore the muttered comments that abounded this time of year, following everywhere she went. People muttering to themselves about how the miller's girl should not be allowed at the festival. How her presence was sure to bring bad luck. Some people were brave enough, or rude enough, to say it to her face, always as a thinly veiled concern. *Wouldn't it be nice to enjoy an evening at home, Serilda? Best for you* and *the village . . .*

But most just talked about her behind her back, mentioning how she'd been at the festival three years ago and there had been droughts all that summer.

And that awful year when she was only seven, when a sickness had come through and killed nearly half the town's livestock the next month.

It didn't matter that there had been plenty of years when Serilda had attended the festival without consequence.

She tried her best to ignore these mutterings, as her father had told her to since she was a child, as she had all her life. But it was becoming more difficult to ignore old superstitions these days.

What if she really was a harbinger of ill fortune?

"You're doing wonderful work," she said, inspecting the buttons that Nickel had sewn onto the face—one black eye, one brown. "What happened here?" She pointed to a place where the cloth had been cut open on the god's cheek and stitched back up with black thread.

"It's a scar," said Fricz, shoving back a flop of blond hair. "I figured the god of death has probably been in a good brawl or two. Needs to look tough."

"Is there any more ribbon?" asked Nickel, who was attempting to make a cloak for the god, mostly out of old towel scraps.

"I have grosgrain," said Anna, handing it to him, "but that's the last of it."

"I'll make do."

"Gerdy, no!" said Hans, snatching a paintbrush out of the little girl's hand. She looked up, her eyes wide.

On the god's face, there was a dark smear of red—a smudgy mouth.

"Now it looks like a girl," snapped Hans.

Gerdrut flushed bright red beneath her freckles—embarrassed and confused. She looked at Serilda. "Is Velos a boy?"

"They can be, if they wish to be," said Serilda. "But sometimes they might wish to be a girl. Sometimes a god might be both a boy and a girl . . . and sometimes, neither."

Gerdrut's frown became more pronounced, and Serilda could tell she hadn't helped matters. She chuckled. "Think of it this way. We mortals, we put limitations on ourselves. We think—Hans is a boy, so he must work in the fields. Anna is a girl, so she must learn to spin yarn."

Anna released a disgusted groan.

"But if you were a god," Serilda continued, "would you limit yourself? Of course not. You could be anything."

At this, some of the confusion cleared from Gerdrut's expression. "I want to learn how to spin," she said. "I think it looks like fun."

"You say that now," Anna muttered.

"There's nothing wrong with learning to spin," said Serilda. "A lot of people enjoy it. But it shouldn't be just a job for girls, should it? In fact, the best spinner I know is a boy."

"Really?" said Anna. "Who?"

Serilda was tempted to tell them. She had shared many stories these past weeks about her adventures in the haunted castle, many more fictional than true, but she'd avoided telling them about Gild and his gold-spinning. Somehow, it had felt like too precious of a secret.

"You've never met him," she finally said. "He lives in another town."

This must have been a dull-enough answer—they didn't press her for details.

"I think I could be good at spinning."

This statement, spoken so quietly, went almost unnoticed. It took Serilda a moment to realize it was Nickel who had said it, his head lowered as his fingers made perfectly tidy stitches on the cloak.

Fricz stared at his twin, momentarily aghast. Serilda was already bristling, ready to come to Nickel's defense when Fricz made whatever teasing comment came to his mind first.

But he didn't tease. Instead, he just gave his brother that lopsided grin and said, "I think you'd be pretty good at it, too. At least . . . you'd be way better at it than Anna is!"

Serilda rolled her eyes.

"So, what am I supposed to do about this mouth?" asked Hans, dark eyebrows bunching.

They all paused to stare at the effigy's face.

"I like it," Anna said first, at which Gerdrut beamed.

"Me too," Serilda agreed. "With those lips and that scar, I think this is the best god of death that Märchenfeld has ever seen."

With a shrug, Hans started mixing up a new batch of egg tempera.

"Do you need more madder root?" Serilda asked.

"I think this will be enough," he said, testing the paint's consistency. He looked almost mischievous when he raised his eyes. "But I know what you could be doing while we work."

She lifted an eyebrow at him, but needed no explanation.

Immediately, the children brightened to an encouraging chorus of *"Yes, tell us a story!"*

"Hush!" said Serilda, looking back toward the schoolhouse's open doors. "You know how Madam Sauer feels about that."

"She's not in there," said Fricz. "Said she still needed to gather some wild mugwort for the bonfire."

"She did?"

Fricz nodded. "She left right after we came out here."

"Oh, I didn't notice," said Serilda. Lost in her own thoughts again, no doubt.

She considered their pleas. Lately, all her stories had featured haunted ruins and nightmare monsters and heartless kings. Burning hounds and a stolen princess. Though the children had been in raptures for most of her tales, she had overheard little Gerdrut saying that she started having nightmares in which *she* was kidnapped by the Erlking, which had filled Serilda with a flood of guilt.

She vowed to make her next story cheerier. Maybe something with a happy ending, even.

But that thought was eclipsed by sudden grief.

There wouldn't be any more stories after this.

She looked around at their faces, smeared with dirt and paint, and had to clench her jaw to keep her eyes from filling with tears.

"Serilda?" said Gerdrut, her voice small and worried. "What's wrong?"

"Nothing at all," she said quickly. "I must have pollen in my eyes."

The children traded doubtful looks, and even Serilda knew it had been a terrible lie.

She inhaled deeply and leaned back on her hands, turning her face toward the sun. "Have I told you of the time I came across a nachzehrer on the road? He was newly risen from the grave. Had already chewed off his burial shroud and the meat of his right arm, straight down to the bone. At first when he saw me, I thought he would run away, but then he opened his mouth and let out the most bloodcurdling—"

"No, stop!" cried Gerdrut, covering her ears. "Too scary!"

"Ah, come on, Gerdy," said Hans, draping an arm over her shoulders. "It isn't real."

"And just how do you know?" said Serilda.

Hans barked a laugh. "Nachzehrer aren't real! People don't come back from the dead and go around trying to eat their own family members. If they did, we'd all be . . . well, dead."

"It isn't *everyone* that comes back," said Nickel matter-of-factly. "Only people who die in terrible accidents, or from sickness."

"Or who kill themselves," added Fricz. "I've heard that can make someone a nachzehrer, too."

"That's right," said Serilda. "And now you know that *I've* seen one, so of course they're real."

Hans shook his head. "The more outlandish the tale, the harder you try to convince us it's more than just a story."

"That's half the fun of it," said Fricz. "So quit your complaining. Go on, Serilda. What happened?"

"No," said Gerdrut. "A different story. Please?"

Serilda smiled at her. "All right. Let me think a moment."

"Another one about the Erlking," said Anna. "Those have been so good lately. I almost feel like I'm in that creepy castle with you."

"And those stories aren't too scary for you, Gerdrut?" asked Serilda.

Gerdrut shook her head, though she was looking a little pale. "I like ghost stories."

"All right, a ghost story, then." Already Serilda's imagination had transported her back to the castle at Adalheid. Her pulse sped up, hearing the screams, the squelch of bloody footprints.

"Once, a long time ago," she began, her voice faint and unsure, as it

often was when she was just beginning to explore a story, not fully knowing where it was about to lead her. "There was a castle that stood above a
deep blue lake. In the castle lived a good queen and a kind king . . . and . . .
their two children . . ." Her brow furrowed. It usually didn't take much for
a story to begin to unfold before her. A few characters, a setting, and off she
went, chasing down the adventure as fast as her imagination could keep up.

But now, she felt like her imagination was leading her straight to an
unclimbable wall, with no hint as to what was on the other side.

Clearing her throat, she tried to push forward anyway.

"And they were happy, beloved by all the people in their kingdom,
and the countryside flourished . . . but then . . . something happened."

The children paused in their work and looked up at Serilda, waiting
and eager.

But as her gaze fell, it landed on the god of death, or at least, this
rather ridiculous embodiment of them.

There were ghosts prowling the halls of Adalheid Castle.

Real ghosts.

Real spirits, full of anger and regrets and sadness. Reliving their vio-
lent ends over and over.

"What happened there?" she whispered.

There was a moment of confused silence, before Hans chuckled.
"Exactly. What happened?"

She looked up, meeting each of their gazes in turn, then forced a
smile to her face. "I've had a brilliant idea. *You* should finish the story."

"What?" said Fricz, his lip curling with distaste. "That's not brilliant
at all. If you leave it up to us, pretty soon Anna will have everyone kissing each other and getting married." He made a face.

"And if she leaves it up to you," Anna shot back, "you'll kill everyone
off!"

"Both options have potential," said Serilda. "And I'm serious. You've
heard me tell plenty of stories. Why don't you give it a try?"

Skepticism flashed across their faces, but Gerdrut quickly perked up. "I know! It was the god of death!" She jabbed a finger into its stuffed side. "They came to the castle and killed everyone!"

"Why would Velos do that?" asked Nickel, looking severely unhappy with the way Serilda had given up so easily and passed her responsibilities on to them. "They don't murder people. They just shepherd their souls to Verloren once they've already passed."

"That's right," said Fricz, growing excited. "Velos didn't kill anyone, but . . . they were there all the same. Because . . . because . . ."

"Oh!" said Anna. "Because it was the night of the wild hunt, and they knew the Erlking and his hunters would be coming to the castle, and Velos was tired of all those souls escaping their clutches. They thought, if they could set a trap for the hunters, then they could claim the souls for Verloren!"

Nickel scowled. "What does that have to do with the king and queen?"

"And their children?" added Gerdrut.

Anna scratched her ear, accidentally smearing paint down one of her braids. "I hadn't thought about that."

Serilda chuckled. "Keep thinking. This is the start of a very exciting tale. I know you'll figure it out."

The children bandied about ideas as they worked. Sometimes the Erlking was the villain, sometimes it was the god of death, once it was the queen herself. Sometimes the townspeople narrowly escaped, sometimes they fought back, sometimes they were all massacred in their sleep. Sometimes they joined the hunt, sometimes they were stolen off to Verloren. Sometimes the ending was happy, but usually it was tragic.

Soon, the story had tied itself into knots, the threads growing ever more tangled, until the children were arguing over which storyline was best, and who should die and who should fall in love and who should fall in love and *then* die. Serilda knew she should interject. She should help them set the record straight, or at least reach some sort of ending that they could all agree on.

But she was lost in her own thoughts, hardly listening to their story as it became more and more cumbersome. Until it no longer resembled the story of Adalheid Castle at all.

The truth was, Serilda didn't want to make up another story about the castle. She didn't want to keep spinning outlandish fabrications.

She wanted to know the truth. What had really become of the people who had once lived there? Why were their spirits never put to rest? Why had the Erlking claimed it as his sanctuary, and abandoned Gravenstone Castle, deep in the Aschen Wood?

She wanted to know about Gild.

She wanted to know about her mother.

But all she had were questions.

And the brutal certainty that she would never have answers.

"Serilda? Serilda!"

She jolted. Anna was frowning at her. "Fricz asked you a question."

"Oh. I'm sorry. I was . . . thinking about your story." She smiled. "It's very good so far."

She was met with five dismayed looks. It seemed they didn't agree.

"What did you ask?"

"I asked if you'll be walking with us during the parade?" said Fricz.

"Oh. Oh, I can't. I'm too old now. And besides, I . . ."

I'll be gone. I'm leaving you, leaving Märchenfeld. Forever.

She couldn't tell them. She hoped it was easier this way, to just leave and never come back. To not have to suffer through their farewells.

But she didn't really believe it would be easier at all.

For sixteen years she'd believed her mother had left her without a goodbye, and there had been nothing easy about that.

But she couldn't tell them. She couldn't risk it.

"I might have to miss the festivities this year."

"You won't be there?" shouted Gerdrut. "Why not?"

"Is it because—" Hans began, but then stopped himself. As a Lind-beck, he had probably heard all about the year that his older brother danced with the cursed girl, and wolves got into their fields.

"No," said Serilda, reaching over to squeeze his hand. "I don't care what everyone says about me, even if I am bad luck."

His frown deepened.

Serilda sighed. "My father and I are going to visit Mondbrück in a few days, and we aren't entirely sure when we'll be back. That's all. But of course I hope to be here for the festival. I would hate to miss it."

THE
CROW
MOON

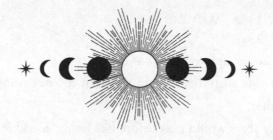

Chapter 20

She'd spotted a black bird flying over the spring market when she was picking out a bunch of onions that morning, and could not tell whether it was a crow or a raven or one of the Erlking's spies. The image had haunted her the rest of the day, those wings spread wide as it circled above the bustling square outside Mondbrück's nearly completed town hall. Around and around. A predator, waiting for the opportune moment to dive for its prey.

She wondered if she would ever again hear a crow's throaty scream without startling.

"Serilda?"

She glanced up from her salmon pie. The main room of the inn was swarming with guests who had come in from nearby provinces to enjoy the market or sell their wares, but Serilda and her father had kept to themselves since they'd arrived two days ago.

"It's going to be all right," her father murmured, reaching across the table to pat her wrist. "It's only one night, and then we will get as far away from here as we can."

She smiled faintly. Her stomach was in knots, a hundred doubts creeping into her thoughts, despite all her father's assurances.

One more night. The hunt might come looking for her at the mill, but they would not find her, and come sunrise, she would be free.

At least, free enough to keep running.

It filled Serilda with dread to think about the next month, and the month after that.

How many years would pass before her father was able to let down his guard? Before they truly felt that they'd managed to get away?

And always, those annoying whispers that it was all for naught. The Erlking might already be done with her. What if they were disrupting their lives and leaving behind everything they'd ever known all because of a stew of unfounded fears?

Not that it mattered now, she told herself. Her father was committed. She knew there was no talking him out of their plan.

She had to accept that her life would never be the same after this night.

She glanced toward the open doorway, where she could see daylight fading into dusk. "It's almost time."

Papa nodded. "Finish your pie."

She shook her head. "I have no appetite."

His expression was sympathetic. She'd noticed that he hadn't been eating much lately, either.

He left a coin on the table and they headed toward the staircase and the room they had let since they arrived.

If anyone was watching—if *anything* was watching—it would appear that they had retired for the night.

Instead, they ducked into a small alcove beneath the steps where earlier Serilda had stowed a couple of jewel-toned traveling cloaks that she'd purchased from a weaver at the market the day before. They had been too expensive, but it was their best chance for slipping out of the inn without being recognized.

She and her father each tossed a cloak on over their clothes and shared a determined look. Papa nodded, then slipped out through the back door.

Serilda waited behind. His spies would be looking for two travelers, her father had insisted. They needed to go separately, but he would be waiting for her. It would not be for long.

Her heart was in her throat as she counted to a hundred, twice, before she pulled up the emerald hood and followed. She hunched her shoulders and shortened her stride, trying to make everything about her different. Unrecognizable. Just in case they were watching.

It was not Serilda Moller who slipped away from the inn. It was someone different. Someone who had nothing to hide and nothing to hide from.

She walked the path she had memorized days ago. Down the long alley, past the public house, with raucous laughter spilling out the doorway, past a bakery closed for the night, past a cobbler and a small shop with a spinning wheel in the window.

She turned and hurried around the square, keeping to the shadows, until she arrived at the side door of the town hall. She usually loved this time of year, when boards were removed from windows to let out the stifling, stale air. When every sprig of grass and tiny wildflower was a new promise from Eostrig. When the market filled with early spring vegetables—beetroot and radishes and leeks—and the fear of hunger abated.

But this year, all she could think about was the shadow of the wild hunt looming over her.

She had just begun to tap on the wood when the door opened. Her father greeted her with anxious eyes.

"Do you think you were followed?" he whispered, shutting the door behind her.

"I have no idea," she said. "Looking around for nachtkrapp seemed like a sure way to make myself appear suspicious."

He nodded and squeezed her in a brief embrace. "It's all right. We'll be safe here." He said it as if he was trying to convince himself as much as he was trying to convince her. Then he shoved a crate full of bricks in front of the door.

Her father had sneaked blankets into what would become the council chamber. He lit a single candle, chasing away the otherwise pitch-black. They said little. There was nothing to discuss that they hadn't already discussed at length these past weeks. Their preparations, their fears, their plans.

Now there was nothing to do but wait for the Crow Moon to pass.

Serilda did not believe she would sleep at all as she curled up on the hard floor, using the new cloak to cushion her head. She tried to tell herself this would work.

The coachman might again come for her at the mill in Märchenfeld. Or, if the king's spies had been paying attention, they might come for her at the Mondbrück inn.

But they would not find her. Not here, in this enormous barren hall full of unfinished woodwork and carts laden with bricks and stones.

"Wait, we mustn't forget," said her father, pulling the candle from its copper base. He tipped it at an angle, so that the flame melted the wax around the wick. It soon dripped down onto the candlestick in a small pool. Once it had begun to cool, Serilda picked up the soft wax and formed it into balls, before pressing it into her ears. The world closed in around her.

Her father did the same, though he made a face as he squished the wax into his ears. It was not a pleasant sensation, but it was a precaution against the call of the hunt. The silence of the night was complete, but the thoughts in Serilda's head became aggressively loud as she laid her head back down on the cloak.

Her mother.

The Erlking.

Spun gold and the god of death and moss maidens fleeing from the hounds.

And Gild. The way he looked at her. Like she was a miracle, not a curse.

She closed her eyes and pleaded for sleep.

☾

Sleep must have finally claimed her, for she was awoken by a muffled *thump* not far from her head. Her eyes snapped open. Her ears were full of a dull roar. She was staring at unfamiliar walls lit with shifting candlelight.

She sat up and spotted the candle rolling around on the wooden floorboards. With a gasp, she grabbed the cloak and threw it over the flame, smothering it before it could start a fire.

Darkness engulfed her, but not before she'd caught sight of her father's figure stumbling away from her.

"Papa?" she whispered, not sure if she was too loud or too quiet. She got to her feet and called to him again. In the night, the moon had risen, and her eyes began to adjust to the light coming in through three small openings that had not yet been filled with leaded glass.

Her father was gone.

Serilda moved to follow him and felt something give beneath her heel. Reaching down, she picked up the glob of wax. Her insides squeezed.

The hunt?

Had they been found? After everything?

No. Perhaps he was only sleepwalking.

Perhaps . . .

She grabbed her cloak and shoes and hurried out into the massive hall beyond the chamber, in time to see him slip around a distant corner. Serilda followed, calling to him again.

He was not heading toward the small back door. Instead, he

shuffled toward the main entrance that opened onto the city square. The massive arched doors were nailed shut with temporary planks of wood to ward off thieves while the building was being constructed. Serilda spied her father in time to see him grab a large hammer left behind by one of the crews.

He swung the hammer, splintering the first board.

She cried out in surprise. "Papa! Stop!" Her voice was still dampened by the wax, but she knew he must be able to hear her. Still, he did not turn around.

Using the tool's handle as leverage, he pried away the first board from the intricately carved door. Then the second.

Serilda's hands fell onto her father's. "Papa, what are you doing?"

He glanced toward her, but even in the dim lighting she could see that his gaze was unfocused. Sweat beaded on his brow.

"Papa?"

With a sneer, he put a hand to her sternum and shoved her away.

Serilda stumbled back.

Her father yanked open the door and rushed out into the night.

Pulse fluttering, she dashed after him. He was moving quicker now, hurrying across the square, toward the inn where they should have been staying. The moon illuminated the square in a silver glow.

Serilda was halfway across the square when she realized he wasn't heading to the inn's entrance, but around to the back. She picked up her pace. Usually she had no trouble keeping up with her father. Her legs were longer and he was not a man to hasten unnecessarily. But now she was out of breath as she darted around the large fountain of Freydon in the square's center.

She turned the corner behind the inn and froze.

Her father had disappeared.

"Papa? Where are you?" she said, feeling the waver in her voice. Then, with clenched teeth, she reached for her ears and pried out the globs of wax. The sounds of the world rushed back around her. Mostly the night was quiet, the revelers from the public houses and ale gardens having long retired. But there was the sound of shuffling not far away.

She realized it was coming from the stables that were shared by the inn and other nearby businesses.

She stomped forward, but before she could duck into the shelter, her father emerged, leading Zelig by the reins.

She blinked in surprise, stepping back. Papa had secured the bridle over Zelig's head, but had not bothered with the saddle.

"What are you doing?" she asked, breathless.

Again, his gaze swept over her without expression. Then he stepped onto a nearby crate and, with a strength and agility she would have been certain her father did not possess, heaved himself up onto the horse's back. His fists grabbed the reins and the old horse lurched forward. Serilda threw herself back against the stable wall to keep from being trampled.

Dazed and frightened, Serilda ran after them, screaming for him to stop.

She did not have to run far.

As soon as she reached the edge of the wide-open square, she froze.

Her father and Zelig were there waiting for her.

And they were surrounded by the hunt. Beside them, Zelig looked small and pathetic and weak, though he was standing as proud as he ever had, as if attempting to fit in with these powerful warhorses.

Dread hardened in her stomach.

She was shaking as she met the Erlking's gaze. He rode at the front of the hunting party, astride that glorious steed.

And there was one horse without a rider. Its coat as dark as ink, its white mane braided with belladonna flowers and sprigs of blackberries.

"How good of you to join us," said the Erlking with a wicked smile.

Then he raised the hunting horn to his lips.

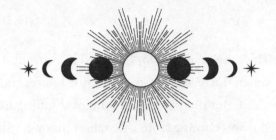

Chapter 21

It could only be a dream. True, many unusual and uncanny things had happened to her these past weeks, and the boundary between truth and fiction felt thinner every day.

But *this*.

This was dream and nightmare and fantasy and horror and freedom and disbelief all churned into one.

Serilda was given the riderless horse, and its strength and power seemed to transfer into her own body. She felt invincible as they raced away from the city. The hellhounds tore across the countryside. The world blurred in her vision and she doubted her horse's hooves were touching the ground at all. Their path was guided by the light of the Crow Moon and the unearthly howl of the hounds. They skimmed over riverbeds. Shot past darkened farmhouses. Crossed over pastures lush with grass, freshly plowed fields, and hillsides singing with early wildflowers. The wind in her face smelled sweet, almost salted, and she wondered how far they had gone. They might have been near the ocean, except that it wasn't possible to travel so far in such a short time.

None of this was possible.

In her daze, Serilda thought of her mother. A young woman, not much older than she was now. Yearning for freedom, for adventure.

Could she blame her for having been tempted by the call of that horn?

Could she blame anyone? When so much of life was rules and responsibilities and cruel gossip.

When you weren't exactly what others thought you should be.

When your heart desired nothing more than to stoke the flames of a bonfire, howl at the stars, dance beneath the thunder and rain, and kiss your lover, languid and soft, in the frothy surf of ocean waves.

She shivered, sure that she'd never had these yearnings before. They felt wanton, but she knew they were hers. Desires she'd never before recognized now clawed their way to the surface, reminding her that she was a creature of earth and sky and fire. A beast of the woods. A dangerous, feral thing.

The hounds chased wild hares, a startled doe, quail, and grouse.

Serilda's mouth watered. She glanced at her father, whose face was caught in speechless bliss. He was at the back of the group, though Zelig was galloping as fast as his old legs would move. Faster than he had likely ever run in his life. Moonlight glistened off his sweat-covered body. His eyes flashed wild and bright.

Serilda turned her head and caught the eye of a woman to her other side. She had a sword at her hip and a scarf tied around her waxen throat, and Serilda vaguely remembered her from the night of the Snow Moon.

Words filtered back to her through her heady thoughts.

I believe she speaks true.

She had believed Serilda's lies of gold-spinning, or at least claimed to. If she had not spoken, would the king and the hunt have murdered Serilda that very night?

The woman smiled at Serilda. Then she dug her heels into her steed's side, leaving Serilda behind.

The moment was fleeting. She wondered if it had even been real.

She tried to lose herself again in the mad, delicious chaos. Up ahead, a man with a cudgel leaned forward from his saddle and swung at their newest quarry—a red fox who was trying desperately to get away, darting back and forth, but trapped in every direction by the hunt.

It was a direct hit.

Serilda didn't know if the fox made a sound. If so, it was too quickly buried beneath the loud cheer and laughter that rose up from the hunters.

Her mouth was watering. The hunt would end in a feast. Their kills served on silver dishes, still swimming in pools of ruby blood.

Turning her face up toward the moon, Serilda laughed along. She released the reins and spread her arms wide, pretending to fly over the fields. Crisp air filled her lungs, bringing with it the most profound elation.

She wished for this night to never end.

On a whim, she glanced back again, to see if her father was flying, too. If he was on the verge of weeping, like she was.

Her smile faded.

Zelig was still charging forward, trying desperately to maintain his speed.

But her father was gone.

（

The drawbridge thundered beneath the horses' hooves as they stampeded across it and beneath the gatehouse. The courtyard was full of figures awaiting the return of the wild hunt. Servants hurried forward to collect the game. The stable boy and a few other hands took the reins of the horses and began leading them toward the stables. The master of the hounds lured the beasts back to the kennel with slabs of bloodied meat.

The moment Serilda slid from her mount, the spell over her shattered. She drew in a sharp breath, and the air was not sweet. It did not fill her with buoyancy. All she felt was horror as she spun around and her gaze landed on Zelig.

Poor old Zelig, who had collapsed onto his side just inside the castle wall. His sides were heaving as he tried to drag in breaths. His entire body was shaking from the exertion of their long ride, his coat covered in a lather of sweat. His eyes had rolled back into his head as he panted.

"Water!" Serilda screamed, grabbing the stable boy's arm as he returned for another steed. But then, worried that she would crush his fragile bones beneath her grip, she quickly released him and jerked her hand back. "Please. Bring this horse some water. Quickly."

The stable boy gaped at her, wide-eyed. Then his gaze darted to something past Serilda's shoulder.

A hand clasped her elbow, swiveling her around. The Erlking's expression was murderous.

"You do not command my servants," he growled.

"My horse is going to die!" she screamed. "He's old! He shouldn't have been pushed so hard tonight!"

"If he dies, he will die having tasted the greatest thrill any gelding could hope to enjoy. Now come. You've wasted enough of my time tonight."

He started to drag her toward the keep, but Serilda yanked her arm from his grip. "Where is my father?" she shouted.

In the next moment, the king had twisted Serilda's braids around his fist and yanked her head back, pressing a blade to her throat. His eyes were piercing, his voice low. "I am not in the habit of asking twice."

She clenched her jaw against the urge to spit in his face.

"You will follow me," he said, "and you will not speak out of turn again."

He released her and stepped back. As he stalked toward the keep's steps, every muscle in Serilda's body tightened with rage. She wanted to scream and rail and grab whatever was in reach and hurl it at the back of his head.

Before she could do anything, a ghost in a blacksmith apron ran out from the keep. "Your Grim! There's a . . . a problem. In the armory."

The Erlking slowed his steps. "What sort of problem?"

"With the weapons. They're . . . well. Perhaps you should see for yourself."

With a low growl, the Erlking swept back through the massive doors, the blacksmith on his heels. Only when the blacksmith turned around did Serilda see the half-dozen arrows jutting from him like pins in a cushion.

Serilda stood, heart still racing, fury still clouding her thoughts. She looked back at Zelig, relieved to see the stable boy carrying a pail of water in his direction.

"Thank you," she breathed.

The boy blushed, not daring to meet her gaze. She looked past him, toward the open gate. The lowered bridge.

Her entire body was sore, but mostly her thighs and rear end, which summoned dizzy memories of charging across the land on the back of that magnificent horse. She had done little riding in her life. She was reminded now that her body was unaccustomed to it.

But she thought she might still be able to run.

If she had to.

"I would not advise that."

The coachman appeared beside her. His warning from before returned to her.

If you run, he will only further relish the chase.

This night had shown her how right he was.

"I believe he told you to follow," continued the coachman. "I would not make him come searching for you later."

"He's already gone. I'll never find him."

"They were heading to the armory. I will show you the way."

She wanted to ignore him. To run. To find her father—who was out there alone. One more victim of the hunt, abandoned in a field or at the edge of the forest. He could be anywhere. What if he was hurt? What if he was—

She exhaled sharply, refusing to allow the word into her thoughts.

He was alive. He would be all right. He had to be.

But if she didn't do as the Erlking wanted, she would never leave this castle alive. She would never be allowed to go find him.

She faced the coachman and nodded.

This time they did not descend into the dungeons but ventured into a series of narrow hallways. Servant halls, if she had to guess, with her limited knowledge of castle architecture. After a dizzying number of turns, they arrived at an open barred door. Beyond it, a large table stood at the center of the room. The walls were hung with shields and various pieces of armor, from chain-mail jerkins to bronze gauntlets. There were a number of bare spots on the walls, too, where weapons might be hung.

The weapons weren't on the walls, though.

Instead, they were hanging, suspended from the tall ceilings. Hundreds of swords and daggers, mallets and axes, javelins and maces, dangling precariously by bits of twine.

Serilda hastily stepped back out into the hall.

"When did he do this?" the Erlking was saying, his voice rough with anger.

The blacksmith shrugged helplessly. "I was in this room just yesterday, my lord. He must have done it since then. Perhaps even after you left on the hunt?" He sounded like he was trying not to be impressed.

"And why wasn't anyone watching the armory?"

"There was a guard posted. There's always a guard posted—"

With a snarl, the king struck the blacksmith on the side of his face. The man was thrown to the side, his shoulder hitting the corridor wall.

"Was that guard posted on the *outside* of this gate?" roared the king.

The blacksmith did not answer.

"Fools, all of you." He jerked a hand toward the hanging weapons. "What are you waiting for? Get one of those useless kobolds to climb up there and start cutting them down."

"Y-yes, Your Grim. Of course. Right away," stammered the blacksmith.

The Erlking swept back out of the room, lips peeled back against his sharp teeth. "And if anyone sees that poltergeist, use the new ropes to string him up in the dining hall! He can hang there until next—"

He stopped abruptly when he spotted Serilda.

For a moment, he looked startled. Clearly, he'd forgotten she was there.

Like a curtain dropping over a stage, his composure returned. His eyes iced over; his sneer shifted from furious to respectably irked.

"Right," he muttered. "Follow me."

Again, Serilda was sped through the castle, past big-eyed creatures gnawing on candles and a ghost girl weeping in a stairwell and an older gentleman playing a sorrowful tune on a harp. They all went ignored by the Erlking.

Serilda had found some measure of calm since leaving the courtyard. Or, at least, her rage had been tempered by a swell of new fear.

Her voice was meek, almost polite, as she dared to ask, "Your Darkness, might I know what's become of my father?"

"You no longer need concern yourself with him," came the abrupt reply.

It was a stab to her heart.

She almost couldn't stand to ask, but she had to know—

"Is he dead?" she whispered.

The king stopped at a doorway and rounded on her, eyes blazing. "He was thrown from his steed. Whether or not the fall killed him, I neither know nor care." He gestured for her to enter the room, but Serilda's heart was trapped in a vise and she didn't think she could move. She remembered seeing him during the hunt. His exulted smile. His wide-eyed wonder.

Could he really be gone?

The king stepped closer, towering over her. "You have wasted my time and yours this night. Sunrise is mere hours away. Either this straw will be gold come morning or it will be red with your blood. That choice is yours to make." Grabbing her shoulder, he shoved her through the door.

Serilda stumbled forward.

The door slammed and locked behind her.

She took in a shuddering breath. The room was twice as large as the prison cell had been—which is to say, still quite small, and still lacking in windows. Empty hooks were spaced along the ceiling. The scent of mildew and misery had been replaced with the smell of salted, drying meats—and the sweet smell of more straw, of course.

A larder, she guessed, though it had been cleared of preserved foods to make space for her task.

Another pile of straw stood in the center of the room, significantly larger than the first, along with the spinning wheel and more stacks of empty bobbins. A candle sat flickering in the corner, already burned down to the height of her thumb.

She stared at the straw, lost in her thoughts. Anguish was crushing her rib cage.

What if he was gone? Forever?

What if she was all alone in the world?

"Serilda?"

The voice was hesitant and gentle.

She turned to see Gild a few steps away, his face taut with concern. His hand hovered in the air, like he'd been reaching out for her, but had hesitated.

No sooner had she laid eyes on him than tears blurred her vision.

With a sob, she threw herself into his arms.

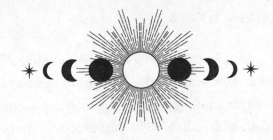

Chapter 22

He held her and let her cry, solid as a rock in the surf. Serilda didn't know for how long. It was an embrace that asked for nothing. He did not stroke her hair or ask what was wrong or try to tell her everything would be all right. He just . . . held her. His shirt was soaked through with her tears by the time she managed to still the tremors in her breaths.

"I'm sorry," she said, pulling back and sniffling into her sleeve.

Gild's arms loosened, but didn't release her. "Please don't be. I heard what happened in the courtyard. I saw the horse. I . . ." She met his gaze. His face was tight with emotion. "*I'm* sorry. This was a terrible night to be pulling pranks, and if he takes his anger out on you . . ."

Serilda rubbed the tears from her lashes. "The armory. That was you."

He nodded. "I'd been planning it for weeks. Thought I was being so clever. I mean it was kind of clever. But he was already in a mood, and now . . . If he hurts you . . ."

Her breath hitched. His voice was thick with distress. The candle-light was catching on golden specks in his eyes.

And he was not flinching away from her. He held her gaze with no apparent disgust.

That alone made her heart skip.

And also . . . there was something *different* about him. She squinted, unable to place it. Her hands settled against his chest and Gild's arms tightened around her waist again, drawing her closer. Until—

"Your hair," she said, realizing what had changed. "You combed it."

His body stilled, and a moment later, pink splotches appeared on his cheeks. He stepped back, his arms falling away. "Did not," he said, self-consciously digging his fingers into his red hair. It still fell loose past his ears, but it was definitely tidier than before.

"Yes, you did. And you washed your face. You were filthy last time."

"Fine. Maybe I did," he spat. "I'm not a schellenrock. I have pride. It's nothing to write a sonnet about." He cleared his throat uncomfortably and looked past her toward the spinning wheel. "There's a lot more straw this time. And a much shorter candlestick."

She sagged. "It can't be done," she said, on the verge of crying again. "I tried to run away. My father and I went to another town. We tried to hide, so he wouldn't be able to find me. I shouldn't have done it. I should have known it wouldn't work. And now, now I think he would take any excuse to kill me."

"The Erlking doesn't need excuses to kill someone." Gild stepped closer again and took her face into his hands. His palms were rough and callused. His skin was cool to the touch, but gentle, as he tenderly brushed aside a strand of hair that was stuck to her damp cheeks. "He hasn't killed you yet, which means he still wants to use your gift. You can take poison on that. We just have to spin the straw into gold. And it *can* be done."

"Why doesn't he just kill me?" she said. "If I were a ghost, wouldn't I be trapped here forever?"

"I'm not sure, but . . . I don't think the dead can use god-gifts. And supposedly, you were blessed by Hulda, weren't you?"

She sniffed again. "That's what he believes, yes."

Gild nodded. Then he swallowed hard and slid his hands away from her waist to grasp her fingers. "I will help you, but I need something for payment."

His words felt distant, almost foreign. Payment? What did payments matter? What did any of this matter? Her father might be dead.

She shut her eyes with a shudder.

No—she couldn't think of that now. She had to believe that he was alive. That she only needed to survive this night and she would soon be with him again.

"Payment," she said, trying to think, though her mind felt clouded. What could she offer as payment? He had already taken the necklace with the girl's portrait—even now she could see a hint of its chain around his neck.

There was still the ring . . . but she did not want to give it to him.

Another idea occurred to her and she met his gaze again, hopeful. "If you spin this straw into gold, then I will spin you a story."

Gild's brow furrowed. "A story?" He shook his head. "No, that won't work."

"Why not? I'm a good storyteller."

He eyed her, thoroughly unconvinced. "All I've wanted to do since the last time you were here is get that horrendous story you told out of my head. I don't think I can stomach another one."

"Ah, but that's just it. Tonight I will tell you what is to become of the prince. Perhaps you will appreciate this ending better."

He sighed. "Even if that did interest me, a story won't fulfill the requirements. Magic requires something . . . valuable."

She glared at him.

"Not that stories aren't valuable," he hastened to add. "But don't you have anything else?"

She shrugged. "Perhaps you could offer your aid as a show of gentlemanly honor."

"Much as I enjoy knowing that you think I might be a gentleman,

I'm afraid I can't. My magic won't work without a payment of some sort. It isn't my rule, but there it is. You'll have to give me something."

"But I have nothing else to offer."

He held her gaze a long moment, as if willing her to speak the truth. The look made her bristle.

"I *don't*."

His shoulders sank. "I think you do." He ran his thumb over the golden band on her finger. "Why not this?" he asked, not unkindly.

The caress made her skin tingle. Something coiled tight in the pit of her stomach. Something she couldn't quite place, couldn't quite name . . . but something she thought might be related to yearning.

But it was smothered beneath her sudden frustration.

"Don't be absurd," she said. "I'm sure you're fond of me, but to ask for my hand in marriage? I'm quite flattered, but we barely—"

"Wha—marriage?" he blurted, jerking away from her in a way that was just a little insulting.

Serilda hadn't meant it, of course, but she couldn't help but scowl.

"I meant the ring," he said, gesturing wildly.

Serilda was tempted to play ignorant, but she felt suddenly bone-weary, and the candlewick was burning too fast, and not a single piece of straw had been spun.

"*Obviously*," she said dryly. "But you can't have it."

"Why not?" he said, challenging. "I somehow doubt it was your mother's."

Her fists clenched. "You don't know anything about my mother."

Gild started, surprised at her sudden anger. "I . . . sorry," he stammered. "*Was* it your mother's?"

She peered down at the ring, tempted to lie, if it would keep him from asking for it again. Every time she saw it, she remembered how she had felt so very alive that night, when she ushered the moss maidens into the cellar and dared to lie bald-faced to the Erlking himself. She had always wondered until that night if she could be as courageous as the heroes in her stories. Now she knew that she could, and this was proof of it. This was all the proof she had left.

But as she was staring at the ring, another thought occurred to her. *Her mother.*

She might be here, somewhere in this castle. Was it possible that Gild *did* know something about her after all?

But before she could gather these thoughts into a question, Gild asked, "I don't mean to pressure you, but tell me again what His Darkness will do to you if this straw has not been spun into gold by morning?"

She scowled.

Then, teeth gritted, she pried the ring from her finger and held it out to him. He snatched it away, quick as a magpie, and tucked it into his pocket. "I accept your payment."

"I should imagine so."

Again, magic pulsed around them, sealing their bargain.

Ignoring the chilly look she was shooting him, Gild rolled out his shoulders, popped the joints of his knuckles, and took his seat at the spinning wheel. He began without fanfare, setting immediately to work, as if he'd been born at a spinning wheel. As if it were as natural to him as breathing.

Serilda wanted to wallow in thoughts of her father, her mother, her necklace and ring. But she didn't want Gild to snap at her like he had the last time. And so she removed her cloak and folded it into a pile in the corner, then rolled up her sleeves, and tried to make herself useful. She helped push the straw in his direction and form the raw mess into neat little bundles.

"The king called you a poltergeist," she said once they had found a steady rhythm.

He nodded. "That's me."

"Then . . . last time. You were the one who set that hound free. Weren't you?"

He grimaced. His foot faltered over the treadle, but he quickly found his pace again. "I didn't *set it free*. I just . . . broke its chain. And maybe left the gate open."

"And maybe almost got me killed."

"Almost. But didn't."

She glared at him.

Gild sighed. "I did mean to apologize. It was bad timing, which seems to be common practice around you."

She grimaced, wondering if Gild had overheard her conversation with the Erlking last time, when she'd told him that people in her village saw her as bad luck.

"But I didn't realize we were expecting a mortal guest." His hands shot up defensively. "I swear I didn't mean any harm. Not to you, at least. The king, he just gets real protective of those hounds, and I thought it'd get under his skin."

"You pull a lot of pranks on the king?"

"Have to do something to stay busy."

She hummed. "But why does he call you the poltergeist?"

"What else should he call me?"

"I don't know, but . . . a poltergeist is a ghost."

He glanced at her, the corners of his mouth twitching. "You do know what sort of castle you're in, don't you?"

"A haunted one?"

His jaw clenched as he focused on the wheel again.

"Yes, but you don't look like the other ghosts." She scanned the top of his head, the tips of his shoulders. "They fade around the edges. Whereas you seem . . . entirely present."

"I guess that's true. I can do things they can't, too. Like popping in and out of locked rooms, for example."

"And weren't *you* blessed by Hulda?" she added. "But that doesn't make sense, if the dead can't use god-gifts, like you said."

He stopped working, his gaze turning thoughtful as the wheel slowed. "I hadn't thought of that." He pondered for a long moment, before shrugging and giving the wheel another turn. "I don't have any answers. I suppose I was probably blessed by Hulda, but I don't know that for sure, or why they would have bothered with me. And I know that I'm not like the other ghosts, but I'm also the only poltergeist here, so I always figured I'm just . . . a different sort of ghost."

She frowned.

He glanced once at the candle, then squared his shoulders. His pace increased as he set to work again. Serilda looked at the candle, too. Her pulse skipped.

There was so little time left.

"If it pleases you," Gild said, replacing a full bobbin with an empty one, "I'll have that story now."

Serilda frowned. "I thought you hated my stories."

"I hated the story you told last time. It's easily the worst thing I've ever heard."

"Then why would you want me to continue?"

"Just figured I'd be able to focus better if you weren't constantly pestering me with questions."

Her lips twisted to one side. She was tempted to throw one of those bobbins at his head.

"Besides," he added, "you do have a talent for words. The ending was awful, but everything before that was . . ." He struggled a moment for the right word, then sighed. "I enjoyed everything before that. And I like listening to your voice."

Warmth rushed into her cheeks at this almost compliment.

"Well. Lucky for you, that wasn't the ending."

Gild paused long enough to stretch his back and shoulders, then smiled at her. "Then I would love to hear more, if you're willing to tell it."

"Fine," she said. "Only because you begged me."

His eyes glinted almost impishly, but then he looked away and grabbed up another handful of straw.

Serilda thought back to the story she had told last time, and immediately felt the comforting pull of a fairy tale. Where terrible things sometimes happened, but good always defeated evil.

Before she'd even begun, she knew it was just the sort of escape her mind and heart needed at that moment. A part of her wondered whether Gild had realized this. But no—he couldn't possibly know her so well already.

"Let's see," she started. "Where did we leave off . . ."

As the sun rose over the Aschen Wood, its golden beams descended over the spires of Gravenstone Castle. The veil's mist evaporated. The haunted night gave way to birdsong and the steady drip of melting snow. As soon as the light beams struck the hellhounds that had attacked the young prince, they turned into clouds of ink-black smoke and vanished into the morning air. In the daylight, the castle, too, was gone.

The prince was badly wounded. Bleeding. Torn. But his heart hurt worst of all. Over and over again, he saw the Erlking driving the tip of his arrow into the princess's small form. The murderer had taken her life, and now even her body was trapped beyond the veil, where he could not honor her with a royal burial, a proper rest. He did not even know if the Erlking would keep her as a ghost or let her travel to Veloren, where someday he might see her again.

Where Gravenstone Castle had just stood, now there were the crumbling ruins of a great shrine. Once, long ago, a temple had stood in this forest clearing. A sacred place once regarded as the very gates to Verloren.

The prince managed to get to his feet. He stumbled toward the ruins—great monoliths of slick black stone jutting toward the sky. He had heard of this place, though never seen it with his eyes. He supposed it should be no surprise that this unholy clearing in the midst of the forest was the place where the Erlking had chosen to build his castle, for there was such a sense of lifelessness and foreboding between these stone columns that no one with any sense would dare enter.

But the prince was beyond sense. He stumbled forward, suffocating beneath the weight of his loss.

But what he saw made him pause.

He was not alone before these black stones. The massive drawbridge over the swampy moat remained, connecting the forest to the ruins, though the wood was rotting and worn on this side of the veil. And there, in the middle of the bridge, lay a crumpled form. The huntress Perchta. Left behind in the realm of mortals.

The prince's arrow had pierced her heart and blood soaked the bridge beneath her. Her skin was pale blue, the very color of the moonlight. Her hair white as fresh snow, now speckled with wine-red blood. Her eyes gazed up toward the brightening sky in something like wonder.

The prince stepped closer, cautious, his body crying in pain from his many terrible wounds.

She was not dead.

Perhaps dark ones, creatures of the underworld themselves, could not die.

But there was such little life left in her. She was no fierce huntress now, but a broken, betrayed thing. Tears made treks down her once-radiant face, and as the prince stepped closer, her eyes shifted to meet his.

She sneered, revealing jagged teeth. "You cannot think that you have defeated me. You are but a child."

The prince steeled his heart against any pity he might have felt for the huntress. "I know I am nothing before you. But I also know that you are nothing before the god of death."

Perchta's expression became confused, but when the prince looked up, she shifted to follow his gaze.

There—in the center of those hallowed stones—a gateway appeared amid a thicket of brambles. It might have been alive once, but now it was a dead thing. An arch of brittle twigs and tangled thorns, dead branches and faded leaves. Beyond the opening, a narrow staircase descended through a gash in the ground, down into the depths of Verloren, over which Velos, the god of death, alone holds dominion.

And there the god stood. In one hand they held a lantern, the light of which never died. In the other they held a long chain. The chain that binds all things, living and dead.

Perchta saw the god and cried out. She tried to stand, but she was too weak and the arrow through her chest would not allow her to move.

As Velos approached, the prince stepped back, bowing his head with deference, but the god paid him no heed. It was rare that the god was able to reclaim one of the dark ones. Once, they belonged to death. Demons, some called them. Birthed in the poisoned rivers of Verloren, creatures born of the cruel deeds and haunting regrets of the dead. They were never meant for the land of mortals, but in the beforetimes, some escaped through the gate, and the god of death had mourned their loss ever since.

Now, as Perchta screamed with rage and even fear, Velos threw the chain around her and, defying all her struggles, dragged her back through the gateway.

No sooner had they descended than the brambles grew together, so thick one could not see through them. An entire hedge of unforgiving thorns disguised the opening amid those towering stones.

The prince collapsed to his knees. Though he was heartened to see the huntress taken away to Verloren, his heart was still broken from the loss of his sister, and his body so weak he thought he might collapse right there on the rotting bridge.

He thought of his mother and father, who would soon awaken. All the castle would wonder what had become of the prince and princess who had disappeared so suddenly in the night.

He wished with all his heart that he could go to them. That he could have been fast enough, strong enough, to rescue his sister and bring her back home to safety.

Just before he allowed his weary eyes to shut, he heard a heavy thumping, felt the vibrations on the bridge. With a groan, he forced himself to look up.

An old woman had emerged from the forest and was hobbling across the bridge.

No. Not just old. She was ancient, as ageless as the tallest oak, as wrinkled as old linens, as gray as the winter sky. Her back was hunched and she walked with a thick wooden cane that was as gnarled as her limbs.

Her vulpine eyes, though, were brilliant and wise.

She came to stand before the prince, inspecting him. He tried to stand, but he had no strength left.

"Who are you?" said the woman, in a tattered voice.

The prince gave his name, with as much pride as he could muster, despite his weariness.

"It was your arrow that pierced the heart of the great huntress."

"Yes. I hoped to kill her."

"Dark ones do not die. But we are grateful that she has finally been returned to Verloren." The woman glanced behind her, and—

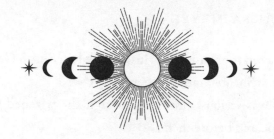

Chapter 23

Serilda yelped, jumping away from the unexpected, feather-soft touch along her wrist.

"I'm sorry!" said Gild, launching himself backward. His leg hit the spinning wheel and sent it toppling onto its side.

Serilda grimaced from the crash, her hands flying to her mouth.

The wheel spun half a turn before coming to a stop.

Gild looked from the fallen wheel, back up to Serilda, grimacing. "I'm sorry," he said again. His face pinched—with an apology, and maybe embarrassment. "I shouldn't have. I know. I couldn't resist, and you were so lost in the story, and I . . ."

Serilda's hand went to cover the bare skin of her wrist, still tingling from his barely-there caress.

Gild followed the movement. His face fell into something like despair. "You're so . . . so *soft,*" he whispered.

A clipped barking laugh escaped her. "Soft! What are you—" She stopped short, her gaze falling on the wall behind the toppled spinning wheel, and all the bobbins that had been empty when her story had begun. They now gleamed with spun gold, like gems in a jewelry case.

She looked down at the floor, completely bare, but for her traveling cloak and the candlestick, still burning strong. "You're finished." She returned her focus to Gild. "When did you finish?"

He considered for a moment. "Just now when Shrub Grandmother showed up. It is Shrub Grandmother, isn't it?"

His voice was serious, almost as though the wizened old woman really had appeared before them.

Serilda pressed her lips against a smile. "Don't spoil the story for yourself."

His smirk turned knowing. "It's definitely her."

Serilda frowned. "I didn't realize you'd stopped. I suppose I could have been helping more."

"You were quite engrossed. As was I—" His last word broke off into something strangled. Again his gaze dipped to her bare arm and suddenly he was turning away, his cheeks flaring red.

Serilda thought of how often he seemed to find reasons to touch her, even when he didn't have to. Brushing her fingers when she handed him the straw. Or the way he had nuzzled her hand the last time, and how the memory sent an unexpected thrill through her even now.

She knew it was only because she was alive. She was not a dark one, cold as ice in the dead of winter. She was not a ghost, who felt like they would dissolve if you so much as breathed on them. She knew it was only because—to this boy who had not touched a mortal human in ages, if ever—she was a novelty.

But that didn't keep her nerves from shivering at every bit of unexpected contact.

Gild cleared his throat. "I would say we have, maybe, half an hour before sunrise. Is there . . . more to the story?"

"There's always more to the story," Serilda said automatically.

A grin like the thaw of spring came over his face. Gild plopped himself down on the floor, crossing his legs and cupping his chin. He reminded her of her charges at the school, attentive and eager.

"Go on, then," he said.

She laughed, then shook her head. "Not until you answer some of my questions."

He frowned. "What questions?"

Serilda sat against the wall opposite him. "For starters, why are you dressed like you're getting ready for bed?"

He sat up straighter, then looked down at his clothes. He raised his arms, his sleeves billowing. "What are you talking about? It's a perfectly respectable shirt."

"No, it isn't. Respectable men wear tunics. Or doublets. Or jerkins. Not just a poufy blouse. You look like a peasant. Or a lord who's lost his valet."

He guffawed. "A lord! That's a fine idea. Don't you see?" He stretched out his legs in front of him, crossing his ankles. "I'm the lord of this whole castle. What else could I possibly want?"

"I'm being serious," she said.

"So am I."

"You make *gold*. You could be a king! Or at least a duke or an earl or something."

"Is that what you think? Dearest Serilda, the moment the Erlking learned of your supposed talent, he brought you here and locked you in the dungeon, demanding that you use your skill to benefit *him*. When people know that you can do *this*"—he gestured at the pile of gold-filled bobbins—"then that is all they care about. Gold and wealth and riches and what you can do for them. It is not a gift, but a curse." He scratched behind his ear, taking the momentary pause to work a kink from his shoulders, before sighing. It sounded sad. "Besides. Nothing that I want can be purchased with gold."

"Then why do you keep taking my jewelry?"

His smile returned, a little impish. "Magic requires payment. How many times do I have to tell you? I'm not making it up just to steal from you."

"But what does that mean, exactly?"

"Just what it says. No payment, no magic. No magic, no gold."

"Where did you learn that? And how did you come to have this gift? Or curse?"

He shook his head. "I don't know. Like I said before, it might be a blessing from Hulda. Or maybe I was born with this magic? I haven't the faintest idea. And learning to take payment for it . . ." He shrugged. "It's just something that I know. That I've always known. At least as far as I can remember."

"And how does he not notice you?"

His look turned questioning.

"The Erlking is going through all this trouble to bring me here to spin this gold, when he has a gold-spinner living in his own castle. Does he not know about you?"

Unexpected panic flared in Gild's eyes. "No, he doesn't. And he can't. If you tell him . . ." He fumbled for words. "I'm trapped enough as it is. I won't be enslaved to him as well."

"Of course I won't say anything. He would kill me if he found out the truth, anyway."

Gild considered this, his momentary alarm fading.

"But that doesn't really answer my question. How can he *not* notice you? You're . . . you're not like the other ghosts."

"Oh, he notices me plenty." This was said with a fair bit of smugness. "But I'm just the resident poltergeist, remember? He notices what I want him to notice, and I want him to notice that I am a complete and utter nuisance. I doubt it's ever crossed his mind that I could be something more, and I'd like to keep it that way."

Serilda frowned. It still struck her as unlikely that the king would be so ignorant about a gold-spinning ghost in his court, even a meddlesome one.

Seeing her suspicion, Gild scooted closer. "It's a big, crowded castle, and he avoids me whenever possible. The feeling is mutual."

"I suppose," she said, sensing that there was more to their history, but that Gild didn't care to reveal it. "And you're sure you're a ghost?"

"A poltergeist," he clarified. "It's a particularly obnoxious kind of ghost."

She hummed, unconvinced.

"Why? What do *you* think I am?"

"I'm not sure, but I've already concocted a dozen stories in my head about you, if not more."

"Stories? About me?" His expression brightened.

"That can't be a surprise. A mysterious stranger who appears magically whenever a fair damsel is in need of rescuing? Who dresses like a drunken earl, but can create gold at his fingertips. Who is flippant and aggravating, but somehow charming, too, when he wants to be."

He snickered. "It was a convincing start, but now I know you're only mocking me."

Serilda's pulse had started to flutter. Never had she been so candid with a boy before. A handsome boy, whose touches, no matter how faint, brought her whole body sparking to life. It would be easiest, she knew, to laugh her comment away. Of course she was making it up.

But he *could* be charming. When he wanted to be.

And she would never forget the feel of his arms around her, comforting her when she needed it most.

"You're right," she said. "The evidence suggests that a maiden needn't be fair at all in order for you to come to her rescue. Which, most confounding, only adds to the mystery."

The silence that followed was suffocating, and Serilda knew that she waited a heartbeat too long, hoping for what? She wouldn't admit it even to herself.

She shook off her disappointment and met Gild's eye again. He was staring at her, but she could not read the look. Confusion? Pity?

Enough of that.

Sitting straighter, she declared, "I think you're a sorcerer."

His eyebrows shot upward in surprise. Then he started to laugh, a great, bellowing sound that warmed her to her toes.

"I am not a sorcerer."

"That you know of," she said, lifting one finger toward him. "You're under some dark spell that's caused you to forget a sacred oath you once made to always come to the aid of a fa—of a worthy maiden when she calls on you."

He fixed her with a look and repeated, "I am not a sorcerer."

Serilda mirrored his expression. "I've watched you spin *straw* into *gold*. You are a sorcerer. You cannot convince me otherwise."

His smile broke through again. "Maybe I'm one of the old gods. Maybe I *am* Hulda."

"Don't think the idea didn't occur to me. But no. Gods are pompous and distant and in love with their own brilliance. You're none of those things."

"Thank you?"

She smirked. "Well, you might be a little in love with your own brilliance."

Gild shrugged, not disagreeing.

She tapped her fingers against her mouth, watching him. He truly was a mystery, and one she felt compelled to figure out—if it was only because she needed the distraction from every horrible thing that wanted to crowd into her thoughts.

He was like no fairy or kobold she had ever heard of, and she did not think he was a zwerge or a land wight or any of the forest folk. True, many stories revolved around the magic ones assisting lost travelers or poor fishermen or desperate maidens—for a price. Always for a price. And in that regard, Gild did seem to fit the description. But he had no wings, no tall ears, no pointed teeth, no devil's tail. He did have a subtle mischief, she had to admit. A teasing smile. An eye for trouble. Yet his mannerisms were thoughtful and precise.

He was magical. A gold-spinner.

A witch?

Maybe.

A godchild of Hulda?

Perhaps.

But nothing felt quite right.

Again, she found herself inspecting his edges. They were as solid as any boy she'd ever met in the village. There was no haziness about him, as though he were about to dissolve into the air. No transparent limbs, no foggy silhouettes. He seemed real. He seemed alive.

Gild held her gaze while she studied him, never flinching, never breaking eye contact, never turning away in embarrassment. A small smile clung to his lips while he waited for her proclamation.

Finally, she declared, "I have made up my mind. Whatever you might be, you are definitely not a ghost."

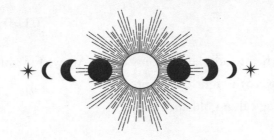

Chapter 24

Gild beamed. "You're certain?"

"I am."

"And why am I not a ghost?"

"You're too"—she struggled for the right word—"alive."

His laugh was hollow. "I don't feel alive. Or at least I didn't. Not until—" His gaze dropped to her hands, her wrists. Back up to her face.

She stilled.

"I would tell you if I had any answers to offer," he said. "But if I'm being honest, I'm not sure it much matters what I am. I can go anywhere in this castle, but I can never leave it. Maybe I'm a ghost. Maybe I'm something else. Either way, I'm trapped here."

"And you've been here a long time?"

"Ages."

"Decades? Centuries?"

"Yes? Maybe? Time is hard to grasp. But I know that I've tried to leave this castle, and I can't."

She chewed on the inside of her lip. Her mind was racing with ideas. Stories. Fairy tales. But she wanted to know the truth.

"Such a long time to be trapped in these walls," she murmured. "How can you stand it?"

"I can't," he said. "But I haven't much choice."

"I'm sorry."

He shrugged. "I like to look out at the city. There's a tower—the one in the southwest corner—with a wonderful view of the docks and the houses. I can watch the people. If the wind is right I can even hear them. Haggling over prices. Playing their instruments." He paused for a long time. "Laughing. I love it when I can hear them laughing."

Serilda hummed in thought. "I think I understand better now," she said slowly. "Your jokes. Your . . . pranks. You wield laughter like a weapon, a protection against your awful circumstances. I think you're trying to create lightness where there is so much dark."

One of his eyebrows lifted with amusement. "Yes. You have it exactly right. I assure you, I only think of daisies and shooting stars and bringing merriment into this dreadful world. I never think at all of how His Foulness will turn blue with anger and he'll spend half a night cursing my existence. That would just be spiteful. Far beneath me."

She laughed. "I suppose spite can be a weapon, too."

"Absolutely. My favorite, in fact. Well. Other than a sword. Because who doesn't love a sword?"

She rolled her eyes at him.

"I met one of the children in town," she said. "A girl named Leyna. She and her friends like to play games on the docks. Perhaps it's their laughter you heard."

Gild's expression turned bittersweet. "There have been many children. Children who have turned into adults who have made more children. Sometimes I feel so connected to them, like I could walk across that bridge and they would recognize me. That they would know me somehow. Even though, if anyone in that city had ever known me, they would be long dead by now."

"You're right," she mused. "There must have been a time before."

"Before?"

"Before you were trapped here. Before you became . . . whatever you are."

"Probably," he said, sounding empty, "But I don't remember it."

"Nothing?"

He shook his head.

"If you were a ghost, then you would have died. Do you remember your death?"

He kept shaking his head. "Nothing."

She sank, disappointed. There had to be some way to figure it out. She racked her brain trying to think of every non-mortal being she'd ever heard of, but nothing seemed to fit.

The candle wavered then. The shadows flickered, and dread dug into Serilda's chest at the thought of the night reaching its end. But a glance told her that the candle was still burning bright, though there wasn't much wick left to burn. The night *would* end soon. The Erlking would return. Gild would be gone.

Relieved that the candle was not yet extinguished, Serilda peered at him.

He was watching her, vulnerable and distressed. "I am so sorry about your father."

She shivered as she was pulled back to the horrible truth she'd been trying to forget.

"But I am not sorry I got to see you again," continued Gild. "Even if that makes me as selfish as any of the dark ones." He looked positively miserable to be confessing this. He knotted his hands in his lap, knuckles going white. "And I hated seeing you cry. But at the same time, I really liked holding you."

Heat rushed into Serilda's cheeks.

"It's just that—" He stopped himself, struggling for words. His voice was thick, almost pained, when he tried again. "Remember when

I told you that I've never met any mortals before? At least, that I know of."

Serilda nodded.

"That never really bothered me. I guess I never gave it much thought. I never realized you would be . . . that someone who's alive would be . . . like you."

"So soft?" she said, with a note of teasing.

He exhaled, embarrassed, but starting to smile. "And warm. And . . . solid."

His gaze fell to her hands resting in her lap. She could still feel the phantom caress from earlier. That delicate brush against her skin.

Her gaze darted across to *his* hands. Hands that, until her, had never touched a human being. They were clutched together, as if he were trying to keep himself from dissolving.

Or from reaching out to her.

Serilda thought of all the touches she took for granted. Even if she had always been something of an outcast in Märchenfeld, she had never been completely ostracized. She'd had her father's all-encompassing hugs. The children who would snuggle against her sides while she told them her tales. Tiny moments that meant nothing. But, to someone who had never experienced them . . .

Nervously wetting her lips, Serilda scooted forward.

Gild tensed, watching with trepidation as she inched closer, until she was sitting beside him, her back against the same wall. Their shoulders almost, but not quite, together. Just close enough that the little hairs on her arms prickled at his nearness.

Holding her breath, she held out her hand, palm up.

Gild stared at it for a very, very long time.

When he finally reached for her, he was trembling. She wondered if he was nervous or frightened or something else?

When the pads of their fingers pressed together, she could feel the tension release from him, and she realized that was the source of his fear. That, this time, he would slip right through her. Or the sensation wouldn't be the same. That whatever warmth or softness he'd felt before would be gone.

Serilda laced their fingers together. Palm to palm. She could feel her heartbeat thundering through her fingers, and she wondered whether he noticed it, too.

His skin was dry, rough, covered in scratches from the straw. Dirt had long been embedded into the edges of his brittle fingernails. He had a scrape on one knuckle that hadn't yet started to scab over.

They were not pretty hands, but they were strong and sure. At least, once he finally stopped shaking.

Serilda knew that her hands weren't pretty, either. But she couldn't help feeling that they fit together, just right.

She and this boy. This . . . whatever he was.

She tried to ward off the thought. He was desperate for human contact. Any human contact. She could have been anyone.

Besides, she thought, looking at the ring he'd slipped onto his pinkie finger, he might have saved her life, but he'd claimed his price for it. There were no favors between them. This was not friendship.

But that didn't keep her blood from burning hotter for every moment that passed with his hand in hers.

It didn't keep her heart from soaring when he leaned his head against her shoulder, letting out a sigh mixed with a sob.

Her lips parted in surprise.

"Are you all right?" she whispered.

"No," he whispered back. His honesty startled her. It was as if his blithe demeanor had dissolved away, leaving him exposed.

Serilda pressed her cheek to the top of his head. "Shall I continue the story?"

He chuckled quietly and seemed to consider, but then she felt his head shaking. He pulled away, enough to look at her. "Why do you say you aren't fair?"

"What?"

"Before, talking about damsels and my . . . heroics." His smile grew cheeky, but only for a moment. "You seemed to be suggesting that you're . . . not beautiful."

Despite his obvious discomfort, he did not look away.

"Are you mocking me?"

His brow pinched. "No. Of course not."

"Can you not see what's before you?"

"I can see precisely what's before me." He reached up with his other hand and, when she didn't pull away, settled the tips of his fingers lightly against her temple. He held her gaze steadily, when so many boys had flinched away with looks of pity, if not outright disgust.

Gild did not flinch.

"What do they mean?" he asked.

She swallowed. A lie would have been easy. She had thought of so many to explain away her eyes.

For so long, she had wondered if the tale her father had told her was just another fabrication.

But now she knew it was the truth, and she did not want to lie to Gild.

"I was marked by Wyrdith," she said, suddenly unable, or unwilling, to move. Every touch was a new revelation.

His eyes widened. "The god of stories. Of course. It's the wheel of fortune."

She nodded. "They mean that I can't be trusted. That I'm bad luck."

Gild considered this for a long time, before giving a subtle grunt. "Fortune determines who will prosper and who will fail. It's all a matter of chance."

"That's what they like to tell you," she said, "but when someone has good fortune, they are quick to thank Freydon or Solvilde, even Hulda. But Wyrdith is only ever credited with bad luck."

"And do people blame you? When they have bad luck?"

"Some do, yes. Being a storyteller doesn't help. People don't trust me."

"Doesn't seem right, to blame you for things you have no control over."

She shrugged. "It can be difficult to prove I'm not at fault."

Especially when she wasn't sure they were wrong. But she didn't want to tell him that. Not when he had, so far, not shied away from her.

Gild let his hand drop back to his lap, which both relieved and saddened her. "You haven't answered my question."

"I've forgotten what it was."

"Why do you think you're not beautiful?"

She flushed. "I would think that's been answered just fine."

"You've told me that you're cursed by the god of stories. That people don't trust you. But that isn't the same thing. Spend enough time with the dark ones and you'll know that sometimes the most untrustworthy things are also the most beautiful."

She pictured the Erlking, in all his unimaginable beauty.

"You just compared me to black-hearted demons. Don't tell me that was a compliment."

He laughed. "I don't know. Maybe." The gold flecks in his eyes glittered in the candlelight, and when next he spoke, it was so quiet that Serilda barely heard him, even right at his side. "This is . . . very new to me."

She wanted to say that this was very new to her, too, but she wasn't entirely sure what *this* was.

Only that she didn't want it to end.

She gathered her courage, wanting to say as much, when the candle began to splutter.

They both looked at it, desperate for it to not go out. For the night to not be over. But the flame was hovering precariously on the last tiny bit of wick, moments from being doused in the dark wax.

As it flickered again, they heard footsteps.

A key in the lock.

"Serilda."

She looked at Gild, wide-eyed, and nodded. "I'm satisfied. Go."

He looked, for the barest of moments, like he didn't know what she was talking about. Then his expression cleared.

"I'm not," he whispered.

"What?"

"Please forgive me this."

He leaned forward and pressed his lips to hers.

Serilda gasped against him.

She did not have time to shut her eyes, to even think about kissing him back, when the key turned. The lock clanked.

Gild vanished.

She was left trembling, her insides like an entire flock of sparrows taking flight. The candle went out. Its light was almost immediately replaced with the torches from the corridor as the door was thrust open and the Erlking's shadow fell over her.

Serilda blinked up at him, but for a long moment, she couldn't really see him. Her thoughts lingered on Gild. The urgency of the kiss. The desire. As if he feared it might be his only chance. To kiss her. To kiss . . . anyone.

And now he was gone.

It took all her mental strength not to reach up and touch her lips. Not to slip away into a daydream, reliving that tremulous moment again and again.

Luckily, the king had eyes only for the gold. He ignored her as he sauntered into the room and eyed the stacks of bobbins.

"I would ask that you keep any fits of displeasure to yourself," he said serenely, as his fingers grabbed one spoke of the spinning wheel and gave it a quick turn. "This spinning wheel is original to the castle. I would hate to see it broken."

Serilda glanced over at him. She'd completely forgotten that the spinning wheel had fallen onto its side.

Gulping, she pushed herself up to standing, making sure to lock out her legs so that her knees did not quake. "Forgive me. I . . . think I fell asleep. I must have kicked it over. I meant no harm."

He smiled slightly as he turned to her. "Congratulations, Lady Serilda. I will not be gutting you this morning after all."

It took a moment for his comment to register in her flustered mind. When it did, she responded dryly, "You have my gratitude."

"And you have mine."

She couldn't tell if he was ignoring her ire, or willfully oblivious to it.

"You must be tired," he said. "Manfred, show her to the tower."

The coachman gestured for Serilda to follow, but she hesitated. She might never have another opportunity as this, and time was not her ally. When the Erlking moved toward the corridor, she gathered her courage and stepped in front of him, blocking his path.

He froze, his surprise evident.

To soften what she knew must be an enormous breach of propriety, she attempted an off-kilter curtsy. "Please. I do not wish to anger you, but . . . I must know what's become of my father."

His eyebrow lifted, even as his expression darkened. "I believe I already answered that question."

"You said that you didn't know."

"And I don't." There was a brittle edge to the words. "If he died during the hunt, then his soul has already been carried to Verloren. I certainly didn't want it."

She clamped her jaw, both livid at his callousness and hurt by her missed chance to see her father one last time, if his ghost had lingered even for a moment last night.

But no—he might be all right. She had to believe that.

"And what of my mother?" she demanded.

"What of your mother?" he asked, his gray eyes sparking impatiently.

She tried to talk fast. "My father told me that when I was but two years old, my mother did not merely leave us." She studied his expression. "She was taken by the hunt."

She waited, but the king appeared . . . disinterested.

"I want to know if you still have her."

"You mean, has her ghost become a permanent part of my retinue?"

He seemed to emphasize the word *permanent,* but it might have been Serilda's imagination.

"Yes, my lord."

The Erlking held her gaze. "We have many talented seamstresses."

Serilda opened her mouth to interject—her mother wasn't *actually* a talented seamstress—but at the last moment, she bit back what would have given up her original fib.

The king continued. "Whether or not one of them is your mother, I haven't the slightest idea nor can I muster a whit of care about it. If she is mine, then she is yours no longer."

It was spoken coldly and decidedly, leaving no room for argument.

"Besides, Lady Serilda," he went on, his voice softening, "it might ease your troubled heart to remember that those who join the hunt come willingly." This time, when he smiled, it was not cheerful—but taunting. "Wouldn't you agree?"

She shuddered, remembering the urging of the deepest, quietest parts of her soul last night when she had heard the call of the horn. When she had been helpless to resist its allure. The promise of freedom, of ferocity, of a night without restrictions or rules.

Understanding passed over the king's eyes, and Serilda felt a spike of shame to know that some part of her craved such wild abandon, and that the Erlking recognized it in her.

"Perhaps there is comfort in knowing that you have this . . . commonality with your mother," he said, smirking.

She looked away, unable to disguise the sense of disgrace that stirred in her gut.

"Now then, Lady Serilda, I might suggest that you not travel so far on the next full moon. When I summon you, I expect you to answer promptly." He stepped closer, a warning in his tone. "If I have to come looking for you again, I will not be so generous."

She swallowed.

"Perhaps it would be best to find accommodations in Adalheid, so that you will not need to waste half the night in travel. Tell the townspeople that they are to treat you as a personal guest of mine, and I am sure they will be most accommodating."

He took her hand and pressed his iced lips to her knuckle. Goose bumps prickled her arm. The moment his fingers loosened, she ripped her hand away and squeezed it into a fist at her side.

His eyes seemed to be laughing at her as he stood to his full height. "Forgive me. I am sure you required some rest, yet it seems we will not have time to settle you into your rooms after all. Until the Chaste Moon, then."

She frowned, confused, but before she could speak, the world shifted. The change was sudden and jolting. Serilda had not moved, but in a blink, the king was gone. The bobbins of gold, the spinning wheel, the lingering scent of straw.

She was still in the larder, but now she was surrounded by rust and decay and stifling musty air, and she was alone.

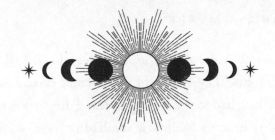

Chapter 25

As Serilda made her way through the empty castle, she heard the rumble of distant thunder and a torrent of rain pounding the outer castle walls. Nearby, something was dripping. Soft and steady. She could feel the dampness in her bones, and even her cloak could not ward off the invading chill. She started to shiver again as she tried to find her way through the maze of halls. The castle looked so different on this side of the veil, with its scattered furniture and torn tapestries. She soon found the source of the dripping sound—a window where a hole in the masonry was letting the rainwater soak through. It was beginning to puddle on the floor.

Serilda held her breath as she passed, expecting the water to turn into blood.

It did not.

She exhaled. Her muscles were knotted and tense, waiting for the haunts of the castle to awaken. Every time she peered around a corner, she expected to see either a deadly monster or a pool of blood or some other horrible thing.

But the castle stayed eerily silent.

The memories of the night before jumbled about in her weary mind. Only the day before, she'd dared to hope that she was safe. That her father was safe. Miles away from Märchenfeld. They'd watched for hollow-eyed ravens. They'd thought they were so careful.

But the Erlking had found her regardless. Found *them* regardless.

If she hadn't been so foolish, if she hadn't tried to run, then her father would be home right now. Waiting for her.

She tried to shove the fear away. Maybe he *was* home right now, waiting for her. Maybe he had awoken, dazed and bruised, with faint memories of the hunt, but altogether all right. She reminded herself that while the hunt did sometimes leave bodies behind after their mad procession, it was more common for those who had been taken to wake up. Befuddled, embarrassed, but more or less intact.

This was probably what had happened to her father.

By now he had probably made his way home, or he would be on his way now, eager to meet her there.

That is what she told herself.

Then she commanded her heart to believe it.

They would soon be together again, and she would not make the same mistake twice. She could see now how foolish they had been, to think they could so easily escape. She wondered if there was any place in all the world where the Erlking and his wild hunt could not find her.

But even as she thought it, another question arose.

Did she still want to escape?

She knew that if she did not find a way out of this, there was only one possible end for her. The Erlking would discover her lies. He would kill her and mount her head on the castle wall.

But she also wanted to know what had become of her mother, all those years ago.

If her mother was a member of this undead court, didn't Serilda owe it to her to try and set her free? To let her spirit find rest, and ultimately be guided down to Verloren? She had only wanted a night of freedom with the hunt. She did not deserve to be trapped here forever.

And then there was the other ghost—or whatever he was—lingering in her thoughts.

Gild.

The kiss was stitched into her mind. Fierce. Desperate. Longing.

Please forgive me this.

She pressed the pads of her fingers against her lips, trying to re-create the sensation. But last night, it was as though the floor itself had fallen out from beneath her.

Now it was just her fingers, going numb with cold.

She rubbed her hands together, blowing on them with her breath. She wanted to believe the kiss had *meant* something, if only because it had been her first. She would not admit it to anyone, but she had spent hours dreaming about just such a moment. She had spun count-less fantasies of being swept away by everyone from princes to well-intentioned scoundrels. She had imagined a romance in which the hero would find her wit, her charm, her bravery all so painfully irresistible, he would have no choice but to gather her in his arms and kiss her until she was dizzy and breathless.

Gild's kiss had been as quick and sudden as a lightning strike.

And left her dizzy and breathless nonetheless.

But why? Much as she yearned to think he did find her irresistible, a practical voice warned her it was probably not so romantic as all that.

He was a prisoner. A young man—trapped and alone inside this cas-tle for only the gods knew how long. Without company, without even the slightest hope for physical tenderness.

Until now.

Until *her.*

She could have been anyone.

Be that as it may, Gild was trapped here, and she wanted to help him. She wanted to help all of them.

She knew it was naive. What could she, a simple miller's daughter, possibly do to defy the Erlking? She needed to be worrying about her own life, her own freedom, not anyone else's.

But she'd had too many fantasies of heroism to ignore the spark of excitement when she thought of rescuing her mother—if she needed rescuing.

Rescuing Gild.

Rescuing . . . everyone.

And, if anything had happened to her father, she would make sure the Erlking paid for it.

She paused suddenly, her thoughts of vengeance scattering as she looked around. She'd been sure she was nearly to the great hall, but the corridor that should have turned to the left was turning to the right, and she found herself questioning every turn she'd taken.

She ducked into a room where a wall of bookshelves displayed nothing but spiderwebs. She peered through the window, trying to orient herself.

The rain was smashing into the water below, the wind causing drifts of fog to scatter across the lake's surface, obscuring the distant shore. From what little she could see, she determined that she was somewhere near the northwest corner of the keep. She was surprised to see a second courtyard below, between the keep and the outer wall. It was so overrun with weeds and rooted saplings that it looked almost like a wild garden.

Then her gaze fell on a tower, and a piece of her conversation with Gild scratched at her thoughts. He had mentioned the southwest tower. It had sounded like his favorite place, where he liked to watch the city, the people.

Curiosity had always been a difficult thing for Serilda to resist.

If Gild was some sort of ghost, could his spirit be lingering in this castle even now? Could he see her? The thought was mostly eerie, but also a tiny bit comforting.

She thought of the drude that had attacked her.

The candelabra that had attacked *it*.

Could it have been . . . ?

She returned to the hall, moving faster now, focusing on every turn to keep herself from getting lost again. At every corner, she paused to be sure there were no malevolent spirits or raging birds. She tried to picture the keep and its numerous spires. A map was beginning to form in her mind. She passed another door open to a spiraling staircase and guessed it was the shorter tower on the western wall.

Still, no sign of life—or death, for that matter. No screams. No nacht-krapp watching her with empty eyes.

She seemed alone. Just her and the quiet thumping of her boots on the threadbare carpet as she continued.

Questions nagged at her with every door she passed. She spied a harp still standing amid yellowed music pages that had been scattered across the floor. A storeroom full of dust-covered wine casks. Wooden chests rotting away and cushioned benches turned into homes for the local rodents.

Until one doorway revealed another spiraling staircase.

She held her skirt aloft as she made her way up into the tower, passing a series of alcoves, empty pedestals, and the statue of an armored knight holding a large shield, though the bottom half of the shield had broken off. On the fourth full turn around the twisting steps, the staircase ended—not at a door, but at a ladder disappearing into an overhead hatch.

Serilda eyed it suspiciously, knowing that while the wood might look sturdy, everything in this castle was suspect. Any one of those wooden rungs might have rot on the inside.

She craned her head, trying to see what was above, but all she could make out were more stone walls and grayish daylight. The noise of the storm was louder here, the rain pounding the rooftop directly overhead.

Serilda reached for the ladder and checked that it was secure before starting to climb, hand over hand. The wood groaned from her weight, but the rungs held. As soon as her head was above the floor hatch, she looked around, afraid that some vengeful spirit might be waiting to throw her out a window, or whatever vengeful spirits did.

But all she saw was one more abandoned room in this dismal castle.

Serilda climbed to the top and stepped off the ladder. Not so much a watchtower intended for defense—those were on the outer walls—but a room designed for beauty. For watching the stars, the lake, the sunrise. The room was circular, with massive clear-glass windows looking out in every direction. She could see it all. The lake. The courtyard. The bridge, shrouded in fog. The mountains—or she was sure she would be able to, when the thick cloud cover had burned off. She could even see the row of stained-glass windows she'd walked past in her explorations before.

And there, the sparkling city of Adalheid.

Except it wasn't so sparkling today. It was actually a sorry sight, under siege by the rain. But Serilda had a good imagination, and it didn't take much effort to picture it as it might be in the sunshine, especially as winter gave way to spring. She pictured the golden light breaking through the clouds. How the painted buildings would shine like seashells, how the tiled roofs would look like little plates of gold. Marigolds and geraniums would overtake the window boxes, and patches of dark earth would be lush with fat cabbages and cucumbers and pole beans.

It was a lovely town. She could see why Gild liked to look at it, especially when he was surrounded by relative gloom all the time. But it also made her sad to think of him here, entirely alone. Craving more.

Something soft and warm, as light as a breath, tickled the back of Serilda's neck.

She gasped and spun around.

The room was empty, as abandoned as it had been the moment she'd climbed the ladder.

Her eyes darted to every corner. Her ears strained to hear above the sound of the storm.

"Gild?" she whispered.

The only response was a shiver that shook her spine.

Serilda dared to shut her eyes. She tentatively lifted one hand, fingers stretching toward nothingness.

"Gild . . . if you're here . . ."

A brush of skin against her palm. Fingers lacing with hers.

Her eyes flew open.

The sensation vanished.

No one was there.

She might have imagined it.

And then—

A scream.

Serilda whirled toward the nearest window and looked down at the castle's exterior wall. She spotted the figure of a man running along the wall-walk, his chain-mail armor glinting silver. He was nearly to the tower when he jerked to a stop. For a moment he was still, his back arched and his face turned toward the sky.

Toward Serilda.

She pressed a hand against the window, her breath steaming the glass.

The man fell to his knees. Blood burbled up from his mouth.

Before he could fall face-first to the stone, he vanished.

And another scream came, from the opposite side of the tower. From the main courtyard.

A child's scream. A child's cry. And another man, pleading, *No! Please!*

Serilda backed away from the window, covering her ears. Afraid to look. Afraid of what she might see, and knowing that she could do nothing to stop it.

What had *happened* in this castle?

With a shuddering breath, she grabbed the ladder and scrambled down. On the fourth rung, the wood cracked and split. She yelped and jumped the rest of the way to the floor. Her legs were shaking as she ran down the steps.

She emerged onto the second level and nearly collided with a squat, wrinkled creature with long pointed ears and a once-white apron now covered in grime.

Serilda lurched backward, afraid that it might be another drude.

But no—it was only a kobold. Harmless goblins that often worked in castles and manor houses. Some considered them to be good luck.

But this kobold was staring at Serilda with fervid eyes, which gave her pause. Was she a ghost? Could she see Serilda?

The creature took a step closer, waving her arms. "Go!" she screeched. "They're coming! Quick, to the king and queen! We must save the—"

Her words were cut off with a strangled gasp. The kobold reached her leathery fingers to her throat as brownish blood began to seep through them.

Serilda turned and fled the other way. It wasn't long before she again found herself dizzy and turned around. Afraid she was going in circles. She stumbled past unfamiliar rooms, through open doorways. She ducked into the servants' halls before emerging into a great ballroom or a library or a parlor, and every corner she turned, there were screams crowding in around her. The rush of panicked footsteps. The metallic stench of blood in the air.

Suddenly, Serilda stopped.

She had found the hallway with the rainbow wash of daylight. The seven stained-glass windows, the seven gods heedless of the girl before them.

She pressed a hand against the ache in her side.

"All right," she said, panting. "I know where I am. I just have to . . . to find the stairs. And they were . . ."

She looked in both directions, trying to retrace her steps from the last time she'd been here. Had the stairway been to the left, or to the right?

She chose right, but as soon as she turned the corner, she knew her mistake.

No—this was the strange hall with the candelabras. The doors all closed, except that last one, with its unusual pale glow, the shadows shifting across the floor, the vivid tapestry she could barely see.

"Go back," she whispered to herself, urging her feet to listen. She needed to get out of this castle.

But her feet didn't listen. There was something about the room. The way the lights shimmered on the stonework.

Like it wanted to be discovered.

Like it was waiting for her.

"Serilda," she murmured, "what are you doing?"

All the candelabras had been knocked over by that invisible force when she'd been here last. They still lay strewn across the hallway. Had it been a poltergeist? *The* poltergeist?

She grabbed the first candelabra that she passed, gripping it like a weapon.

Only once the edge of the tapestry came into view did she remember. Last time, this door had slammed shut.

It should not have been open now.

Her brow furrowed.

NO!

The cry attacked her from all directions. Serilda cowered, knuckles tight around the iron candelabra.

The roar came from everywhere. The windows, the walls—her own mind.

It was furious. Terrifying.

Get out!

She stepped back, but did not run. Her arms trembled under the candelabra's weight. "Who are you? What's in that room? If I could only see—"

The door dividing her from the tapestry slammed shut.

GET!

In unison, the rest of the doors along the hallway started to open, then slam, then open—*BANG-BANG-BANG*—one after another. An angry chorus, a thundering melody.

OUT!

"No!" she yelled back. "I need to see what's in there!"

A screech drew her eyes toward the rafters. A drude was dangling from a chandelier, its talons clacking together, teeth bared as it prepared to lunge for her.

She froze. "All right," she breathed. "You win. I'll leave."

It hissed.

Serilda backed out of the hallway, clutching her makeshift weapon. As soon as she reached the windows, she dropped the candelabra and ran.

Her path was surer this time. She didn't stop at the throne room, didn't stop for anything. She ignored the cacophony of screams and crashes and the permeating smell of blood. The occasional movement in the corner of her eye. A shadow figure reaching for her. Fingers grasping. The noise of footsteps racing in every direction.

Until the entry hall, with the massive carved doors shut tight against the drumming rainstorm. Her escape.

But she wasn't alone.

She drew up short, shaking her head, pleading with this castle to leave her be, to let her go.

A woman was standing just inside the doors. Unlike the kobold and the man on the castle wall, this woman *looked* like a phantom, like a ghost in a fairy tale. She was not old, exactly. About the age of Serilda's father, she guessed. But she had the sorrowful air of someone who had seen too much hardship in her years.

Serilda glanced around, searching for another exit. Surely there were other doors that led in and out of the keep.

She would have to find them.

But before she could back around the nearest corner, the woman turned her head. Her gaze fell on Serilda. Her cheeks were stained with tears.

And . . . Serilda recognized her. Hair tightly braided and a scabbard at her hip. Only, the last time she'd seen the woman, she had been riding atop a powerful steed. A scarf tied around her throat. She had smiled at Serilda.

I believe she speaks true.

Serilda blinked, startled. For a moment, the woman seemed to recognize her, too.

But then pain clouded the phantom's expression. "I taught him as well as I could, but he wasn't ready," she said, her voice thick with unshed tears. "I failed him."

Serilda pressed a hand to her chest. The suffering in the woman's voice was tangible.

Slumping forward, the woman placed one palm on the massive door and let out a sob. "I failed them all. I deserve this."

Serilda started to move closer, wishing she could do something, anything to ease her torment.

But before she could reach her, a thin red line appeared around the woman's neck. Her sobs abruptly silenced.

Serilda cried out, leaping backward as the woman collapsed, her body sprawling across the entryway floor.

Her head rolled a few more feet, landing mere steps away from Serilda.

The woman's eyes were open wide. Her mouth twitched, forming silent words.

Help us.

"I'm sorry," Serilda gasped. "I'm so very sorry."

She couldn't help anyone.

Instead, she ran.

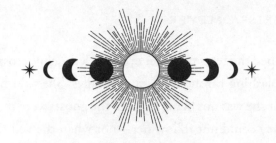

Chapter 26

She was nearly to the drawbridge when she spotted a form lying in the shade of the wayfaring tree. Serilda drew up short, her heart sputtering. A sharp stitch dug at her side.

First, she thought, *Monster*.

But no. She recognized that chestnut coat, that dark brown mane.

Her second thought—*Dead*.

Her heart was pounding as she approached, tears already gathering in her eyes. Zelig lay on his side, eyes shut, perfectly still.

"Oh . . . Zelig . . ."

Startled, the horse's head lifted, its frightened eyes landing on her.

Serilda gasped. "Zelig!" She ran to him, dropping her hands over his head as he gave a whimpering neigh. He nuzzled her palm, though she suspected he was searching for food as much as he was showing affection. She didn't mind. She was already sobbing in relief. "Good boy," she whispered. "Good boy. It's all right now."

It took a couple of tries for the old horse to get his hooves beneath him and scramble up to standing. She could tell he was still exhausted from the night before. Serilda found his tack discarded beneath the weeds a few feet away, and the horse didn't balk as she put the bridle over his head. She hoped that he was as grateful to see her as she was to see him.

Now she only needed to find her father.

Serilda wiped the tears from her eyes and led Zelig across the bridge, his hooves splashing through the rain puddles. She told herself again and again that she was not being chased. The ghosts were trapped inside the castle. They could not follow her—not when the veil was in place, at least.

She was all right.

The streets of Adalheid were empty. There were no townspeople this time to gawk at Serilda as she and the horse emerged from the ruins. The mist off the water slowly cleared, revealing the timber-decorated buildings along the shore, water pouring down from the eaves and forming rivulets along the cobblestones.

She was eager to start for home immediately and see whether her father had made it back yet—to make sure he was okay—but Zelig needed food, so with a heavy heart, she turned in the direction of the Wild Swan. Maybe she could stable Zelig there for a few days and see if someone else might be willing to drive her to Märchenfeld, or near to it. But she knew it wasn't likely, not in this weather. Too risky for cart wheels to get stuck when the mud was so thick.

The stable behind the inn was full of sweet hay and even had a bucket at the entrance full of small, bright red apples. Serilda led Zelig to an empty stall. He immediately bent his head toward the trough, eager to gorge himself on fresh water. Serilda left a few apples within his reach and headed toward the inn.

She stepped through the door and, leaving a little trail of rainwater as her cloak was soaked through, headed straight for the roaring fireplace at the back of the public house. It was a quiet morning, with only a few tables occupied, likely by guests staying at the inn. Serilda doubted many of the townspeople would be braving this weather, no matter how good the breakfast food was.

The air smelled of fried onions and bacon. Serilda's stomach warbled as she tapped a gentle knock on the oak table.

"Well, if our local specter isn't back," said Lorraine, emerging from the kitchen with a platter of food. She deposited the food at the table by the window and approached Serilda, hands on her hips. "Locking up for the hunt last night, I wondered if you might be turning up again today."

"Not entirely by choice," said Serilda. "But here I am. Might I bother you for another cup of cider?"

"Of course, of course." But Lorraine didn't immediately head back to the kitchen. Instead, she studied Serilda for a long moment. "I must say. I've lived in this town all my life, and never once have I heard of the Erlking abducting a human and then letting them go, unharmed. Now, I'm not saying that isn't a good thing, but it's making me nervous, and I know I'm not the only one. The dark ones are terrifying, but at least they're predictable. We've found ways to live in their shadow, even prosper. You don't suppose that this *arrangement* you've got with the Erlking is going to be changing that, do you?"

"I would hope not," said Serilda, a little shaky. "But if I'm being honest, I'm not sure how much I yet understand that arrangement. Right now, I'm mostly focused on trying to keep him from killing me."

"Smart girl."

Remembering what the Erlking had said shortly before sunrise, Serilda wrung her hands. "I should tell you that the Erlking has all but ordered me to return on the Chaste Moon again. He suggested that I should ... er ... stay here in Adalheid, so there is less distance to travel when he summons me. He said that the people here would be accommodating."

A sour look came over Lorraine's face. "I'm sure he did."

"I'm not meaning to take advantage of your hospitality, I swear it."

Lorraine chuckled. "I mostly believe that. Don't worry. It's easy to be generous in a town like Adalheid. We've all got more than we need. Besides, that castle is full of more darkness than my root cellar and more ghosts than a graveyard. I can venture a guess as to what you've been through."

Some of the tension in Serilda's shoulders evaporated at her kind tone. "Thank you. I don't have coin with me this time, but next time I return from Märchenfeld I will be more prepared—"

Lorraine cut her off with a wave of her hand. "I won't risk angering the hunt, whether you have coin or not. I have a daughter to think about, you know."

Serilda swallowed. "I do know. I truly don't wish to be a burden, but if I could let a room during the full moon?"

Lorraine nodded. "Consider the Wild Swan your second home."

"Thank you. You will have payment."

Lorraine shrugged. "We'll figure that out when the time comes. At least you won't feel that you have to con Leyna into buying your breakfast this time."

Serilda flushed. "She told you about that?"

"She's a good girl, but terrible at keeping secrets." She seemed to hesitate over something, then heaved a sigh and crossed her arms. "I do want to help you. It's something of my nature, and Leyna was quite taken with you, and . . . well. You don't strike me as the sort who goes out *looking* for trouble, which is a habit I can't tolerate."

Serilda shifted her weight. "No, but it does find me often enough."

"So it seems. But I'm not going to talk around the hot porridge. You should know that the people here are frightened. They saw a human girl coming out of that castle the morning after the hunt, and it's got us spooked. The hunters don't stray much from routine. People are worried what it might mean. They think you could be a . . . "

"A bad omen?"

Lorraine's expression was sympathetic. "Precisely. Your eyes don't help matters."

"They never have."

"But what worries *me*," Lorraine said, "is that Leyna seems to be under the impression that you're out for some sort of revenge. That you intend to kill the Erlking."

"Oh? Children and their imaginations."

Lorraine lifted an eyebrow, her expression challenging. "Perhaps it was a misunderstanding, but that is the story she's been telling to anyone who will listen. Like I said, not much for secrets, that child."

Serilda shrugged off her cloak, growing warm despite her damp clothes. Serilda hadn't asked Leyna *not* to tell anyone. In fact, she'd fully expected her to spread the story to the other children. She shouldn't have been surprised.

What was odd was that, at the time, she'd had no reason to seek personal vengeance against the Erlking. That was before she knew that he really had taken her mother. That was before her father had been thrown from his horse during the wild hunt. That was before this spark of hatred had begun to smolder in her chest.

"I assure you," she said, "I don't mean to bring any trouble."

"I'm sure you don't," said Lorraine. "But let's not imagine that the dark ones care for your good intentions."

Serilda lowered her eyes, knowing she was right.

"For your sake," Lorraine continued, "I hope you were merely trying to impress a fanciful little girl. Because if you truly think you're going to do harm to the Erlking, then you're a fool. His wrath is not to be tried, and I will not have my daughter, or my town, taking any part in it."

"I understand."

"Good. I'll bring you that cider, then. Breakfast, too?"

"If it isn't too much to ask."

After Lorraine had bustled away, Serilda hung her cloak on a peg beside the hearth and settled into the nearest table. When the food arrived, she dug into it hungrily, surprised yet again at how hungry the ordeal at the castle had left her.

"You're back!" said an excited voice, as Leyna plopped herself into the seat across from her, eyes shining. "But how? My friends and I were watching the roads all day yesterday. Someone would have noticed you coming back to the city. Unless"—her eyes widened—"were you brought by the hunt? *Again?* And he still hasn't killed you?"

"Not yet. I guess I've been lucky."

Leyna looked unconvinced. "I told Mama I thought you were brave, but she said you might be trying to get to Verloren before your time."

Serilda laughed. "Not on purpose, I swear it."

Leyna didn't entertain a smile. "You know, we're always told to stay away from that bridge. Until you, I'd never once heard of anyone crossing over and coming out of it, well, alive."

"You've heard of people coming out of it dead?"

"No. The dead ones just get trapped there."

Serilda sipped at her cider. "Will you tell me more about the castle, and the hunt? If you don't mind."

Leyna thought for a moment. "The wild hunt emerges every full moon. And also on the equinoxes and the solstices. We lock our doors and windows and put wax in our ears so we won't hear them calling to us."

Serilda had to look away, her heart squeezing to remember how her father had insisted they do the same. Had he not put the wax in deep enough? Or had he clawed it out in his sleep? Perhaps it didn't matter. Everything had gone wrong, and she didn't know if it would ever be right again.

"Even though everyone says that the hunt will leave us alone," Leyna continued. "They don't take kids, or ... anyone from Adalheid. Still, adults always get nervous around the full moons."

"Why doesn't the hunt take people from here?"

"Because of the Feast of Death."

Serilda frowned. "The what?"

"The Feast of Death. On the spring equinox, the day when death is conquered at the end of winter, making way for new life. It's coming up in just a few weeks."

"Right. We have a festival in Märchenfeld, too, but we call it Eostrig's Day."

Leyna's gaze turned haunted. "Well, I don't know about Märchenfeld. But here in Adalheid, the spring equinox is the most terrifying night of the year. That's when the ghosts and the dark ones and the hounds all leave the castle and come out into the city. We prepare a feast for them, and have animals for them to hunt. And they set up a big bonfire and make a lot of noise and it's very frightening, but also sort of fun, because Ma and I usually end up reading books by the fire all night long, since we can't really get any sleep."

Serilda gaped at her, trying to picture it. A city willingly inviting the wild hunt to run rampant through their streets for a full night? "And because you prepare this celebration for them, they agree to not take anyone for the hunt?"

Leyna nodded. "We still have to put wax in our ears, though. In case the Erlking changes his mind, I suppose."

"But why don't you just leave? Why stay, so close to the Erlking's castle?"

The girl's brow furrowed, like this idea might never have occurred to her before. "This is our home."

"Lots of places can be home."

"I suppose. But Adalheid . . . well. There's good fishing. Good farmland outside the walls. And we get lots of merchants and travelers passing through from Nordenburg, heading to the northern ports. The inn's usually busy, especially once the weather warms. And . . ." She trailed off, looking like she wanted to say more, but knew that she shouldn't. Serilda could see her debating with herself. But the look soon passed, and she seemed almost eager when she asked, "Have you actually met any of the ghosts in the castle? Are they all terrible?"

Serilda frowned at the change in topic. "I've met a few. The stable boy seemed nice enough, though I can't say I actually *met* him. And there's a coachman. He's . . . surly. But he has a chisel stuck in his eye, and that would probably make me surly, too."

Leyna made a disgusted face.

"And there's a boy about my age. He's actually been helping me. He's a bit mischievous, but I can tell he has a good heart. He told me that he cares about the people in this town, even if he can't meet any of you."

Leyna, though, looked a little disappointed.

"What is it?" asked Serilda.

"Is that all? You haven't met a fairy? Or a goblin? Or some magic creature that can—I don't know—make . . . gold?" She almost squeaked this last word.

"Gold?" stammered Serilda.

Leyna grimaced and hastily waved her hands. "Never mind. That's silly."

"No! No, it isn't. It's just . . . this boy I mentioned. He can make gold. Out of straw. Out of . . . well, just about anything, I suppose. How did you know?"

Leyna's expression shifted once again. No longer disappointed, she looked almost ecstatic as she reached forward and gripped Serilda's hands. "You *have* met him! But he's a boy? Are you sure? I always pictured Vergoldetgeist as a helpful little hobgoblin. Or a kindhearted troll. Or—"

"Vergoldetgeist? What's that?"

"The Gilded Ghost." Leyna's face pinched with guilt. "Mama wouldn't want me telling you this. It's something of a town secret, and we aren't meant to talk about it with strangers."

"I'm not a stranger," said Serilda, her heart fluttering. "What exactly is the Gilded Ghost?"

"He's the one that leaves the gold." Leyna glanced toward the kitchen, ensuring that her mother was out of sight, and lowered her voice. "After the Feast of Death, there are gifts of gold left all over the rocks on the north side of the castle. Sometimes they fall into the lake. Most of it gets picked up by the fishermen after the feast, but you can sometimes still find pieces they missed. We like to go diving for them in the summer. I've never found anything, but my friend Henrietta once found a golden cuff that was stuck between two rocks. And Mama has a small figurine that her grandpa pulled out of the water when he was young. Of course, we don't keep most of it. A lot of it gets sold or traded. But I'd say just about everyone in town has one or two trinkets from Vergoldetgeist."

Serilda stared at her, picturing Gild's quick fingers, the fast-spinning wheel. Straw transformed into gold.

Not just straw. He could turn almost anything into gold. He'd told her as much.

And that's what he did. And every year, he gave the gifts he'd made, crafted from his spun gold, to the people of Adalheid.

The Gilded Ghost.

You may call me Gild.

"That's why the town has prospered," Serilda whispered.

Leyna chewed on her lower lip. "You won't tell anyone, will you? Ma says, if word ever got out, we'd be overrun with treasure hunters. Or Queen Agnette would hear about it and raise all our taxes, or send the military to collect the gold." Her eyes grew wider by the moment as she began to realize what a betrayal of her own town she might have committed.

"I won't tell a soul," said Serilda, grateful that, here at least, she didn't yet have a reputation for being an unforgivable liar. "I can't wait to tell him that you thought he was a troll." At least, she hoped she'd have a chance to tell him, even if that did mean being stolen away by the Erlking yet again.

Or did it?

"Why do you think he leaves the gold on the equinox?"

Leyna shrugged. "Maybe he doesn't want the Erlking to know? And that's the only night of the year when everyone else comes out to enjoy the feast. I figure it's likely the only night when Vergoldetgeist is left alone in the castle."

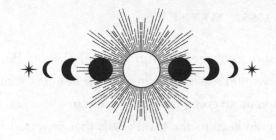

Chapter 27

Lorraine had let Serilda borrow a saddle, despite her admonishments that to try to ride home in this weather was ludicrous. Serilda insisted that she had to go, though she couldn't bring herself to explain why.

Images of the hunt kept returning to her in flashes. One moment her father was there, and the next he was gone. She didn't even know where they had been when it happened. She didn't know where the hunt had taken her, how far they had traveled.

But she knew that if Papa was all right, he would have gone home. He might be waiting for her even now.

She pulled on Zelig's reins, pausing beneath the shelter of Adalheid's city gate. The rain had let up somewhat, but she had already lost the warmth from the inn's fire. She knew it wouldn't be long before she was shivering, dampness seeping into her skin.

Father would chastise her. Warn that she would catch her death.

Oh, how she hoped he would be there to chastise her.

She peered out toward the dirt road stretching past the town. The rain had turned much of it to mud, battering down the thick brush on either side. Straight ahead, the road disappeared into the Aschen Wood, the gray line of trees mostly hidden behind a shroud of fog.

Home lay in that direction. She would not hurry Zelig, knowing he must still be sore from the hard ride the night before. But even at his slow pace, they could reach home in a couple of hours at most.

But it would mean going through the forest.

Or they could keep to the main roads that traversed the edges of the woods, meandering west through flat fields and farmlands, before eventually turning south for a straight path toward Nordenburg. It was the route that the chicken cart had taken, and she knew it would take much longer. She might not make it home before nightfall. She didn't even know if Zelig had the strength to carry her all that way.

Zelig snorted and thumped his hoof impatiently against the ground while Serilda considered.

The forest was not welcoming to humans. Yes, they might pass through on occasion—generally without harm, even—but that was under the relative protection of an enclosed carriage. With just Zelig, slow as he was, she would be vulnerable, a temptation to the creatures that lurked in the shadows. The dark ones might be hidden behind the veil, but the forest folk were not always known for kindness, either. For every tale of a headless ghost stalking the night, there were twenty of mischievous land wights and curmudgeonly imps wreaking havoc.

Thunder crooned overhead. Serilda did not see the lightning, but she felt the charge on the air. Her skin prickled.

A moment passed before the skies opened and another downpour ravished the countryside.

Serilda scowled at the sky. "Honestly, Solvilde," she muttered. "What a time to water your garden. You couldn't wait until tomorrow?"

The sky did not respond. Nor, for that matter, did the god.

It was an old myth, one of countless tales that blamed the gods for everything. Rain and snowstorms were the fault of Solvilde; uneven stitches on a piece of embroidery were a trick of Hulda; a plague, the work of Velos.

Of course, as Wyrdith was the god of fortune, nearly everything could be placed on their shoulders.

It hardly seemed fair.

"All right, Zelig. We'll be fine. Let's go home."

Tightening her jaw, she flicked the reins and they set off toward the Aschen Wood.

The storm offered no mercy, and by the time the road met the tree line, she was once again soaked through to her chemise. Zelig froze at the edge of the forest, great gobs of rainwater splattering onto the muddied road, while before them, the trees' shadows disappeared into mist and gloom.

Serilda felt a tug behind her navel, like a rope was tied to her insides, gently pulling her forward.

She inhaled sharply, her breath wavering.

She was simultaneously repelled by the woods and drawn to it. If the trees had a voice, they would have been chanting a dark lullaby, calling her closer, promising to envelop her and keep her. She hesitated, gathering her courage, feeling the tendrils of old magic reaching out to touch her, before vanishing in the gray light of day.

The woods were both living and dead.

Hero and villain.

The dark and the light.

There are two sides to every story.

Serilda was dizzy with fear, but she gripped the reins and dug her heels into Zelig's side.

He whinnied loudly and reared his head. Rather than trotting forward, he backed away.

"Go on, now," she encouraged, leaning forward to pat the side of his face. "I'm here." She urged him forward again.

This time, Zelig lifted up onto his hind legs with a desperate squeal. Serilda cried out, clutching the reins tighter to keep from being thrown off.

As soon as his hooves hit the dirt again, Zelig turned and bolted away from the woods, back toward Adalheid and safety.

"Zelig, no!" she shouted. At the last minute, she was able to swerve him away from the city gate, heading toward the western road instead.

He slowed to a canter, though his breaths were still quickened.

With a frustrated groan, Serilda glanced back over her shoulder. The woods had been swallowed up again in mist.

"Suit yourself," she grumbled. "We'll go the long way."

(

The rain stopped somewhere before Fleck, but Serilda did not dry out the entire ride. Dusk was approaching by the time Märchenfeld finally came into view, tucked into its valley by the river. Though equal parts cold and miserable, Serilda was overcome with happiness to be home. Even Zelig's steady clomping steps seemed to pick up at the sight.

As soon as they reached the mill, she tied Zelig to the hitching post, promising she would be back with his supper, and ran into the house. But she had no sooner opened the door than she knew Papa wasn't home. There was no fire in the hearth. No food simmering in the pot. She'd forgotten how barren they'd left the house, having sold off so many of their belongings before leaving for Mondbrück. It felt like entering the home of a stranger.

Cold. Abandoned.

Decidedly unwelcoming.

A loud grinding noise drew her attention toward the back wall. It took her exhausted mind a moment to place it.

The mill.

Someone was operating the mill.

"Papa," she breathed, running back outside. Zelig watched drows-ily as she scampered through the yard, hopping over the gate that sur-rounded their small garden, and rushed around to the gristmill. She yanked open the door and was greeted by the familiar smell of grinding stone and timber beams and rye grain.

But she stopped cold again, her hopes crashing to the wooden planks at her feet.

Thomas glanced up from adjusting the millstones, startled. "Ah—you're back," he said, starting to smile, though something in Serilda's expression must have given him pause. "Is everything all right?"

She ignored him. Her gaze darted around the mill, but no one else was there.

"Serilda?" Thomas took a step toward her.

"I'm fine," she said, the words automatic. They were the easiest lie, one that everyone told from time to time.

"I'm glad you're home," said Thomas. "I was having some trouble with the water gate sticking earlier, and thought your father could offer some suggestions."

She stared at him, fighting back tears. She'd had so much hope.

Miserable, unfounded hope.

Swallowing, she gave her head a shake. "He's not home."

Thomas frowned.

"He stayed in Mondbrück. I had to return to help with the school, but Father . . . the work isn't finished yet on the town hall, so he wanted to stay."

"Ah, I see. Well. I'll just have to figure it out myself, then. Do you know when he plans to be back?"

"No," she said, digging her fingernails into her palms to keep away the threatening tears. "No, he didn't say."

Serilda waited for him.

She remembered smelling sea salt in the air during the hunt. He could have fallen as far away as Vinter-Cort for all she knew. It could take days, even a week, and that was if he was able to find transportation. He likely had not had coin with him. He might have to walk. If that was the case, it might take even longer.

She clung tightly to these hopes, and tried to keep up appearances in town. Everyone was so busy preparing for Eostrig's Day that no one paid her much attention. She feigned an illness to keep from going to the school. She spent her days going through the mindless motions of sweeping out their house, sewing a new dress for herself, as the few articles of clothing she owned had been left behind in Mondbrück, and spinning—when she could stand it.

She spent many hours staring at the horizon.

She could not sleep at night. The house was too eerily quiet with no rumbling snores coming from the next room.

When Thomas had questions about the mill, she told him that she would write to her father and let him know once she'd heard a response, even going so far as to walk into town to post the fake letter.

When she saw nachtkrapp, she threw stones at them until they flew away.

They always came back.

But her father never did.

Eostrig's Day

THE
SPRING
EQUINOX

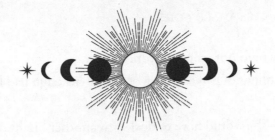

Chapter 28

She had been dreading this visit all week. Had, on more than one occasion, tried to persuade herself that it was not necessary.

But she knew that it was.

She needed to know more about Adalheid. She needed to know when and how and why the Erlking had claimed the castle. What had happened to leave its walls haunted by so many brutally murdered spirits. Whether or not there had been a royal family who had ever lived there, and what had become of them. She needed to know when and how the citizens of Adalheid had entered into this strange relationship, in which they prepared a feast on the equinox, in exchange for the hunt leaving them and their children alone.

She didn't know which answers, if any, would be useful to her, which was why she would learn as much as she could. She would arm herself with knowledge.

Because knowledge was the only weapon she might hope to wield against the Erlking. The man who had taken her mother. Who left her father to die in the middle of nowhere. Who thought he could imprison Serilda and force her into servitude. The man who had killed so many mortals. Stolen so many children.

Maybe there was nothing she could do against him. In fact, she was rather certain there was nothing she could do against him.

But that would not stop her from trying.

He was a blight of evil on this world, and his reign had lasted for far too long.

But first—she would have to deal with another blight of evil.

Taking in a bracing breath, Serilda lifted her fist and knocked on the door.

Madam Sauer lived less than a mile from the schoolhouse, in a one-room cottage surrounded by the nicest garden in all Märchenfeld. Her herbs, flowers, and vegetables were the envy of the town, and when she wasn't educating the children, she could usually be heard lecturing her neighbors on soil quality and companion plantings. Mostly unsolicited advice that, Serilda suspected, went largely ignored.

Serilda did not understand how someone with such a dismal personality could coax such life from the earth, but then, there were many things in this world that she did not understand.

She did not wait long before Madam Sauer yanked open the door, already wearing a scolding look.

"Serilda. What do you want?"

She attempted a withering smile. "Good day to you as well. I'm looking for that book that I added to the school's collection a few weeks past. I could not find it at the schoolhouse. Might you know where it is?"

Madam Sauer's gaze narrowed. "Indeed. I've been reading it."

"I see. I'm so sorry to have to ask, but I'm afraid I need it back."

The woman's lip curled. "You *did* steal it, didn't you?"

Her jaw clenched. "No," she said slowly. "It is not stolen. It was borrowed. And I now have the opportunity to return it."

With a loud huff, Madam Sauer stepped back and threw open the door.

Thinking this might be an invitation, though it wasn't entirely clear, Serilda took a hesitant step inside. She had never been in the schoolmistress's house before, and it was not what she'd expected. It smelled strongly of lavender and fennel, with bundles of various herbs and flowers hung to dry by the hearth. Though Madam Sauer kept the schoolhouse tidy as a toadstool, the shelves and tables of her little home were littered with mortars and pestles, bundles of twine, dishes overflowing with pretty colored rocks and dried beans and pickled vegetables.

"I have the utmost respect for libraries," said Madam Sauer, picking up the book off a small table beside a rocking chair. She spun back to face Serilda, brandishing the book like a mallet. "Sanctuaries of knowledge and wisdom that they are. It is most shameful, Miss Moller, most shameful indeed that one would dare to steal from a library, of all places."

"I didn't steal it!" said Serilda, puffing out her chest.

"Oh?" Madam Sauer opened the front cover and held it up so that Serilda could see the words written in dark brown ink in the corner of the first page.

Property of Professor Frieda Fairburg and the Adalheid Library

She snarled. "I didn't steal it," she said again. "Professor Fairburg gave it to me. It was a gift. She didn't even ask that I return it, but I plan to anyway." She held out a hand. "May I have it back, please?"

The witch pulled the book away from her reach. "Whatever were you doing in Adalheid, of all places? I thought you and your father had been traveling to Mondbrück all this time."

"We have been traveling to Mondbrück," she said through her teeth. "My father is in Mondbrück at this very minute." The words only barely caught in her throat.

"And *you*?" said Madam Sauer, stepping closer while holding the book behind her back. She was shorter than Serilda, but her wrinkled glower made Serilda feel about as big as a mouse. "Where have you been returning from the day after the past two full moons? That is most peculiar behavior, Miss Moller, and one I cannot accept as a harmless coincidence."

"You don't have to accept anything," said Serilda. "My book, please."

Her insides were quivering, more from anger than anything else. But it was also disconcerting to know that the schoolmistress had been watching. Or perhaps she was repeating the gossip from town. Perhaps other townsfolk had noticed her comings and goings, always around the full moons, and the rumors were beginning to circulate.

"So that you can return it to Adalheid? Are you going there today? On the equinox of all days?"

Her words dripped with accusation, and Serilda didn't even know what she was being accused of. "Do you want me to return it to the library or not?"

"I'm trying to warn you," snapped the old woman. "Adalheid is a wicked place! Anyone with the slightest bit of common sense would do well to stay far away from it."

"Oh? You've visited there often, have you?"

Madam Sauer faltered, long enough for Serilda to reach around and snatch the book away from her.

She let out a disgruntled cry.

"I'll have you know," Serilda added, "that Adalheid is a lovely town full of lovely people. But I agree that you should stay away from it. I daresay you would not fit in."

Madam Sauer's eyes blazed. "Selfish child. You are already a blight on this community, and now you will bring wickedness upon us!"

"This may come as a surprise to you, madam," said Serilda, her voice rising as her temper overcame her, "but your opinion is not required."

Turning, she stormed from the house, slamming the door so hard behind her that Zelig, tied to the fence post, gave a jump and a whinny.

She paused, fuming, before she turned and thrust open the door again.

"Also," she said, "I will not be attending the Eostrig's Day festival. Please give the children my heartfelt apologies and tell them how very proud I am of their work on the god figures this past month."

Then she slammed the door again, which was awfully satisfying.

Serilda expected the witch to come charging after her, slinging more insults and warnings. Her fingers were shaking as she tucked the book into a saddlebag and untied the reins. It had felt good to yell, when she had been swallowing her enraged screams all month.

Serilda hauled herself into the saddle and spurred the horse down the road—toward Adalheid.

☾

She did not try to take the forest route, knowing that Zelig would refuse again. As the sun traced its path across the sky, she was glad they had gotten an early start. It would be far into the afternoon by the time she arrived.

She still thought of the Hunger Moon, when the coachman had first appeared at her doorway. She had been nervous then, even a little excited. There might have been moments when she'd been afraid, but she realized now that she had not been afraid enough. She had approached it all like a great story and had loved every moment she'd spent telling the children about her exploits, knowing they only half believed her.

But now . . .

Now her life was balanced precariously on the tip of a sword, and every direction was fraught with danger. Fate was closing in around her, and she couldn't imagine how to escape it. Her father was gone. She knew now that she could never escape the Erlking, not unless he chose to let her go. Eventually he would find out the truth, and she would pay the price.

And she knew she should be terrified. She knew it.

But mostly she was livid.

This was just a game to the Erlking. Predator and prey.

But to her, it was her life. Her family. Her freedom.

She wanted him to pay for what he had done. Not just to her, but to countless families, spanning centuries.

She tried to use the long hours to concoct some sort of plan for this night. It wasn't as though she could just stroll up to the Erlking, grab his hunting knife, and plunge it into his heart.

For starters, even if, by some miracle, she actually succeeded in such a plot—she wasn't even sure if that would kill him.

She wasn't even sure he *could* be killed.

But that didn't keep the fantasy at bay.

At least, if she failed, she intended to go down with the drums and trumpets. For now, she tried to focus on practical measures she could take on this, the night of the springtide. But even then, her thoughts quickly became muddled. She knew she must try to sneak into the castle. She would find Gild. If Leyna was right, he would be alone. She needed to talk to him. To ask if he might know anything about her mother. To ask about the history of the castle, and if the Erlking had any weaknesses.

And, if she were being honest, she simply wanted to see him again.

Thoughts of Gild came with their own persistent fantasies.

The last moments of the Crow Moon had been overshadowed by her fears for her father, but she could not think of Gild without remembering that hasty kiss pressed against her lips. Hungry and wanting and then, simply, *gone.*

She shivered at the memory, but not from cold.

What had he meant by it?

There was a small, quiet, practical voice that kept reminding her how much she should be dreading this return to Adalheid and its haunted castle. But the truth was, she wasn't dreading it.

She wasn't dreading it at all.

Because this time, she was returning of her own volition. She was Serilda Moller, godchild of Wyrdith, and she would be controlled by the Erlking no longer.

At least, that was what she tried to tell herself as her ancient steed clomped slowly, steadily along the road.

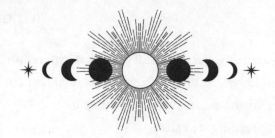

Chapter 29

She had barely passed through the gates of Adalheid when it became clear that the springtide celebrations here were quite different from those in Märchenfeld. There were no banners dyed in pink and green hung over the windows and doors. Instead, the doors she passed were decorated with garlands made of bones. At first the sight made her shudder, but she could tell these were not human bones. Chickens and goats, she guessed, or perhaps even wild hares or swans from the lake, all strung with twine and left to dangle from pegs. When a strong breeze came through, they rattled musically against one another, a sorrowful chime.

As the lake came into view, she saw a crowd gathered near the docks, but there was no cheerful music or robust laughter. Back home, the festivities would have been well underway by now, but the air here felt somber, almost oppressive.

The only similarities were the tantalizing aromas of roasting meats and fresh bread.

Serilda dismounted and walked Zelig the rest of the way toward the docks, where a number of tables had been set up on the street beside the lakeshore. The townsfolk bustled about, focused on their tasks as they set out a proper feast. Plates of sausages and salted pork, rhubarb tarts drizzled with honey and fresh strawberries, hard cheeses and shelled

chestnuts, sweet cakes and steaming hand pies, platters of roasted car-
rots, ramps, and buttered radishes. There was drink, too; kegs of ale,
barrels of wine.

It was lovely, and Serilda's stomach gurgled at the tempting aromas.

But none of the townsfolk helping to prepare the feast looked at all
excited about it. This feast was not for them. As Leyna had described,
as the sun set, the castle's residents would emerge and the streets of
Adalheid would be overtaken by dark ones and spirits.

Her attention went to the castle ruins, somehow still looking gloomy
and gray despite the sunlight that glistened off the water's surface.

Though at first the townsfolk were too busy to notice Serilda in their
midst, eventually her presence started to draw attention. Murmurs followed. People paused in their work to stare at her, curious and suspicious.

But not outright hostile. At least, not yet.

"Pardon," hollered a voice, startling Serilda. She turned to see a
young man pushing a cart toward her. She apologized and hastened
out of his path. The cart was making an awful lot of racket, and as he
pushed past her, Serilda peeked over the edge to see an assortment of
live animals crowded inside. Hares and weasels and two small foxes,
plus a cage full of pheasants and grouse.

The man pushed the cart toward the bridge, where a group of men
and women stepped forward to help him unload, leaving the birds
inside their cage and tying the rest of the animals to a post.

"Miss Serilda!" Leyna ran up to her, a basket of sugared strudel in
her arms. "You came!"

"Hello again," she said, her stomach grumbling as the smell of sweet
custard wafted toward her. "My, those look good. May I?"

A look of horror crossed Leyna's face and she pulled the basket out
of reach before Serilda had even lifted her hand. "It's for the feast!" she
hissed, lowering her voice.

"Well, yes, I figured," said Serilda, glancing at the overflowing tables. Bending forward, she whispered, "I doubt anyone will notice?"

Leyna gave a hasty shake of her head. "Better not. It isn't for us, you know."

"But do the hunters really have such impressive appetites?"

Leyna made a sour face. "Seems a waste to me, too." She approached the table and Serilda shifted a few trays so Leyna had a place to set the basket.

"It must be vexing to work so hard, only to give it away to the tyrants who lurk in that castle."

"It can be," said Leyna with a shrug. "But once everything is ready, we'll head home and Mama always has some extras set aside for us. Then we'll spend the night reading ghost stories by the fire and sneaking glimpses of the Feast of Death through the curtains. It's positively horrifying, but also one of my favorite nights of the year."

"You aren't afraid to spy on them?"

"I don't think they care much about us, so long as we provide the feast, and the game. Though last year, I swear one of the ghosts looked up at me the exact moment I peeked through the curtains, like they'd been waiting for it. I shrieked, nearly gave Mama a heart attack. I was sent to bed after that." She shuddered. "Didn't get much sleep though."

Serilda grinned. "What about Vergoldetgeist? Have you ever seen him during your spying?"

"Oh no. All the gold shows up on the north side of the castle. We can't see it from the town. They say he's the only one who doesn't come out to the party, and maybe he's bitter about not being invited."

"How do they know he's the only one that doesn't come?"

Leyna opened her mouth, but hesitated, her brow furrowing. "I have no idea. That's just how the story goes."

"Perhaps the Gilded Ghost *is* bitter about not being included, but

I don't think he cares much for the dark ones, so it's probably just as well."

"Did he tell you that?" asked Leyna, eyes shining, eager for any tid-bit of gossip from the walls of the castle.

"Oh yes. It isn't such a secret. He and the Erlking are not fond of each other."

A teasing smile came over Leyna's cheeks. "You like him, don't you?"

Serilda tensed. "What?"

"Vergoldetgeist. Your eyes turn extra gold when you talk about him."

"They do?" Serilda pressed her fingers to the corner of her eye. She'd never heard of the golden wheels changing before.

"Is *that* a secret?"

"My eyes?"

"No!" Leyna laughed. "That you are taken with a ghost."

Heat rushed into Serilda's cheeks. "That's silly. He's helping me, is all." She bent closer. "But I do have a secret, if you wish to hear it."

Leyna's eyes widened and she leaned in.

"I've decided to go into the castle tonight," she said. "When the dark ones are all at their feast, I'm going to sneak in and see if I can find the Gilded Ghost and talk to him."

"I knew it," Leyna breathed. "I knew that was why you'd come today." She bounced on the balls of her feet, though Serilda couldn't tell if she was excited, or trying to keep warm as the sun sank into the lake. "How are you going to get past the feast?"

"I was hoping you might have some ideas."

Leyna bit her lower lip, considering. "Well, if it were me—"

"Leyna!"

They both jumped and turned around. Serilda was sure they could not have looked any guiltier if they'd each been holding a piece of cake from the feast table.

"Hello, Mama," said Leyna as her mother picked her way through the crowd.

"Professor Fairburg has got two more baskets to bring down. Run on and help her, would you?"

"Of course, Mama," Leyna chirped before darting down the street.

Lorraine paused a few feet from Serilda. "I can't say I'm surprised to see you back here again." She smiled, but it wasn't that same cheery, dimpled smile she'd had before. If anything, she seemed a bit frazzled. Which was to be suspected, Serilda supposed, given the occasion.

"Everyone seems so busy," said Serilda. "Is there anything I can do to help?"

"Oh, we're just about finished. Not a moment too soon, as per usual." She nodded toward the horizon, where the sun was just kissing the distant city wall. "Every year I tell myself, I'll be extra prepared. We'll be ready by noon! But somehow, there's always more to do than I think."

As she spoke, another cart arrived carrying yet more hunting game—mostly rabbits, from what Serilda could see.

"I wasn't expecting to see you until the full moon," said Lorraine. She started to walk along the feast tables, adjusting platters and small clay vases full of herbs. "Has the Erlking requested your presence for the equinox as well?"

"Not exactly, no," said Serilda. "But Leyna was telling me something of the feast, and I wanted to see it for myself. Besides, I have questions for the Erlking. And since he doesn't seem interested in conversation on the nights of the full moon, when he is busy with the hunt, I thought this might be a better opportunity."

The mayor froze and stared at her as if she'd started speaking another language. "You mean to . . . have a conversation? With the Erlking? During the Feast of Death?" She barked a laugh. "Oh, dearest! Do you not understand who he is? What he's done? If you approach him tonight, of all nights, to . . . to ask questions?" She laughed again.

"You'll be asking him to skin you alive! To pluck out your eyeballs and feed them to the hounds. To tear your fingers off one by one and—"

"All right, thank you. I see your point."

"No, I don't think you do." Lorraine stepped closer, all signs of mirth erased. "They are not human, and they have no sympathy for us mortals. Can't you see that?"

Serilda gulped. "I don't think he will kill me. He still wants gold from me, after all."

Lorraine shook her head. "You seem to be playing a game for which you do not know all the rules. Heed my advice. If the king is not expecting you tonight, then take a room at the inn and stay put until morning. Otherwise you are risking your life for nothing."

Serilda's gaze swept toward the castle. "I do appreciate your concern."

"But you're not going to listen to me."

Serilda pursed her lips apologetically.

"I have a daughter. You might be older, but I recognize that look all the same." Lorraine stepped closer, lowering her voice. "Do not anger the Erlking. Not tonight. Everything must go perfectly."

Serilda was startled by the vehemence in Lorraine's tone. "What do you mean?"

Lorraine gestured toward the tables. "You think we do all this to be good neighbors?" She shook her head, a shadow eclipsing her eyes. "There was a time when our children would go missing, too. But our ancestors began tempting the hunt with this feast on the spring equinox, the gift of game to be hunted in our streets. We hoped to appease them, to gain their favor, so they would leave our city and our families alone." Her face pinched with distress. "My heart aches, of course, for the loved ones who go missing from other towns, especially when I hear of innocent children being taken. I can only imagine the pain a parent would feel. But because of this feast, they are not taken from Adalheid, and I will not risk you interfering."

"But you are still afraid," said Serilda. "You might have found a way to make peace with the dark ones, but you are still afraid of them."

"Of course I'm afraid of them! Everyone should be. *You* should be far more afraid of them than you seem to be."

"Madam Mayor!"

Lorraine looked past Serilda's shoulder, then straightened as the librarian, Frieda, hurried toward them with Leyna on her heels.

"They're bringing out the god of death," said Frieda. She paused with a smile at Serilda. "Hello again. Leyna told me you would be watching the spectacle with us. It's terrifying, but . . . still a sight worth seeing."

"With . . . us?" asked Lorraine.

Frieda flushed, but Leyna stepped forward with a wily grin. "I invited Frieda to stay at the inn tonight! It's far too scary to be home alone during the Feast of Death."

"If it isn't any trouble . . . ," said Frieda.

"Oh! No, no trouble at all. I believe we have spare rooms available for you and for the young miss." She glanced at Serilda. "If you are planning to stay, that is?"

"A room would be much appreciated, thank you."

"Good. It's decided, then."

"We should hurry, shouldn't we?" said Leyna. "It's getting dark."

"Indeed it is." Lorraine started toward the castle bridge, where townspeople—many carrying lanterns as dusk claimed the city—had gathered around the tables and the leashed animals. Serilda lingered toward the back of their group. When Leyna noticed, she slowed her steps so that Serilda could catch up.

"Why is she mad at you?" Leyna whispered.

"I don't think she's mad, just worried," Serilda answered. "I can't say that I blame her."

Ahead, a group of people carried what looked like a scarecrow painted up like a skeleton. Together, they attached it to a small plain boat waiting off the dock nearest the castle bridge, where Serilda had seen Leyna and her friends playing all those weeks before.

"We make effigies of the gods, too, in Märchenfeld," she told Leyna. "So they can watch over the festival and give us their blessings."

Leyna shot her a baffled look. "Blessings?"

She nodded. "We give them flowers and gifts. It isn't the same here?"

With a cackle, Leyna gestured toward the skeletal figure. "We only make Velos, and we give it to the hunters, along with all the quarry. You saw the hares and the foxes?"

Serilda nodded.

"They'll be released so the hunt can chase them through the city. Once they've all been captured, they kill them and throw the meat onto the god of death and . . . and then the hounds have *their* feast."

Serilda cringed. "That sounds gruesome."

"Mama says it's because the dark ones are at war with death. Have been ever since they escaped Verloren."

"Maybe," said Serilda. "Or maybe this is one way he can get revenge."

"Revenge for what?"

Serilda glanced down at the girl, thinking about the story she'd told to Gild about the prince slaying the huntress Perchta, and the god of death taking her spirit back to Verloren.

But that was just a story. One that had woven itself in her mind's eye, like a tapestry on the loom, each thread gradually adding to the image until the scene slowly took shape.

It was not real.

"Nothing," she said. "I'm sure your mother is right. The god of death kept the dark ones trapped in Verloren for a long time. I'm sure they're still resentful about it."

At the front of the crowd, Madam Mayor started to make a speech, thanking everyone for their hard work and explaining to them why this night was so important, though Serilda doubted anyone needed reminding.

At one point, she looked about to say something more, but then her gaze darted to Serilda and she caught herself, instead stammering out something about breakfast at the public house tomorrow morning, in celebration of another successful feast.

Serilda glanced up at the castle, wondering if Lorraine had been about to mention the town's resident benefactor—Vergoldetgeist. She had a feeling that the breakfast was an annual tradition every bit as much as the preparation of this feast for the dark ones was, and that tomorrow all of Adalheid would gather around eagerly to see what gifts of gold their fishermen and divers brought home.

"Leyna," she whispered. "Do you know who this castle belonged to before it belonged to the Erlking?"

Leyna frowned up at her. "What do you mean?"

"Surely the dark ones didn't build it. It must have been the home of mortals at some point. Royalty, or at least nobility. A duke or a count perhaps?"

Leyna curled her lips up close to her nostrils in a way that Serilda knew Madam Sauer would have found most unseemly. It was an endearing, tough-thinking look. "I suppose so," the girl answered slowly. "But I don't remember anyone ever talking about it. It must have been a long time ago. Nowadays, it's just the Erlking and the dark ones. And the ghosts."

"And Vergoldetgeist," Serilda murmured.

"Shh!" said Leyna, tugging on Serilda's wrist. "You aren't supposed to know about that."

Serilda whispered a distracted apology as the mayor finished her speech. Candles and lanterns were lit, allowing her to more clearly see the effigy they had made. It hardly resembled the one she'd watched the children make for the Märchenfeld celebration. This likeness was taken seriously. Cloaked in black robes and looking fearsomely realistic with its skull's head and sprigs of poisonous hemlock sewn to its hands. Would the hellhounds devour those, too? Would it not harm them? Maybe it strengthened them, she reasoned. Kindling for the fires in their bellies.

The figure was anchored to a tall wooden column and surrounded by alder branches, a nod to Erlkönig, the Alder King.

As the last stripes of purple light began to fade, the townsfolk started toward their homes. Lorraine and Frieda headed to the inn, walking, perhaps, a hair closer to each other than was strictly necessary. Lorraine occasionally glanced back, making sure Leyna was following.

"If you still wanted to get in to that castle," Leyna said, "I'd take a boat, row up along the far side of the drawbridge, then climb up the rocks just under the gate. It isn't as steep on that side, and you should be able to get over the rail."

Leyna gave Serilda instructions about which boat to use and when she should go. "As long as there's no one watching the gate, that is," the girl said.

"Do you think there will be?"

Leyna shook her head, though she seemed uncertain. "Just don't go until after they've started the hunt. They'll all be so busy watching the games and eating our food, they won't even notice you."

Serilda smiled. "You've been marvelously helpful."

"Yes, well . . . don't get killed; otherwise, I'll feel horrid about this."

Serilda squeezed her shoulder. "I don't plan to." With a quick glance toward Lorraine and Frieda, Serilda sidestepped into a narrow alley, disappearing into the shadows and separating herself from the crowd.

She waited for the noise of footsteps and chatter to fall silent before peeking out from her hiding spot. Seeing the streets empty, she scurried quickly down to the docks, staying to the shadows as much as she could. It was easier on a night like this, when the people of Adalheid took their lanterns inside.

Before her, the castle stood, a waiting monster perched above the lake.

And then the last sliver of sunlight fell behind the horizon and all at once the spell that kept the Erlking's castle hidden behind the veil slipped away like an illusion. Serilda gasped. If she had looked away for even a moment, she would have missed the transformation. One moment, hulking darkness. And the next, Adalheid Castle stood in all its glory—the watchtowers lit with flickering torches, the stained-glass windows of the keep shimmering like jewels. The narrow bridge itself, its crumbling walls mended, now glistened beneath the light of a dozen torches reflected in the black water below.

Seen like this, in such stark contrast to the ruins of a moment before, the castle was truly breathtaking.

She had just reached the dock where Leyna said she would find the boat that belonged to the Wild Swan when a new sound echoed across the lake.

The low, haunting bellow of a hunting horn.

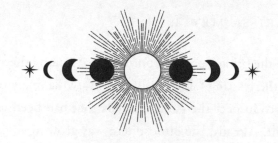

Chapter 30

Having nowhere to hide on the wide-open dock, Serilda flattened herself against the wooden boards and hoped that her cloak would disguise her in the shadows. The castle gates opened with a rumble and groan. She lifted her head high enough to watch them pour through.

It was not a stampede, like she had come to expect from the wild hunt. But then, tonight was not a hunting moon.

The king walked at the helm of their parade, while the dark ones fanned out behind him, some on horses and others on foot. Even from afar she could see that they were dressed in finery. Not sumptuous velvet gowns and feathered caps, like the royal family in Verene might have worn. But in their own way, the hunters had prepared for an evening of revelry. Their jerkins and doublets were trimmed with gold, their capes lined with fur, their boots fastened with pearls and gems. They still looked as though they might commandeer a stallion and chase after a stag at any moment, but they were prepared to do so with inarguable elegance.

The ghosts followed. Serilda recognized the one-eyed coachman and the headless woman. Their clothing remained the same as always: a bit old-fashioned and covered in their own blood.

It was not long before the undead inhabitants of Adalheid Castle had filled up the bridge, pouring onto the road along the water. Some approached the feasting tables with delight, while many of the hunters gathered to inspect the game animals that had been left for their entertainment. Already, the atmosphere was growing jovial. Some of the ghost servants took to pouring ale and wine and passing overflowing goblets among the crowd. A quartet of gore-splattered musicians struck up a song that was lively if also a touch discordant to Serilda's ear, as if their instruments hadn't been tuned in a few centuries.

Serilda strained to get a better look at the ghouls. Would she recognize her mother if she was among them? She knew so little about her. The inclination was to look for a woman close to her father's age, but no, she would have been in her early twenties when she went missing. Serilda wished she had asked her father more questions. What did her mother look like? Dark hair and a chipped tooth was all the information she had. What color were her eyes? Was she tall, like Serilda was, or did she have the same small brown freckles like constellations on her arms?

She searched the faces of every woman she could see, hoping to feel a surge of recognition, a surge of *anything,* but if her mother was among them, she couldn't tell.

The howls of the hellhounds made Serilda duck again. On the bridge, the master of the hounds appeared, gripping a dozen leashes as the hounds strained and growled to get free. They had seen the quarry at the end of the bridge.

"Hunters and spirits," rang the Erlking's voice. "The immortal and the lifeless." He took the crossbow off his shoulder and notched an arrow. A group of apparitions gathered around the trembling prey. The hunters on their horses gripped the reins, lascivious grins darkening their faces. "Let the hunt begin." The Erlking fired the arrow—straight into the heart of the god of death. It landed with a sickening thump.

Cage doors were thrown open. Ropes were slashed.

The hounds were released.

Terrified animals scattered in every direction. Birds flapped toward the nearest rooftops. Hares and ferrets and badgers and foxes scampered into yards, down alleyways, around buildings.

The hounds gave chase, the hunters not far behind.

A raucous cheer erupted from the crowd. Wine splashed as goblets were toasted. The tempo of the music increased. She had never imagined a castle of ghosts could make so much noise, or sound so . . . cheerful.

No—that wasn't the right word.

Riotous was better.

Serilda was amazed how much it reminded her of Eostrig's Day in Märchenfeld. Not the hunting, but the joviality, the merriment, the celebratory air.

If the dark ones hadn't been callous murderers, she might have wished to join them.

As it was, she recalled Leyna's warning, to wait until they were distracted by the hunt before making her move.

Staying as low as she could, she slowly crept forward.

Though there were dozens of boats moored along the dock, it was easy to spot the one that belonged to the White Swan. It was not the biggest, the newest, the nicest—not that Serilda was a particularly qualified judge of boats—but it was painted the same bright blue as the front of the public house, with a white swan on the side.

Serilda had never been in a boat before, much less unmoored and rowed one herself, and she spent perhaps far too much time staring down at the sun-faded wood benches and the fraying rope looped and knotted around an iron stand, trying to figure out if she should untie the rope before or after climbing in. And once she was in, how much would the boat sway under her weight, and how exactly was she going to use those two measly oars to steer herself around all the other boats squeezed in like sausages along this pier?

She pulled the edge of the boat closer, until it thunked hollowly against the dock. After another moment's hesitation, she sat down on the ledge and stuck her feet into the boat, testing its sway. It dipped low under the pressure, but buoyed easily back up. Exhaling, she clambered awkwardly inside, sinking down to the floor, where a small puddle of cold water soaked into her skirt.

The boat didn't sink. So that was encouraging.

It took another minute for her to unknot and unwind the rope. Then, using the end of one of the oars, she shoved away from the dock. The boat rocked treacherously and clonked time and again against the sides of its neighbors as she tried to steer it away. She cringed at every noise, but a boisterous archery tournament had started up as some of those who had not gone after the hunting quarry gleefully turned the god of death into a pincushion.

It took her ages to get onto open water. The boat was an uncontrolled spinning top, and she was grateful that the lake's surface was relatively still, otherwise she would have been at its mercy. As it was, she found she had better luck using the oars to shove away from other boats than she did using them to actually row, but once she had left the confines of the narrow marina, she had no other choice. Situating herself with her back to the castle, as she'd seen the fishermen do, she took hold of both oars with tight fists and started to rotate them in stiff, awkward circles. It was much harder than it looked. The water resisted, the oars felt strange and unrelenting in her hands, and she was constantly forced to correct her course as the boat turned too far in one direction and then the other.

Finally, a couple of lifetimes later, she found herself in the shadow of the castle, just beneath the drawbridge.

From this angle, the structure was huge and ominous. The walls and watchtowers stretched upward toward the star-dappled sky, blocking the moon from her view. Gigantic boulders made up its foundation, surrounded by gently lapping water, which might have been peaceful if not broken by the ghostly cheers of the revelers on the shore.

Serilda paused and craned her neck, trying to see any place where she might safely land and be able to climb out, but it was so dark that all she could make out were glistening wet rocks, nearly indistinguishable from one another.

After a number of attempts to run the boat ashore, Serilda was finally able to grab hold of a sharp-tipped boulder and loop the rope around it. She tied the best knot she could and hoped that the boat would still be here for her when she returned for it . . . then she hoped that she would return for it at all.

Tying her skirts to keep them from tangling underfoot, she scrambled inelegantly from the boat and started to climb. The rocks were slick, many covered with slimy moss. She tried not to think about what creatures might be hiding under the jagged stones, claws and scales and sharp little teeth waiting for a vulnerable hand to slip by.

She was doing a poor job not thinking about it.

Finally, she made it to the lowered drawbridge. The bridge was empty, but she couldn't see much of the courtyard beyond the gate, and had no way of knowing if it was inhabited or not.

"Oh well," she said, with a bracing nod. "I've come this far."

With a series of grunts and groans, she hauled herself up onto the bridge. She collapsed atop the planks in a heap, but quickly pushed herself up to all fours and glanced around.

She saw no one.

She sprang to her feet and dashed through the castle gates, before throwing herself against the inside of the castle wall.

She scanned the bailey, taking in the stables, the kennels, the collection of storage and outbuildings around its edges. She saw no one, and could hear nothing beyond her own breathing, her own heartbeat, the distant thunking of arrows and the cheers and hollers that followed, and much-closer snuffles and snorts from the bahkauv in the stables.

According to Leyna's story about Vergoldetgeist, Gild would most likely be on the outer wall of the castle, perhaps in one of the towers facing the other side of the lake. She figured it would take a bit of guesswork to figure out how, exactly, to get up there. She had never been around to the back side of the castle or on the outer walls at all, but she was starting to get a feel for how everything was laid out.

She took a moment to scan the tops of the castle walls, but while there were flickering torches along the parapets, she saw no movement, and no Gild.

She wanted to see him. Was almost aching to see him, and she told herself it was because she needed to ask if he knew whether or not her mother might be among the king's court. It was a mystery that wouldn't stop gnawing at her.

But there was another mystery gnawing at her, too. It hadn't been a part of her plan, but now, standing in the courtyard, with those shimmering stained-glass windows looking down at her from the castle keep, she wondered if she would ever have another chance to explore this castle while the veil was down and the court was absent.

Perhaps a quick look, she told herself. She only wanted to peek behind that door, to see the tapestry that had caught her attention.

Then she would find Gild.

It wouldn't take long, and she had all night.

With another glance around, she scurried across the bailey and into the keep.

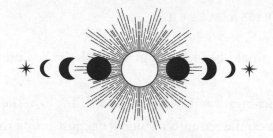

Chapter 31

Somehow, the castle was even eerier on this side of the veil, with its tapestries and paintings and furniture all tidy and clean, fires burning in the hearths and torches lit in every corridor and chandelier, and yet—not a soul to be found. As if there had been life a moment ago, but that life had been snuffed out like a candle flame.

By now, she knew enough of the passages to find her way easily to the stairwell that led up to the hall of gods, as she'd taken to calling the room with the stained-glass windows. She had only ever been in that hall during the day, when bits of glass were shattered, the leading broken, the decor made of fat, dusty cobwebs.

It was different at night. The light came from the standing candelabras, not the sun, and while still lovely, the windows did not sparkle and gleam.

Her steps were quick as she rounded the corner. The narrow hall stood before her, windows to one side, shut doors on the other. Chandeliers dripping with wax instead of spiders.

The door at the far end was shut, but she could see a hint of light spilling out from the gap onto the floor.

Even knowing the castle was empty, she moved cautiously, her feet padding into the soft carpet.

Her pulse was a drumbeat in her ears when she reached the door, afraid that it would be locked. But when she pulled on the latch, it opened easily.

She held her breath as it swung backward. The light she'd seen came from a single candle set onto a stone ledge just inside the door. She stepped into the room, letting her eyes adjust to the dimness.

Her gaze fell on a curtain of sheer lace hung from the ceiling, draped around a cage in the center of the room.

She froze. Cages were for animals. What kind of creature would be kept in such a room? She squinted, but could barely make out a lumpy form behind the bars, unmoving.

Asleep?

Dead?

Holding completely still, she shifted her gaze to the wall where she had seen the tapestry.

She frowned.

The tapestry was there, but in a reversal of the mortal world, it was not pristine as it had appeared on the other side of the veil. Here, it hung in shreds. She could make out a bit of the background scenery, a lush garden at nighttime, lit by a silver moon and dozens of lanterns. In the garden stood the figure of a bearded man wearing an ornate doublet and a golden crown. But something was off about him. His eyes too large, his smile a toothy grimace.

Serilda inched closer, even as quiet dread began to gnaw at her.

Once her eyes adjusted to the dim candlelight, she froze. The tapestry did not depict the face of an honored king. It depicted a skull. A corpse dressed in fine regalia.

The man was dead.

Shaking now, she reached for one of the shreds of woven fabric and caught sight of a second figure, smaller and ripped in two, but clearly a girl by her poufed skirt and ballooned sleeves and . . .

Thick ringlet curls.

Her heart thundered.

Could it be the girl from the locket?

Serilda reached for the next scrap, when, from the corner of her eye, a dark shadow lunged toward her.

Her scream collided with its shrill cry. Serilda barely had time to raise her arms. The monster sank its talons into her shoulder, its shriek flooding her thoughts.

And she was no longer in the castle.

She was standing in front of the schoolhouse in Märchenfeld, or— what had been the schoolhouse, recognizable for its yellow-painted shutters. But it was on fire. Black smoke filled the air. Serilda started to cough, trying to cover her mouth, when she heard their screams.

The children.

They were inside.

They were trapped.

Serilda started to rush forward, ignoring the stinging in her eyes, but a hand grabbed her shoulder, holding her back.

"Do not be a fool," came the voice of the Erlking, preternaturally calm. "You cannot save them. I told you, Lady Serilda. You should have done as I asked."

"No!" she gasped, horrified. "I have! I've done everything you asked!"

"Have you?" The question was met with a low chuckle. "Or have you been trying to sell me a lie?" He spun her around to face him, his gaze bitter in its coldness. "This is what happens to those who betray me."

His face faded away, replaced with a cascade of images, too grotesque to process. Papa's body facedown in a field while scavenger birds picked at his insides. Anna and her two younger siblings locked in a cage while goblins jeered and stabbed them with sticks. Nickel and Fricz fed to the hellhounds, ripped to shreds by their merciless teeth. Leyna and her mother together as a flock of nachtkrapp came at them again and again—their sharp beaks targeting their vulnerable eyes, their kind hearts, the hands that tried desperately to hold on to each other. Gild pinned like a moth to an enormous spinning wheel that whirred and whirred and whirred . . .

A feral roar reached her across the plain of nightmares.

The claws on her shoulder were torn away. The shriek was silenced.

Serilda tried to climb back to consciousness, but the nightmares clung to her, threatening to drag her back. Somewhere beyond the darkness, she could hear a fight. The drude's angry hisses. The strikes and grunts of a battle.

His voice—*You will not touch her again!*

She didn't think it was possible, but Serilda managed to pry her eyes open. They immediately shut again, flinching away from the faint candlelight. But in that moment she'd seen him. A figure armed with a sword, an actual sword. Except, instead of flashing silver and steel, it appeared to be made of gold.

She squinted her eyes open again, lifting one arm to block her view of the candle.

She was just in time to see Gild driving the weapon clean through the drude's belly.

A gargling sound. The stench of entrails.

Another beat of wings, another deafening cry.

She gasped. "Gild!"

The second drude dove for his head, claws dragging along his scalp.

Gild roared and yanked the sword out of the first drude's body. In one ferocious swing, he turned and cut off one of the second attacker's wings.

The sound it made was agony and horror as it collapsed to the ground. Sitting back on its haunches, its one wing flapping uselessly, it hissed at Gild with its sharp pointed tongue.

Fury twisted Gild's face as he lunged, stabbing it in the chest, where a heart might have been.

The drude's hiss turned into choking. Black liquid spilled from its mouth as it slumped forward onto the blade.

Panting hard, Gild yanked the sword away, letting the drude crumple in a heap beside its peer. Two grisly piles of bruise-purple skin and leathery wings.

He stood for a long while, gripping the hilt, his eyes darting madly around the room. He was shaking.

"Gild?" Serilda whispered, her voice hoarse from screaming.

He spun toward her, wide-eyed. "What is wrong with you?" he yelled.

She jolted. His anger helped her shed some of the lingering paralysis from the nightmares. "What?"

"One battle with a drude wasn't enough?" He held his hand toward her. "Come on. There will be more coming. We have to go."

"You have a sword?" she said, a little dazed, as he pulled her to her feet. To her surprise and a bit of disappointment, he yanked his hand away from her the moment she was standing.

"Yes, but I'm out of practice. We got lucky. Those things can torture me every bit as easy as they can torture you."

He stuck his head out into the hall, making sure it was empty, before waving for Serilda to follow him. She started to, but they hadn't rounded the corner before her legs gave way and she collapsed against the wall.

Gild wheeled back to her.

"Sorry," she stammered. "I'm just . . . I can't stop shaking."

Sympathy flashed across his features. Stepping closer, he took her elbow, infinitely more gentle than he'd been moments before. "No, I'm sorry," he said. "You're hurt . . . and scared."

She hadn't been thinking about her shoulder, but once he mentioned it, she could suddenly feel the sting where the drude's talons had dug into her.

"So are you," she said, watching as a slim trail of blood made its way down Gild's temple from the wounds in his scalp. "Hurt."

He winced. "It's not so bad. Let's keep moving. I'll help you walk."

He carelessly tossed the sword off into a corner so he could support her around the waist, one hand gripping hers tight as they passed the stained-glass windows and headed back down the stairs. He led her into the great hall and set her down in front of the fireplace. The rubin-rot wyvern peered down at them from its place above the mantel, eyes glittering with the light of a hundred candle flames. Its lifelike appearance made Serilda uneasy, but Gild seemed hardly to notice it, and so she tried not to be bothered, either.

Kneeling, Gild reached for her forehead, as if he intended to check for a fever. But then he froze and reeled his hand backward, tucking it close to his chest instead. A flicker of anguish passed over his face, but was gone in an instant, replaced with concern.

"How long did it have you before I got there?"

Serilda started to sit up straighter, and again Gild's fingers flexed toward her. The movement was brief before he was pressing both of his palms into his knees instead. She looked down at his hands, noting the way his fingers were clawed, his knuckles going white.

"I don't know," she said. "It happened so fast. What time is it?"

"Maybe . . . two hours after sunset?"

"Not long then, I don't think."

He exhaled a long breath, some of the worry clearing from his brow. "Good. They can torture you for hours, until your heart stops. When you can't handle any more terror, and you just sort of . . . give up." He met Serilda's eyes. "What were you thinking, going back there?"

"How do you know I've been there before?"

He reacted as if this was a ridiculous question. "After the Hunger Moon! When you were running for your life. Then you show up on the equinox, when the king didn't even summon you, and head straight back to that room of horrors?"

Despite his lecture, Serilda felt her heart expand. "It was you. With the candelabra. You attacked the drude last time, too."

"Of course it was me! Who did you think it was?"

She had thought . . . had even hoped. But she hadn't been sure.

Ignoring his frustration, she asked, "How did you find me? How did you know I was there?"

Gild rocked back on his heels, withdrawing inch by inch. "I was in the gatehouse when I saw you creeping across the courtyard." He shook his head, and he looked pained when he added, "I thought maybe you were looking for me."

"I was!"

He scowled. Unconvinced, and rightfully so.

"I was going to," Serilda amended. "I just thought this would be my best chance to see what's in that room."

"Why do you care what's in that room? *Drudes* are in that room!"

"I thought the castle would be empty! Everyone was supposed to be at the feast!"

He barked a laugh. "Drudes don't go to parties."

"And now I know that," she snapped, then tried to temper her irritation. If she could only make him understand. "There's something in there. A . . . a tapestry."

His expression became more bewildered. "There are hundreds of tapestries in this castle."

"This one is different. On my side of the veil, it isn't destroyed like everything else. And when I went in tonight . . . there was a cage. Did you see it?" She leaned forward. "What would the Erlking be keeping that needs a cage?"

"I don't know," he said, shrugging. "More drudes?"

She rolled her eyes. "You don't understand."

"No, I don't. You could have been killed. Doesn't that matter to you?"

Something in his tone gave her pause. Something bordering on panic.

"Of course I care," she said, quieter now. "But I also feel there's something . . . important. You said you can go anywhere in this castle. Don't you ever go in there?"

"*No*," he said. "Because, again—and I cannot stress this enough—that is where the drudes are. And it is a terrible idea to cross paths with a drude. I avoid them whenever I can, and you should, too."

She crossed her arms and pouted. She wanted to tell him she would, but the frustration from not having any questions answered, no mysteries solved, was nagging at her. "What if they're protecting something? Something the Erlking doesn't want anyone to find?"

Gild opened his mouth, readying another glib retort, but then he hesitated. Frowning, he closed his mouth again, considering her. Then he sighed, his gaze falling to Serilda's hands. He shifted forward and she thought he was going to reach for her hands, take them into his. Instead, he settled his palms on the lounge cushions on either side of her knees.

Careful not to touch her.

"The Erlking has his secrets," he said, "but whatever is in that room, it isn't worth risking your life. Please. Please don't try to go there again."

Her shoulders fell. "I . . . I won't go there again . . ."

Relief stole across his features.

". . . unprepared."

He tensed. "Serilda—no. You can't—"

"Where did you get a sword anyway?"

Gild glowered at the change of subject, then huffed and pushed himself to standing. "The armory. Erlkönig keeps enough sharp, deadly things to arm an entire militia."

"I've never seen a golden sword before."

Gild started to drag a hand through his hair, then paused and pulled it away, looking down at the smear of blood on his fingers.

"Here." Standing beside him, her legs no longer threatening to collapse, she lifted the corner of her cloak and reached for his brow. Gild flinched away.

"Hold still. It won't hurt."

His gaze flashed to hers, as if insulted. But he didn't move again as she dabbed at the blood, already drying on his brow.

"Gold is a terrible choice for a weapon," he said as she worked, his voice strangely distant, his gaze glued to her face. "It's a very soft metal. Dulls easily. But a lot of magic creatures are averse to gold, including drudes."

"There," she said, letting the edge of her cloak fall. "That's a bit better, though we'll need water to wash off the rest."

"Thank you," he murmured. "Your shoulder?"

"It will be all right." She glanced down to see the tears that the drude's talons had left in the fabric. "I'm more worried about my cloak. It's my favorite. And I'm not the best at patchwork."

His smile was hesitant. Then, as if suddenly realizing how close they were, he took a step back.

Serilda felt a prickle of hurt. The last time she'd seen him, he'd been so eager to hold her hand, to embrace her while she cried, even to give her that frantic kiss.

What had changed?

"I didn't just come here to see that room," she said. "I did come to find you. As soon as I heard about the Feast of Death, and that the king and his court would not be in the castle, I thought . . . I don't know what I thought. I just wanted to see you again. Without being locked up with a pile of straw for once."

He looked almost hopeful when she said this, even as he wrung his hands and took yet another step away from her. "Believe it or not, this is an important night for me."

"Oh?"

He smiled, the first real smile she'd seen on him all night. That impish, dimpled look again. "In fact, maybe you'd like to help."

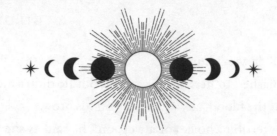

Chapter 32

You spend all year making these?" said Serilda, crouched over the crate full of small golden trinkets. She picked up a figurine shaped like a horse, crafted entirely of braided gold wire, similar to the golden strands she'd seen him spin from straw.

"That, and saving your life," said Gild, leaning against the parapet. "I like to keep busy."

She sent him a good-natured glare. Standing, she peered over the wall's edge, down at the rocks far below and the lake reflecting a path of moonlight.

"What do you suppose the Erlking wants the gold for?" she asked. "Somehow I doubt his motives are as benevolent as yours."

Gild scoffed. "Indeed. I suspect a few of these pieces will go toward paying off the feast he's enjoying right now."

He did not try to hide his resentment.

"And yet," added Serilda, "what need does he have for riches?"

Gild shook his head, staring down at the rocks, though it was too dark to see the pieces they'd already tossed down for the divers and fishermen of Adalheid to find.

"I don't know. He was storing it in the undercroft beneath the keep. I popped in every once in a while to see if it had been moved, but he didn't seem to be doing anything with it. Then, after the Crow Moon,

I went in one day and it was gone. All of it." He shrugged. "Maybe he was worried I was going to try to steal it. I may have been planning as much." His eyes twinkled with a hint of mischief, but it was quickly doused. "But I don't know where he's moved it to. Or what he wants it for. You're right, though. I've never known him to take an interest in human riches before. Or really, anything other than hounds and weapons and the occasional feast. And servants. He enjoys being waited on."

"Are all the servants ghosts?"

"No. He also has the kobolds, the goblins, the nachtkrapp . . ."

She pressed her lips together, wondering if she should tell Gild that the nachtkrapp had been watching her ever since the start of the new year.

Not that it mattered now. She wouldn't be trying to run away again.

"Are *you* one of his servants?" she asked instead.

He glanced at her, eyes glittering. "Of course not. I'm the poltergeist."

She rolled her eyes. He seemed far too proud of his role as the resident troublemaker. "Do you know what they call you in Adalheid?"

His grin brightened. "The Gilded Ghost."

"Exactly. Did you come up with it?"

He shook his head. "I don't remember when I had the idea to start leaving gifts for them. I did it at first to amuse myself, and wasn't entirely sure anyone would ever find them here on the back side of the castle. Not many people like to venture close to a haunted castle, after all. But when someone discovered a few of the presents, they all started coming back for more. It's my favorite time of the year, after Eostrig's Day, when I can stand up here and watch them searching for the gold below. It's the only time people are close enough for me to hear them, and I remember, a long time ago, hearing them talking about their . . . *benefactor.* Vergoldetgeist. I figured they had to mean me. And I hope . . . I mean, I want them to know the ghosts in this castle aren't cruel."

"They know," she said, taking his arm. "It's largely because of your gifts that Adalheid has flourished all these years. They're very appreciative, I assure you."

Gild smiled, but it was suddenly tight as he extricated his arm. Taking the horse figurine, he paced farther down the wall.

Serilda's heart sank. "What's wrong?"

His expression was all innocence as he turned back to her. "Nothing's wrong." He reeled back his arm and threw the horse toward the lake.

Serilda leaned over the wall, but it was too dark to see much. She heard a quiet *plink-plink* as the horse hit the rocks, followed by a *splash*.

"I like to spread them out," he said. "Some in the water, some on the rocks . . . makes it kind of a game, you know? Everyone likes games."

Serilda wanted to mention that the townsfolk probably liked the gold more than the game, but she didn't want to ruin his fun. And it *was* sort of fun, she realized, as she took a golden butterfly and a golden fish and tossed them out onto the rocks below. While they "worked," Serilda told Gild more about Leyna and Lorraine and Frieda, the librarian. Then she told him about Madam Sauer and the schoolhouse and her five favorite children in the world.

She did not tell him about her father. She didn't trust herself not to start crying.

Gild seemed as eager to hear her stories—real stories for once—as he'd been to hear the tale of the stolen princess, and Serilda realized he was starved for news of the outside world. For human connection, not just physically, but emotionally, too.

It didn't take long before the crate was empty, but they made no move to leave, content to stand side by side looking out at the calm waters.

"Do you have any friends here?" she asked tentatively. "Surely you must get along with some of the other ghosts?"

He shifted away, idly pressing a finger to the wound on his head.

"I suppose. Most are nice enough. But it's complicated when they're not . . ." He searched for the right word. "When they aren't exactly their own masters?"

Serilda turned to face him. "Because they're servants to the Erlking and the dark ones?"

He nodded. "It isn't just that they're servants, though. When he takes a spirit for his court, he takes control of them. He can make them do whatever he wants. There's enough of them now that most of them are more or less left alone, unless someone's unlucky enough to be one of the king's favorites. Sometimes I think Manfred would rather stab his other eye than take one more order. But what choice does he have?"

"Manfred? That's the coachman, isn't it?"

He nodded. "He's sort of become the king's best man, to his endless chagrin, I think, though I've never heard him say as much. Capable to a fault."

"What about you?"

He shook his head. "I'm different. I've never had to follow orders, and I don't know why. And I'm grateful for that, of course. But at the same time—"

"Being different makes you an outcast."

He fixed a look on her, surprised, but Serilda just smiled. "Exactly. It's hard to be close to someone when you can't trust them. If I tell them anything, I risk it being reported back to the king."

Serilda licked her lips, a motion that caught Gild's attention before he quickly turned his gaze back toward the lake. Her insides fluttered, and she couldn't help but think of the last time she'd seen him, when he'd kissed her, quick and desperate, then vanished.

Standing so close to him now, the memory made her dizzy. She cleared her throat and tried to shake it away, reminding herself of the question she'd most wanted to have answered tonight.

"I know all the ghosts here died horrible deaths," she said carefully.

"But . . . did they all die here? In the castle? Or does the king collect them from . . . from his hunts, too?"

"Sometimes he brings in other spirits. But it's been a while. I think maybe the castle was starting to feel a bit crowded for his taste."

"What about . . . maybe, sixteen years ago? Do you remember a woman spirit being brought back?"

Gild frowned. "I'm not sure. The years tend to all run together. Why?"

She sighed and told him the story her father had told her about her mother being lured away by the hunt when Serilda was just two years old. When she was finished, Gild looked sympathetic, even as he shook his head.

"Most of the ghosts I know have been here as long as I have. He does occasionally bring spirits that he found on the hunt . . . but it's difficult for me to keep track of time. Sixteen years . . ." He shrugged. "I suppose she could be here. Can you describe her?"

She told him what her father had told her. It wasn't much, but she thought the chipped tooth would be memorable, at least. When she was done, she could see that he was thinking hard. "I can ask around, I suppose. See if anyone remembers leaving behind a baby girl."

Her heart lifted. "Would you?"

He nodded, but he looked unsure. "What was her name?"

"Idonia Moller."

"Idonia," he repeated, committing it to memory. "But, Serilda, you must know, the king doesn't bring many spirits back from the hunt. Most of them he just . . ."

Disappointment scratched at Serilda's insides. She remembered the vision given to her by the drude of her father lying facedown in a field. "Leaves to die."

His expression was so forlorn. "I'm sorry," he said.

"Don't be. That would be better. I'd rather she was in Verloren, at peace." She said it, but she didn't know if she meant it. "You will try to find her, though? To see if she's here?"

"If it will make you happy, of course."

The comment surprised her, along with how simply he said it. She didn't know if his asking about her mother would make her happy—she supposed that depended on what he did or didn't learn—and yet. The thought that he might care about her helped warm some of those places that had gone cold inside.

"I know it isn't the same thing," he added, "but I don't remember my mother, either. Or my father for that matter."

Her eyes widened. "What happened to them?"

He gave a soft, resentful laugh. "I have no idea. Maybe nothing. It's another way I'm different. Most of the others remember *something* of their life before. Their families, what sort of job they did. Most of them worked here in the castle, some even knew one another. But if I lived here, no one remembers me, and I don't remember them."

Serilda started to reach for him, but then, recalling how he had pulled away every time she'd moved near, she clenched her hand into a fist and slumped against the wall instead. "I wish there was some way to help you. To help all of you."

"I wish that every day."

A cackling laugh echoed around them. Serilda stiffened and instinctively grabbed Gild's arm.

"Just a hobgoblin," he said, his voice low as he gave her hand a squeeze. "They're supposed to patrol the walls once in a while. Make sure that no one sneaks into the gatehouse and raises the drawbridge while everyone's in town."

His tone held some humor in it. Serilda peered at him, skeptical.

"I got away with it two years in a row, once. But I think I did him a favor, encouraging him to give them more responsibility. No one wants an idle hobgoblin around. Their idea of fun is to put out all the fires in the keep, then hide the kindling."

"You must get along great, then."

He smirked. "Hiding the kindling might have been my idea."

The laughter turned to loud whistling—a jaunty tune that split through the night. It seemed to be coming closer.

"Come on," said Gild, tugging her back toward the tower. "If it sees you, I can't trust it not to tell Erlkönig."

They were halfway down the tower steps when Gild seemed to realize that he was still holding Serilda's hand. He immediately let go, dragging his fingers along the mortar lines in the wall instead.

She frowned.

"Gild?"

He did not look back at her, but made a small questioning grunt.

She cleared her throat. "You don't have to tell me if you don't want to, but . . . I can't help but notice that you're . . . that you don't want to be touched tonight. And that's . . . well, that's your choice, of course. It's just that, before, you always seemed—"

He paused so fast that Serilda nearly crashed into him.

"What do you mean, *I* don't want to be touched?" he said, spinning to face her with a tremulous laugh.

She blinked. "Well, that's certainly how it seems. You keep pulling away from me. You haven't wanted to be close to me all night."

"Because I can't—!" He stopped himself, inhaling sharply. He grimaced, as if biting back his reaction. "I'm sorry. I owe you an apology. I know I do," he said, the words like a skittish rabbit darting between them. "But I don't know how to say it."

"An apology?"

He squeezed his eyes shut. He looked a little bit like a petulant child who *really* didn't want to say he had done wrong, but would under threat of no dessert.

"I shouldn't have kissed you before," he said. "It wasn't . . . gentlemanly. And it won't happen again."

Her breath hitched. "Gentlemanly?" she asked, her brain catching on one of the few words that didn't sting.

He opened his eyes, clearly irritated. "Despite what you might think, I'm not entirely without honor." But then he ducked his head away, his expression swinging almost instantly from annoyed to apologetic. "I regretted it the moment I left you. I am sorry."

Regretted it.

These words alone were enough to curdle every last fantasy Serilda had entertained these past weeks. But rather than let them sadden her, she took hold of the second emotion that cropped up in their wake. Anger.

She crossed her arms and walked down a few more steps so they were at eye level. "Why did you then? I wasn't encouraging you."

"No, I know. That's exactly it." His hands flailed, though his anger seemed to be matching hers stride for stride.

Which was ridiculous. What did he have to be angry about?

"I don't expect you to understand. And . . . I won't try to make excuses. I'm sorry. That's all there is to say."

"I disagree. I think I'm owed some explanation. It was my first kiss, I'll have you know."

He groaned, running a hand down his face. "Don't tell me that."

"Oh, look at me, Gild. You can't possibly think I have a bevy of suitors waiting for their chance to sweep me off my feet. I'd gotten rather used to the idea of spinsterhood."

His face contorted into something almost pained. He opened his mouth, but soon shut it again. Collapsing one shoulder against the wall, he let out a heavy sigh. "It was mine, too."

It was a quiet confession, one Serilda wasn't sure that she'd heard correctly. "What?"

"No—I shouldn't say that. I don't know if it's true. But . . . if I ever did kiss anyone, I have no memory of it, so as far as I'm concerned, it was my first. And until I met you, I was sure I would never . . ." He glanced at her, then quickly tore his gaze away. "I cannot . . . to have met you . . . I thought it was impossible. I thought . . ."

His voice was flooding with emotion, and Serilda's pulse hiccupped. Suddenly she understood what he was trying to say.

"You've been alone," she said softly. "You thought you'd always be alone."

"You asked me if I had any friends here. And I do like some of the other ghosts, care about them even. But I've never . . ." His gaze became searching. "I've never felt anything like . . . like this. I've certainly never wanted to kiss anyone before."

And just like that, the spark of hope in her chest reignited.

Even if, realistically, she knew it wasn't such a victory, to be compared to a bunch of undead spirits.

"I can imagine how hard this has been for you," she said, "especially to think there would be no end to it. I can see how you might . . . feel drawn to the first girl who . . . to me." She lifted her chin. "For what it's worth, I'm not angry about the kiss."

It was true.

She wasn't angry.

Though she was still a little hurt.

She had already known it to be true, but now it was confirmed. She could have been anyone. He would have felt desperate to touch *anyone*.

She couldn't pretend otherwise.

And though physical affection was not something to be forced, or to ever be stolen, it occurred to her in that moment that it might be a gift she was willing to give. Not as payment. Not as a bargaining chip. Not because she felt guilty.

But because she wanted to.

"Gild," she said softly. Stretching her hand forward, she slipped her palm against his and threaded their fingers together, one by one. His whole body seemed to tense. "I'm not expecting anything from you. I mean, I hope that if the Erlking continues to threaten me, you might continue to help. But besides that . . . it isn't as though I'm in love with you. And I know you won't ever be in love with me."

His brow twitched into a furrow, but he didn't respond.

"I'm hoping that maybe we can be friends. And if a friend ever needed an embrace or to hold my hand for a while or . . . just to sit and be together, I wouldn't mind."

Gild was silent for a long time, staring at their interlaced fingers like he was worried she would pull away.

She didn't pull away. She didn't disappear.

Finally, he brought his other hand forward as well, so that her one hand was clasped tight between both of his. Leaning closer, he lightly rested his forehead against hers, his eyes closed.

After a moment's hesitation, Serilda snaked her free arm up around his shoulders. He shifted his body closer, then lowered his head, their temples grazing. Her breath caught, as she half expected his lips to find hers. But instead, he nestled his face into the crook of her neck. A second later and his arms had both come around her, pulling her body to his.

Serilda inhaled deeply, searching for a scent that she would forever tie to this moment. She could still remember dancing with Thomas Lindbeck, two years ago to this very night, and how he had carried the grassy scent of his family's farm with him. Her father always smelled of wood smoke and flour from the mill.

But if Gild had carried a scent in life, it was gone now.

Still. His arms were strong. The tickle of his hair against her cheek and his linen collar on her throat were real enough.

They stayed that way for what felt like ages and no time at all. Maybe she had taken his hand thinking she was doing him some sort of favor, but once her body melted into his embrace, she realized how much she'd needed this, too. The sense that this boy wanted to be holding her as much as she wanted to be holding him.

For a time she thought she could feel his heartbeat drumming against her, until she realized that it was her own beating for them both. It was this thought that stirred her out of her cocoon. As soon as she started to move, Gild pulled away, and she was startled to see red around his eyes. He'd been so still, she hadn't realized he'd been crying.

Serilda pressed her palm against his chest. "You don't have a heartbeat."

"Maybe I don't have a heart," he said, and she could tell he meant it as a joke, and so she allowed herself to smile. At the boy who craved an embrace as much as she did. Who was, literally, weeping at the sensation of being held.

"I doubt that."

He started to smile, as if she'd given him a compliment. But the look was short-lived as the haunting cry of the Erlking's hunting horn intruded on their sanctuary. They both tensed, their arms tightening around each other.

"What does that mean?" asked Serilda, checking the sky, but it was still dark, no signs yet of dawn. "Are they coming back?"

"Not yet, but soon," he said. "The hunt is over, and it's time to feed the hounds."

Serilda grimaced, recalling Leyna's description of how the hunters would throw the captured animals' carcasses onto the effigy of the god of death and let the hounds tear it apart.

"Do you . . . want to watch?" asked Gild.

She made a face. "Not even a tiny bit."

He chuckled. "Me either. Would you . . ." He hesitated. "Would you like to see my tower?"

He looked so endearingly nervous, his cheeks flushing in a way that highlighted the wash of freckles, that Serilda couldn't temper her grin. "If there's time?"

"We aren't far."

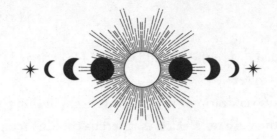

Chapter 33

In the mortal realm, the upper room of the southwest tower had been barren and dusty. But on this side of the veil, Gild had created a haven for himself, with layers of rugs and furs on the floor and some blankets and pillows no doubt pilfered from other rooms in the castle. A stack of books, a candlestick, and on one side of the room, a spinning wheel.

Serilda crossed to the windows and peered out toward Adalheid. She caught a glimpse of the hounds fighting over the meat that had been hung from the effigy's body and quickly tore her gaze away.

Her attention landed on the Erlking instead, as if his presence had an unavoidable magnetism. He stood apart from the crowd, standing on the very edge of the nearest dock. He was staring out at the water, his sharp features glowing beneath the light of the torches on the bridge. Unreadable, as always.

His presence, even across the lake, was a threat. A shadow. A reminder that she was his prisoner.

Once His Darkness has you, he does not like to let you go.

Serilda shivered and turned away.

She picked up one of the books. It was a small volume of poetry, though she was unfamiliar with the poet. It had been read so many times, the pages were falling out of the binding.

"Have you ever been in love?"

Her head snapped up. Gild was leaning against the far wall. There was a tension in his stance, one bare foot flat against the wall in a forced mimicry of nonchalance.

It took a second for the question to sink in, and once it did, Serilda guffawed. "What makes you ask that?"

He nodded at the book. "It's mostly love poetry. Painful to slog through at times, all overwrought metaphors and flowery prose, everything having to do with pining and yearning and longing . . ." He rolled his eyes, reminding Serilda a little bit of young Fricz.

"Why do you have it then, if you despise it so much?"

"There is limited reading material in this castle," he said. "And I notice you didn't answer the question."

"I thought we'd established that there is no one in Märchenfeld who would ever be interested in me."

"So you've said, and . . . I have questions about that, too. But not being loved doesn't preclude someone from *loving*. It might have been unrequited."

She grinned. "Despite your apparent disdain for this poetry, I think you're a romantic."

"Romantic?" He balked. "Unrequited love sounds awful."

"Absolutely horrid," agreed Serilda with another laugh. "But only a romantic would think so." She sent him a cheeky grin, and his frown returned.

"You're *still* avoiding the question."

She sighed, peering up toward the ceiling rafter. "No, I've never been in love." Thinking of Thomas Lindbeck, she added, "I thought I was once, but I was wrong. Satisfied?"

He shrugged, his gaze clouding. "I can't remember anything about my life before, and somehow I still have regrets about it. I regret not knowing what it's like to fall in love."

"Do you think you might have been? Before?"

"There's no way to know. Although, I feel like, if I had been, then surely I would remember *that*. Wouldn't I?"

She didn't respond, and after a while he was forced to look up at her. To see her sly grin.

"What?" he asked.

"Romantic."

He scoffed, even as his face pinkened. "Just when I'm starting to think I enjoy talking to you."

"I'm not mocking you. I would be a hypocrite if I was. All my favorite stories are about love, and I've spent an inordinate amount of time thinking about what it would be like, and wishing . . ." She trailed off, her pulse sputtering as she realized what dangerous territory she was treading into, with the only boy who had ever looked at her with something close to desire.

"I know," said Gild, startling her. "I know all about wishing."

She believed him. She believed that he *did* know. The pining and the yearning and the longing. The unbearable desire for someone to tuck a stray hair behind her ear. To press a kiss against the back of her neck. To hold her on long winter nights. To look at her like she was the one he wanted, the one he would always want.

She didn't remember stepping close to him, but suddenly, she was there, near enough to touch. But Gild didn't glance down at her lips this time. His focus was on her gold-spoked eyes. Unflinching.

"I don't think it's superstition that they're afraid of," he said.

She froze. "What?"

"All these boys that supposedly aren't interested in you because they think you'll bring them bad luck? Well . . . maybe that's true, but . . . it has to be more than that."

"I don't know what you mean."

His hand came up to graze her cheek before he tenderly tucked a lock of hair behind her ear.

Serilda nearly dissolved.

"I know I've barely met you," he said, his voice fighting to not tremble, "but I can tell that you are worth all the bad luck in the world." Having said it, his shoulders jerked upward in an uncomfortable shrug, and for a moment she thought he wouldn't go on. When he finally did, she could tell it was a struggle for him, and she realized that he, too, might be realizing how dangerous this conversation had become. How fleeting, how tenuous, how . . . unfathomable. "I think they pretend not to be interested, because they can tell you're destined for something else."

She took another half step toward him.

He came a half step closer to her, their bodies almost touching.

"And what am I destined for?" she whispered.

His fingers brushed ever so lightly against the back of her hand, sending a current along her nerves. Her breath caught.

"You're the storyteller," he said, with the start of a smile. "You tell me."

What was she destined for?

She wanted to dwell on it, to really consider what might be possible in her future. But she couldn't think of it now, when all her thoughts were overwhelmed by the present.

"Well," she started, "I doubt many girls from Märchenfeld can claim to be friends with a ghost."

Gild's smile slipped. His jaw clenched briefly. "It's been a long time since I lived in proper society," he said, "but I suspect that friends don't often have reason to kiss each other."

Warmth rushed up her neck. "Not often, no."

His gaze fell to her lips, his pupils dilated. "May I kiss you again anyway?"

"I certainly wish you would," she breathed, leaning into him.

His hand slipped up her arm, cradling her elbow, tugging her closer. His nose brushed against hers.

When an enraged scream echoed from the base of the tower. "Poltergeist! Where are you?"

They jumped apart as if the hellhounds themselves were upon them.

Gild let out a stream of muttered curses.

"Who is that?" Serilda whispered.

"Giselle. The master of the hounds," he said, grimacing. "If she already found it, they must be coming back. We've got to hide you."

"Found what?"

Gild gestured at the ladder. "I'll explain. Go, go!"

Footsteps echoed below. Heart thundering, Serilda swung her leg onto the ladder and hastened down the rungs. She reached the lower level and spun around, only to nearly crash right into Gild. His hand clamped over her mouth, stifling her startled scream. Then he took her wrist and pressed a finger to his mouth, urging her to be quiet, before tugging her toward the stairs.

The footsteps below grew louder.

"I don't care what you've got against those mutts!" hollered Giselle. "I'm responsible for them, and if you keep pulling these stunts, the king will have *my* head!"

Where was Gild taking her? There was only this narrow stairway. They would run right into her.

They came to the alcove containing the statue of the knight and his shield, no longer broken. Gild ducked into it, yanking Serilda in beside him. He pressed her into the corner, where they could both be shrouded in darkness, and craned his head until they were cheek to cheek, perhaps trying to hide his copper-colored hair.

Serilda reached for her hood and pulled it up. It was large enough that, when they were this close to each other, it swept fully over the back of Gild's head. Taking the cloak's sides, she wrapped her arms around his shoulders, shrouding them in charcoal gray, the same color as the stone walls, the same color as nothingness.

Gild moved into her, his body pressed along her length. His fingers spread out across her back. The sensation was enough to make her light-headed, and all she wanted was to close her eyes and turn her face, just the tiniest bit, and place a kiss against his skin. Anywhere that she could reach. His temple, his cheek, his ear, his throat.

She wanted him to do the same to her.

But she forced herself to keep her eyes open, watching through the tiny gap in the cloak's fabric, as the master of the hounds turned the corner, grumbling to herself.

She and Gild both tensed.

But the dark one marched right past the alcove without stopping.

They listened as the footsteps stomped upward toward the tower.

"She'll come back down in a second," Gild said, so quiet she almost couldn't hear him, despite his breath dancing across her ear. "Best we wait until she's gone."

Serilda nodded, happy for the chance to catch her breath, though it was difficult with Gild's hands on her waist, sending waves of heat through her body. Her entire being was humming, tingling, caught between Gild and the stone walls. She wanted desperately to thread her fingers into his hair. To pull his mouth to hers.

But while her blood simmered inside, outside she was motionless. As still as the statue that half hid them from view.

"What did you do?" she whispered.

He made a guilty face. "Before you got here, I may have mixed up some crushed holly berries with the hounds' bedding."

She stared. "What does that mean?"

"Hellhounds don't do well with holly. Even just the smell of it can upset their stomachs. And . . . they just ate a *lot* of meat."

She winced. "That's disgusting."

They heard footsteps again, and Serilda shut her eyes, for fear they might catch the light.

A second later, Giselle stormed back down the steps, muttering to herself about *that damned poltergeist*.

Once the tower was quiet again, they released mutual exhales.

"Do you think...," Serilda started, barely a whisper, hoping he wouldn't detect the aching behind the words, "it might be safest for me to just wait here, and sneak out after sunrise? When the veil is in place again?"

He pulled away, enough to meet her gaze. His fingers squeezed gently, bunching the fabric at her waist.

"I just feel it would be very dangerous for me to be seen," she said.

"Yes," said Gild, a little breathless. "I think that would be for the best. The night is almost over anyway." His gaze dipped again to her mouth.

Serilda crumbled. She finally allowed her hands the freedom they'd been craving, letting her fingers trail up his neck until they were buried in his hair. She pulled him to her, their mouths meeting. There was a moment in which Serilda overflowed with needs she didn't know what to do with. The need to be closer, when such a thing was not possible. The need to feel his hands at her waist, her back, her neck, her hair, everywhere, all at once.

But that first wave of craving ebbed, and something gentler replaced it. A kiss that was tender and unhurried. Her own fingers abandoned his hair to splay out across his shoulders and trail down his chest, even as his hands traced poetry across her spine. She sighed against him.

She didn't know how long they had, but she did not want to waste a moment of it. She wanted to live inside this alcove, in the surround of his arms, in these new sensations that made her feel weightless and hopeful and terrified all at once.

It felt like making a promise. That this would not be the last kiss. That she would return. That he would be waiting.

And then—

It was over.

Her hands closed around empty air. The arms supporting her vanished, and she would have collapsed if she hadn't had the wall at her back. Her eyes snapped open, and she was alone in the alcove.

The statue's shield was broken. The pedestal sported a collection of chipped corners and a blanket of cobwebs.

She shivered.

The equinox was over.

Was Gild still there? Invisible, untouchable, just out of her reach?

Could he still see *her*?

Swallowing hard, she stretched her fingers out into the nothingness, searching for a chill, a shock, a warm breeze. Some sign to know she wasn't alone after all.

She felt nothing.

With a heavy sigh, she wrapped the cloak around her shoulders and stepped out of the alcove. She was just about to descend the steps when her gaze caught on the broken shield, and the words scribbled into the thick layer of dust.

Will you come back?

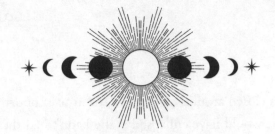

Chapter 34

Lorraine's expression was dark when Serilda entered the Wild Swan, her lips pinched in disapproval. All she said as she handed Serilda a key to one of the upstairs rooms was "I had your things brought in from the stables."

The room wasn't luxurious like those inside the castle, but it was comfortable and warm, with soft quilts on the mattress and a little desk with writing parchment and ink by the window. Her items from the saddlebags had been set neatly onto a cushioned bench.

Serilda sighed with quiet gratitude, then promptly climbed into bed.

It was well past noon by the time she managed to peel her eyes open again. The sounds of the city rumbled up from the streets below. Wagon wheels, braying mules, children singing a rhyming song to welcome the spring. *Oh, if only it were warm and green, with birdsong evermore. Just give us this, dear Eostrig, and we will not ask for more.*

Serilda pulled herself out of bed and went to change out of her clothes, only to find her shoulder throbbing in agony. She hissed and pulled down the sleeve to see the gouges left by the drude, now caked over with dried blood.

She debated asking Lorraine for help cleaning and bandaging the wound, but the mayor already seemed anxious enough over Serilda's comings and goings from the castle, and she didn't think adding an attack from a nightmarish beast would help matters.

More careful this time, she wriggled out of her dress and chemise and used the provided washcloth and basin to clean the wounds as well as she could. After inspecting the wounds, she determined that they were not as deep as she'd thought, and as the bleeding had already stopped, she figured that a bandage wouldn't be necessary.

When she was done, she sat down at the little vanity to comb out her hair. There was a small mirror and Serilda paused, catching sight of her own eyes. Mirrors were a rare luxury in Märchenfeld, and she'd only seen her reflection a handful of times over the course of her life. It always startled her, to see the gold-spoked wheels looking back at her. It always gave some clarity to why no one ever wished to look her in the eye.

But she did not shy away. She peered at the girl gazing back, thinking not of the countless people who had turned away from her, but of the one boy who hadn't. These were the eyes that Gild had peered into with such open intensity. These were the cheeks his fingers had caressed. These were the lips . . .

Pink blossomed across her face. But she wasn't embarrassed. She was smiling. And that smile—she thought, somewhat bewilderingly—was beautiful.

☾

Leyna was waiting for Serilda by the fireplace when she left her rooms.

"Finally!" she cried, bouncing to her feet. "Mama forbade me to bother you. I've been waiting for *hours*. Was beginning to worry you'd died up there."

"I desperately needed the rest," said Serilda. "And now I desperately need nourishment."

"I'll bring you something." She dashed away into the kitchen while Serilda slumped in a chair. She had brought the library book with her, and she settled it on her lap and flipped it open to the title page.

The Geography, History, and Customs of the Great Northern Provinces of Tulvask.

Serilda made a face. It was precisely the sort of scholarly text that Madam Sauer adored, and she despised.

But if it helped her understand anything of that castle, it would be worth suffering through.

She started flipping through pages. Slowly at first, then quicker, once she saw that the first chapters were all an in-depth analysis of the unique geographical details of these provinces, starting with how the basalt cliffs had impacted early trade routes and led to the port city of Vinter-Cort becoming a hub of merchant activity. There was talk of shifting borders. The rise and fall of early mining towns in the Rückgrat Mountains. But only one mention of the Aschen Wood, and the authors had not even called it by name. *The mountain foothills are largely forested and home to a wide array of natural beasts. Since the earliest recordings of civilization in the area, the forests have been considered inhospitable and have remained largely unsettled.*

She came to a series of chapters on prominent settlements and the resources that had encouraged their growth. Serilda yawned, turning past sections on Gerst, Nordenburg, Mondbrück. Even Märchenfeld was given a small mention for its thriving agricultural community.

She scanned the pages of dense text. Occasionally there were splatters of ink where the author's quill tip had snapped. Occasionally there were words crossed out, a small error fixed. Occasionally there were illustrations. Of the plants. The wildlife. The landmark buildings.

Then she turned a page and her heart snagged.

An illustration of Adalheid Castle filled up half a page. The colored dye was still vibrant, despite the book's age. The image did not show the castle in ruins, but as it had once been. As it was on the other side of the veil.

Dignified and glorious.

She began to read.

The origins of Adalheid Castle, presented here in its original state, have been lost to time and remain unknown to contemporary historians. As of the turn of the century, however, the city of Adalheid had become a prosperous community along the routes connecting Vinter-Cort and Dagna on the coast with—

Serilda shook her head, her hopes sagging. She turned back to the previous page. No other mention of Adalheid.

Frustrated, she finished reading the page, but the author made no further mention of the city's mysterious past. If they cared at all that no one knew about the castle and city's origins, it did not show in their writing. A few pages later, and the book's focus shifted to Engberg in the north.

"Here you are," said Leyna, using her toe to drag a small table a bit closer and setting down a platter of dried fruits and salted meats. "You missed the midday meal, so it isn't warm. Hope you don't mind."

Serilda slammed the book shut, scowling.

Leyna blinked at her. "Or . . . I could see if we have any meat pies left over?"

"This is lovely, thank you, Leyna. I'd only hoped that this book might have a bit more useful information on this city." She tapped her fingers against the cover. "For so many towns, it presented a well-researched and incredibly dull account, stretching back multiple centuries. Not so with Adalheid."

She met Leyna's gaze. The girl looked like she was trying hard to share in Serilda's frustration, but that she didn't entirely understand what she was talking about.

"It's all right," said Serilda, picking up a dried apricot from the plate.

"I'll just have to make a visit to the library today. Would you care to join me?"

Leyna's face brightened. "Really? I'll go ask Mama!"

☾

"See the fishing boats?" said Leyna, pointing as they walked along the cobbled roads off the shore of the lake.

Serilda's gaze had latched on to the castle—specifically, on the southwest tower, wondering whether Gild might be up there, watching, even now. Dragging her thoughts back, she followed Leyna's gesture. Normally the boats were spread throughout the lake, but now a number of them could be seen clustered near the far end of the castle.

"Searching for gold," said Leyna. She side-eyed Serilda. "Did you see him again? Vergoldetgeist?"

The question, so innocently asked, brought back a wave of feelings that made Serilda's insides flutter. "I did," she said. "In fact, I helped him toss some of his gifts down to the rocks and the lake." She beamed to see Leyna's eyes widening in disbelief. "There will be many treasures to be found."

Adalheid was radiant in the sunlight. Flower boxes overflowed with geraniums, and vegetable patches were rich with cabbages and gourds and new seedlings for the summer.

Ahead of them, near the docks, many of the townspeople were cleaning up after the festivities of the night before. Serilda felt a tug of guilt. She and Leyna should probably offer to help. It might help to ingratiate her to the townspeople who still saw her as a bad omen.

But she was eager to get to the library. Eager to uncover some of the castle's secrets.

"I'm so jealous," said Leyna, her shoulders drooping. "I've been wanting to go inside that castle my whole life."

Serilda stumbled.

"*No,*" she said, more sharply than she'd meant to. She eased her tone, settling a hand on the girl's shoulder. "There is good reason that you all stay away. Remember, when I'm there, it's usually as a prisoner. I've been attacked by hellhounds and drudes. I've watched ghosts relive their awful, gruesome deaths. That castle is full of misery and violence. You must promise never to go in there. It isn't safe."

Leyna's expression tightened bitterly. "Then why is it all right for you to keep going back?"

"I haven't been given a choice. The Erlking—"

"You had a choice last night."

The words evaporated off Serilda's tongue. She frowned and stopped walking, crouching so that she could grasp Leyna's shoulders. "He killed my father. He may have killed my mother, too. He means to keep me as a prisoner, a servant—perhaps for the rest of my life. Now listen. I don't know if I can ever be free of him, but I do know that as things stand now, I have no power, no strength. All I have are questions. Why did the dark ones abandon Gravenstone and claim Adalheid instead? What happened to all those spirits in there? What does the Erlking want with all of this spun gold? What *is* the Gilded Ghost, and who is he, and what happened to my mother?" Her voice hitched as tears prickled at her eyes. Leyna's gaze, too, had become glossy. Serilda took in a shaky breath. "He is hiding something in that castle. I don't know if whatever that is can help me, but I do know that if I do nothing, then someday he will kill me, and I'll become just one more ghost haunting those walls." She slid her palms down to take Leyna's hands into hers. "That's why I went back to the castle, and why I'll keep going back. That's why I need to go to the library and learn all that I can about this place. That's why I *need* your help . . . but also, why I can't allow you to put yourself in danger. Can you understand that, Leyna?"

Leyna slowly nodded.

Serilda gave her hands a squeeze and stood. They continued walking in silence, and had crossed the next street before Leyna asked, "What is your favorite dessert?"

The question was so unexpected that Serilda had to laugh. She thought about it for a moment. "When I was young, my father would always bring home honey walnut cakes from the markets in Mondbrück. Why do you ask?"

Leyna glanced over toward the castle. "If you do become a ghost," she said, "I promise to always set out honey walnut cakes during the Feast of Death. Just for you."

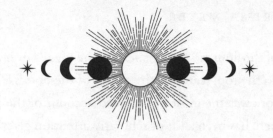

Chapter 35

Serilda had not expected the Adalheid library to be anywhere near as grand as the great library in Verene, which was associated with the capital's university and heralded for both its ornate architecture and its comprehensive collection. It was a marvel of scholarly achievement. A haven for art and culture. She had known the library in Adalheid would not be *that*.

Yet she couldn't help feeling a tiny twinge of disappointment when she walked in and found that the Adalheid library was only a single room, not much larger than the Märchenfeld schoolhouse.

It was, however, overflowing with books. Shelves and stacks of them. Two large desks piled high with thick tomes, with more piles on the floor, and bins in one corner packed full of old scrolls. Serilda felt immediately comforted by the scent of leather and vellum, parchment and binding glue and ink. She inhaled deeply, ignoring the odd look that Leyna gave her.

It was the scent of stories, after all.

Frieda, or Madam Professor as Leyna called her, was ecstatic to see them, and became more delighted still when Serilda tried to explain what she was looking for—even though she wasn't entirely sure what that was herself.

"Well, let's see," said Frieda, picking her way around an overflowing desk to one of the floor-to-ceiling shelves. She tugged over a ladder and climbed up to the top, scanning the spines of the books. "That book I gave you before was the most generalized account of the area. I don't know that there has been a lot of scholarly attention given to our city, specifically, but . . . here I have ledgers from our city council dating back at least five generations." She started pulling out the books and flipping through them, then handed a few down to Serilda. "Treasury holdings, trade agreements, taxes, laws . . . does this interest you?" She handed Serilda a codex so frail that Serilda thought it might disintegrate in her hands. "A written account of work orders and payments made on public buildings during the last century? We've had some truly remarkable artisans receive their start in Adalheid. A number of them went on to work on some of the prominent structures in Verene and—"

"I'm not sure," interrupted Serilda. "I'll take a look. Anything else?"

Frieda pursed her lips and returned her focus to the shelf. "These here are ledgers. Accountings of merchant holdings, employee earnings, taxes paid. Ah, here's a historical account of the town's agricultural expansion?"

Serilda tried to look hopeful, but Frieda must have been able to tell that this was not what she was looking for, either.

"Don't you have anything about the castle? Or the royal family who used to live there? They must have been a prominent part of this community to have built such an incredible fortress. There must be some records of them?"

Frieda gave her a long, strange look, then slowly climbed down from the ladder.

"To be perfectly honest," she said, pressing a finger to her lips, "I'm not sure there ever was a royal family inhabiting that castle."

"But then who was it built for?"

Frieda shrugged. "Perhaps as a summer house for a duke or an earl? Or it may have been for military use."

"If that was the case, surely there would be records of *that*, then."

Frieda's expression shifted, as if a light were coming over her. Her gaze traveled back up to the tomes on the top shelf. "Yes," she said slowly. "One would think so. I . . . I suppose I never considered it."

Serilda tried to tame her irritation, but how could a town's librarian never have considered the history of its most notable landmark? And one with such a terrifying reputation, at that?

"What about the Erlking and the wild hunt?" she asked. "When did he abandon Gravenstone and come to reside in Adalheid Castle?"

"Well, now, that is an interesting question," said Frieda. "But we have to consider that the existence of Gravenstone might be nothing more than folklore. It may never have existed at all."

Serilda shook her head. "No, the Erlking himself told me that he had left Gravenstone because it held painful memories for him, and had come here to Adalheid instead. And he mentioned a royal family. He said they weren't using it anymore."

The color slowly drained from Frieda's face. "You . . . you really have . . . *met* him?"

"Yes, I really have. And I'll almost certainly be meeting him again on the next full moon, which is not that far away, and I would love to know something more about that castle and the ghosts who occupy it before I do." She set down the books that Frieda had already given her, though nothing yet had struck her as particularly helpful. "Isn't there any documentation about who built the castle? What methods they used? What quarry the stone came from? You mentioned artisans before. The keep has incredible stained-glass windows and iron chandeliers as big as this room, and in the entry hall the columns are carved with the most ornate imagery. It would have been an ambitious undertaking. Someone must have commissioned all of that, probably hired the most accomplished craftworkers from all over the realm. How can there not be any record of it?"

Frieda's eyes were shining, awestruck. "I don't know," she whispered. "No one alive has ever seen the things you're talking about. No one other than you, that is. All we see are ruins. But judging from the architectural style, I would estimate the castle was built . . . perhaps five hundred, six hundred years ago?" Her brows pinched as she looked around at the books surrounding them. "I don't disagree with you. You're right. One would expect there to be some records. But I can't think of anything I've ever seen that gave insight into our local history beyond . . . maybe two or three centuries ago."

"And nothing at all about a royal family?" Serilda persisted, feeling desperate. There must be *something*. "Birth or death records, family names, coat of arms?"

Frieda's mouth opened and closed. She looked a little lost, and Serilda had the impression that it was rare for her to be stymied.

"Maybe there were records," said Leyna, "but they were destroyed?"

"That does happen," said Frieda. "Fires and floods and the sort. Books are fragile."

"There was a fire?" said Serilda. "Or . . . a flood?"

"Well . . . no. Not that I know of."

Sighing, Serilda scanned the piles of books. How could a town so successful and wealthy, situated on the edge of the Aschen Wood to one side, along a well-traveled trade route to the other, have no concept of its own history? And why was it that she seemed to be the only one who had ever noticed how peculiar that was?

She gasped. "What about a cemetery?"

Frieda blinked at her. "Pardon?"

"You must have one."

"Well, yes, of course. The cemetery is right outside the city wall, just a short walk from the gate." Frieda's eyes widened with understanding. "Right. That's where we've buried our dead since the city was founded. Which would mean—"

"Since the castle was built," said Serilda. "Or even earlier."

Frieda gasped and gave a snap of her fingers. "There are even grave-stones there that are something of a local mystery. They're quite promi-nent, intricately carved, mostly of marble, if I remember correctly. They're works of art, really."

"And who is buried there?" asked Serilda.

"That's the mystery. No one knows."

"You think it could be royalty?" asked Leyna, bouncing with excite-ment.

"It seems odd that it wouldn't be marked as such," said Frieda. "And we can't discount the possibility that there could be tombs beneath the castle itself, so it isn't guaranteed that whoever lived there would be buried with the rest of the townsfolk."

"But there's a chance," said Serilda. "Will you take me to see them?"

The cemetery was acres and acres of gray headstones as far as she could see. Clusters of blue and white wildflowers were scattered among the stones and tucked among the roots of mature chestnut trees, their spring blossoms like white candlesticks among the boughs. Serilda scanned the engravings, saddened, though not surprised, to see how many of the gravestones belonged to children and newborns. She knew such was common, even in a town as prosperous as Adalheid, where disease could so easily take root in a small body. She knew of a number of women in Märchenfeld who spoke openly about their miscarriages and babes being stillborn. But knowing the realities of life and death did not make it any easier to see.

In the distance, closer to the road, she noticed a small hill where the gravestones were not tall and exquisitely carved, but nothing more than large plain stones laid out in a tidy grid. Hundreds of them.

"What are those?" she asked, pointing.

Frieda's expression was sorrowful as she answered. "That's where we bury the bodies left behind by the hunt."

Serilda's feet stuttered and came to a stop. "What?"

"It doesn't happen after every full moon," said Frieda, "but it happens often enough that . . . well. There have been so many. We usually find them by the forest, but sometimes they'll have been left right outside the city gates. We wait a week or so to see if anyone comes to claim them, but that's unusual. And of course, we have no way of knowing who they are or where they came from, so . . . we bury them there, and hope they find their way to Verloren."

Serilda's hands shook. Those victims of the hunt were forever lost to their loved ones. Forever without a name or history, with no one to place flowers upon their grave or leave a drop of ale when they honored their ancestors beneath the Mourning Moon.

Was her mother among them?

"Do you . . . do you happen to recall if there was a young woman found about sixteen years ago?"

Frieda looked at her with obvious curiosity. "Do you know someone who was taken by the hunt? I mean, other than yourself, of course."

"My mother was. When I was only two years old."

"Oh, dear. I am so sorry." Frieda took her hand and offered a sympathetic squeeze. "That, at least, is something I might be able to help with. We keep a record of every body we find. The date they were found and any distinguishing characteristics, any items that were found on their person, that sort of thing."

Serilda's heart lifted with hope. "You do?"

"There, see?" said Frieda, her eyes brightening. "I knew there would be something in my library that you would find useful."

"Look," said Leyna, pointing to a shared tombstone for *Gerard and Brunhilde De Ven*. There's my great-grandparents." She walked a bit farther, before pausing. "And my papa. I don't normally come to visit him except during the Mourning Moon."

Ernest De Ven. Beloved husband and father.

Stooping, Leyna plucked some butterbloom flowers and arranged them neatly on her father's stone.

Serilda's heart tugged. In part because she knew the sorrow of losing a parent so young, and in part because she could not lay flowers on her father's grave.

The Erlking had stolen *that* from her, too.

But maybe the records of bodies would hold at least one answer for her.

Frieda gave Leyna a side squeeze as they started walking down the rows again. "There," she said, pointing as they crested a short hill. "You can see them."

Shoving aside thoughts of her parents, Serilda felt excitement clawing at her insides. Even from here she could tell that the stones in this back corner of the cemetery were different. Larger, older, more resplendent, shaded beneath enormous oak trees. Some were carved into statues of Velos with their lantern, or Freydon holding aloft a tree sapling. Some were covered by pillared monuments. Some stood taller than Serilda.

The closer they got, the more the age of the stones became apparent. Though the marble still shone white beneath the sun, many of the corners were crumbling and worn. The plants in this distant corner were overgrown, as if there was no one alive who cared to maintain the area around these markers.

From the way that Frieda had described them, Serilda had suspected there to be no inscriptions at all, but she saw that wasn't true. She stepped closer, rubbing her fingers over the face of one of the stones. The death date was nearly four hundred years ago. The size of the marker suggested that whoever was buried here had been wealthy or respected or both.

But their name was missing. It was the same on the second stone. And, as Serilda made her way to each marker, she saw it was the same on them all. Birth years, death years, an occasional heartfelt benediction or a poetic verse.

But their names were absent.

If these were the resting places of royalty—perhaps even generations of kings and queens, princes and princesses—how could there be no record of them? It was as if they had vanished. From memory, from the pages of history, from their own gravestones.

"Look," said Leyna. "This one has a crown."

Serilda and Frieda went to stand beside her. The gravestone before Leyna did indeed have what looked to be a monarch's crown carved into the top of the stone.

But it was not this that made Serilda suck in a startled gasp.

Leyna glanced at her. "What is it?"

Crouching before the stone, Serilda peeled away some of the ivy that had started to claim it, revealing the etching underneath.

A tatzelwurm entwined around the letter *R*.

"Does that mean something?" asked Leyna.

"The *R* could be the first initial of a name?" suggested Frieda.

Serilda tugged off more of the ivy until she could see all the stone's face, but where the name of the deceased should have been, there was only stone, polished and smooth.

"How odd," murmured Frieda, leaning closer and feeling the stone for herself. "It's as smooth as glass."

"Is it possible that—" started Leyna, before hesitating. "I mean, could the names have been erased? Perhaps someone came through and polished them away?"

Frieda shook her head. "That would mean sanding down the material, which would leave grooves where the words had been. These look like they were never engraved at all."

"Unless they were erased with magic?" said Leyna. She spoke hesitantly, like she was afraid Serilda and Frieda might laugh at the thought.

But Serilda just looked up, meeting the librarian's shadowed gaze.

No one spoke for a long time, considering the possibility. In the end, nobody laughed.

THE
CHASTE
MOON

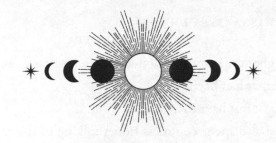

Chapter 36

Serilda thought the full moon would never come. Every night she looked out at the moonlight dancing on the lake's surface and watched as it grew—first a teasing crescent, then gradually waxing night after night.

During the day, she helped around the inn where she could and spent hours gazing at the castle, wondering if Gild was in his tower, gazing back at her through the veil. She yearned to go back and was constantly resisting the desire to cross that bridge, but then she would remember the screams and the blood and the drudes, and she would force herself to have patience.

She kept busy with her attempts to uncover more of the mysteries of the castle and the hunt, but she felt that she was running into a stone wall at every turn. The ledgers of dead bodies left behind after the hunt held no clues to her mother's disappearance. There had not been any bodies found that Mourning Moon. The closest possibility was a young woman found a few months previously on the Lovers' Moon, but Serilda did not think her father would have been so mistaken on the timing.

She did not know what to make of the revelation. Her mother might have been killed inside the castle walls, and her body never found.

Or she might have been abandoned somewhere far away from Adal-heid, as her father had been.

Or she might not have died at all.

Serilda had also spent countless hours talking to the townspeople, asking what they might know about the castle, its inhabitants, their own family histories. Though there were still some who were afraid of Serilda and wanted to chastise her for tempting the wrath of the Erl-king, most of the citizens of Adalheid were happy to talk to her. She figured it didn't hurt that Vergoldetgeist had been most generous this year, and the whole town seemed to be celebrating their good fortune, even if they always fell quiet about their new riches whenever they noticed Serilda in their midst.

In speaking with the townspeople, Serilda learned that many had had families living in Adalheid for generations, and some could trace their lineage back a century or two. She even discovered that the for-mer mayor she had seen at the public house after the Hunger Moon had a journal long passed down through his family. He was most eager to share it with Serilda, but when she flipped back through the pages, she found entire columns of text missing, pages left blank.

It was impossible to tell for sure, but from the context of the sur-rounding entries, she suspected the missing pages all had to do with the castle and the royals who she was sure had once lived there.

In the evenings, she earned her keep at the inn by telling tales to whoever was gathered around the fireplace in the public house once they had finished their evening bread. She did not tell stories about the dark ones, worried that they would be too frightening for those who knew all too well that the Erlking was not merely a story for amusement. Instead, she regaled the citizens of Adalheid with tales of witches and their newt familiars. The old spinster who slew a dragon and the moss maiden who climbed to the moon. Cruel sirens who trapped sailors in their watery castles, and kindly land wights who rewarded worthy peasants with a wealth of jewels.

Night by night, the crowd grew in the public house, as word of their new resident storyteller spread.

Night by night, Serilda waited.

When the full moon finally arrived, it was as if a mourning shroud had fallen over the city. All day long, the villagers were quiet and subdued as they went about their business. When Serilda asked, Lorraine said it was always that way on the full moons, but that the Chaste Moon tended to be the worst. With the Feast of Death behind them, this night would determine whether or not the wild hunt was satisfied and would leave the families of Adalheid be.

The public house that evening was the emptiest Serilda had seen all week. Half an hour before sunset, the last guests retired to their rooms.

"But can't I hear a story?" Leyna pleaded. "Serilda can tell me one in her room?"

Lorraine gave a shake of her head. "We do not invite ourselves into our guests' rooms."

"But—"

"And even if you were invited, we retire early on the full moon. I want you fast asleep before the witching hour. No arguments."

Leyna scowled, but no arguments were made as she trudged up the stairs to the rooms she and her mother shared. Serilda tried to hide that she was grateful for Lorraine's intervention. She was not in a storytelling mood tonight, distracted by her own anticipation.

"Serilda?" asked Lorraine, extinguishing the lanterns around the public house until it was lit only by the embers in the hearth. "I don't mean to be insensitive—"

"I won't be here," said Serilda. "I have every reason to believe the

Erlking will summon me, and I would not dream of bringing his attention to you and Leyna."

Relief flashed across Lorraine's face. "What will you do?"

"I'll go to the castle, and . . . wait."

Lorraine grunted. "You're either very brave or very foolish."

Sighing, Serilda stood from her favorite seat beside the fire. "May I return tomorrow?"

Lorraine's face wrinkled with unexpected emotion. "Dear girl. I most certainly hope that you will."

Then she reached her arms forward and embraced Serilda. It startled her and filled her with more warmth than she would have expected. She had to squeeze her eyes shut to ward off the threat of tears.

"Thank you," she whispered.

"Be safe," commanded Lorraine. "And make sure that you have everything you need before you go. I will be locking the door behind you."

The sun had dipped beneath the city wall when Serilda left the Wild Swan. In the east, the Chaste Moon was glowing somewhere behind the Rückgrat Mountains, tingeing their distant peaks in silver. This moon was meant to symbolize newness, innocence, rebirth. But one would not have known that this was the month of such tender optimism walking along the dim streets of Adalheid. As night settled over the city, lights vanished from the windows. Shutters were closed and latched. Shadows overtook the castle ruins, slumbering on their solitary island.

Soon they would awaken.

Soon the hunt would come storming through the town and into the mortal world. The hellhounds would howl, the horses would stampede, the riders would seek out what prey they could find—magic creatures like those whose heads graced the castle's halls, or moss maidens and forest folks, or humans who weren't wise enough, or superstitious enough, to sequester themselves behind locked doors.

Serilda arrived at the bridge just as the moon was cresting the mountains, casting its sheen across the lake. As before, she wasn't fully prepared for the moment when its beams struck the ruins of the castle, transforming it from desolate ruins to a home worthy of a king.

Even if he was a wicked one.

Standing alone beyond the drawbridge, Serilda had never felt so insignificant.

The portcullis began to rise, groaning and creaking with the complaints of ancient timbers and iron hinges. In the next moment, the howls began, sending a chill down her spine. She swallowed hard and tried to stand straighter as a blur of movement within the bailey captured her attention.

The wild hunt.

A torrent of fiery hellhounds, enormous war steeds, flashing armor.

Riding straight for her.

Serilda yelped and raised her arms in a pathetic attempt to protect herself.

The beasts ignored her. The hounds moved around her like water around a rock. The bridge shook as the horses surged past, armor clanging in her ears and the cry of the hunting horn drowning out every thought.

But soon the cacophony faded to distant shouts as the hunters sped through the town and into the countryside.

Shaking, Serilda lowered her arms.

An obsidian horse stood before her, as still as death. She lifted her gaze. The Erlking stared down at her from his perch. Examining her. He looked almost pleased to see her.

She swallowed hard and tried to curtsy, but her legs were trembling and her curtsies weren't the greatest on the best of days. "You requested that I stay close, my lord. In Adalheid. The townspeople here have indeed been most accommodating."

She figured this bit of praise was the least she could do for the community that had so embraced her these past weeks.

"I am glad of it," said the Erlking. "I would not have had the pleasure of crossing your path this night otherwise, and this will give you ample time to complete your work." He tilted his head, still eyeing her. Still *reading* her.

Serilda held very still.

"Your skills have thus far surpassed expectations," he added. "Perhaps I shall owe you a reward."

She gulped, unable to tell if he wanted a response. Was this her chance to ask him for something? But what would she ask of him? To be left alone? For him to give up all his secrets? For Gild to be set free?

No—there was no reward he would give her that she would actually want, and she could never let on that she knew Gild, the poltergeist he so despised. And if he knew that the true gold-spinner had been inside his castle all this time, she didn't know what he would do to Gild.

But she knew exactly what he would do to her.

"Manfred will meet you in the courtyard. He will take you to the spinning wheel." Then a hint of a smile, and not a nice one, touched his mouth. "I do hope you will continue to impress me, Lady Serilda."

She smiled wryly. "I trust you'll be taking the hunt into the Rückgrat foothills tonight?"

The Erlking paused, on the verge of dismissing her. "And why is that?"

She tilted her head to one side, the picture of innocence. "There have been rumors that a great beast has been seen prowling around the mountains, beyond the Ottelien border, I believe. You hadn't heard?"

He held her gaze with the barest spark of intrigue. "I had not."

"Ah. Well. I thought a new conquest might make a fine addition to your decor, but perhaps that distance is too far to travel in one night.

Nevertheless, I hope you'll enjoy hunting your . . . foxes and deer and little woodland creatures. My lord." She curtsied and turned away.

She was nearly to the bridge when she heard the snap of reins and thunder of hooves. Only when the king had vanished did she let her smile overtake her.

Let him enjoy his wild goose hunt tonight—and with a touch of luck, be kept far away from this castle until sunrise.

The coachman was in the courtyard, waiting patiently while the stable boy latched the two bahkauv to the carriage. They both glanced up with bewildered looks as she made her way across the stones, and Serilda wondered if she was the first human to ever dare intrude upon them when the moon was full, especially as the hunt had departed only moments before.

She hoped her eagerness didn't show. She knew that she should be terrified. She knew her life was in danger, and her lies could be discovered with hardly a slip of her tongue.

But she also knew that Gild was inside these walls, and that gave her more comfort—and impatience—than was likely warranted.

She was trying to ignore the frightening possibility that she might be falling in love with a ghost, one who was trapped inside the castle of the Erlking himself. She had mostly succeeded in not thinking about all the practical dilemmas that would cause. There was no hope of a future, she told herself again and again. There was no hope for happiness.

And again and again, her brittle heart responded that it didn't quite care.

Though she thought it probably should.

Nevertheless, as the coachman told the stable boy that the beasts would not be necessary this night, and tried to hide how pleased he was about it, Serilda felt a flush of exhilaration.

Again she was led into the castle keep, through corridors that were becoming more familiar with every passing visit. She was beginning to be able to connect them with the ruins she saw during the day. Which chandeliers still hung, now draped with cobwebs and dust. Which pillars had collapsed. Which rooms were full of brambles and weeds. Which pieces of furniture, so stately and ornate in this realm, were toppled and broken on the other side of the veil.

When they passed the staircase that led up to the hall with the stained-glass gods and the mysterious room with the tapestry, Serilda's steps slowed. There was nothing to be seen from down here, and yet she couldn't keep from craning her head.

When she faced forward again, the coachman was watching her with his good eye. "Looking for something?" he drawled.

Serilda tested a smile. "It's such a labyrinth here. Don't you ever get lost?"

"Never," he said mildly, then gestured to an open doorway.

Serilda expected another hall, or perhaps a staircase.

Instead, she saw straw. Mounds and mounds and *mounds* of straw.

She gasped, amazed at the sheer amount of it. Enough to fill an entire hayloft. Enough to fill the gristmill, wall to wall, floor to ceiling, and have yet more spurting out the chimney.

All right, that might have been a slight exaggeration.

But only *slight*.

And, again, there was the spinning wheel and the mountain of empty bobbins and the sickly sweet smell that choked her.

Impossible.

"He can't . . . I can't possibly do all this!" she said. "It's too much."

The coachman cocked his head to one side. "Then you will risk his disappointment."

She frowned, knowing that to argue was pointless. This man—this ghost—wasn't the one setting these tasks, and the Erlking had just ridden off for a night of sport.

"I suppose it's for your benefit that you arrived early," he continued. "More time to complete your work."

"Was he hoping I would fail?"

"I think not. His Grim is"—he searched for the word, before finishing dryly—"an optimist."

It almost sounded like a joke.

"Do you require anything more?"

An extra week, Serilda wanted to say. But she shook her head. "Only peace to do my work."

He bowed and left the room. Serilda listened for the turn of the lock, then faced the straw and the spinning wheel, hands planted on her hips. This was the first room she'd been brought to that had windows, though she wasn't entirely sure what it might have been used for before it was converted into her prison. There were a few scarce pieces of furniture that had been pushed up against the walls to make room for the straw—a blue velvet settee, a couple of high-backed chairs, a desk. Perhaps it had been a study or a parlor, but with the lack of decoration on the walls, she assumed it had not been put to much use in a long time.

Inhaling a long breath, Serilda laced her fingers and started to pace nervously as she spoke to the empty air. "Gild, you're not going to like this."

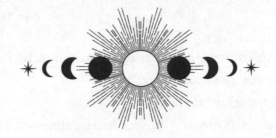

Chapter 37

One moment the air was empty.

The next, Gild was there, mere inches in front of her.

Serilda collided into him with a yelp. She stumbled backward—her hands instinctively grabbing for his shoulders—and pulled him back with her. They both fell, Serilda landing on her back on the pile of straw. Gild landed on top of her with a grunt, his chin smacking her shoulder, making his teeth crack loudly near her ear. His knee struck her hip, as he barely managed to keep from crushing her under his weight.

Serilda lay in the straw, disoriented and breathless, a dull pain thrumming in her backside.

Gild pushed himself up with one hand and rubbed his chin, grimacing.

"Still alive," moaned Serilda, copying Anna's favorite phrase.

"Makes one of us," Gild said. He met her gaze, laughter in his eyes. "Hello again."

Then he glanced down, to where Serilda's hands were caught between their bodies. Her hands, entirely of their own mind, were pressed against his chest. Not pushing him away.

Color burst across his face. "Sorry," he said, pulling back.

As soon as he did, a sharp pain burned across Serilda's scalp. She cried out, leaning toward him. "Stop, stop! My hair!"

Gild froze. A lock of Serilda's long hair had caught on the button of his shirt's collar. "How did that happen?"

"Meddlesome elves, no doubt," said Serilda, trying to shuffle into a better position where she could start untangling the hair, bit by bit.

"They're the worst."

Serilda paused in her work to meet his eyes, catching the silent humor glittering in them. This close, in this light, she could see that they were the color of warm amber.

"Hello again," he said quietly.

The most innocent of words.

Spoken quite un-innocently.

A second later, he was no longer the only one blushing.

"Hello again," she responded, suddenly bashful.

Serilda might have spent hours this past week dreaming about seeing him again or, to be more accurate, kissing him again, but she didn't know if her expectations were realistic.

Their relationship was . . . odd.

She knew that.

She couldn't quite tell how much of his affection was the act of a lonely boy who yearned for *any* amount of intimacy . . . and how much might be because he legitimately liked her.

Gods be told, she wasn't entirely sure how much her own yearning was based on the same.

Could this really be the start of love?

Or perhaps it was nothing more than hasty passion and a recipe for mistakes—as Madam Sauer would have said. She was always quick to chastise the girls in the village who fell too easily into the arms of a handsome boy.

But this was Serilda's story, and this was *her* handsome boy, and if it was a recipe for mistakes—well, she was grateful for now to at least have been handed some of the ingredients.

In the space between her uncertain *hello* and these scattered thoughts, Gild had started to smile.

And Serilda couldn't help smiling back.

"Stop it," she said. "I'm trying to untangle us."

"I'm not doing anything."

"You're distracting me."

"I'm just lying here."

"Exactly. It's *very* distracting."

He laughed. "I know I shouldn't be so happy to see you. I assume the Erlking wants you—" He cut himself off as he looked up to take in the room, overflowing with straw. He let out a low whistle. "Why, that greedy monster."

Serilda managed to free the last bit of hair. "Can you do it?"

Gild sat up. There was no hesitation as he gave a firm nod. Relief flooded through Serilda, even as she saw his shoulders droop.

"What's wrong?"

His expression was baleful as he looked back at her. "I guess I was hoping we might have a bit of time . . . together . . . that didn't involve this." He grimaced. "I mean, to talk. To . . . just . . . be with each other, not to—"

"I know," said Serilda, her entire body flushing hotter than before. "I was hoping that, too."

He reached for her hand and bent to press his mouth against her knuckles. A thrill ignited across Serilda's nerves. She couldn't help thinking of how he had taken her hand the first night they'd met.

It had surprised her then.

It elated her now.

"Maybe," she said, "if we work very hard, we can have it done with time to spare."

His eyes glinted. "I like a challenge." Again, his warmth was short-lived. "But, Serilda, I hate this, but . . . I must ask for payment."

She stilled. A rush of coldness swept from her hand, still clasped in his, all the way to her heart. "What?"

"I wish I didn't have to," he hastened to add, almost pleadingly. "But the balance of magic requires it—or at least, this magic does. Nothing can be given for free."

Serilda pulled away. "You spin gold all the time. All those gifts for the villagers. You can't tell me you're receiving *payments* for those."

He flinched, as if she'd struck him. "I do that for me. Because I want to. It . . . it's different."

"And you don't *want* to help me?"

With a groan, he yanked a hand through his hair. Lurching to his feet, he grabbed a handful of straw and sat down at the spinning wheel. His shoulders were taut as he gave the wheel a spin and pounded his foot against the treadle.

As he had done a thousand times before, he fed the straw through the maiden hole. But it did not emerge a sleek, glistening thread of gold.

It emerged as straw. Brittle and frayed.

He kept trying. His brow pinched. His eyes determined. Gathering another handful. Forcing it through. Trying to wind it around the bobbin when it continually broke. When it continually, stubbornly refused to be turned to gold.

"I don't understand," whispered Serilda.

Gild grabbed the wheel, stopping it mid-spin, and heaved a defeated sigh. "Hulda is the god of labor and hard work. Not just for spinning, but farming, woodworking, weaving . . . all of it. I've thought maybe they don't like their gifts to be given away for free because . . . hard work deserves compensation." He shrugged helplessly. "I don't know. I could be wrong. I don't even know for sure if what I have *is* a gift from Hulda. But I do know that I can't do this as a favor, no matter how much I want to. It doesn't work that way."

"But I have nothing more to give."

She looked at the necklace, its chain visible behind his collar. At the engraved ring on his finger, the seal the same that she'd seen in the cemetery.

Then, with a flash of inspiration, she beamed and gestured at his chest. "How about a lock of hair?"

His brows drew together and he glanced down, noticing the knot of hair that had been left behind, still tangled around the shirt's button.

His lips twisted to one side as he peered back up at her.

"What?" she asked. "Sweethearts give each other locks of hair all the time. It must be a coveted treasure."

Surprise, and a hint of hope, flashed across his face. "Are we sweethearts?"

"Well…" She hesitated. She wasn't sure what else they could be after their kiss in the stairway alcove on Eostrig's Day, but it wasn't a question she'd ever had to answer before. She wanted to answer honestly, tell him what she truly wanted to say. But it felt safer to tease. So instead, she responded, "You did just take me for a tumble in the hay, didn't you?"

She watched him closely, delighted to see his face shift from confused to mortified, pink blotches darkening his freckled cheeks.

Laughter exploded out of her.

"Yes, yes, you're very clever," he muttered. "I don't think a lock of hair will sufficiently pay for pounds and pounds of spun gold."

She pouted. Considering. Then—another thought. "I will give you a kiss!"

He grinned, but it was pained. "I would accept it in a heartbeat."

"Are you sure you have a heartbeat? I've tried to listen for it before and was unconvinced."

He chuckled, but the sound was hollow, and Serilda felt a jolt of guilt to be teasing him. He looked truly sorry as he opened his palms to her. "I cannot take a kiss, though I wish I could. It must be gold for . . . well, something with tangible value. Not a story. Not a kiss."

"Then name your price," she said. "You can see everything I have in my possession. Will you take my cloak? There are some holes from the drude, but it's in decent shape. Or maybe my boots?"

He groaned, casting his gaze skyward. "Are they worth anything?"

"They're worth something to me."

She was irritated at the anger rising inside her. She could tell that Gild was being honest—she knew enough about lies to know the difference. He didn't want to be having this conversation any more than she did.

Yet here they were. Discussing payment, when her life would be forfeit if this wasn't done.

"Please, Gild. I have nothing of value and you know it. It was sheer luck that I had the locket and the ring to begin with."

"I know that."

Serilda chewed on her lower lip for a moment, considering. "What if I promised to give you something in the future?"

He shot her a disgruntled look.

"No, truly. I don't have anything of value now, but I'll promise to give you something of value when I can."

"I don't think that will work."

"Why not?"

"Because . . ." He shook his head, as frustrated as she was. "Because the likelihood of you actually having something to offer in the future is so slim. Do you think you're suddenly going to come into an inheritance? Discover some long-lost family heirlooms?"

"You don't need to sound so dismissive."

"I'm trying to be realistic."

"But would it hurt to try?"

He groaned. "I don't . . . I don't know. Maybe not. Just let me think."

"We don't have time for this! This is so much straw; it's already going to take most of the night, and if he comes back and I've failed, you know what will happen to me."

"I know. I *know*." He crossed his arms over his chest, glowering at nothing. "There must be something. But—great gods, Serilda. What about next time? And after that? This can't go on forever."

"I don't know! I'll think of something."

"You'll think of something? It's been months. Do you think he's suddenly going to get bored with you? Just let you go?"

"I said I would think of something!" She was shouting now, the first hints of desperation clawing at her. For the first time it occurred to her that Gild might actually say *no.*

He might leave her. The work undone. Her fate sealed.

Because she had nothing more to offer.

"Anything," she whispered, reaching for him, gripping his wrists. "*Please.* Do this for me one more time and I'll give you . . ." A thought struck her and she let out an exalted laugh. "I'll give you my firstborn child!"

He balked. "What?"

She gave a chagrined smile, a helpless shrug. And though the words had been said in jest, she was already beginning to wonder.

Her firstborn child.

The likelihood that she would ever conceive a child was so minuscule. Ever since the fiasco with Thomas Lindbeck, she'd felt resigned to a future of solitude. And given that the only other boy who had captured her interest was *dead* . . .

What did it matter if she promised away a nonexistent child?

"Assuming I live long enough to birth any children," she said. "Even you have to admit that's a good deal. What could possibly be more valuable than a child?"

He held her gaze, his expression intense and, she thought, just the tiniest bit saddened.

Under the soft fabric of his sleeves, she imagined that she could feel his pulse. But no, it was only her own heartbeat, fluttering in her fingers. And in the sudden silence, she caught the tremulous rhythm of her own shallow breaths.

The moments ticking by, too fast.

The candle flickering in the corner.

The spinning wheel, waiting.

Gild shivered and tore his gaze from her face. He looked down at her hands, then pried his arms away.

Serilda released him, heart sinking.

But in the next moment, he'd taken her fingers into his. His head lowered, avoiding her gaze, as he wrapped his fingers around hers.

"You are very persuasive."

Hope skittered inside her. "You'll do it? You'll accept that offer?"

He sighed, the sound long and drawn out, as if it physically pained him to agree to this. "Yes. I will do this in exchange for . . . your firstborn child. *But*"—his grip tightened, squashing the jolt of euphoria that threatened to have her throwing her arms around him—"this bargain is binding and unbreakable, and I fully expect you to stay alive long enough to fulfill your end of it. Do you understand me?"

She gulped, feeling the magical pull of the bargain. The air pressing in around her. Stifling, squeezing in against her chest.

A magical bargain, binding and unbreakable. A deal struck beneath the Chaste Moon, with a ghostly thing, an unliving thing. A prisoner of the veil.

She knew she couldn't really promise to stay alive. The Erlking would have her killed as soon as it pleased him to do so.

And yet, she heard her own words as if whispered from a distant place. "You have my word."

The air shuddered and released.

It was done.

Gild flinched and pulled away.

He wasted no time in settling himself at the spinning wheel and beginning the task. He seemed to work twice as fast as he had before, his jaw set and his eyes focused only on the straw being fed into the wheel. It was magic itself to watch him. The confident movements of his fingers, the steady thump of his foot on the pedal, the deft way his hands tied the golden threads onto the bobbin as they emerged twinkling from the wheel.

Serilda once again set about assisting him as well as she could. The night passed quickly. It seemed that every time Serilda dared to glance at the candle, another inch had been lost from the wax. Her fears rose as she tried to estimate how much work they had done. She surveyed the pile of straw, picturing what it had been when she'd first arrived. Were they halfway through? More? Was there yet any sign of the sky lightening outside the castle walls?

Gild said nothing. He hardly moved but to accept each new handful of straw she handed him, always maintaining the steady spinning of the wheel.

So much for all her fantasies of romance, she thought dryly, then chastised herself for it. She was grateful—endlessly grateful that Gild was here, that she would live another night, despite the Erlking's impossible demands.

If they finished, that is.

The piles of straw slowly dwindled and the pile of sparkling bobbins grew, until there was a wall of gold thread glistening near the door.

Whir . . .

Whir . . .

Whir . . .

"I've been asking around to see if there are any spirits named Idonia."

Serilda blinked. Gild was not looking at her. His focus never left his work. He seemed tense after their bargain. She supposed she felt pretty tense, too.

"And?" she asked.

He shook his head. "Nothing so far. But I have to be careful who I ask. Don't want it getting back to His Darkness, or he might get suspicious of us."

"I understand. Thank you for trying."

"If I do find her . . . ," he started uncertainly. "What should I tell her?"

Serilda considered. It seemed like an impossible hope at this point. What were the chances, that of all the hunt's victims, her mother would be one the king had deigned to keep in his servitude? Her search felt futile, especially when she was supposed to be worrying about herself, her own servitude.

"Just tell her that someone is looking for her, I suppose," she said.

At this, Gild did glance up, looking like he wanted to say more. But he hesitated for too long, then eventually returned his focus to his work.

"Shall I continue our story?" Serilda suggested, eager for a distraction. Something that didn't have to do with her mother or her firstborn child or this rotten predicament she was trapped in.

Gild sighed, relieved. "I wish you would."

The old woman stood on the bridge before the prince, her face in a permanent scowl, yet her eyes alight with wisdom.

"By returning Perchta to the land of the lost, you have done us a great service, young prince," she said. Then she gestured toward the surrounding woods, and a group of figures began to emerge into the dappled sunlight. Women of all ages, with skin that gleamed in every shade, from tawny gold to darkest brown, and tufts of lichen sprouting between antlers and horns.

They were moss maidens, and in that moment, the prince knew that he was in the presence of their leader, Pusch-Grohla, the Shrub Grandmother herself.

"Ha! I knew it was her!"

"Oh, yes, you're very clever, Gild. Now hush."

Shrub grandmother was not known for being kind to the humans who ventured too close to the forest folk. She often demanded that mortals complete impossible tasks and punished them when they failed.

Or—sometimes—rewarded them for deeds of kindness and courage.

One could never be sure of her mood, but the prince knew enough to show respect. He lowered his gaze.

"Stop groveling," she snapped, thumping the end of her walking stick so hard it broke through one of the rotted boards. "Can you stand?"

He tried to get to his feet, but one leg buckled from his weight.

"Never mind," growled the old woman. "Do not kill yourself to impress me."

She walked past him, staring up at the black stones, where the gate to Verloren had stood. "She will do everything she can to escape. Perchta will never be content to be a prisoner of the underworld. She is most cunning." She nodded, as *if agreeing with herself.* "If she ever returns, the creatures of this world will once again be in danger of her arrows and blades, her fathomless brutality." She turned to the women gathered at the edge of the woods. "Until that day, we will stand watch over this gate. We will ensure that no one ever comes out of Verloren, that the gods themselves will not open these doors to allow the huntress passage. We must stay vigilant. We must keep guard."

The moss maidens nodded, their expressions fierce.

Hobbling up to the stones, Shrub Grandmother lifted her walking stick over her head and said an incantation, the words languid and solemn. The old language. The prince watched, speechless, as the tall black monoliths tipped toward the center of the brambled clearing. The ground thundered as they struck the earth. Branches splintered and groaned.

When she was finished, the gates to Verloren had been sealed, permanently trapping Perchta in the afterworld.

She turned back to the prince, something almost like a smile stretching across her toothless mouth. "Come, young prince. You require healing."

The moss maidens built a hammock of branches and vines, and together, they carried the wounded prince into the woods. He tried to look back as he was taken away. To see if there was any hint that Gravenstone Castle stood hidden behind the veil, and his sister's body, perhaps her ghost, somewhere just beyond his reach. But all he saw was an impassable field of brambles and thorns.

The forest folk took the prince to Asyltal, their home and sanctuary, a place so hidden by magic that the Erlking himself had never found it. There, Shrub Grandmother and the moss maidens, in all their expert knowledge of healing herbs, nursed the prince back to health.

He did not know that behind the veil, the Erlking was pondering his revenge.

The dark ones do not mourn, and neither would the wicked Erlking. Only fury was allowed inside his black heart.

Fury, and a burning need for retaliation against the boy who murdered the only being he had ever loved.

As the days passed behind the veil, the Erlking began to concoct a terrible plan. He would ensure that the prince would soon come to know the same fate he had dealt upon the Erlking himself. A future without peace, without joy.

Without end.

The days passed slowly as he crafted his vengeance.

As the moon began to wax, on the far side of the forest, the young prince recovered from his wounds. He told Shrub Grandmother that he must return home, to tell his family the sad news of his sister, yet also to let them rejoice that he himself was not lost.

Shrub Grandmother agreed that the time had come for him to return to his people. With much gratitude for their healing magic, the prince bestowed on the moss maidens what gifts he had in his possession—a small locket and a golden ring. Then, with a grateful bow, the prince set off for his home. He did not know until he left Asyltal that nearly a full month had passed, and he would be returning home beneath the glow of a full moon. He quickened his pace, eager to see his mother and father again, no matter how his heart ached to tell them what had become of their beloved princess.

But he could not reach the castle before the sun had set, and as he made his way through the encroaching darkness, he heard a sound that chilled his very soul.

Howls and the soulless croon of a hunting horn.

The wild hunt had returned.

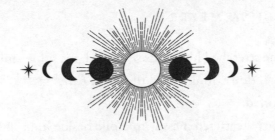

Chapter 38

It was the silence that brought Serilda back to the present.

The wheel had stopped spinning.

She looked over to see Gild watching her, his chin cupped in both hands, leaning forward on the stool like a rapt child. But in the next moment, his brow had furrowed.

"Why did you stop?" he asked.

"Why did *you* stop?" she said, jumping up from the settee, where she'd settled at some point during her tale. "We don't have time to—"

She paused and looked around.

The straw was gone.

They were *done.*

Gild grinned widely. "I said I could do it."

"What time is it?" She looked at the candle, startled to see that it was still as tall as her thumb. Planting her hands on her hips, she glared at Gild. "Are you telling me that those first two nights, you were intentionally going *slow*?"

He shrugged, his eyes widening, a picture of sincerity. "I had nothing better to do with my time. And I was enjoying the stories."

"You told me you hated the story that first night."

He shrugged, then rolled his shoulders a few times to work out their stiffness. As he stretched his hands overhead, his spine emitted a series of loud pops. "I don't think I used the word *hate*."

Serilda scoffed.

Bobbins were scattered messily in a pile beside him, since he hadn't paused to organize any of them and Serilda had been too distracted in her storytelling to complete her end of the work. She walked around the spinning wheel and started stacking them against the wall. She wasn't entirely sure why she bothered. Some servant would come in, scoop them up, and take them away for whatever the king was doing with so much golden thread, but she felt guilty for not having helped much tonight.

As she set the bobbins into neat rows, they shone like little beacons in the candlelight, as pretty as gems. The amount of straw had made the task seem like an impossible feat, but Gild had done it with time to spare. She couldn't help feeling impressed.

As she went to set the last bobbin of thread on the top of the last stack, she hesitated and looked down at the glistening gold.

What *was* it worth?

She still wasn't entirely sure that it was real. Or—she believed it was real here, on this side of the veil, in the realm of ghosts and monsters. But if it crossed over into the sunlight, would it vanish like morning mist?

But no, the gifts that Gild gave to the people of Adalheid were real enough. Why wouldn't this be as well?

Before she could second-guess herself, Serilda pulled back her cloak and tucked the bobbin, heavy with gold, into her dress pocket.

"What is he doing with it all?" she murmured, stepping back to inspect Gild's work in all its shimmering glory.

"Nothing good, I'm sure," he said, so close that she imagined she could feel his breath tickling the back of her neck.

Had he noticed her taking the bobbin?

She turned to face him. "And you're all right with that? I know you're helping me, but . . . you're also helping him. Adding to his riches."

"It isn't wealth he wants," Gild said with calm conviction. "He has something else in mind for this." He sighed. "And—no. I'm not all right with it. I want to throw it into the lake to make sure he never gets any of it." He looked back at her, his expression tormented. "But I cannot let him hurt you. Erlkönig can have his gold if it keeps you safe."

"I'm sorry that I keep bringing you into this. I will find a way out of it, somehow. I keep thinking that . . . at some point, he'll have enough, and he won't need me . . . or *you* anymore."

"But that's just the thing. Once that happens, you'll be gone forever. And I know that's a good thing. I don't want you trapped here like I am. I don't want anyone else to suffer here. There's already plenty enough suffering in this castle as it is." He paused. "And yet . . ."

He didn't have to say it. She knew what words he was searching for, and she was tempted to put him out of his misery. To say the words for him, because words had always been her haven, her comforts . . . whereas Gild seemed to agonize over every one. At least, when he was being honest, like this. When he was so vulnerable.

Finally, he shrugged. "And yet, I don't want you to leave, knowing that you'll never come back."

Her heart squeezed. "I wish I could take you with me. I wish we could both be free of him. Run away from here . . ."

His expression was hopelessly sad. "I'll never be free of this place."

"What happens if you do try to leave?"

"I get as far as the drawbridge, or the lake—I've tried jumping off the walls more times than I can count. But then . . ." He snapped his fingers. "I'm back inside the castle. As if nothing happened."

A shadow passed over his features. "The last time I tried it, ages ago, I reappeared in the throne room and the Erlking was sitting there, like he'd been waiting for me. And he just started laughing. Like he knew how hard I was trying to get away, and that I never would, and seeing me struggle was the most fun he'd had since . . . I don't know. Since he caught the wyvern probably." He met Serilda's gaze again. "That was when I decided that if I was going to be trapped here, I would at least spend my time making life as miserable for him as possible. I can't *really* do anything to him. There's no point in trying to fight him or kill him. But I can really, truly annoy him. That probably sounds childish, but . . . sometimes it feels like all I have."

"And here I am," she whispered, "asking you to spin gold. For *him*."

Reaching forward, he took one of her braids between his fingers, running his thumb along the strands. "It's worth it. You've been the most brilliant distraction I could have asked for."

She bit the inside of her cheek, then did what her body had been yearning to do since he'd first appeared. She tied her arms around his neck and pressed her temple to his. Gild's arms were quick to surround her, and she knew she wasn't the only one who had been testing the strength of her will, to see how long she could go without falling into his arms.

She shut her eyes, squeezing them until little flashes of golden light appeared on the darkness of her eyelids.

She would find a way out of this mess, and she had a feeling that she would have to do it sooner rather than later. After all, she'd already promised Gild her firstborn child in exchange for his help. What would she offer next time, and the time after that?

And yet, to her dismay, the thought of running away and escaping the Erlking's grasp brought her no comfort. It only made her heart feel like it was being squeezed in a vise.

What if this was the last time that she ever saw Gild?

Her pulse sped up as she slipped her fingers into his hair and turned her head, pressing a kiss just below his ear.

He inhaled sharply, his arms tensing around her.

The reaction encouraged her. She hardly knew what she was doing as she caught the tender flesh of his earlobe between her teeth.

Gild groaned, startled, even as he leaned into her, his fingers clutching at the back of her dress.

Then he was pushing her away.

Serilda gasped. Her cheeks were flushed, her heartbeat racing.

Gild's eyes were molten as he stared at her.

"I'm sorry," she breathed. "I don't know what I was—"

His fingers found the back of her head, tangling in her hair, as he pulled her back to him. His mouth found hers. Ravenous.

Serilda met him in kind. Her body was burning up in the confines of her dress. She felt light-headed, barely able to keep up with the sensations on her skin as Gild's hands left trails of frazzled warmth on her neck, her back, along the sides of her rib cage, the curve beneath her breasts.

She pulled away only when she needed to breathe. Trembling, she fitted her hands against Gild's chest. He may not have had a heartbeat, but he was solid beneath her touch. Under the thin linen there was strength and tenderness. Her thumb caressed the dip of his collarbone and she leaned forward, suddenly desperate to kiss that spot of bare flesh underneath his open collar.

"Serilda . . ."

Her name was a throaty plea, a yearning, a question.

She met his eyes and realized that she wasn't the only one who had started shaking. Gild's hands were on her hips, gathering the fabric of her skirt into fistfuls.

"I've never . . . ," he started, his eyes tracing the lines of her face, from her brow to her chin to her swollen mouth.

"Me either," she whispered back, nervous all over again. "But I'd like to."

He exhaled and tipped his head forward, pressing their foreheads together. "Me too," he breathed, with a bit of a chuckle. "With you."

His hands slid up the back of her dress, and she could feel little tremors in his fingers as they found the laces and began to untie them.

Slowly.

Tediously slow.

Agonizingly slow.

With a frustrated huff, Serilda pushed Gild backward until his legs hit the settee. She tumbled on top of him, encouraged by the sound of his laughter, teasing and warm, before Serilda's mouth effectively silenced it.

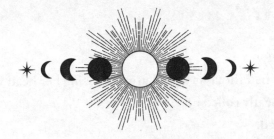

Chapter 39

She was liquid gold. A pool of sunshine. A lazy nap on a summer's day.

Serilda could not remember when she had last slept so soundly, but then, she'd never slumbered encircled by protective arms, a firm chest flush against her back. At one point she'd started to shiver, and she wondered with a rush of misery if she would open her eyes and find herself alone in the castle ruins. But no—she was just cold, with no blanket to snuggle beneath. Gild had helped her back into her dress, tenderly kissing each of her shoulders before pulling up the fabric of her sleeves and retying the laces. They'd easily dozed off again. Serilda knew she was smiling, even in her half-dreaming state.

Utterly content.

Until a shadow fell over her, eclipsing what little light was making the windows glow indigo blue.

Serilda squinted her eyes open.

Then sat up, flustered, but alert.

She shot to her feet, flinching at the crick in her neck, and dipped into a curtsy. "Your Grim. Forgive me. I was—we were—"

She hesitated, unsure exactly what she was apologizing for. She glanced back, suddenly terrified of what the Erlking would do if he found Gild in here, with her, but . . .

Gild was gone.

What she had thought was an arm pillowing her head was her traveling cloak, neatly rolled up.

She blinked.

When had he left?

In all her spiraling emotions, Serilda was most surprised at the twinge of regret that he had not woken her to say goodbye.

She chastised herself and faced the king, rubbing sleep from her eyes. "I . . . must have fallen asleep."

"And enjoyed the most pleasant of dreams, it would appear."

Embarrassment knotted her insides, worsening when the Erlking's curious look turned almost glib. "Dawn approaches. Before the veil separates us, there is something I would like to show you."

Her brow pinched. "Me?"

The king smiled—the overpowering smile of a victor. The smile of a man who always got what he wanted, and had little doubt he would this time as well. "Your presence continues to be of surprising advantage, Lady Serilda. And I am in a generous mood." He held out a hand.

She hesitated, recalling the icy feel of his skin. But, with little choice, she braced herself and settled her hand into his. A chill swept down her spine, and she could not fully disguise the shudder that his touch elicited. The king's grin widened, as if he liked having this effect on her.

He led her from the room. Only once they were in the corridor did Serilda remember her cloak, but the king was walking briskly and she had a feeling that he would not appreciate the delay if she asked to return for it.

"This has been an exhilarating night," said the Erlking, whisking her down a long stairway that spilled out into a wide conservatory. "In addition to your diligent work, our hunt achieved a most glorious prize, with some thanks owed to you."

"Me?"

"Indeed. I hope you aren't the sensitive sort."

"Sensitive?" she asked, more bewildered by the moment and unable to fathom why he was being so nice to her. In fact, the Erlking, who usually struck her as ominous and more than a little morose, now was bordering on . . . *chipper*.

It made her nervous.

"I know there are mortal girls of weak constitution, who feign repulsion at the captivity or slaughter of wild animals."

"I'm not sure the repulsion is *feigned*."

He snorted. "Show me a lady who does not enjoy a tender cut of venison on her table, and I will concede the point."

Serilda had no argument for that.

"To your question," she said a bit hesitantly, "I do not think myself to be particularly sensitive, no."

"I hoped as much." The king paused before a set of wide double doors that Serilda had never seen before. "Few mortals have ever witnessed what you are about to behold. Perhaps the night will exhilarate us both."

A flush burst hot across her face. His words brought back flashes of intimacy and pleasure that she was trying hard not to think about in this most inopportune moment.

Gild's body. Gild's hands. Gild's mouth . . .

The Erlking shoved open the doors, letting in a rush of cool air, the melodic rhythm of a light rainfall, the thick scent of sage.

They emerged onto a covered stone walkway that ran the length of the northern side of the keep. Before them, half a dozen steps led down to a large garden hemmed in by the fortress's tall outer walls. The garden was neat and precise, segmented into squares by tall boxwoods. Within each square was a centerpiece—a tiered fountain or a topiary in the shape of a lyre-playing nymph—surrounded by patches of bluebells and poppies and star-shaped edelweiss. In the corner far to Serilda's right, the segments were more practical, though no less lovely, filled with spring vegetables, herbs, and fruit trees.

Serilda had not stopped to wonder about how the dark ones fed themselves. Clearly they *did* eat, or else they would have had no interest in the feast the citizens of Adalheid prepared for them. But she wasn't sure if they *needed* to eat, or if they simply enjoyed it. Either way, she'd had an image of their feasts being made entirely of the food claimed during the hunt—wild boar and venison and game birds. Clearly, she'd been mistaken.

The Erlking did not give her time to properly take in the splendid view of the gardens. Already he was at the base of the steps, and Serilda hastened to keep up with him, jogging down the central path that led straight through to the far wall while a mist of drizzling rain clung to her skin. She shivered, wishing she had her cloak.

Her gaze caught on a statue in one of the garden patches, standing ominously over a swath of black roses. She stumbled and paused.

It was a statue of the Erlking himself, clothed in his hunting gear, the crossbow in his hands. It was carved of black stone, granite perhaps. But the base was different. A light gray, like the castle walls.

She blinked, surprised at what struck her as a blatant display of vanity. The king had been eager to show off his trophies in the castle—the taxidermy and mounted heads. But he had not struck her as particularly . . . well, *vain*.

She shook herself from the daze and hurried to keep up, for the king evidently had no intention of waiting for her. She passed a couple of undead gardeners. A man with enormous shears jutting from his back was pulling weeds from one of the beds, and a woman whose head seemed permanently cocked at an odd angle, as if her neck might have been broken, was pruning a hedge of topiaries into the shape of a long-tailed serpent. There were more ghosts milling about the gardens in the distance, but as she neared the back castle wall, Serilda's attention was drawn away from the patches of lush foliage.

Her steps slowed as she was led through a wrought-iron gate that had not been visible from the palace steps. It led onto a narrow, tidy lawn here at the back part of the gardens, what might have been used for lawn bowling.

All around its perimeter stood a series of ornate cages. Some were small enough to hold a house cat, others nearly as big as the mill's waterwheel, all lit by the blaze of a hundred torches burning at the edges of the lawn.

Some of the cages were empty.

But others . . .

Her mouth fell open and Serilda could not make it close. She wasn't sure that what she was seeing was real.

In one cage, an elwedritsch, a plump birdlike creature covered in scales instead of feathers, with a rack of slender antlers sprouting from its head. There was its cousin, the rasselbock, a rabbit in size and form, but also sporting antlers like a roebuck. In the next cage, a bärgeist, an enormous black bear with glowing red eyes. And there were creatures she had no names for. A six-legged oxlike creature that bore a protective shell on its back. A beast the size of a boar, covered in shaggy fur that, on closer examination, might not have been fur at all, but sharp porcupine-like quills.

A sound almost like a gasp, almost a laugh, escaped her as she spotted what appeared at first to be an average mountain goat. But as it hobbled closer to its food dish, she saw that the legs on the left side of its body were significantly shorter than the legs on the right side. *A dahut.* The creature whose fur Gild had said was his favorite to use for spinning.

She wandered closer, shaking her head in wonder. Only a few feet from the dahut's cage, she could see that it indeed had great patches where the fur had recently been sheared off in haphazard strips. She doubted the dahut cared much, especially as the days grew warmer, but something told her the Erlking and his hunters would be most annoyed at the random patches of fur that occasionally went missing.

She shook her head, trying to smother her grin.

It was easy to do when she stepped back and took in the caged beasts all at once. They were a mixture of peculiar and regal, but they all looked cramped and miserable in their enclosures. Many were despondently curled up in the far corners, shying away from the rain and watching the dark ones with wary eyes. A couple had visible open wounds that had not been tended to.

"All these miraculous beasts," muttered a haughty voice, "and the mortal wants to see the dahut."

Serilda startled. Forcing her attention away from the creatures, she saw that she and the Erlking were not alone. A cluster of dark ones in their hunting gear stood gathered at the far end of the lawn, near an enormous but empty cage. It was a man who had spoken, with bronze skin and hair like flaxen gold, a broadsword on his back. When he saw that he had her attention, he raised an eyebrow. "Is the little human afraid of the beasts?"

"Hardly," Serilda said, standing straighter. "But I prefer natural charm over vanity and brute strength. I've never seen a creature so purely guileless. I'm rather smitten."

"Lady Serilda," said the Erlking. She jumped, and the stranger smirked. "We have little time. Come, I wish to show you our newest acquisition."

"Concern yourself not with her, Your Grim," yelled the man, "for the human has poor taste in beasts."

"Your opinion was not solicited," said the king.

The man's jaw tensed, and Serilda couldn't help the smug tilt of her chin as she brushed past him.

She had not gone a dozen steps when a deafening noise, like metal on metal, made her stop. Serilda grimaced and pressed her hands to her ears.

The dark ones all around her laughed. Even the Erlking seemed momentarily amused, before turning proudly back to the source of the sound.

Through another gate on the far side of the lawn, a number of hunters and servants were leading a gigantic beast forward. Each was gripping the end of a long rope that had been looped around the creature's neck and body. There were two dozen captors, at least, yet Serilda could tell by their straining muscles and grunts that it was taking all their efforts to drag the animal forward.

Her stomach dropped. "It's a tatzelwurm," she whispered in disbelief. "You've captured a tatzelwurm."

"Found roaming the foothills in Ottelien," said the Erlking. "Precisely as you said it would be."

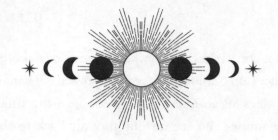

Chapter 40

The creature was three times as long as Serilda was tall, most of its
body consisting of a long serpentine tail covered in shimmering
silver scales that whipped and writhed as the hunters yanked
on the ropes. It had no hind legs, but two front arms, each with thick
corded muscles and three claws that looked like daggers in the torchlight as it scraped at the earth, trying to get purchase against its captors. Its head was distinctly feline, like an enormous lynx, with fierce,
slitted yellow eyes, long silken whiskers, and tufts of black hair sprouting from its wide pointed ears. Its mouth and nose had been muzzled,
but it could still emit that grating screech and deep, throaty growls. A
wound on one side of its body was steaming and oozing blood that, in
this light, appeared to be as green as the grass.

"Prepare the cage!" shouted a woman, and Serilda recognized Giselle,
the master of the hounds. One of the hunters heaved open the door to
the enormous empty cage.

Serilda stepped back, not wanting to be anywhere near the tatzelwurm if it managed to break free—and it seemed to have a good chance.

"Breathtaking, isn't it?" said the Erlking. She glanced up at him,
speechless. His eyes were fixed on the capture, his expression glowing.
He appeared almost gleeful, his pointed teeth revealed behind upturned
lips, his blue-gray eyes mesmerized by the beast.

Serilda realized that she had been wrong to think he was being kind to her before. He'd merely wanted to gloat about his new trophy. And who better to admire its awe-inspiring nature than a mortal peasant?

As the hunters hauled the tatzelwurm into the cage, the Erlking turned his smile toward Serilda. "We owe you our gratitude."

She nodded dully. "Because I told you where to find it." She tried not to let on how this baffled her. She'd made it up. She'd been lying.

But evidently, she'd also been right.

"Yes," said the Erlking, "but also because without your gift, we would have had to leave the creature paralyzed. As my wyvern, if you've seen it. A fine decoration this would make, but . . . I prefer to enjoy my captures in a more spirited state. Full of vigor. But we could not have transported it so far without your precious gift."

"What gift?" she said, having no earthly idea what he was talking about.

He laughed merrily.

The tatzelwurm was dragged into the cage. The hunters slipped back out, locking the beast in, leaving only the master of the hounds inside. She set about undoing the ropes that were still tied around the creature's body.

Ropes that glittered when they caught the light of the torches.

Serilda clamped her teeth together to hold back a cry.

They were not ropes, but chains.

Slender golden chains.

"The thread you made was barely enough to braid together into these ropes," said the king, confirming her suspicions. "But what you provided us with tonight should be enough to capture and hold even the greatest of beasts. This was a test, to see if the chains would serve their purpose. As you can see, they worked magnificently."

"But . . . why gold?" she said. "Why not steel or rope?"

"Not *gold*," he said, a lilt in his voice. "Spun gold. Did you not know the worth of such a god-gift? It is perhaps the only material that can bind a creature of magic. Steel or rope would have no chance on a creature such as this." He chuckled. "Magnificent, isn't it? And finally mine."

She swallowed hard. "What are you planning to do with it?"

"That remains to be seen," he said. "But I have some grand ideas." His voice had darkened, and Serilda pictured the tatzelwurm stuffed and mounted, another piece in the king's collection.

"Come," he said, offering Serilda his elbow. "These gardens are not easily navigated on the other side of the veil, and sunrise draws near."

Serilda hesitated for perhaps a moment too long before she accepted his arm. She looked back only once, as the master of the hounds was slipping out of the cage with her arms full of chains. Perhaps she was also the gamekeeper, Serilda thought, now that she knew there was game to be kept. As soon as she was out, they slammed shut the cage door and locked the heavy latches.

The tatzelwurm released another earsplitting wail. Before it had sounded furious. Now Serilda heard an agony of a new sort. Devastation. Loss.

Its gaze fell on Serilda. There was clarity in its slitted eyes. Fury, yes, but also brilliance, an understanding that seemed unnatural on its feline features. She could not help but feel that this was not some mindless beast. This was not an animal to be kept in a cage.

This was a tragedy.

And it was her fault, at least in part. Her lies had led the king to the tatzelwurm. Somehow, she had done this.

Serilda turned away and let the king lead her back down the path, tidy garden patches spread out to either side and the castle glowing before them. Over the eastern wall, a hint of rose touched the sparse purple clouds.

"Ah, we have dallied too long," said the king. "Forgive me, Lady Serilda. I do hope you can find your way."

She looked up at him, a new trepidation filling her. For as much as she hated this man—this *monster*—at least she knew what sort of monster he was. But on the other side of the veil, the castle held too many secrets, too many threats.

As if sensing her mounting fear, the Erlking gently pressed his hand over hers.

As if he meant to comfort her.

Then a beam of golden sunlight struck the tallest tower of the keep and the king vanished like mist. All around her, the gardens grew wild and unkempt, the trees and shrubs overgrown, the boxwoods sprawling in all directions. The path beneath her feet was overtaken by vines and weeds. She could still make out the pattern of square patches, and some of the stonework still stood—a fountain here, a statue there—but always faded and chipped, some having toppled over.

The stately castle was reduced to ruins once more.

Serilda sighed. She was shivering again, and though the morning was damp, she thought it was as much from the nearness of the Erlking a moment ago.

Could he still see her from his side of the veil, like looking through a window? She knew that Gild could. After all, he had protected her from the drude that first morning. Perhaps all the inhabitants of this castle could watch her, when she saw nothing but disarray and abandonment. With Gild, the idea was comforting. With the others, not so much.

Knowing that in any minute the screams would begin, Serilda lifted her skirts and hurried along the path, dodging the overgrowth. The gardens might be forsaken, but they were full of life. Many of the plants had thrived and germinated, untended, and not all of them weeds. The air smelled of mint and sage, the aromas made more pungent by the wet earth, and she noticed many herbs running amok through the once-tidy beds. A variety of birds perched in the tree branches, whistling their morning songs, or hopped about on the ground, picking at worms and critters. In her hurry, Serilda startled a grass snake, which in turn startled her as it slithered fast into a patch of heather.

She was nearly to the castle steps when Serilda tripped. She lurched forward, landing hard on her hands and knees with a grunt. Rolling onto her backside, she looked down at her palm, which had landed on a musk thistle. Grumbling, she picked out the tiny spines, before rolling up her skirt to check her knees. Her left was barely bruised, but the right was bleeding from a shallow scrape.

"Not nice," she snapped, kicking her heel at the rock that had tripped her, hidden beneath an overgrown weed. The rock, almost perfectly round, rolled away a couple of feet.

Serilda sat up straighter.

Not a rock.

A *head*. Or at least, the head of a statue.

She stood and approached the stone. After rolling it over with her toe to make sure there were no deadly insects hiding on it, she stooped and picked it up.

It was worn from the weather, the nose broken off, along with a few pieces of a headdress. Its features were feminine, with a full, stern mouth and delicate ears. Turning it over, Serilda saw more clearly from the back of the head that it was not a headdress she wore, but a crown, which time had chipped away to a circlet of uneven stubs.

Serilda looked around, searching for the statue's body, and spotted a toppled figure behind a shrub that had yet to sprout leaves for the season. At first, it looked like just a mound of rock covered in moss, but on closer inspection, she saw it was two figures standing side by side. One in a gown. The other in a long tunic and fur-trimmed mantle. Both were headless.

More searching revealed a broken scabbard and . . . a hand.

Setting down the head, Serilda picked up this lost limb, broken off just above the wrist and missing the thumb and first two fingers. She brushed away a clump of lichen that clung to its surface.

Her eyes widened.

On the hand's fourth finger was a ring.

She looked closer, squinting. Though worn by time, the ring's seal was recognizable.

The *R* and the tatzelwurm.

Had Gild seen this statue before? Was that why the symbol had been familiar to him?

Or was there a deeper meaning here? If this seal was on the ring of a statue—a *queen's* statue, from the looks of the crown—it might have been a family crest. That matched her theories about the gravestones.

But what royal family?

And what had become of them?

Serilda realized, peering around the garden, that she was near the same plot of land where the statue of the Erlking had stood on the other side of the veil.

That statue would have been right . . . *there.*

Serilda used the stone hand to peel back a thick covering of vines, and it was right where she thought it would be. The statue's base, where she assumed this king and queen, now broken to pieces, had once stood regally above their gardens.

There were words carved into it.

Excitement skittered through her. Serilda cleared away the grime and debris, using her breath to blow away the layers of dust that filled up the engraving, until finally she could read the words.

THIS STATUE ERECTED TO COMMEMORATE THE ASCENSION OF
QUEEN
AND HER HUSBAND
KING
THEIR MOST GRACIOUS MAJESTIES
TO THE THRONE OF ADALHEID

She read them again.

And again.

That was it?

No—there should be names.

She felt around the blank plains of the stone, but there were no more words.

Queen and King who?

Serilda traced the words with her thumb, then brushed her fingers against the wide-open spaces where names should have been.

It was nothing but solid stone, smooth as glass.

Which was when she heard the first scream.

Disgruntled, Serilda picked up her skirts and fled.

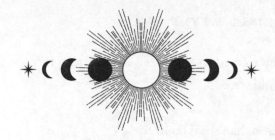

Chapter 41

Clouds had swept in and it had started to rain again. Serilda sat at the edge of the dock, her feet dangling above the water, mesmerized by the faint droplets making infinite rings across the surface. She knew she should go back to the inn. Her dress was soaked through and she had started shivering some time ago, especially without her beloved cloak. Lorraine would be worried, and Leyna would be eager to hear her tell of another night in the castle.

But she could not bring herself to get up. She felt like if she only stared at the castle long enough, it might spill out some of its secrets to her.

She yearned to go back. Was tempted to cross that bridge even now. To take her chances with the monsters and the ghouls.

But that was a fool's mission.

The castle was dangerous, no matter which side of the veil she was on.

A flock of black birds rose up above the ruins, cawing at some spotted prey. Serilda stared at them, watching their black bodies swirl and dive before they settled back down out of sight again.

She sighed. Nearly two weeks had passed since Eostrig's Day and the Feast of Death and all she'd learned was that the Erlking was using the spun gold to hunt and capture magical creatures, and that there definitely had been a royal family who once inhabited this castle but somehow they seemed to have been erased from history, and that her feelings for Gild were . . .

Well.

More intense than she'd realized.

A part of her wondered if she had been too hasty last night. If *they* had been too hasty. What had passed between them had been . . .

The perfect word eluded her.

Maybe the word *was* perfect. A perfect fantasy. A perfect moment caught in time.

But it had also been unexpected and sudden, and when she woke to find Gild gone and the Erlking towering over her, that illusion of perfection dissolved.

There was *nothing* about her growing intimacy with Gild that was perfect. She needed him if she was to survive the Erlking's demands. She was constantly indebted to him. She'd paid him with her two most valuable belongings and now the promise of her firstborn child, and regardless of whether or not it was the magic that demanded such sacrifices, it didn't seem like a basis for an enduring relationship.

They had gotten carried away, that was all. A boy and a girl who had been given few opportunities for romance, overcome with fervid desire.

Serilda blushed deeply at having thought those words.

Overcome with . . . with heightened longing.

That sounded a bit more respectable.

They were hardly the first couple to tumble into bed together—or, in their case, an old settee—with little forethought. And they would by no means be the last. It was one of the favorite pastimes of the women in Märchenfeld, to tsk and tut over which unwed boys and girls had become, in their opinion, a little *too* close. But it was relatively harmless gossip. There was no law against it, and if pressed, most of those same women would gladly talk about *their* first tumble, with a smidgen of roguish, wanton pride, and always followed up with the disclaimer that it was all a *long* time ago, before they met the love of their life and settled down in marital bliss.

Serilda knew that not every first intimacy was a happy one. She had heard tales of men and women alike who had believed themselves in love, only to later find those feelings were unrequited. She knew there could be shame attached to giving so much of oneself. She knew there could be regrets.

She chewed on the inside of her cheek, trying to determine whether *she* felt any shame. Whether *she* had regrets.

And the more she thought of it, the more it became clear that the answer was . . . no.

Not yet, at least.

Right now, she just wanted to see him again. Kiss him again. Hold him again. Do . . . other things with him. Again.

No. Not ashamed.

But she couldn't fulfill any of those wishes. And if there were any tricky, difficult feelings, that was the source of them. He was trapped behind the veil, and she was here, staring at a castle where ghosts moaned and cried and suffered through their deaths over and over again.

A breeze kicked up from over the water. Serilda shuddered. Her dress was soaked, her hair saturated. Little droplets had begun to slide down her face.

A fire would be nice. Dry clothes. A cup of warm cider.

She should go.

But instead of getting up, she tucked her hands into her dress pockets.

Her fingers wrapped around something and she gasped. She'd forgotten all about it.

She pulled out the bobbin, half expecting to see it wound with scratchy straw. But no, she was holding a handful of fine spun gold.

She laughed with surprise. It felt a little bit like a gift, even if, technically, she had stolen it.

A new sound intruded on her thoughts. A jangle. A clatter.

Serilda hid the bobbin against her body and glanced around. There were fishing boats out on the lake, their crews casting nets and lines, occasionally hollering information at one another that Serilda couldn't make out. The road at her back sported a handful of carts, their wheels rattling loudly on the cobblestones. But with the dreary weather, the town was mostly quiet.

There it was again—a musical, hollow jingle, a bit like wind chimes.

It sounded close.

As if it were coming from under the dock.

Serilda had just begun to tip forward to peer over the edge when a hand appeared a few steps away from her, gripping the wooden boards. A puddle of lake water splattered around brownish-green skin. The hand was made of thick knobby fingers connected by slimy webbing.

Serilda gasped and lurched to her feet.

The hands were followed by enormous buglike eyes peering over the dock, glowing faintly yellow. A patch of river-weed hair clung to an otherwise bald, bulbous head.

Its eyes landed on Serilda and she took another step back. She tucked the bobbin of gold thread back into her pocket, then cast around for something she could use as a weapon. There was nothing, not even a stick.

The creature threw its elbows up onto the dock and began to shamble up.

Should she run? Call for help?

Despite the way her heart was racing, the creature was not *particularly* threatening. As it emerged onto the dock, she could see it was the size of a young child. And yes, it was a strange, hideous thing, with lumps and bulges all along a slimy body, and sinewy froglike legs that kept it lowered into a crouch. She would have thought for sure it was some odd animal born of a forest swamp, except that it was not entirely naked. It wore a coat crafted of woven grasses and covered in small shells. It was the shells that clacked and jingled with every move it made.

Except now, it had fallen silent. Motionless. Its mouth, which stretched wide across its face, stayed in a flat line. Studying her.

She studied it back, her pulse steadying.

She *knew* this creature.

Or, at least, she knew what it was.

"Schellenrock?" she whispered. A river bogeyman, usually harmless, most notable for the coat of shells that chimed like little bells wherever it went.

Not malicious.

At least, not in any of the stories she'd ever heard. Sometimes it even helped lost or weary travelers.

With a wary smile, Serilda lowered herself to a crouch. "Hello there. I won't hurt you."

It blinked—one eyelid closing at a time. Then it lifted a webbed hand toward her and crooked one of its fingers.

Beckoning.

It did not wait for her reaction.

The schellenrock turned and scampered past her, before lowering itself back down into the lake's shallows with a jangle and a splash.

Serilda glanced around to see if anyone was watching, but a woman pushing a cart full of manure had paused to chat with a neighbor in the overhang of their front door, and no one was watching Serilda, or her unexpected visitor.

"I suppose I might be a lost and weary traveler," she said, following the creature. She climbed down onto the shore, which was more rock than sand. As soon as it was sure that she was following, the schellenrock took off, speeding through the shallow water on hands and feet, staying close enough to the shore that it was easy for Serilda to keep pace with it.

It was leading her straight toward the cobblestone bridge that connected the castle to the town, and unless it expected her to swim out into the lake to go beneath the drawbridge, they would soon reach a dead end.

But the schellenrock did not swim out farther into the lake. Once they reached the bridge, constructed of rocks and boulders that were slick with algae, the creature climbed up over a few rocks and vanished.

Serilda froze.

Was she imagining things?

A moment later, the creature appeared again, its yellow eyes peering out at her from the rocks, as if asking why she had stopped.

Serilda approached with a bit more caution. Fitting her hands onto the damp stones, she pulled herself up to where the schellenrock was waiting for her. The climb was easy enough, so long as she was careful not to slip.

The river creature disappeared again, and when Serilda peered into the space where it had gone, she saw that there was a little alcove in this wall of rocks. And tucked into it—invisible from the shore or the docks—was a small cave, leading away from the castle, underneath the city.

Or, perhaps, a tunnel.

Or a hiding place for a schellenrock, she supposed.

A small part of Serilda wondered if it would be best *not* to follow. This cave looked dark and dank and all manner of unwelcoming.

But she had heard, and told, enough stories to know that it was never wise to ignore the summons of a magical creature. Even a lowly, peculiar one like this little river monster.

As the schellenrock crept into the mouth of the cave, Serilda hastily tied back her braids and followed.

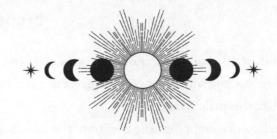

Chapter 42

er initial reaction had been accurate. The cave *was* dark and dank and entirely unwelcoming. It also smelled of dead fish. She had to stay crouched the entire time and her legs were aching something terrible; and there was standing water on the cave floor that the schellenrock kept kicking up behind it and splattering into Serilda's face.

And she couldn't see. The only light came from the schellenrock's faintly illuminated eyes, which might have let *it* see well enough, but left Serilda in the dark.

The path was mostly straight, though, and Serilda could tell that they were traveling beneath the city. She tried to gauge how far they had gone, and wondered how long this tunnel went for, and very much hoped that it had an opening at the other end and she wasn't being led to an unsavory death.

Just when she was beginning to think her thighs couldn't take any more and she would have to start crawling on her hands and knees—*not* a tempting proposition—she saw a spot of light up ahead and heard the burble of water.

They emerged.

Not in the town or out in the fields . . .

But in a forest.

Serilda had no sooner marveled at how gratifying it could feel to stretch one's legs after they'd been crouched for far too long, than a shiver prickled along her spine.

The creature had brought her into the Aschen Wood.

They were standing in a shallow creek bed, surrounded by ancient trees, their boughs so thick she could barely make out the sky above, sheltering them from the rain. The air was still damp and chilled, and great globs of rainwater fell from the branches.

The schellenrock hurried off down the creek, its webbed feet splashing in the shallow water, part hopping, part hobbling, leading Serilda deeper into the wood.

Her boots squelched with every step. She knew she should be afraid— the woods were not friendly to humans, especially those who entered them on foot or ventured off the road, and she was definitely off the road. But mostly she was curious, even excited. She wanted to pause and drink it in, this mysterious place she'd been dreaming of her whole life.

The one time she'd ever been beyond the edge of the woods was a few short months ago, on the night of the Hunger Moon, when the king had first summoned her and the carriage traversed the little-traveled road through the forest, when it had been too dark to see anything.

Papa had never dared enter the woods, not even on horseback. She doubted he'd have traveled through the woods if he had an entire royal guard to accompany him. His fears made more sense to her now. The Erlking had lured away her mother, and most people believed that the Erlking still resided in Gravenstone Castle, which lay deep in the heart of the forest.

Regardless whether the king now called Adalheid his home, the Aschen Wood remained a treacherous place. Serilda had always feared it, just as she'd always been drawn to it. What child could resist the allure of such magic? The image of fae creatures dancing on toadstools and water sprites bathing in the brooks and songbirds with glowing feathers alighting on the branches overhead.

But it was not quite the landscape of evocative color and song she'd always pictured. Instead, everywhere she looked there was a chorus of gray and green. She tried to think of it as pretty, but for the most part, it struck her as a palette of uninterrupted gloom. Spindly black tree trunks and branches drooping with strings of lichen and fallen logs crumbling under the weight of thick moss and fungi the size of wagon wheels.

There was a sense of eternity here. This was a place where time didn't exist, where even the smallest sapling might be ancient. Unchanged and unchanging.

But of course, it wasn't unchanging. The forest was alive, but in quiet, subtle ways. The fat spider spinning its intricate web among a patch of bloodberry thorns. The rumbling call of toads along the banks of a murky pond. The haunted cry of crows eyeing her from the boughs, occasionally answered by the lonely song of the warblers. Together with the incessant rainfall, it made a somber melody. The quiet drumbeat on the canopy overhead, paired with steady drips pummeling the lower leaves, thumping down into the bed of undergrowth and pine needles.

Serilda's nerves tingled with imagined threats. She kept a close eye on those crows, especially the ones who landed overhead and waited for her to pass underneath, watching like greedy scavengers. But they were only birds, she assured herself again and again. Not bloodthirsty nachtkrapp, spying for the Erlking.

The coat of the schellenrock jangled loudly, startling Serilda. She realized it had gotten quite far ahead and was standing on a fallen log, eyelids alternating in slow blinks.

"Sorry," she said, smiling.

If the creature *could* smile, it didn't. But that might also be because a fly had started to buzz around its head, catching its attention, and while Serilda made up the distance, the schellenrock stuck out a whip-like black tongue and swallowed the fly whole.

Serilda buried a grimace. When the creature's gaze returned to hers, she had found her polite smile again. "Is there a place we can rest? Just for a few minutes?"

In answer, the schellenrock hopped off the log and headed up the bank of the creek, where the foliage was dense and the ground was a patchwork of gnarled roots and ferns and brambles.

Sighing, Serilda grabbed hold of a thick root sticking out of the clay and hauled herself up after it.

Yes, the forest was bleak, she thought, weaving and ducking around the branches that clawed at her as she passed. But there was a serenity to it, too. Like a sad concerto played in a minor key that made you weep just to hear it, though you could never quite tell why.

It was the smell of earth and fungi. Of that damp, sodden smell after a good rain. It was the tiny purple wildflowers unfurling near the ground, so easy to miss among the prickly weeds. It was the fallen tree trunks that were rotting away, giving life to new saplings, wrapped up in tender, spindly roots. It was thrumming insects and an entire menagerie of croaking frogs.

The path, if it could be called a path, curved along the edge of a swamp overrun with swamp grass and weeping willows. A pool speckled with algae and enormous lily pads was fed by a small brook. The schellenrock clambered over to the other side, its shells clinking merrily, but when Serilda went to follow, her foot slid ankle deep into the mud. She gasped and threw her arms wide, barely managing to catch her balance before she fell into the swamp.

On the other side of the pool, the schellenrock paused to look back at her, as if wondering what could be the problem.

Serilda scowled and pulled her boot from the mud with a gloopy, sucking noise. She backed up onto drier land. "Isn't there another . . ."

She trailed off, spotting, not much farther down the brook, a little footbridge made of birch twigs and mortared stones. "Ah! Like that."

The schellenrock rattled its shells loudly.

"It's not much farther," Serilda called back, pausing to wipe her muddied boot on a patch of moss. "And this will be much easier for me."

It rattled again, a bit panicky. Serilda frowned and glanced back at its wide eyes, now unblinking.

"What?" she said, taking a step onto the bridge.

Oh . . . hello . . . lovely thing.

Serilda stilled. The voice was a whisper and a melody. The rustle of leaves, the soothing burble of water.

Pulling her attention away from the schellenrock, Serilda looked ahead to see a woman standing on the other side of the little bridge.

She was crafted of silk and moonbeams, in a long white dress, with dark hair that hung nearly to her knees. Her face, though lovely, was not flawless like the dark ones'. She had thick, dark eyebrows over acorn-brown eyes, and impish dimples just above the corners of her mouth. Still, mortal as she might look, the ethereal light emanating from her made it clear that she was something unearthly.

And judging from the schellenrock's reaction . . . dangerous.

But Serilda did not feel threatened. Instead, she felt drawn to this woman, this being.

The woman's smile grew wider, her dimples more pronounced. She giggled, and it was parade bells and shooting stars. She stretched a hand toward Serilda.

An invitation.

Will you dance with me?

Serilda made no decision. Already her hand was reaching out, eager to accept the offer. She stepped forward.

Something crunched beneath her foot.

Startled, Serilda looked down.

Ah—nothing but a birch twig.

She went to kick it down into the brook, but paused.

A warning, deep in her mind, shouting at her.

This was no twig.

This was a bone.

The entire bridge was crafted of them, mixed in with the mortar and rocks.

Heart thrumming, she began to step back, meeting the woman's eye again.

The smile fell, overcome with a desperate plea.

Don't go, whispered the voice. *You alone can break this curse. You can set me free. All it takes is a dance. One little dance. Please. Please, don't leave me . . .*

Another step back. Her foot landed on soft mossy ground.

The woman's brittle sorrow morphed again, now a vicious sneer. She lunged forward, her fingers reaching to grab Serilda—to claw or strangle or shove her, Serilda didn't know.

She lifted a hand to protect herself.

A wooden staff smacked the woman's hands away. She released a shriek of pain and reared back.

A figure leaped onto the bridge, between Serilda and the glowering woman. Lithe and graceful, with moss where hair might have been, growing between tall fox ears.

"Not this one, Salige," came a stern voice.

A familiar voice.

It took Serilda a moment to recall the moss maiden's name. Basil? Purslane?

No.

"Parsley?" she asked.

The moss maiden ignored her, her eyes on the woman. Salige, she'd said.

Wait—*salige*. That was not a name, but a type of spirit. The salige frauen—malicious spirits that haunted bridges and graveyards and bodies of water. That demanded a dance from travelers, begging them to break a curse . . . but usually ended up killing them.

I found her first, hissed the salige, baring pearlescent teeth. *She could break the curse. She could be the one.*

"So very sorry," said Parsley, holding her quarterstaff like a shield in front of her as she slowly backed away, forcing Serilda off the bridge. "But this human is already spoken for. Grandmother wishes to have a word with her."

The spirit screamed, a sound of frustrated agony.

But when Parsley turned and grabbed Serilda's arm, yanking her away, the spirit did not follow.

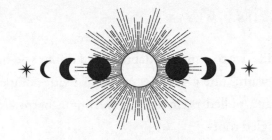

Chapter 43

re you really taking me to see Shrub Grandmother?" said
Serilda, once the bridge with the salige was far behind them
and her heartbeat had begun to slow. "*The* Shrub Grandmother?"

"I would tame your awe before we arrive," said Parsley, a bit snarly.
"Grandmother does not respond well to flattery."

"I can try," said Serilda, "but I cannot guarantee."

The moss maiden moved like a fawn among the branches, quick and
graceful. In her path, Serilda felt more like a wild boar crashing through
the woods, but she was comforted to know that the schellenrock, at
the back of their odd little party, was the noisiest of all with its coat of
shells, and Parsley wasn't telling *it* to be quiet.

"Thank you," she said. "For rescuing me from the salige. I suppose
now I'm in *your* debt."

Parsley paused beside an enormous oak tree, one that stretched so
high Serilda could not see the top of it when she craned her neck.

"You're right," said the maiden, holding out her hand. "I'll take back
my ring."

Coldness swept across Serilda's skin. "I . . . left it at home. For safekeeping."

Parsley smirked and Serilda could sense that she didn't believe her.

"Then you will have to remain indebted, for I doubt you have anything else I would want." She grabbed a curtain of vines draped across the tree's trunk and pulled them aside, revealing a narrow opening just above the tangled roots.

"Go on," she said, with a nod at the schellenrock. It ducked inside, its shells jangling. Parsley turned to Serilda next. "After you."

She stepped into the hollow trunk and was greeted by impenetrable blackness—no sign of the river monster. Squeezing her shoulders, she crouched low so as to fit through, and inched into the tiny shelter, stretching out her hand. She expected to feel the rough, cobwebbed insides of the tree, but found only emptiness in the dark.

She took another step, then another.

On the seventh step, her fingers brushed—not wood, but fabric. Thick and heavy like a tapestry.

Serilda pushed the fabric aside. Gray light spilled forward. As she emerged from the tree, her breath caught.

A dozen or so moss maidens formed a tight circle around her, each one gripping a weapon—spears, bows, daggers. One had a very poisonous-looking wolf spider perched on her shoulder.

They were not smiling.

She spotted the schellenrock crouched behind the group, just as one of the maidens handed him a small wooden bowl teeming with wriggling bugs. He licked his wide lips before enthusiastically burying his face in the bowl.

"You," said one of the maidens, "are very loud, and very cumbersome."

Serilda stared at her. "I'm sorry?"

The maiden cocked her head to the side. "We have been waiting. Come."

They formed a circle around Serilda and led her down the winding paths. She did not know where to look first.

The space before her was cavernous—not a clearing exactly, for towering trees still blocked out the sky far overhead, cloaking the world in dim shadows. But the undergrowth had been cleared out, replaced with meandering walking paths thick with spongy moss. And there were houses everywhere, though unlike any houses Serilda had seen before. These abodes were built into the ancient trees themselves. Wooden doors tucked into the spaces between roots, and windows carved from the natural knots scattered along the trunks. Thick branches curved to form winding staircases. Higher boughs held cozy nooks and balconies.

She could still hear the steady patter of raindrops far overhead, and the occasional drizzle fell down into this wooded sanctuary, but the gloom of the forest had been replaced with something cozy and charming, almost quaint. She spotted little shade gardens bursting with sorrel, arugula, and chives. She was mesmerized by the glow of twinkling lights that floated whimsically everywhere she looked. She didn't know whether it was fireflies or fairies or some magic spell, but the effect was enchanting. She felt like she'd just stepped into a dream.

Asyltal.

The sanctuary of Shrub Grandmother and the moss maidens.

She glanced back once, hoping that Parsley would be coming, too, but there was no sign of her almost-ally.

"Our sister had to return to her duties," said one of the maidens.

"Duties?" asked Serilda.

Another maiden released a wry laugh. "Just like a mortal to think that all we do is bathe in the waterfall and sing to hedgehogs."

"I didn't say that," said Serilda, affronted. "Judging from your weaponry, I suspect you spend a great deal of time dueling and competing in target practice."

The one who had laughed shot her a fierce look. "Don't forget it."

Serilda spotted more maidens lingering around the village, tending to the gardens or lounging in hammocks made of thick vines. They watched Serilda with little interest. That, or they were just really good at hiding it.

Serilda, on the other hand, was so distracted she nearly toppled down a set of stairs. One of the maidens grabbed her elbow at the last second and pulled her back onto the path.

They were standing at the top of an amphitheater cut into the side of a small valley. At the bottom was a circular pool, emerald green and dotted with lily pads. A grassy island in the center held a circle of moss-covered rocks. Two women were seated, waiting.

Serilda gasped—with relief, and an unexpected amount of joy—to recognize Meadowsweet.

The other was an elderly woman who sat cross-legged on her rock. Though, as Serilda was led down the steps, she realized that *elderly* could not be the right word. *Ancient* might be better, *ageless* better still. She was small, but broad, with a hunched back and wrinkles as deep as canyons cut into her pale face. Her white hair hung thin and tangled down her back, picking up twigs and bits of moss. She was dressed simply in layers of fur and dirt-smudged linen, though on her head was a delicate diadem with a large pearl resting against her brow. Her eyes were as black as her hair was white, and they stared unblinking at Serilda as she approached, in a way that made her stand straighter.

"Grandmother," said one of the maidens, "this is the girl who has caught the interest of Erlkönig."

Serilda couldn't help it. A delighted smile stretched across her face. This was the leader of the moss maidens, the source of nearly as many fairy stories as the Erlking himself. The great, the ferocious, the most peculiar Shrub Grandmother.

Pusch-Grohla.

She did her best to curtsy. "This is incredible," she said, with a bit of disbelieving laughter in her voice as she recalled the story of the prince and the gates of Verloren she'd been telling Gild. "I was just talking about you."

Pusch-Grohla smacked her lips a couple of times, then leaned her head toward Meadowsweet. Serilda imagined she was going to whisper something to the maiden, but instead, Meadowsweet demurely turned to the old woman and began picking through her knotted white hair. After a second, she picked something out and flicked it away toward the water. Lice? Fleas?

Nothing was said while Meadowsweet dutifully found two more bugs, and the rest of the maidens who had led Serilda to this place fanned out and claimed stones around the circle, leaving Serilda standing in the middle.

Once they were settled, Pusch-Grohla sniffed and sat up straight again. She never took her gaze from Serilda.

When she spoke, her voice was thin as watered-down milk. "This is the girl who stuffed you into an onion cellar?"

Serilda frowned. To say it that way made her sound like a villain, rather than the hero.

"She is," said Meadowsweet.

Pusch-Grohla sucked on her front teeth for a moment, and when she spoke again, Serilda noticed that a few of those teeth were missing, and the ones she did have didn't quite fit her mouth, or each other. As though they'd been borrowed and repurposed from a helpful mule. "Is there a debt owed?"

"No, Grandmother," said Meadowsweet. "We were happy to show our gratitude, although"—Meadowsweet glanced at Serilda's throat, then down to her hand—"you do not wear our gifts?"

"I have hidden them away for safekeeping," she said, keeping her tone even.

It wasn't entirely a lie. Behind the veil, they were most securely hidden, and she knew Gild would keep them safe.

Pusch-Grohla leaned forward, staring straight through Serilda in a way that reminded her of a hawk watching the skittering path of a mouse across the fields.

Then she smiled. The effect was not so much jolly as disconcerting.

It was followed by a loud, wheezing laugh, as she pointed a crooked finger with swollen knuckles toward Serilda. "You honor the god of lies with that clever mouth. But, child"—her countenance dissolved into sternness—"do not think to lie to *me*."

"I would not dare . . . ," said Serilda. She hesitated, not sure what to call her. "Grandmother?"

The woman sucked her teeth again, and if she cared one way or the other what Serilda called her, it did not show. "My granddaughters gave gifts worthy of your assistance. A ring and a necklace. Very old. Very fine. You had them with you when Erlkönig summoned you on the Hunger Moon, and you have them with you no longer." Her gaze turned sharp, almost hostile. "What did the Alder King give to you in exchange for these trinkets?"

"The Alder King?" Serilda shook her head. "I didn't give them to *him*."

"No? Then how is it you have spent three moons in his care, and yet you remain alive?"

She looked briefly at Meadowsweet and the gathered maidens. There was not a friendly face among them, but she could not blame them for being mistrustful, especially knowing that the dark ones made a game of hunting them for sport.

"The Erlking believes that I can spin straw into gold," she started. "A blessing from Hulda. That was the lie I told him when I was hiding Meadowsweet and Parsley, yes, in an onion cellar. Three times now, he has summoned me to the castle in Adalheid and asked me to do just that, and threatened to kill me if I failed. But there is a . . . a ghost in the castle. A boy who is a true gold-spinner. In exchange for that magic, and for saving my life, I gave him the necklace and the ring."

Pusch-Grohla was silent a long time, while Serilda shifted uncomfortably from foot to foot.

"And what did you give as payment on the third moon?"

She stilled, holding the old woman's gaze.

Memories flashed in her thoughts. Searing kisses and caresses.

But no. That wasn't what she was asking, and it certainly hadn't been payment for anything.

"A promise," she answered.

"God-magic does not work on promises."

"Evidently it does."

Testy surprise flashed through Pusch-Grohla's eyes, and Serilda shrank back a bit.

"It was a promise for . . . for something very valuable," she added, embarrassed to say more. She didn't think she could adequately explain what had led to such a deal being struck, and she didn't want Pusch-Grohla to see her as the sort of person who would carelessly bargain away her firstborn child.

Even if she was. Evidently.

She turned her attention to Meadowsweet. "I am sorry, though, if the necklace held special meaning for you. May I ask, who was the girl in the portrait?"

"I do not know," said Meadowsweet, with no apparent regret.

Serilda flinched. It had not occurred to her that the portrait could hold as little sentimental meaning for the moss maiden as it had for her. "You don't?"

"No. I had that locket for as long as I can remember, and do not recall where it came from. As to its special meaning, I assure you, I value my life more."

"But . . . it was so beautiful."

"Not as beautiful as snowdrop flowers in winter," said Meadow-sweet, "or a newborn fawn taking its first shaky steps."

Serilda had no argument for this. "What of Parsley's ring? It had a seal on it. A tatzelwurm entwined around the letter *R*. And I saw the seal on a statue in Adalheid Castle, too, and in the cemetery outside the city. What does it mean?"

Meadowsweet frowned and looked to Pusch-Grohla, but the old woman's face was blank as slate as she studied Serilda.

"I don't know that, either," Meadowsweet answered. "If Parsley knew, she never said, but I don't believe she was any more sentimental over that ring than I was about the necklace. When we venture into the world, we all know to keep trinkets with us, in case payment is required. They are to us as your human coins are to—"

"This boy," interrupted Pusch-Grohla, unnecessarily loud. "The one who spun the gold. What is his name?"

It took Serilda a moment to change the direction of her thoughts. "He goes by Gild."

"You say he is a ghost. Not a dark one?"

She shook her head. "Definitely not a dark one. The townspeople call him Vergoldetgeist. The Gilded Ghost. The Erlking calls him a pol-tergeist."

"If he is one of the Alder King's dead, then the king controls him. He would not be fooled by this charade."

Serilda swallowed, thinking of her conversations with Gild. He seemed proud to be known as the poltergeist, but it was clear to them both that he was not like the other ghosts in the castle.

"He is a prisoner in the castle, like the other spirits who have been trapped by the king," she said slowly. "But he is not controlled by the king. He is not a servant like the others. He's told me that he doesn't know what he is, exactly, and I believe he is telling the truth."

"And he claims to have been blessed by Hulda?"

"He . . . doesn't know where his magic came from. But that seems to be the most likely possibility."

Pusch-Grohla grunted.

Serilda wrung her hands. "He is one of many mysteries I've encountered during my time in Adalheid. I wonder if you might be able to shed light on one of the others?"

One of the maidens made a derisive sound. "This is not a social call, little human."

Serilda felt her hackles rise, but she tried to ignore her. When Pusch-Grohla had no response, she dared to plunge ahead. "I have been trying to learn more about the history of Adalheid Castle, to find out what happened there. I know it used to be home to a royal family, before the Erlking claimed it for himself. I've seen their graves, and a statue of a king and queen. But no one knows anything about them. And *you*, Grandmother, are as old as this forest. Surely if anyone would remember something about the family who built the castle, or who lived there before the dark ones, it would be you."

Pusch-Grohla studied Serilda for a long moment. When she finally spoke, her voice was quieter than Serilda had yet heard it.

"I have no memories of royalty in Adalheid," she said. "It has always been the domain of the Erlking and the dark ones."

Serilda clenched her teeth. That wasn't true. She *knew* that wasn't true.

How could even this woman, as old as an ancient oak, not remember? It was as if entire decades, perhaps centuries, of the city's history had been erased.

"If you uncover a different truth," Pusch-Grohla added, "you will tell me immediately."

Serilda sagged, wondering if she was imagining the troubled look in the woman's sharp eyes.

"Grandmother," said one of the moss maidens, her voice thick with concern, "what possible use could Erlkönig have for this spun gold? Other than—"

Pusch-Grohla lifted a hand, and the maiden fell silent.

Serilda glanced around the circle, at their fierce and beautiful faces shadowed with worry. "Actually," she said slowly, "I do have some idea what the king wants the gold for."

Reaching into her pocket, she took out the bobbin full of gold thread. Stepping forward, she held it out to Shrub Grandmother. The old woman tipped her head toward Meadowsweet, who took the bobbin and held it up before the woman's eyes, turning it to catch the light.

"He's been taking these threads and braiding them together into ropes," said Serilda.

Around her, the maidens tensed, their concerned looks darkening.

"Last night, the wild hunt used these ropes to capture a tatzelwurm."

Pusch-Grohla's attention snapped back to her.

"The king told me that spun gold is perhaps the only material that can hold magical creatures like that."

She opted not to mention how she had inadvertently told him where to find the beast.

"Indeed," said the woman, her voice brittle. "Blessed by the gods, it would be unbreakable."

"And . . . is it?" Meadowsweet asked hesitantly. "Blessed by Hulda, I mean."

Pusch-Grohla looked like she'd bitten a lemon as she glared at the spool of gold. "It is."

Serilda blinked. So Gild really had been god-blessed? "How can you tell?"

"I would know it anywhere," said Pusch-Grohla. "And I assure you, the Alder King will be using it to hunt more than the tatzelwurm."

"It's this coming winter," murmured Meadowsweet. "The Endless Moon."

It took Serilda a moment to understand what they were suggesting.

The Endless Moon, when a full moon coincided with the winter solstice.

She inhaled sharply.

It had been nineteen years since the last one—the night that, supposedly, her father had helped the trickster god and wished to have a child.

"You think he means to go after one of the gods," she said. "He wants to make a wish."

Pusch-Grohla gave a loud snort. "A wish? Perhaps. But there are many reasons one might hope to capture a god."

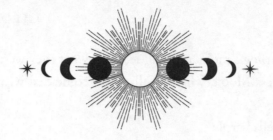

Chapter 44

Grandmother," said Meadowsweet, gripping the golden thread in both hands, "if he does try to make a wish—"

"We all know what he would ask for," muttered the maiden who had threatened Serilda before.

"We do?" said Serilda.

"No, Foxglove, I would not give him so much credit," said Pusch-Grohla.

"But he might," said Meadowsweet. "We cannot know what he would want, but it is possible—"

"We cannot know," said Pusch-Grohla. "Let us not attempt to read his blackened heart."

Meadowsweet and Foxglove exchanged a look, but no one else spoke.

Serilda looked between the three of them, her curiosity burbling. What *would* the Erlking wish for? He already had eternal life. An entourage of servants to do his bidding.

But the memory of her own made-up story whispered to her, answering the question.

A queen.

A huntress.

If this were a fairy tale, that is what he would wish for. True love must be victorious, even for a villain.

But this was not one of her stories, and while the Erlking might be a villain, it was difficult to picture him using a god-given wish to return his lover from the underworld.

What else?

"How much gold has this poltergeist spun for him?" asked Pusch-Grohla.

Serilda considered, picturing all that straw, all those bobbins. Stacks and stacks and stacks of them.

"The gold from the first two nights made enough rope to capture the tatzelwurm," she said. "And he told me that what was done last night would be enough to . . . to capture and hold even the greatest of beasts."

The greatest of beasts.

Pusch-Grohla's mouth twitched to one side. She took a hold of the walking stick beside her and thumped it on the ground. "He cannot be given any more."

Serilda clasped her hands in the same way she did when she was trying to speak patiently and practically with Madam Sauer. "I don't disagree. But what would you have me do instead? He has threatened my life if I don't do what he asks."

"Then forfeit your life," said one of the moss maidens.

Serilda gaped at her. "I beg your pardon?"

"Imagine what harm could come from Erlkönig claiming a god-wish," the maiden said. "It is not worth the life of one human girl."

Serilda glowered. "Would you be so blithe if it were *your* life we were discussing?"

The maiden lifted an eyebrow. "I am not *blithe*. Erlkönig has been hunting us and the creatures of this world for centuries. If we were to be captured, he would attempt to torture us into confessing the location of our home." She gestured around to the surrounding glen. "And we would die with honor before speaking a word."

Serilda glanced over at Meadowsweet, who met her gaze without flinching.

The Erlking had been hunting her and Parsley. He had mentioned having their heads to decorate his wall. But never had it crossed her mind that he might have tortured them first.

"The hunt threatens all living things," said Pusch-Grohla, "human and forest folk alike. My granddaughter speaks true. That gold is a weapon in his hands. We cannot allow Erlkönig to capture a god."

Serilda looked away. She knew they wanted her to swear that she would not give the king any more of what he wanted. That she wouldn't ask Gild to help her. That she would accept death over aiding the king again.

But she didn't know if she could promise that.

She glanced around the circle, taking in the assorted weapons propped against rocks and laid across laps. For the first time since coming here she wondered if she was safe in the presence of the moss maidens. She did not believe they intended her harm, but what would they do if she did not promise what they wanted? She had the sudden uncomfortable sensation that she'd unwittingly found herself caught in the middle of an age-old war.

But if this was a war, what was her role to play in it?

Shrub Grandmother muttered something to herself, too low for anyone to hear. Then she tipped her head toward Meadowsweet and gently knocked the end of her walking stick against her own scalp. Meadowsweet set to lousing her hair again, picking through for bugs while Pusch-Grohla considered.

After four more critters had been flicked away, Pusch-Grohla straightened. "There is a rumor that he does not kill all the beasts he captures in the wood. That some are kept in his castle—for added sport, or breeding, or to train his hounds."

"Yes," said Serilda. "I've seen them."

Pusch-Grohla's expression darkened with thinly veiled loathing. "Does he hurt them?"

Serilda stared, considering the small cages, the untended wounds, the way some of the creatures trembled in silent fear when the dark ones walked past. Her heart squeezed tight.

"I think he might," she whispered.

"Those creatures were our responsibility, and we failed them," said Pusch-Grohla. "Anyone who aids Erlkönig and his hunters must be our enemy."

She shook her head. "I have no desire to be your enemy."

"I care little of your desires."

Serilda's hands clenched. That seemed to be a common theme among these age-old beings, regardless of which side of the war they fell on. Nobody cared for the mortals caught in the middle.

"It doesn't matter," she said weakly. "I have nothing else to offer as payment for the magic. Gild cannot continue to spin gold to save my life, and he won't do the work for free."

"He can't," said Meadowsweet. "Hulda's magic requires balance and balance is obtained through reciprocity. Nothing taken for granted."

"Fine, then," said Serilda, with a shrug that was more nonchalant than she felt. "No doubt the king will summon me again on the Awakening Moon and Gild will not be able to help me and I will fail his task and he will take my life. It seems I have already lost."

"Yes," said Pusch-Grohla. "You are very much sitting in the ink."

"We could kill her now," suggested Foxglove. She did not even bother to whisper it. "It would solve the problem."

"It would solve *a* problem," Pusch-Grohla countered. "Not *the* problem. This Vergoldetgeist would still be within Erlkönig's grasp."

"But Erlkönig doesn't know that," said Meadowsweet.

"Hm, yes," said the old woman. "Perhaps it would be best if the girl never returned to Adalheid."

Gooseflesh speckled Serilda's arms. "I've tried running from him. It didn't work."

"Of course you cannot run from him," said Foxglove. "He is the leader of the wild hunt. If he wants you, he will find you. Erlkönig relishes nothing more than tracking his prey, luring them into his grasp, and striking."

"Yes, I know that now. It's just, we'd thought, I'd thought maybe there was a chance. He can only leave the veil under a full moon. My father and I had sought to travel far enough away that he would not be able to travel so far in one night."

"Do you think the boundaries of the veil end at his castle walls? He can travel anywhere he wishes to, and you will have no idea that he is right there at your side, following your every move."

Serilda shuddered. "Believe me, I've realized my mistake. But *you* have been hiding from him for ages. He cannot find this place. Perhaps, if I could . . ." She trailed off as the expressions darkened around her. Even Meadowsweet looked aghast at what Serilda was suggesting. "Could stay here?" she finished lamely.

"No," said Pusch-Grohla simply.

"Why not? You don't want me returning to Adalheid, and despite the array of sharp weapons around here, I don't think you are prepared to murder me, either."

"We do what we must," growled Foxglove.

"That is enough, Foxglove," said Pusch-Grohla.

The moss maiden lowered her head. Serilda couldn't help the burble of enjoyment she felt at seeing her chastised.

"I cannot offer you sanctuary," said Pusch-Grohla.

"Cannot? Or will not?"

Pusch-Grohla's knuckles tightened around her staff. "My granddaughters are capable of withstanding the call of the hunt. Are you?"

Serilda froze, her mind flooding with foggy memories. A powerful steed beneath her. The wind tossing her hair. Laughter spilling from her own lips. Blood splattered across the snow.

Her father—there one moment. Gone the next.

Shrub Grandmother nodded knowingly. "He would find you even here, and your presence would be putting us all at risk. But you are correct. We will not be killing you. You once saved two of my granddaughters, and while that debt was paid, my gratitude remains. Perhaps I have another way."

She unbent her legs and used the walking stick to stand on top of her rock, so that she was nearly eye level with Serilda. She beckoned her closer.

Serilda tried not to look afraid as she approached.

"You understand the repercussions should Erlkönig amass enough golden chains to capture a god, do you not?"

"I believe I do," she whispered.

"And you will never seek to implore this Vergoldetgeist to spin more gold for that monster?"

She swallowed. "I swear it."

"Good." Pusch-Grohla hummed. "I am keeping this gold thread. In exchange, I will try to help you be free of him. I cannot promise it will work, and should it fail, we will rely on you to keep your promise. If you betray us, then you will not live to see another moon."

Despite her threat, hope fluttered in Serilda's chest. It was the first time in a long while she'd dared to think freedom might be possible.

"I will speak with my herbalist to see if we can prepare a potion suitable for one in your condition. If it is possible, then I will send a message to you by sundown tonight."

Serilda's brow furrowed. "My condition?"

The woman's mouth tightened into a thin smile. She lowered the staff and beckoned Serilda closer. And closer still, until Serilda could detect the scent of damp cedar and cloves on her breath.

The old woman was silent a long time, studying Serilda, until the corner of her mouth lifted tauntingly. "Should we fail, and the king summons you again, you will tell him nothing of this visit."

"You have my word."

The woman cackled quietly. "One does not get to be as old and admired as me by trusting every brittle creature that dares to make a promise." She tipped her staff forward, plunking it lightly against Serilda's forehead. "You will remember our conversation, but should you ever try to find this place again, or lead anyone to us, your words will turn to gibberish and you will become as lost as a cricket in a snowstorm. If I wish to communicate with you, I will send word. Understand?"

"Send word how?"

"Do you understand?"

Serilda gulped. She was not sure that she did, but she nodded anyway. "Yes, Shrub Grandmother."

Pusch-Grohla nodded, then thwacked her stick on the side of her rock. "Meadowsweet, have the girl returned to her home in Märchenfeld. We do not wish for her to come to any harm in the forest."

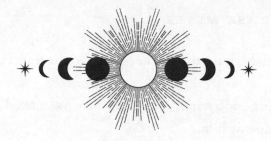

Chapter 45

She did not immediately realize what she had promised. Or what it would mean. The truth, when it hit, was as startling as a thunderclap.

She would never see Gild again.

Or Leyna. Lorraine. Frieda. Everyone who had been so kind to her. Who had accepted her more easily than almost anyone in Märchenfeld ever had.

She would never know what had become of her mother.

She would never know the secrets of Adalheid Castle and its royal family, or understand why the dark ones had abandoned Gravenstone, or why drudes seemed to be guarding a room with a tapestry and a cage, or figure out whether or not Gild really was a ghost, or if he was something else.

She would never see him again.

And she couldn't even say goodbye.

She managed to hold her tears inside until the moss maidens abandoned her at the edge of the forest. In every direction she saw emerald-green pastures. A herd of goats grazed on a hillside.

There was a flurry of noise from a crop of fig trees, and a moment later, a flock of crows took to the skies, swirling in the air for a few long minutes before soaring over to a different field.

She started down the road on her own, and the tears came flooding forward.

He wouldn't understand. After what they had shared, she felt like she was abandoning him.

An eternity of loneliness. Of never again feeling warm embraces, gentle kisses. *Her* torment would eventually end. She would grow old and die, but Gild . . . he would never be free.

And he would never know what had become of her.

He would never know that she had started to love him.

She hated that these were the thoughts clawing at her most, when she knew she should be grateful that Shrub Grandmother offered to help her. From the beginning, she'd known it was possible that she would either die at the Erlking's hand or be in service to him for the rest of her life, and perhaps even beyond. But now there might be a different fate for her, one that didn't involve her desperate and foolish attempts to avenge her father and murder the Erlking (a fantasy that even she could not believe might actually happen). It was remarkable. It was a gift.

She didn't like to give much credit to her godparent, but she couldn't help wondering if the wheel of fortune had finally turned in her favor.

Though Pusch-Grohla had not been sure that whatever she was planning would work.

If it did not . . . if it failed . . . then nothing had been solved. She still could not escape. She was still a prisoner.

And now she knew that, no matter what happened, she could never ask Gild to spin straw for her again. By asking Gild to help her, she was helping the Erlking. She'd known this—they'd both known this. But his reasons had seemed . . . unimportant before. Certainly, whatever he needed the gold for, it was worth saving her own life. She'd told herself that, and been convinced it was true.

But now she knew better.

What would the king do if he captured a god? If he claimed a wish? Would he return Perchta from Verloren?

This possibility was terrible enough. The stories of the Erlking and the wild hunt were wretched—stolen children and a trail of lost spirits. But the stories of Perchta were a thousand times worse, tales she would never tell the children. Whereas the Erlking liked to give chase to his prey and brag of his conquests, Perchta had liked to play. They say that she enjoyed letting her prey think it had escaped, slipped away . . . only to stumble back into her trap. Over and over again. She liked to wound the beasts of the forests and watch them suffer. She was unsatisfied by a quick death, and no amount of torment seemed to slake her bloodlust.

And those were animals.

The way she toyed with mortals was no better. To the huntress, humans were just as viable prey as stags and boar. Preferred, even, because they had enough sense to know they had no chance against the hunt, but they kept fighting anyway.

She was cruelty incarnate. A monster through and through.

She could not be unleashed on the mortal world again.

But maybe the Erlking's wish would not be to summon Perchta from the underworld. What else might such a man long for? The destruction of the veil? Freedom to reign over mortals, not only his dark ones? A weapon, or dark magic, or an entire army of the undead to serve him?

Whatever the answer, she didn't want to find out.

He could not get his wish.

It might be too late. They might have already spun enough for him to hunt and capture a god on the Endless Moon. But she had to hope that wasn't the case. She had to hope.

She crested a hill and saw the familiar roofs of Märchenfeld in the distance, tucked into its little valley by the river. Any other day, her heart might have lifted to be so close to home.

But it wasn't truly a home, not anymore. Not with her father gone.

She glanced toward the sky. There was still a couple of hours until sunset, when Pusch-Grohla had promised to send word and tell Serilda whether or not she would be able to aid her. A couple of hours until she might be given some idea of her fate.

When the mill came into view, Serilda felt no sense of the joy and relief she had when she'd returned after the Hunger Moon.

Except—there was smoke curling up from one of the chimneys.

She paused and at first she thought that someone was in her home. That, maybe, *Papa* was in her home—!

But then she realized that the smoke was coming from the chimney behind the house, in the gristmill, and that flutter of hope sank back into the pain of loss.

Only Thomas Lindbeck, she thought, working in her father's absence. As she made her way down the hill, she could see that the Sorge River was higher now than when she'd left, swelling from the melting snow in the mountains. The waterwheel was churning at a good clip. If the mill wasn't already in demand from their neighbors, it would be soon.

She knew that she should go talk to Thomas. Thank him for keeping everything running while she was gone. Maybe she should even tell him the truth. Not that her father had been taken from the wild hunt and thrown from his horse, but that he had an accident. That he was dead. That he would never be coming back.

But Serilda's heart was too heavy and she didn't want to talk to anyone, least of all Thomas Lindbeck.

Pretending that she hadn't noticed the smoke, she went into her home. Shutting the door behind her, she spent a moment looking around at the barren room. There was a chill in the air and dust on every surface. The spinning wheel, which they hadn't been able to sell before leaving for Mondbrück, had thin lines of spiderwebbing on the spokes.

Serilda tried to picture a future in which she could stay here. Was there any hope that Pusch-Grohla could help her in a way that she might actually be safe from the Erlking? That she could keep her childhood home?

She doubted it. Probably she would have to run somewhere still. Somewhere very far away.

But this time she would be alone.

If it was possible at all. He was a hunter. He would come for her. He would never stop coming for her.

Who was she to think that would ever change?

With a heavy heart, she sank onto her cot, though there were no longer any blankets. She stared at the ceiling she'd been staring up at her whole life, and waited for the sun to set, and this mysterious messenger to come to her aid.

Or to confirm her fears—that there was no hope at all.

She had been wallowing in these thoughts for some time when she began to notice a strange noise.

Serilda frowned and listened.

Scuffling.

Chewing.

Probably rats had gotten into the walls.

She made a face, wondering if she cared enough to try and set traps for them. Probably not. They would be Thomas's problem soon enough.

But then she felt guilty. This was her father's mill, his life's work. And it was still her home, even if it no longer felt that way. She couldn't let it fall into disrepair, not so long as she could do something about it.

She grumbled and sat up. She would need to go into town for the traps, and that would have to wait until tomorrow. But for now she could at least try to figure out where they had gotten in.

She shut her eyes and listened some more. At first there was silence, but after a while she heard it again.

Scratching.

Gnawing.

Louder than before.

She shuddered. What if it was an entire family of rats? She knew the millstones and waterwheel could be loud, but still, hadn't Thomas heard that? Was he already so derelict in the work her father had entrusted to him?

She swung her legs over the cot. Crouching down, she inspected where the walls met the floor, searching for small holes that the vermin might have gotten in. She saw nothing.

"Must be on the mill side," she muttered. And again, she wanted to ignore it. And again, she chastised herself for those thoughts.

At least, if Thomas was still there, she could chastise *him* for his negligence. Rodents were drawn to mills—to the scraps of wheat and rye and barley left behind in the process. It was imperative that they were kept clean. She supposed he ought to learn this now if he was going to become the new miller of Märchenfeld.

With a huff, she rebraided her hair, still filthy from the trek through the underground tunnel and the forest, and headed out, rounding the corner toward the mill.

The millstones were not in operation when she pulled open the door, and from this side of the wall she could hear the noises much louder.

She strode in. The room was sweltering hot, as if the fire had been roaring for days.

A figure was bent over near the fireplace.

"Thomas!" she shouted, angry hands on her hips. "Can't you hear that? There are rats in the walls!"

The figure stiffened and stood tall, his back to Serilda.

Apprehension shot through her. The figure was shorter than Thomas Lindbeck. Broader in the shoulders. Wearing clothing that was filthy and tattered.

"Who are you?" she demanded, gauging how close she was to the tools that hung on the wall, in case she needed to grab a weapon.

But then the figure started to turn. His movements were jerky and stiff. His face pale.

But his eyes met hers and suddenly her head was spinning, her chest tight with disbelief. "Papa?"

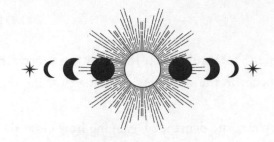

Chapter 46

He shambled a couple of steps toward her, and though Serilda's first instinct was to sob and throw herself into his arms, a second, stronger instinct kept her feet rooted to the ground.

This was her father.

And *not* her father.

He was still wearing the same clothes as when he'd been lured away by the hunt, but his shirt was little more than dirt-crusted and blood-stained tatters. His shoes were missing entirely.

His arm was . . .

It was . . .

Serilda didn't know what to make of it, but her stomach turned at the sight and she thought she might heave onto the gristmill floor.

His arm looked like a haunch of pork strung up over the butcher's table in the market. Most of the skin was gone, revealing flesh and gristle beneath. Near his elbow, she could see all the way to the bone.

And his mouth. His chin. The front of his chest.

Covered in blood.

His *own* blood?

He took another step toward her, running his tongue along the edges of his mouth.

"Papa," she whispered. "It's me. Serilda."

He had no reaction, other than a spark of something in his eye. Not recognition. Not love.

Hunger.

This was not her father.

"Nachzehrer," she breathed.

His lips pulled back, revealing bits of flesh stuck in his teeth. As if he despised the word.

Then he lunged for her.

Serilda screamed. Yanking open the door, she ran out into the yard. She would have thought him to be slow, but the promise of flesh seemed to have awoken something in him and she could feel him at her back.

Fingernails grabbed the cloth of her dress. She was thrown to the ground. The breath was knocked from her and she rolled away a few feet, before stopping on her back. Her father's mutilated body stood over her. He was not breathing hard. There was no emotion at all in his eyes beyond that dark craving.

He dropped to his knees and grasped her wrist in both arms, eyeing it like a blood sausage.

Serilda's other hand flailed around until her fingers landed on something hard. As her father bent his head toward her flesh, she swung the rock at the side of his head.

His temple caved in easily, like a rotten fruit. He dropped her arm and snarled.

With a yowl, Serilda swung again, but this time he dodged back and scampered from her reach, reminding her of a feral animal.

His expression was more wary now, but no less eager, as he crouched a few feet away, trying to determine how to get at his supper.

Serilda sat up, trembling, gripping the rock, bracing for him to come at her again.

He seemed distressed as he stared at her. Afraid of the rock, but not willing to let his prey go. He lifted his hand and gnawed absently on his pinkie finger—until she heard the bone snap and the tip of the finger disappeared between his teeth.

Serilda's stomach kicked.

He must have decided that her flesh would be better than his own, because he spit out the digit and lurched at her again.

This time, she was more prepared.

This time, she remembered what to do.

She curled her legs closer so he would not try to grab her feet, then lifted her arms in front of her face like a shield.

And as soon as he was close enough, she jabbed her hand forward and shoved the stone into his open mouth.

His jaw locked around it, the end of the rock jutting a few inches beyond his bloodied lips. His eyes widened and for a moment his jaw continued to work, his teeth grinding against the stone, as if he meant to try and devour it. But then his body slumped, the energy draining away, and he collapsed onto his back, arms and legs hitting the earth with soft thuds.

Serilda scrambled to her feet. She was covered in sweat. Her pulse was racing, her breaths ragged.

For a long time, she couldn't bring herself to move, afraid that if she took a single step in any direction, this monster would rear back to life and come at her again.

He looked dead now. A corpse with rotting flesh and a rock stuck in its jaw. But she knew she had only paralyzed him. She knew that the only way to truly kill a nachzehrer was . . .

She shuddered. She didn't want to think about it. She didn't want to do it. She didn't think she could—

A shadow appeared in the corner of her vision. Serilda cried out, as a square-headed shovel swung overhead.

It landed with a sickening thump, the shovel's edge being driven through the monster's throat. The figure stepped forward, placed a foot on the shovel's head for leverage, and shoved, severing the head clean through.

Serilda swayed on her feet. The world darkened around her.

Madam Sauer turned and shot her a disgruntled look. "All those disgusting stories you tell, and you don't know how to kill a nachzehrer?"

(

Together, she and Madam Sauer had carried the body to the river, filled his clothes with stones, and let it and the disembodied head sink to the bottom. Serilda felt like she was living in a nightmare, but she hadn't yet woken up.

"He was my father," Serilda said despondently, once some of the shock had passed.

"*That* was not your father."

"No, I know. I would have done it. I just . . . needed a moment."

Madam Sauer snorted.

Serilda's heart was heavy as one of the rocks that had dragged her father's body to the bottom of the river. She had known he was gone for months now. She had not expected him to come back. And yet, there had always been a slim hope. A tiny chance that he might still be alive and trying to make his way back to her. She had never given up on him completely.

Yet, somehow, the truth had been even worse than her nightmares. Not only had her father been dead all this time, he'd been a monster. An undead thing, feasting on his own flesh, making his way back to his daughter—not out of love, but hunger. Nachzehrer came back from the dead so they could devour their own family members. To think that her simple, shy, warm-hearted father had been reduced to such a fate made her stomach roil. He hadn't deserved such a fate. Serilda wished she could have a moment alone. She needed quiet and solitude. She needed a good, long cry.

But as she trudged back to the cottage, Madam Sauer followed stubbornly behind.

Serilda spent a moment looking around and wondering if she should offer food or drink, but she didn't have anything *to* offer.

"Would you go change?" Madam Sauer snapped, making herself comfortable on Serilda's cot, which was the only remaining piece of furniture beside the spinning wheel's stool. "You smell like a slaughter-house."

Serilda looked down at her muck-covered dress. "I have nothing to change into. I have one other dress, but it's in Adalheid. The rest of my clothes were taken to Mondbrück."

"Ahh, yes. When you tried to *run*." Her tone was derisive.

Serilda blinked at her and sat on the other side of the cot. Her legs were still shaky from the ordeal. "How did you know?"

Madam Sauer raised an eyebrow at her. "It's what you told Pusch-Grohla, isn't it?"

At Serilda's perplexed look, Madam Sauer heaved a drawn-out sigh. "Shrub Grandmother did tell you to expect aid, did she not?"

"Yes, but . . . but you're . . ."

The old woman stared at her, waiting.

Serilda gulped.

"You know Shrub Grandmother?"

"Of course I do. The moss maidens came to me this evening and explained your difficult situation. I've been trying to keep an eye on you since the Snow Moon, but you just had to run off to Mondbrück, then Adalheid. If you would ever deign to listen to me—"

"You know the *moss maidens*?"

Madam Sauer balked. "Great gods. And you were *my* pupil? Yes, I know them. Also, keep your voice down." She glanced toward the windows. "I do not think his spies yet know of your return to Märchenfeld, but we cannot be too careful."

Serilda followed her look. "You know about the Erl—"

"Yes, yes, enough of that." Madam Sauer impatiently flicked her hand through the air. "I sell them herbs. The forest folk, obviously, not the dark ones. Also poultices, potions, and the like. They have good healing magic, but not much grows in Asyltal. Not enough sun."

"Wait," whispered Serilda, astonished. "Are you telling me that you're *actually* a witch? A real one?"

Madam Sauer gave her a look that could curdle milk.

Serilda clasped a hand over her mouth. "You are!"

"I have no magic in me," she corrected. "But there is magic in plants, and I am quite good with them."

"Yes, I know. Your garden. I just never thought . . ."

Except, she had thought. A hundred times she'd thought of her as a witch, called her as much behind her back. She gasped. "Do you have an alpine newt for a familiar?"

The woman's expression turned baffled. "What are you—? No, of course not!"

Serilda's shoulders sank, more than a little disappointed.

"Serilda—"

"Is that why the moss maidens were here?"

"Hush!"

"Sorry. Is that why the moss maidens were here, on the Snow Moon last winter?"

Madam Sauer nodded. "And I understand that Shrub Grandmother was grateful for your involvement in seeing two of her granddaughters returned unharmed, which is why she has sent me to see if I might be able to help you."

"But how can you help me? I can't run away from him. I already tried that."

"Of course you can't. At least, not alive."

Serilda's heart skipped. "What does that mean?"

"It means you're lucky. A death draft takes time to prepare, but we have until the Awakening Moon. It's a desperate solution. A bit like trying to milk the mice. But it just might work." She pulled a stiletto knife from her skirts. "To start, I will need some of your blood."

THE
AWAKENING
MOON

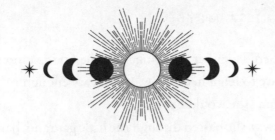

Chapter 47

The sun was bright overhead. A cool breeze made the air comfortable and sweet. Serilda stood in the garden that normally would be starting to flourish with peas and asparagus, beans and spinach, but this year, in her absence, had mostly gone to weeds. At least the cherry and apricot trees were growing heavy with fruit. The fields in every direction were bright green, and far off to the south, Serilda could see a herd of sheep in their fluffy coats grazing on one of the hills. The river was running strong and she could hear the constant creaking and splashing of the waterwheel behind the mill.

Altogether, it was as perfect as a painting.

She wondered if she would ever see it again.

Sighing, she glanced toward her mother's hazelnut tree. The nachtkrapp was there again, in its favorite spot among the boughs. Always watching through those empty eyes.

"Hello again, good Sir Raven," Serilda called. "Found any plump mice this morning?"

The nachtkrapp turned its head away, and Serilda wondered whether she was just imagining the haughty snub.

"No? Well. Just be sure to leave the hearts of the local children alone. I'm rather fond of them."

It ruffled its feathers in response.

Sighing, Serilda let her gaze linger on the house a moment longer. She didn't have to feign her sorrow. It was easy enough to pretend this was the last time she would be seeing it.

Turning away, she passed through the little gate and, barefoot, made her way down to the river, to her favorite spot, where a little pool of calm water split off from the shallower rapids. As a child, she had spent hours here building castles out of mud and rocks, catching frogs, lying in the shade of a whispering willow tree and pretending to see sprites dancing among its boughs. Now, she questioned if it had all been pretend. There were times when she'd been convinced that she really had seen magic. Papa would laugh when she told him, swinging her up into his arms. *My little storyteller. Tell me what else you saw.*

She sat down on a rock that jutted from the side of the shallow bank, where she could dip her toes into the water. It was refreshingly cool. Silver minnows darted in and out of the dappled sunlight, and a cloud of tadpoles gathered between two moss-covered rocks. Soon there would be a chorus of toads every night, which usually lulled her to sleep, though her father had liked to complain about the racket.

She took in everything. The clusters of spiny quillwort sprouting up from the shallow water. The ruffled mushrooms that had sprung up against a fallen tree trunk.

She waited until she could feel their presence. She was becoming good at spotting them now, and with a glance around she spied three nachtkrapp tucked into the shadows around her.

She rested her palms behind her on the sun-warmed stone. "You can come out. I'm not afraid of you. I know you're here to keep track of me, to make sure I don't try to run away. Well, I'm not running away. I'm not going anywhere."

One of the nachtkrapp cawed softly, its wings bristling.

But they did not come closer.

"How does it work? I've wondered all year. Can he see me through your eyes? Or, your eye sockets . . . as it may be. Or are you always having to fly back to the castle and report to him, like carrier pigeons?"

This time, a louder, unruly cry from the bird highest up in the tree.

Serilda smirked. Sitting up, she slipped one hand into her pocket, feeling the smooth sides of the vial, how it fit perfectly into her palm.

"Whichever it is, I have a message for Erlkönig. I hope you'll pass it along."

Silence.

Serilda licked her lips and tried to sound rebellious.

No—she *felt* rebellious.

And she meant every word.

"Your Darkness—I am not your servant. I am not a possession for you to claim. You have stolen from me my father and my mother. I will not let you have my freedom, too. This is *my* choice."

She pulled the vial from her pocket. She was not afraid. She'd been preparing for this all month.

A *caw*, almost a shriek, echoed through the trees, so loud it startled a flock of woodlarks farther down the river. They took to the sky in a frantic escape.

Serilda uncorked the vial. Inside shimmered a liquid the color of ruby wine. It gave her hope that it might even taste good.

It did not.

As the potion hit her tongue, she tasted rot and rust, decay and death.

A night raven dove for her, knocking the vial from her hand, its talons leaving three deep scratches across her palm.

Too late.

Serilda stared at the blood rising on her hand, but already her vision was starting to blur.

Her pulse slowed.

Her thoughts grew thick and heavy. Filling up with an uncanny sense of dread, coupled with . . . peace.

She lay back, her head sinking into the patch of moss that clung to the bank. She was surrounded by the smell of earth, and she distantly thought how odd that it could be both the smell of life and the smell of death.

Her lashes fluttered.

She gasped then, or tried to, though air wasn't coming into her lungs like it should have been. Blackness was edging across her vision. But she remembered—she only just remembered.

She'd nearly forgotten. Her hand scrabbled through the mud, searching. She felt like her limbs were trapped in molasses. Where was it?

Where was . . .

She'd almost given up when her fingers found the branch from the ash tree she'd left here last week. Madam Sauer had insisted it be ash.

Don't let go.

She'd insisted. This had been important.

Serilda didn't know why.

Nothing seemed important anymore.

The scratches on her palm stung dully as she tried to hold on tight, but she no longer had control over her fingers.

She no longer wanted control.

She wanted release.

She wanted freedom.

Visions of the hunt sped through her vision. The wind stinging her eyes. The raucous cheers in her head. Her own lips pursed as she howled at the moon.

The bellows of the night ravens sounded far away now. Angry, but fading into nothing.

She had started to close her eyes when she saw it through the trees.

An early moon rising in the east, though dusk was still hours away. Competing for attention with the guileless sun, not to be ignored.

The Awakening Moon.

How fitting.

Or, if this did not go well—how ironic.

She wanted to smile, but she was too tired. Her heartbeat was slowing. Too slow.

Her fingers went cold, then numb. Soon she could feel nothing at all.

She was dying.

She might have made a mistake.

She wasn't sure she cared.

Hold tight, the witch had told her. *Don't let go.*

The silhouette of a black bird flashed through her vision, soaring northwest. Toward the Aschen Wood, toward Adalheid.

Serilda closed her eyes and sank into the ground.

She let go.

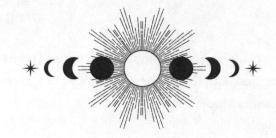

Chapter 48

Serilda lay on her side, staring at her own face, watching herself die. The wisps of dark hair that curled around her ears. The eyelashes against pale cheeks—quite dark, quite pretty—but never noticed because all anyone ever saw were the wheels in her eyes. She had never thought of herself as pretty, because no one else had ever told her she was. Other than Papa, and that hardly counted. All she ever heard was that she was odd and untrustworthy.

But she *was* sort of pretty. By no means a breathless beauty, but lovely in her own way.

Even as the last bits of color drained from her cheeks.

Even when her lips began to turn blue.

Even when her limbs began to spasm, her fingers twitching against the branch at her side, before they finally stilled and sank into the grass and mud.

Unlike all those lost souls in Adalheid Castle, hers was a soft death. Peaceful and quiet.

She felt the moment the last breath left her. Serilda looked down, pressing a hand to her body's chest. Her eyes widened as she noticed that the edges of her hand were wisping into the air like morning dew struck by the first ray of sunlight.

Then she started to fade. Her body was pulling apart. There was no pain. Just dissolving. Returning to the air and the earth, her spirit fading into everything and nothing.

Ahead of her, across the river, she spied a figure in emerald green robes, a lantern lifted high in one hand.

Beckoning her. Their presence was a comfort. A promise of rest.

Serilda took a step forward and felt something solid beneath her heel. She looked down. A stick. Nothing more.

But then—she remembered.

Hold tight.

Don't let go.

She gasped and bent down, reaching for the branch that had been stolen from an ash tree at the edge of the Aschen Wood. At first, her fingers wouldn't take hold. They slipped right through.

But she tried again, and this time, she felt the roughness of the bark.

On the third attempt, her hand wrapped around the limb, clutching it with the little bit of strength left to her.

Her spirit slowly came back together, tethered to the land of the living.

She looked up again and wondered if that was a smile worn by the god of death, before Velos and the lantern faded away.

This time, she did not let go.

(

In the hours that passed, Serilda found that she very much disliked being dead. She was gravely bored.

That's precisely how she would describe it, she thought, when she told this story to the children.

Gravely bored.

They would find it funny.

It *was* funny.

Except that it was also true. There were no people about, and even if there were, she doubted they would be able to see or communicate with her, not so long as there was daylight. She didn't know for sure—she'd never been a spirit before—but she didn't think she was the sort of traumatized, half-corporeal spirit like those that haunted the castle. She was just a wisp of a girl, all mist and rainbows and starlight, wandering along the riverbank and waiting. Even the frogs and the birds paid her no heed. She could scream and wave her arms at them, and they went right on chirping and croaking and ignoring her.

She had no jobs to complete. No one to talk to.

Nothing to do but wait.

She wished she had taken the potion at sundown. If only she'd known. The waiting was almost as tedious as spinning.

Finally, after an age and a year had seemingly passed, the sunset lit the horizon on fire. Indigo blue stretched across the sky. The first stars winked down upon the village of Märchenfeld. Night descended.

The Awakening Moon shone bright overhead, called such because the world was finally growing lush with life once more.

Except for her. Obviously. She was dead or dying or something in between.

Hours passed. The moon painted the river with streaks of silver. It alighted on the tree boughs and kissed the slumbering mill. The frogs began their concert. A colony of bats, invisible against the black sky, squeaked overhead. An owl cooed from a nearby oak.

She tried to guess at the time. She kept yawning, but that seemed to be mostly out of habit. She was not really sleepy, but she couldn't tell if that was merely because of her nerves keeping her awake, or if wandering spirits had no need of rest.

The night must be half through, she thought. Halfway until morning. Soon, the Awakening Moon would be over.

What if the hunt didn't come tonight?

Was it enough that the nachtkrapp had witnessed her demise? Would that convince the Erlking that he had lost her forever?

Would it keep him from ever looking for her again?

Though she thought she should be growing more confident as time ticked on, she felt the opposite. Anxiety clutched at her. If this didn't work, then by morning, nothing would be changed.

And if the hunt didn't come, how would she know whether or not this had—

A howl crept across the fields.

Serilda stilled. The owl, the bats, the frogs all fell silent.

She hurried to the hiding place she'd decided on while the sun was still high, climbing up into the boughs of the oak tree. She did not know if the Erlking would be able to see her, and Madam Sauer had not known, either. But collector of souls that he was, she dared not risk it.

It would have been a difficult climb, made more so by the fact that she could not let go of the ash branch even for a second. But her spirit form was almost weightless and she no longer had to worry about scrapes or bruises or falling to her death. Soon she was tucked into the branches, lush with leaves.

Once settled, she did not have long to wait. The howls grew closer, soon joined by the cacophony of hooves. This was no aimless search for prey.

They were coming for her.

She spotted the hounds first, their bodies alight with embers. They must have been able to track her scent, for they did not hesitate at the cottage, but raced straight toward the riverbank and Serilda's lifeless body lying in the mud. The hounds formed a ring around the figure, growling and pawing at the ground, but none of them touched her.

The Erlking and his hunters arrived moments later. The horses halted.

Serilda held her breath—needlessly, as there was no breath to hold. Her fingers grasped the limb of the ash tree.

The Erlking nudged his steed closer, so that he was looking down upon Serilda's body. She wished she could read his expression, but his face was turned toward the ground, his curtain of black hair hiding what little she might have seen.

The moment drew out. She could sense the hunters growing restless.

Finally, the king dismounted his horse and knelt over the body. Serilda craned her neck, but she could not see what he was doing. She thought he might have picked up the empty vial. Perhaps he traced her cheek with the pad of his thumb. He might have put something into her palm.

Then he rejoined the hunt. With a single wave of his arm, they disappeared back into the night.

Afraid that they would return, Serilda stayed in the oak tree while the howls faded away. As the first hints of light emerged in the east, she finally made her way back to the ground. She approached her body with both curiosity and dread.

Watching herself die had been strange, but seeing herself *dead* seemed like a different matter entirely.

But it was not her colorless skin or utter stillness that she took notice of first.

It was the gift that the Erlking had left behind.

In her corpse's hand was one of the king's arrows, tipped with shining gold.

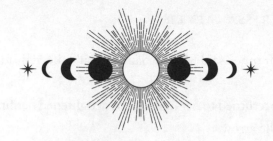

Chapter 49

Madam Sauer arrived just past dawn. Serilda was waiting, standing barefoot in the river and marveling at how the water passed right through her without so much as a ripple.

When she saw the witch approaching over the hill, she broke into a grin and started to wave, but evidently not even a witch could see her.

Trudging through the mud, she sat down beside her body and waited, watching curiously as Madam Sauer crouched over her body and felt for a pulse at her throat. Then she noticed the arrow. The witch stilled, a scowl creasing the corners of her lips.

But she soon gave herself a shake and took a new vial from the folds of her skirts. Uncorking it, she lifted the body's head and let the liquid dribble between her parted lips.

Serilda could almost taste it. Clover and mint and peas fresh from the vine. She closed her eyes, trying to discern more of the flavors—

And when she opened them again, she was lying on her back, staring up at a lavender sky. Her gaze slid over to Madam Sauer, who gave her a satisfied smirk.

It worked, she said, or tried to say, but her throat was dry as parchment and the words came out as little more than a raspy breath.

"Take your time," said Madam Sauer. "You've been dead nearly a full day."

As feeling returned to her limbs, Serilda tightened her fingers around the shaft of the arrow.

"A parting gift?" asked the witch.

Still unable to speak, Serilda smiled weakly.

With the older woman's help, she managed to sit up. Her backside was soaked through, her cloak and the hem of her dress caked with mud. Her skin was cold to the touch.

But she was alive.

After some coughing and a lot of throat clearing and drinking some water from the river, finally Serilda found her voice. "It worked," she whispered. "He thinks I'm dead."

"Do not praise the day before the evening," warned Madam Sauer. "We will not know for sure that the ruse was successful until the next full moon. You should hide until then, and have wax for your ears, perhaps even chain yourself into bed. And I would advise that you never return to this place again."

The thought of it made Serilda dizzy with sadness, but also a fair amount of hope. Was she really free?

It seemed almost possible.

The rest of her life was before her.

Without her father. Without the mill. Without Gild . . . but also without the Erlking.

"I will help you."

She glanced up, surprised at the expression of softness on Madam Sauer's face.

"You are not entirely alone."

Serilda could have wept with gratitude for such simple words, even if she wasn't yet sure that she believed them.

"I feel I owe you an apology," she said, "for all those mean-hearted stories I told about you over the years."

Madam Sauer huffed. "I am not some weak-willed daisy. I care nothing for your stories. If anything, I rather like knowing that the children are afraid of me. As they well should be."

"Well, I find it rather heartening to know that you are a witch. I like it when my lies turn into truths."

"I would tell you to keep that to yourself, but . . . well, no one will believe you even if you do tell them."

The loud, rapid clop of a galloping horse drew their attention toward the road. To the north of the mill, a little bridge passed over the river, and they could see a single rider on a horse racing across. Serilda climbed to her feet, and for a short, gleeful moment, she imagined her father returning with Zelig.

But no—Zelig had been left behind in Adalheid, and her father was never coming home.

It wasn't until the man started yelling that Serilda recognized him. Thomas Lindbeck.

"Hans! Goodman Moller!" he called, breathless. Panicked. "Serilda!"

With a quick glance to the witch, Serilda lifted her heavy, wet skirts and climbed up the riverbank toward him. She didn't relish the idea of having to explain such an early visit from the schoolmistress or why she was covered in river filth, but—what did it matter?—everyone already thought she was odd.

Thomas stopped his horse by the garden gate, but did not dismount. He cupped his hands together and yelled again. "Hans! Seril—"

"I'm here," she said, startling him so badly he nearly toppled off his horse. "Father is still in Mondbrück." She and Madam Sauer had thought it best to continue that lie. Soon, she would tell everyone that her father had gotten sick and she needed to travel to Mondbrück to care for him. From there, Madam Sauer would spread the rumor that he had died, and Serilda, in her grief, had decided to sell the mill and never return. "And Hans certainly isn't here. Whatever is the matter?"

"Have you seen him?" Thomas asked, trotting the horse closer. By all accounts, it was almost unforgivably rude for him to stay perched on his horse staring down at her, but his expression was so harried, Serilda hardly noticed. "Have you seen Hans? Has he been here this morning?"

"No, of course not. Why would he—"

But Thomas was already yanking on the reins, swerving the horse around in the other direction.

"Wait!" Serilda cried. "Where are you going?"

"Into town. I have to find him." His voice started to break.

Lurching forward, Serilda grabbed for the reins. "What's going on?"

Thomas met her eyes and, to her astonishment, did not flinch away. "He's gone. Went missing from his bed last night. If you see him—"

"Last night?" Serilda interrupted. "You don't think . . ."

The haunted look that twisted his face was answer enough.

When children went missing on the night of a full moon, it was easy to guess what had become of them.

She set her jaw. "I'm coming with you. I can help look. Drop me off in town and I'll go to the Weber farm to see if they've heard anything, and you can check with the twins."

He nodded and lent his elbow as she leaped up into the saddle behind him.

"Serilda."

She jolted. She'd almost forgotten about the witch.

"Madam Sauer!" exclaimed Thomas. "What are you doing here?"

"Consulting with my assistant over this week's lessons," she said quite easily, as if lying was not a punishable offense after all. In different times, Serilda might have pointed out her hypocrisy.

Madam Sauer fixed a stern gaze on Serilda, one that had often made her feel as if she were barely an inch tall. "You should not be riding."

Serilda frowned. Riding. The horse?

"Why ever not?"

Madam Sauer opened her mouth, but hesitated. Then shook her head. "Just—be careful. Don't do anything rash."

Serilda exhaled. "I won't," she said.

Madam Sauer's expression darkened.

Just one more lie.

Thomas dug his heels into the horse's sides and they dashed off. He did as Serilda had suggested, dropping her off at the crossroads so that she could run the rest of the way to the Weber farm while he went to look for Hans at the twins' home.

Serilda refused to think the impossible. Would the hunt have taken Hans to punish her? To send her a warning?

If the Erlking had taken him . . . if the hunt had done this and Hans was gone, killed or stolen behind the veil . . . then it was her fault.

Maybe not, she tried to tell herself. They had only to find him. He was hiding. Playing a prank. Which was out of character for the stalwart boy, but maybe Fricz had set him up to it?

But all those desperate pleas shattered as soon as the Weber cottage came into view. As idyllic as always, surrounded by pastureland and grazing sheep, Serilda felt an ominous chill sweep over her.

The Weber family were all gathered on their front stoop. Little Marie was clutching at her grandmother. Baby Alvie was swaddled in his mother's arms. Anna's father was trying to saddle their horse, a speckled gelding that Serilda had always thought was one of the finest-looking horses in town. But the man's movements were clumsy, and as she approached, she could see that he was trembling.

Her eyes searched their faces, all gripped with terror. The elder Mother Weber had a handkerchief pressed against her mouth.

Serilda searched and searched. The garden, the front door left open, the road and the fields.

All the family was there . . . except for Anna.

As Serilda got closer, they all startled and turned toward her with flitting hope that immediately came crashing back down.

"Miss Moller!" cried Anna's father, tightening the bridle. "Do you have word? Have you seen Anna?"

She swallowed hard, and slowly shook her head.

Their expressions fell. Anna's mother buried her face into her daughter's hair and sobbed.

"We woke up and she was just . . . gone," said Anna's father. "I know she's headstrong, but it isn't like her to just—"

"Hans is missing, too," Serilda said. "And I worry"—her voice caught, but she forced out the words—"I worry they aren't the only ones. I think the hunt—"

"No!" bellowed Anna's father. "You can't know that! She's just . . . she's just . . ."

A black shape in the sky drew Serilda's eye upward to a patchy pair of wings showing glimpses of blue sky between the feathers. The nachtkrapp circled lazily above the field.

The king knew.

His spies had been watching all year, and he knew. He knew precisely which children Serilda taught, the ones she adored. The ones that would hurt her the most.

"Goodman Weber," said Serilda, "I'm so very sorry, but I must take this horse."

He jolted. "What? I need to go find her! My daughter—"

"Was taken by the wild hunt!" she snapped. While he was stunned speechless, she snatched the reins and sprang up into the saddle. The family cried in outrage, but Serilda ignored them. "Forgive me!" she said, trotting the horse far enough away that Anna's father couldn't grab her. But he didn't make a move, just gawked, speechless. "I will bring him back as soon as I can. And if I can't, then I will leave him at the Wild Swan in Adalheid. Someone will return him, I promise. And I hope . . . I will try to find Anna. I will do everything I can."

"What in all of Verloren are you doing?" Anna's grandmother hollered, the first to find her voice. "You say she's been taken by the wild hunt, and now you think . . . what? That you're going to *get her back*?"

"Precisely," said Serilda. Pressing her foot into the stirrup, she cracked the reins.

The horse bolted from the yard.

As she passed through Märchenfeld, she saw that nearly everyone had emerged from their homes and were gathered near the linden tree at the town's center, talking in frightened whispers. She spied Gerdrut's parents, her mother's belly round with child, crying while her neighbors tried to comfort her.

Serilda's lungs squeezed until she thought she would not be able to breathe at all. This road did not travel past the twins' home, but she did not have to see their family to know that Fricz and Nickel would be missing, too.

She lowered her head and urged the horse to run. No one tried to stop her, and she wondered if any of them would guess at her guilt.

This was her fault.

Coward. Fool. She wasn't brave enough to face the Erlking. She wasn't smart enough to trick him out of this game.

And now five innocent children had been taken.

The road blurred beneath the horse's hooves as she left the town behind. The morning sun glistened off fields of wheat and rye, but ahead of her the Aschen Wood loomed, dense and unwelcoming. But she wasn't afraid of it anymore. There might be monsters and forest folk and creepy salige, but she knew the true dangers lurked beyond the wood, inside a haunted castle.

She was nearly to the woods when the birds caught her eye. At first she thought it was more nachtkrapp, an entire flock of them swarming above the road. But as she drew closer she could see it was just crows, cawing and screeching at her as she approached.

Her gaze fell.

Her lungs sputtered.

A figure lay half across the road and half in the ditch.

A child, with two dark braids and a pastel-blue nightgown streaked with mud.

"Anna?" she breathed. The horse had barely slowed before she was jumping out of the saddle and racing toward the figure. The girl was lying on her side, facing away, and she might be merely sleeping or unconscious. That was what the wild hunt did, she told herself, even as she was falling to her knees at Anna's side. They lured people from their homes. Tempted them with a night of wild abandon, then left them cold and alone on the edge of the Aschen Wood. So many had woken up disoriented, hungry, maybe embarrassed—but alive.

It had been a threat, that was all.

Next time would be worse.

The king was toying with her. But the children would be all right. They had to be—

She grabbed Anna's shoulder and rolled her onto her back.

Serilda cried out and fell backward, pushing herself away. The image seared into her mind.

Anna. Skin too pale. Lips faintly blue. The front of her nightgown painted red.

There was a ragged hole where her heart had been. Muscle and sinew gaping open. Bits of cartilage and broken rib bone visible in the thick, drying blood.

This was what the scavenger birds had been feasting on.

Serilda staggered to her feet, backing away. Turning, she braced herself on her knees and heaved into the ditch, though there was little to come up but bile and whatever remained of the witch's potions.

"Anna," she gasped, swiping at her mouth with the back of her hand. "I'm so sorry."

Though she didn't want to see it again, she forced herself to look Anna in the face. Her eyes were wide-open. Her face frozen in fear.

She had never stopped moving. Always with her acrobatics and her tricks. Always dancing, fidgeting, rolling through the grass. Madam Sauer had chastised her nonstop, while Serilda had loved it about her.

And now.

Now she was *this*.

It wasn't until she palmed the tears from her eyes that she saw the second body, a little farther up the road, half buried in the brambles that grew wild in the summer.

Bare, muddied feet and a linen nightshirt down to his knees.

Serilda stumbled closer.

Fricz was on his back, his chest as cavernous as Anna's had been. Silly Fricz. Always laughing, always teasing.

Tears streaming fast down her cheeks now, Serilda dared to look past him. To take in the full stretch of road between these two murdered children and the Aschen Wood.

She saw Hans next. He had grown so tall this spring, and she'd barely been around to notice. He had always idolized Thomas and his other brothers. He had so yearned to grow up.

His heart had been ripped clean out of him.

Or—eaten out of him, for Serilda wondered if this was the work of the nachtkrapp.

Perhaps a gift for their loyal service to the hunt.

It took longer, but finally she found Nickel, too. He was lying on his stomach in a tiny creek that would eventually meet up with the Sorge.

His honey-colored hair was dark and matted with blood. He had lost so much of it that the downstream current was tinted pink.

Sweet Nickel. More patient, more empathetic, than any of them.

Weary and heartbroken, Serilda returned for the horse before she continued her search. She held it by the reins so it wouldn't run off as she walked slowly along the road, searching as far as her eyes could see.

But she reached the shadows of the trees, having found no one else.

Little Gerdrut was not there.

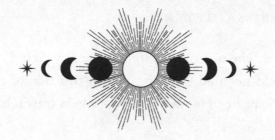

Chapter 50

She blindfolded the horse so it would not spook as they entered the Aschen Wood. To take the long path around the forest was unthinkable—and besides, this was clearly the way the hunt had gone. In the daylight, they would have vanished back behind the veil, but what if Gerdrut was still here in the woods? Serilda's eyes darted back and forth along the edges of the road, searching the brambles and weeds, the thick overgrowth crowding onto the dirt path. Looking for signs of scavengers and blood and a tiny, crumpled body abandoned in the wild.

For once, the forest held no allure for her. Its mystery, its dark murmurs. She paid them no heed. She did not search the distant trees for signs of forest folk. She did not listen for whispers calling to her. If any apparition waited to dance upon a bridge, if any beast wished to coax her into their realm, they were disappointed. Serilda had thoughts only for little Gerdrut, the last missing child.

Could she still be alive? She had to believe. She had to hope.

Even if that meant the Erlking was holding her, a treasure to coax Serilda back to his domain.

She emerged from the trees with no answers to her questions. There was no sign of the child, not in the woods, not at the edge of the forest as Adalheid's wall came into view.

By the time she was riding through the city, Serilda was certain that she would not find Gerdrut. Not on this side of the veil. The Erlking had kept her. He wanted there to be a reason for Serilda to come back.

And so, here she was. Terrified. Desperate. Full of a guilt almost too painful to bear. But more than that, a rage had begun to simmer from her fingertips to her toes, building inside her with suffocating force.

He had killed them as if it was nothing. Such brutal deaths. And what for? Because he felt slighted? Betrayed? Because he wanted to send Serilda a message? Because he needed more *gold*?

He was a monster.

She would find a way to rescue Gerdrut. That was all she could care about right now.

But someday, somehow, she would avenge the others. She would find a way to repay the Erlking for what he had done.

The horse reached the end of the main thoroughfare, the castle looming before her. She turned and headed toward the inn, ignoring the curious glances that followed her. Always, her appearance made such a stir in this town, even if many of the townspeople had grown familiar with her. But today, her expression must have been its own warning. She felt like she was a dark cloud rolling along the shore, full of thunder and lightning.

No one dared speak to her, but she could feel their curiosity at her back.

Serilda alighted from the horse before it had come to a complete stop, and hastily tied it to a post in front of the inn. She barged in through the doors, her heart choking her.

She ignored the faces that turned toward her and marched straight to the bar, where Lorraine was putting a cork back into a bottle.

"Whatever's got into you?" she asked, looking like she was tempted to tell Serilda to go back outside and try coming back in with a better attitude this time. "And why is your dress covered in mud? You look like you slept in a pigsty."

"Is Leyna all right?"

Lorraine froze, a flicker of uncertainty flashing in her eyes. "Of course she's all right. What's happened?"

"You're sure? She wasn't taken last night?"

Lorraine's eyes widened. "Taken? You mean—"

The door to the kitchen swung open, and Serilda exhaled sharply when Leyna burst through, a tray of cured meats and cheeses in her hands.

She broke into a smile at the sight of Serilda. "Another night at the castle?" she said, her eagerness for more stories brightening her eyes.

Serilda shook her head. "Not exactly." She turned back to Lorraine and, suddenly conscious of the silence of the restaurant, lowered her voice. "Five children went missing from Märchenfeld last night. Four of them are now dead. I think he still has the fifth."

"Great gods," Lorraine whispered, pressing a hand to her chest. "So many. Why . . . ?"

"No one went missing from Adalheid?" she asked hurriedly.

"Not that I—no. No, I'm sure I would have heard."

Serilda nodded. "I have a horse posted outside. Will you stable it for me? And"—she gulped—"if I don't come back, could you please send word to the Weber family in Märchenfeld? The horse belongs to them."

"If you don't come back?" asked Lorraine, setting down the bottle. "What are you—"

"You're going to the castle," said Leyna. "But it isn't the full moon. If he took someone behind the veil, you can't reach them."

As if by instinct, Lorraine wrapped an arm around Leyna and tugged her against her side, squeezing her. Protecting her. "I heard something," she whispered.

Serilda frowned. "What?"

"This morning. I heard the hounds, and I remember thinking it was so late . . . The hunt doesn't usually come back so close to dawn. And I heard them crossing the bridge . . ." She swallowed hard, her brow tight with sympathy. "For a second, I thought I heard crying. It—it sounded like Leyna." She shuddered, wrapping her second arm around her daughter. "I had to get up and go check on her to be sure she was still asleep, and of course it wasn't her, so I started to think it might have been a dream. But now . . ."

A cold lump settled in the pit of Serilda's stomach as she started to back away from the bar.

"Wait," said Leyna, trying unsuccessfully to wriggle out of her mother's hold. "You can't get behind the veil, and the ghosts—"

"I have to try," said Serilda. "This is all my fault. I have to try."

Before they could try to talk her out of anything, she rushed from the inn. Down the road that curved along the shore of the lake. She didn't hesitate as she stepped onto the bridge, facing the castle gate. Anger sparked inside her, coupled with that twisting, sickened feeling. She imagined Gerdrut crying as she was carried across this very bridge.

Was she crying even now? Alone, but for the specters and the dark ones and the Erlking himself.

She must be so afraid.

Serilda stormed across the bridge, fists clenched at her sides, her body burning from the inside out. The castle ruins loomed ahead, the leaded and oft-broken windows clouded and lifeless. She passed through the gate, uncaring if there were an entire army of ghosts waiting to scream at her. She didn't care if she came across headless women and ferocious drudes. She could ignore all the cries of every victim this castle had ever devoured, so long as she got Gerdrut back.

But the castle stayed silent. The wind shook the branches of the wayfaring tree in the bailey, now full of vibrant green leaves. Some of the brambles that had sprouted like weeds now held red berries that would ripen to purple-black by the end of summer. A bird's nest had been built in the overhang of the half-collapsed stables, and Serilda could hear the trill of hatchlings calling for their mother.

The sound enraged her.

Gerdrut.

Sweet, precocious, brave little Gerdrut.

She entered the shadow of the entryway. This time, she did not waste time ogling the state of things, the utter devastation that time had wreaked here. She kicked her way through the brush and debris of the great hall, startling a rat who squealed and dove out of her way. She tore down the cobwebs that hung like curtains, through one doorway and then another until she reached the throne room.

"Erlkönig!" she shouted.

Her hatred echoed back to her from a dozen chambers. Otherwise the castle was still.

Stepping over a patch of broken stone, Serilda approached the center of the room. Before her stood the dais and the two thrones, held in whatever spell protected them from the destruction that had claimed the rest of the castle.

"Erlkönig!" she yelled again, demanding to be heard. She knew he was here, shrouded behind the veil. She knew he could hear her. "It's me you wanted, and I'm here. Give back the child and you can keep me. I'll never run again. I'll live here in the castle if you want, just give Gerdrut back!"

She was met with silence.

Serilda glanced around the room. At the shards of broken glass that littered the floor. The sprouts of thistles claiming the far corner, driven to live despite the lack of sunlight. At the chandeliers that had not lit this room for hundreds of years.

She looked back at the thrones.

She was so close. The veil was here, pressing against her. Something so ephemeral, it took nothing more than the light of a full moon to tear it down.

What might be happening to Gerdrut, just beyond her reach. Could she see Serilda? Was she listening, watching, begging Serilda to save her?

There had to be a way through. There had to be a way to get to the other side.

Serilda pressed her palms above her ears, urging herself to *think*.

There must be a story, she thought. Some hint in one of the old tales. There were countless fairy stories of well-meaning girls and boys falling into a well or diving into the sea, only to find themselves in enchanted lands, in Verloren, in the realms beyond. There had to be a clue as to how one could slip through the veil.

There was a way. She refused to accept otherwise.

She squeezed shut her eyes.

Why hadn't she thought to ask Madam Sauer? She was a witch. She probably knew a dozen ways to . . .

She gasped, her eyelids flying open.

Madam Sauer was a witch.

A witch.

How many times had she told the children this very thing? It had been a lie, then. A silly story, even a cruel-hearted one at times, but nothing serious. She had merely been poking fun of their grumpy teacher, whom they all shared a mutual dislike for.

But it hadn't been a story.

It had been real.

She had spoken the truth.

And how many times had she told the once-ridiculous tale that she had been marked by the god of lies?

But—her father really had made a wish upon one of the old gods. She really was marked by Wyrdith. Shrub Grandmother had confirmed it. Serilda had been right all along.

She was the godchild of the god of lies, and yet, somehow . . . all her lies were coming true.

Could she do it on purpose?

Could she tell a story and *make* it true? Or was this part of the magic of her gift, part of the wish granted to her father all those years ago?

She might be marked as a liar, but there would be truths in her words that no one could see. Maybe she wasn't a liar at all, but more like a historian. Maybe even an oracle.

Telling stories of the past that had been buried for too long.

Creating stories that might yet come to be.

Spinning something out of nothing.

Straw into gold.

She imagined the audience before her. The Erlking and his court. All his monsters and ghouls. His servants and attendants—those battered spirits—who, on this side of the veil, had to endure their deaths over and over again.

Gild was there, too, trapped somewhere in these walls. As lost as any of them.

And Gerdrut.

Watching her. Waiting.

Serilda inhaled deeply, and began.

There was once a young princess, stolen by the wild hunt, and a prince, her elder brother, who did all he could to rescue her. He rode through the forest as fast as he could, desperate to catch the hunt before she was taken forever.

But the prince failed. He could not save his sister.

He did, however, manage to vanquish Perchta, the great huntress. He shot an arrow through her heart, and watched as her soul was claimed by the god of death and dragged back to Verloren, from whence all the dark ones had once escaped.

But Perchta had been loved, adored. Almost worshipped. And the Erlking, who had never known true loss until that day, vowed that he would have vengeance on the human boy who had stolen his lover from the world of the living.

Weeks passed as the prince healed from his wounds, tended to by the forest folk. When he finally returned home to his castle, it was under the bright silver light of a full moon. He walked across the bridge and through the gates, surprised to find them unguarded. The watchtowers abandoned.

As the prince stepped into the courtyard, a stench engulfed him, one that nearly stopped his heart.

The unmistakable smell of blood.

The prince reached for his sword, but it was too late. Death had already come to the castle. No one had been spared. Not the guards, not the servants. Bodies were sprawled across the courtyard. Broken, maimed, torn to pieces.

The prince ran into the keep, shouting to anyone who might hear him. Desperately hoping there might be someone who had survived. His mother. His father. The nursemaid who had often comforted him, the sword master who had trained him, the tutors who had taught and scolded and praised him into adulthood, the stable boy who had sometimes joined in his childhood mischief.

But everywhere he went, he saw only the echo of violence. Brutality and death.

Everyone was gone.

Everyone.

The prince found himself in the throne room. He felt ripped to shreds at the extent of the massacre, but when his eyes fell on the dais, it was rage that overtook him.

The Erlking sat on the king's throne, a crossbow on his lap and a smile on his lips, while the bodies of the king and queen had been strung up like tapestries on the wall behind him.

With a wail of fury, the prince raised his sword and began to charge the villain, but in that same moment, the Erlking fired an arrow tipped in pure gold.

The prince screamed. He dropped the sword and fell to his knees, cradling his arm. The arrow had not gone completely through but remained lodged in his wrist.

With a snarl, he looked up and staggered back to his feet. "You should have aimed to kill," he told the Erlking.

But the villain merely smiled. "I do not want you dead. I want you to suffer. As I have suffered. As I will continue to suffer for the rest of time."

The prince claimed the sword with his other hand. But when he again went to charge for the Erlking—something tugged on his arm, holding him in place. He looked down at the bloodied arrow shaft trapped in his limb.

The Erlking rose from the throne. Black magic sparked in the air between them.

"That arrow now tethers you to this castle," he said. "Your spirit no longer belongs to the confines of your mortal body, but will be forever trapped within these walls. From this day into eternity, your soul belongs to me." The Erlking lifted his hands and darkness cloaked the castle, spreading through the throne room and out to every corner of that forsaken place. "I lay claim to all of this. To your family's history, your beloved name—and I curse it all. The world will forget you. Your name will be burned from the pages of history. Not even you will remember the love you might have known. Dear prince, you will be forever alone, tormented until the end of time—just as you've left me. And you will *never understand why. Let this be your fate, until your name, forgotten by all, should be spoken once more."*

The prince slumped forward, crushed beneath the weight of the curse.

Already the words of the spell were stealing through his mind. Memories of his childhood, his family, all that he had ever known and loved, were pulling apart like threads of spun yarn.

His last thought was of the stolen princess. Bright and clever, the keeper of his heart.

While he could still remember her, he looked at the Erlking with tears gathering in his eyes and managed to choke out his last words before the curse claimed him.

"My sister," he pleaded. "Have you trapped her soul in this world? Will I ever see again?"

But the Erlking merely laughed. "Foolish prince. What sister?"

And the prince could only stare, dumbfounded and hollow. He had no answer. He had no sister. No past. No memories at all.

✦

Serilda exhaled, shaken by the story that had spilled out of her and the lurid visions it had conjured. She was still alone in the throne room, but the smell of blood had returned, thick and metallic. She looked down to see the floor awash with it, dark and congealed, its surface the sheen of a black mirror. It pooled at her feet, to the base of the throne's dais, covering the broken stones, splattered across the walls.

But there was one place, only a few steps in front of her, that was untouched. A perfect circle, as if the blood had struck an invisible wall.

Serilda swallowed hard against the lump that had begun to clog her throat as she told the story. She could see it all clearly now. The prince standing amid the bloodshed in this very room. She could picture his flame-red hair. The freckles on his cheeks. The flecks of gold in his eyes. She could see his fury and his sorrow. His courage and his devastation.

She had seen it all herself—how he wore these emotions in the set of his shoulders and the quirk of his lips and the vulnerability in his gaze. She had even seen the scar on his wrist, where the arrow had pierced him. Where the Erlking had cursed him.

Gild.

Gild was the prince. This was his castle and the stolen princess was his sister and—

And he had no idea. He didn't remember any of it. He *couldn't* remember any of it.

Serilda inhaled a shaky breath and dared to finish the story, her voice barely a whisper.

"The Erlking's wicked spell was cast, his gruesome revenge complete. But the massacre that happened in that castle . . ." She paused with a shudder. "The massacre that happened here was so horrific that it tore a hole into the veil that had long separated the dark ones from the world of the living."

In response to her words, the blood on either side of that untouched circle began to flow upward. Two thick rivulets, the color of burgundy wine and thick as molasses, crawled toward the ceiling. When they were not much taller than Serilda herself, they moved inward and drew together, forming a doorway in the air. A doorway framed in blood.

Then, from the center of the doorway, the blood dripped . . . upward.

In slow, steady drops.

Climbing toward the rafters.

Serilda followed its trail, up.

Up.

To a body hung from the chandelier.

Her stomach lurched.

A child. A little girl.

For a moment, she thought it was Gerdrut and she opened her mouth to scream—

But the rope turned with a creak and she could see that it was not Gerdrut. The girl's face was almost unrecognizable.

Almost.

But she knew it was the princess she'd seen in the locket.

The kidnapped child.

Gild's sister.

Serilda wanted to rail. To howl. To tell the old gods and whoever was listening that this was not how the story was meant to end. The prince should have defeated the wicked king, saved his sister, saved them all.

He should never have been trapped in this horrid place.

He should never have been forgotten.

The Erlking was not supposed to win.

But even as her tears built up, Serilda clenched her teeth and refused to let them fall.

There was still one child who might be saved tonight. One heroic deed to perform.

With tightened fists, she stepped through the tear in the veil.

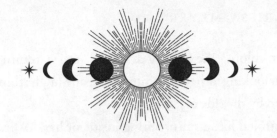

Chapter 51

The blood was gone. The castle returned to its splendor.

Serilda had only ever seen the throne room as part of the castle ruins. This was where the pool of blood had leaked between the brittle weeds and clung to her footsteps. Where the two thrones on the dais alone seemed to have been preserved in time, untouched by the centuries of neglect. They looked the same now as they did on the mortal side of the veil, but now the rest of the room was as pristine to match them. Vast chandeliers lit with dozens of candles. Thick carpets and fur skins and black velvet drapes hung behind the dais, framing the thrones. Pillars carved from white marble, each one depicting a tatzelwurm climbing toward the ceiling, its long serpentine tail spiraling all the way to the floor.

And there was the Erlking, waiting for her upon his throne.

Beside him, a sight that brought a shuddering gasp from Serilda's lips.

Hans. Nickel. Fricz. Anna.

Their little ghosts standing to either side of the throne, holes in their chests and their nightgowns stained with blood.

"Serilda!" Anna cried. She started to run off the dais, but was blocked by the king's crossbow.

She whimpered and fell back, clutching at Fricz.

"How miraculous," the Erlking drawled. "You've returned from the dead. Though looking rather unkempt. Why, one might think you spent the night dead by the side of a river."

Hatred burbled like a sulfur spring inside of her. "Why would you take them? Why would you do this?"

He shrugged mildly. "I think you know the answer to that." His fingers drummed against the crossbow handle. "I told you to stay close. To be present in Adalheid when I summoned you. Imagine my disappointment to find you were not in Adalheid. I was forced to search for you yet again—but no one was home at the mill in Märchenfeld." His eyes crystallized. "How do you think that makes me feel, Lady Serilda? That you could not be bothered to bid farewell. That you would rather *die* than assist me with one simple favor." A haughty smile touched his dark-tinted lips. "Or at least, pretend to."

"I'm here now," she said, trying to keep the tremor from her voice. "Please let them go."

"Who? *Them?* These darling little ghouls? Don't be absurd. I've claimed them for my court, now and forever. They're mine."

"No. Please."

"Even if I could *let them go,* have you considered what that would mean? Let them go home? I'm sure their families would be thrilled to have sad little ghosts haunting their sad little cottages. No, best they stay with me where they can be made useful."

"You could free their spirits," she said around a sob. "They deserve peace. They deserve to go to Verloren, to rest."

"Speak not of Verloren," he growled, sitting taller. "When Velos gives me what is mine, then I will consider releasing these souls, and not a moment sooner." His rush of anger passed as quickly as it had risen, and he leaned against one arm of the throne, resting the crossbow in his lap. "Speaking of what is owed to me, I have another task for you, Lady Serilda."

She thought of her promise to Pusch-Grohla. She had sworn she would not help the Erlking anymore.

But she was a liar, through and through.

"You took one more child," she said through gritted teeth. "If you want any more gold from me, then you will let her go. You will return her to her family, unharmed."

"You are hardly in a position to be making demands." He sighed, almost melodramatically. "She is a pretty thing, for a human. Not as pretty as the Adalheid princess. Now, *she* was a gift my love would have doted on like no other. Sweet, charming . . . *talented*. They say she was blessed by Hulda, just like you, Lady Serilda. Her death was such a waste. As will yours be, if it comes to that."

"You're trying to goad me," said Serilda through her teeth.

The Erlking smiled quite viciously. "I take my enjoyment where I can."

Serilda swallowed and glanced behind her, unsure how she should feel to see that the doorway back to the mortal world was still there.

She could leave. Could he follow her? She suspected not. If it was so easy, surely he would not have stayed confined to the veil, allowed freedom but one night each cycle of the moon.

But she couldn't leave.

Not without Gerdrut.

Her gaze traveled up toward the rafters, but the princess who had been hung from the chandelier was gone. Her body would have been disposed of long ago. Buried or tossed into the lake. Serilda knew her ghost was not here in the castle. Either she'd been left behind in Gravenstone, or sent on to Verloren. Otherwise, she was sure she would have noticed her among the ghostly servants, and Gild would have known immediately who the portrait depicted.

Gild.

Where was Gild? Where were any of the ghosts? The castle felt eerily quiet, and she wondered if the Erlking could force their silence when it pleased him to do so.

She fixed her gaze on the king again, trying hard not to think about the four trembling children beside him. The ones she had already failed.

She would not fail Gerdrut, too.

"Why did you abandon Gravenstone?" she asked, and was pleased at the surprise that flashed over his face. "Was it truly because you couldn't stand to be in the place where Perchta had fallen? Or did you choose to claim this castle as another layer of revenge against the prince who killed her? It must have felt quite satisfying at first. Do you sleep in his quarters and listen to the moans and cries of the ones you murdered all night long? Does that please you?"

"You enjoy a mystery, Lady Serilda."

"I like a good story. I like when one takes an unexpected turn. What's interesting to me is that I don't think even *you* have figured out the final twist in this tale."

The Erlking's lips curled with amusement. "That the little mortal girl will be saving everyone?"

Serilda clicked her tongue. "Don't spoil the ending for yourself," she said, proud of how brave she sounded. Though in reality, she hadn't been thinking of her own role in this tale at all. *They say she was blessed by Hulda.* That was it—the real reason the Erlking had wanted the princess. Not just for Perchta to dote on, not just because the child was so beloved among her people. He had believed that *she* was the goldspinner. He had taken her for her magic, probably so she could spin golden chains for his hunts.

To this day, centuries later, he still didn't know. He'd taken the wrong sibling.

Of course, Serilda wasn't about to tell him that.

"The story still hasn't revealed whether or not you kept the princess's ghost," she said. "Did you release her to Verloren, or is she still in Gravenstone? I understand why you couldn't bring her back here, of course. The love the prince felt for her was so strong—surely, if he saw her, he would know that she was his sister and that he loved her very much. I think that's why I haven't seen the king and queen, either. You didn't keep their ghosts. You couldn't risk them recognizing each other, or their son. Maybe it wouldn't break the curse entirely. Maybe their family and their name would still be forgotten by everyone, even themselves, but . . . that wasn't the point, was it? You wanted him to be alone, abandoned . . . without love. Forever."

The Erlking's face was that cold mask he favored, but she was coming to know his moods, and she could see the tension in his jaw.

"How do you know the things you do?" he finally asked.

Serilda had no answer for him. She could hardly tell him that she'd been cursed by the god of lies, who somehow, it seemed, was as much the god of truths.

No. Not the god of lies. The god of stories.

And every story has two sides.

"You brought me here," she said. "A mortal in your realm. I've been paying attention."

His mouth quirked to one side. "Tell me—do you know the family's name? Have you solved *that* mystery?"

She blinked.

The family's name.

The prince's name.

Slowly, she shook her head. "No. I don't."

She wasn't sure, but she thought he might have seemed relieved at this.

"Unfortunately," he said, "I am not a fan of fairy stories."

"That *is* unfortunate, as you are in so many of them."

"Yes, but I am always cast as the villain." He craned his head. "Even *you* cast me as the villain."

"It is hard not to, my lord. Why, just this morning you abandoned four children by the side of the road, their hearts devoured by nacht-krapp and their bodies left to the rest of the scavengers." Her chest squeezed and she dared not look at the spirits standing at the king's side, knowing she would dissolve into tears if she did. "I think you rather like playing the villain."

Finally, a real smile graced his features, down to the sharp points of his teeth. "And who is the hero of this story?"

"I am, naturally." Serilda hesitated a moment, before adding, "At least, I hope to be."

"Not the prince?"

It felt like a trap, but Serilda knew better. She laughed lightly. "He's had his moments. But no. This is not his story."

"Ah." He clucked his tongue. "Perhaps you are trying to save *him,* then."

Her smile wanted to fade but she clung to it. Of course she wanted to save Gild. She desperately wanted to save him from the torment he'd endured these hundreds of years. But she could not let the Erl-king know that she had met the poltergeist, or that she finally knew the truth of who and what he was.

"Once I've met him, I will let you know," she said, keeping her tone light. She made a show of looking around the throne room. "Is he here? You tethered him to this castle, so he must be around somewhere?"

"Oh, he is," said the Erlking. "And I regret it more days than not. He is a constant thorn in my side."

"Then why not release him from the curse?"

"He deserves every bit of suffering he's been given and more."

Serilda gritted her teeth. "I will keep that in mind, when I finally cross his path." She lifted her chin. "If we have a deal, then I am ready to complete your task."

His pale eyes glinted in the torchlight. "Everything is already prepared for you."

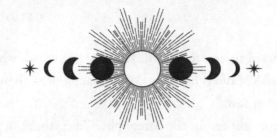

Chapter 52

As the king strode past her, Serilda ushered the children to her sides. Touching them, she remembered how it had first felt when Manfred had helped her into the carriage, so many months ago.

They were real. They were solid. But their skin was brittle and delicate and cool to the touch. They felt like they would crumple to ash, but that didn't prevent her from squeezing them into a giant hug in a hasty attempt to give some comfort.

The Erlking cleared his throat impatiently.

She gripped Anna's and Nickel's hands and followed after him, ignoring how the sensation made her skin crawl. Fricz and Hans huddled at their sides.

The king led them to the courtyard.

Emerging into daylight was bewildering enough. The castle was not ruins. She really had forced her way to this side of the veil, and now she was in the bailey beneath the bright sun. Her feet stalled.

A spinning wheel sat in the center of the yard, beside a cart laden with straw. It was a small pile, not much larger than a barrel of wine.

And all around it, gathered within the looming stone walls, were the residents of Adalheid Castle.

The hunters. The servants. The bruised stable boy, the one-eyed coachman, the headless woman. Hundreds of undead humans, and at least as many kobolds. All silent and still, their eyes upon her as she stepped into their midst.

As a group, their ephemeral figures were more pronounced. Their cumulative silhouettes wisping upward like smoke off the last remnants of a bonfire. They seemed so tenuous, as though a breath could blow them away.

She could not keep herself from scanning their faces, searching for a woman who might look a little bit like her. Hoping that one of these ghostly women might recognize the child she'd once loved, now full grown.

But if her mother was there, Serilda did not recognize her.

Her attention drifted toward the dark ones. Their graceful forms and cunning eyes. All dressed in the finest of furs and leather armor and hunting gear. They were the nobles of this castle, and as such, they stood apart from the ghostly entourage, their expressions unreadable.

The contrast between the two groups was stark. The dark ones in all their pristine, unearthly beauty. The ghosts with their battered bodies and bleeding wounds.

Then there were the creatures—nightmare drudes, snarling goblins, the soulless nachtkrapp.

All the court was there, and they were waiting for *her*.

Serilda's stomach dropped. *No.*

This would not work. There would be no more dungeons. No locked doors. The king intended for her to give a demonstration. She was his prize, and he was ready to show her off to his kingdom, just as he'd once showed off the tatzelwurm to her.

She swallowed hard and glanced around again. She didn't realize she was looking for Gild until disappointment at his absence clawed at her.

Not that it mattered.

He could not spin for her, not in front of everyone. And even if he could . . . she'd promised herself that she would not allow him to. Not again.

But that was before.

Before the children had been taken.

Before she'd realized he still had Gerdrut. That she could still save her.

"Behold," said Erlkönig, the Alder King, his eyes locked on Serilda's but his voice raised for the gathered crowd, "the Lady Serilda of März-enfeld, godchild of Hulda."

She did not look away.

"On the Snow Moon, this girl told me that she had been blessed with the gift of gold-spinning, and these past months, she has proven her worth, to me and to the hunt." His lips curled upward. "As such, I thought that tonight, in celebration of our victorious hunt of the tatzel-wurm, I would invite Lady Serilda to honor us all with the splendor of her gift."

Serilda tried not to fidget under his stare and the curious silence around her, though her insides were roiling. She signaled to the chil-dren to wait on the steps and approached the king, trying not to let him see how she was trembling.

"Please, Your Grim," she whispered, angling her face away from the crowd. "I have never spun before an audience. I am not accustomed to such attentions, and would far prefer—"

"Your preferences mean little here," said the Erlking. One slender eyebrow arched. "Dare I say, they mean nothing at all."

One of the ravens squawked, as if laughing at her.

She exhaled slowly. "And yet, I am sure that I will be more efficient if I could just have some peace and solitude."

"I should think you would be adequately motivated to impress me."

She held his gaze, searching for another excuse. Any excuse.

"I'm not sure my magic will work if people are watching."

He looked as though he were tempted to laugh. Leaning toward her, he whispered, with careful enunciation, "You will persuade it to work, or the child will be mine."

She shuddered.

Her brain turned, grasping at anything. But she could see that the king would not be moved.

Panic set in as she faced the spinning wheel. She thought of that first night beneath the Snow Moon, and how she had managed, at least temporarily, to persuade the Erlking that she could spin straw into gold. She thought of the first night in the castle, when Gild had appeared so suddenly, as if summoned by her very desperation.

She wondered how many miracles one girl was allowed.

Her footsteps felt leaden as she cast another look around the bailey, silently pleading for anyone, anything that could help her. But who could help her but Gild? Where *was* Gild?

It didn't matter, she told herself. He could do nothing here, not before all these witnesses.

No help was coming. She knew that.

But it didn't keep her from hoping. Maybe he had some prank planned. Maybe she'd lied before. Maybe she did want to be rescued. Maybe she was never meant to be the hero at all.

She glanced back at the children on the steps to the keep, her heart in agony over all that had happened.

Then she froze, finally spotting him.

Her mouth fell open, and she barely bit back the cry that wanted to escape.

He was strung up on the outer face of the keep, just beneath the seven stained-glass windows depicting the old gods. Gold chains bound his arms from wrists to elbows, attached to anchors somewhere over the parapets.

He was not struggling. His head was drooped forward, but his eyes were open. His expression was shattered as he met Serilda's gaze.

She didn't realize that she'd taken a step toward him until the king's voice startled her back to herself.

"Leave him be."

She froze. "Why—" Then, remembering that she was not supposed to have met Gild before, she cleared the hurt from her brow and faced the king. "Who is he? What has he done to be chained up like that?"

"Only our resident poltergeist," the king said mockingly. "He dared to steal something that was mine."

"Steal something?"

"Indeed. A bobbin was missing from your previous night's work, disappeared before my servants could even collect the gold. I am sure it was the poltergeist, as he has a habit of causing trouble."

Serilda's stomach dropped.

"But I will not tolerate his mischief on such an occasion. Besides, you see, my lady? Your labors have already served me well. Not many things can hold him, but chains crafted from magicked gold? They have worked just as I'd hoped."

She swallowed hard and looked back. Gild's jaw was locked. Misery mixed with anger across the planes of his face.

It was too far for her to see the chains clearly, but Serilda had no doubt they were crafted of strands of pure gold, woven into an unbreakable chain.

Her heart ached.

He had made his own prison, and he had done it for her.

But to stare a second longer would lead to suspicions, and the king could not know that it was Gild who had the gift of spinning, not her. If he knew what the cursed prince was truly capable of, he would no doubt find new ways of torturing him until Gild agreed to spin all the gold he wanted.

And if she knew Gild at all, she knew that he would endure the torture rather than do anything this monster demanded of him.

For eternity.

She forced herself to turn away. To face the spinning wheel.

A story, some sneaky voice whispered as she took a seat on the stool. What she needed was a great lie. Something convincing. Something that would get her out of this predicament and also let her keep her head, and rescue Gerdrut.

That was a lot to ask of a simple fairy tale, and her mind was blank. She doubted she could have recited a nursery rhyme in that moment, much less spun a story as grand as she needed.

She gave the wheel a turn with her fingers, as if testing it. She pressed her foot against the treadle. She tried to appear contemplative as her fingers skimmed across the empty, waiting bobbin.

What a picture she must make. The charming peasant girl at her spinning wheel. She had become a spectacle.

She reached into the cart for a handful of straw, taking the opportunity to glance around once more. Some of the ghosts were leaning forward, craning their necks to see.

She pretended to inspect the straw in her hands.

A lie.

I need a lie.

Nothing came.

Wyrdith, god of stories and fortune, she pleaded silently. *I have never asked you for anything, but please hear me now. If my father did help you, if you did give me your blessing, if I am truly your godchild, then please. Spin your fortune's wheel. Let it land in my favor.*

Serilda's hand shook as she picked out the longest piece of straw and took in a staggered breath. She had seen Gild do this so many times.

Was it at all possible that his magic might have transferred into her? That one could *learn* to be a gold-spinner?

She gave the wheel another spin.

Whir . . .

Her foot pressed against the treadle, increasing its speed.

Whir . . .

She moved the straw toward the maiden hole, as she had moved countless knots of fresh-sheared wool since she was a child. The straw scratched at her palms.

Whir . . .

It did not wrap around the bobbin.

Of course it didn't.

She'd forgotten to tie the leader yarn.

Face heating with embarrassment, she fumbled to secure one end of the straw onto the bobbin. She could hear rustling in the audience, but from the corner of her eye, the Erlking stood perfectly still. He might have been a corpse himself.

With the leader yarn attached as well as she could get it, and knotted to the next strand of straw, she tried again.

Whir . . .

One only had to feed it through.

Whir . . .

The wheel would twist the wool.

Whir . . .

The yarn would wrap around the bobbin.

But this was straw, and it quickly frayed and snapped.

Her heart pounded as she looked down at the remaining strands, dry and worthless in her unmagical grip.

She could not keep herself from glancing up, though she knew it was a mistake. Gild was watching her, his face full of anguish.

Funny how that look made so many things pristinely clear. There had remained a number of treacherous doubts these past weeks, after she had given so much to him, and taken so much in return. Everything he did came with a price. A necklace. A ring. A promise.

But he couldn't have looked at her like that if she meant nothing to him.

A spark of courage ignited in her chest.

She had told Gild that she would stay alive long enough to deliver to him the payment she owed. Her firstborn child.

The bargain had been made with magic, binding and unbreakable.

"You have my word," she murmured to herself.

"Is something wrong?" said the Erlking, and though his words were subdued, they had an unmistakable sharpness beneath them.

Her gaze snapped back to him. She blinked, startled.

Not so much by the presence of the Erlking, but by the cool shiver traipsing down her spine.

Her firstborn child.

She dropped the straw. Both hands went to her stomach.

The Erlking frowned.

She and Gild had made love on the night of the Chaste Moon. An entire moon cycle had passed, and she'd been so caught up in her worries and planning that she hadn't realized until that moment . . .

She'd missed her blood cycle.

"What is the matter?" growled the Erlking.

But Serilda barely heard him. The words were turning through her mind, a spinning wheel of blurring, impossible things.

Your condition.

You should not ride.

Firstborn child.

Firstborn child!

The progeny of a girl cursed by the god of lies and a boy trapped behind the veil. She couldn't picture such a creature. Would it be a monster? An undead thing? A magicked thing?

It wouldn't matter, she tried to tell herself. She had struck a deal with Gild. Though she knew he had accepted the offer with as much dismay as she'd made it, both of them thinking it would never come due, she also knew that Gild had meant it when he'd said their bargain was unbreakable.

She had no claim to this being inside her. No more than a cask can claim the wine or a bucket can claim the milk.

And yet.

A feeling she had never known rose up in her as her fingers pressed softly into her abdomen.

A child.

Her child.

An icy hand snatched her wrist.

Serilda gasped and looked up into the Erlking's frosted eyes.

"You are testing my patience, miller's daughter."

And that was when it came.

The story. The lie.

That was not entirely a lie.

"My lord, forgive me," she said, not having to feign her breathlessness. "I cannot spin this straw into gold."

One lip curled upward, revealing a sharp canine tooth that reminded her too much of the hounds he cherished.

"And why is that?" he asked, his tone a promise of regret if she dared to defy him.

"I fear it isn't proper to say . . ."

His eyes flashed murderous.

Serilda leaned toward him, whispering so that only he could hear. "Your Darkness, the god-given magic that flowed through my veins is gone. I can no longer summon it to my fingers. I am no longer a gold-spinner."

Shadows eclipsed his face. "You play a dangerous game."

She shook her head. "I swear, this is no game. There is good reason for the loss of my magic. You see . . . it seems that my body now harbors a gift far more precious than gold."

He squeezed her wrist until it hurt, but she didn't yelp. "Explain."

Her other hand had never left her stomach, and now she looked down, knowing that his gaze would follow.

"I am no longer a gold-spinner, because that magic now belongs to my unborn child."

His grip loosened, but he did not let go. She waited a few seconds before daring to meet his gaze again. "I am sorry to have disappointed you, my lord."

Skepticism still clung to his porcelain features, but they were quickly overshadowed by a fury unlike anything she'd ever seen.

Serilda tried to shrink away, but he did not let go.

Instead, he yanked her to her feet and started toward the castle keep, all but dragging her in his wake. "Redmond!" he bellowed. "You are needed in the throne room. *Now.*"

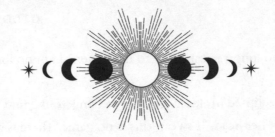

Chapter 53

The Erlking threw Serilda down into the center of the throne room and marched onto the dais. She pushed back her hair to look up at him.

Fear thrumming through her, she swallowed hard and rose to her knees. "Your Darkness—"

"Silence!" he roared. He looked like a different creature altogether, his face contorted into something decidedly unlovely. It hardly looked like him, who was usually so full of elegant composure. "This is a great disappointment, Lady Serilda." Her name sounded like a snake's hiss on his tongue.

"With all due respect, most people see babies as a gift."

He snarled at her. "Most people are idiots."

She clasped her hands pleadingly. "I could not have foreseen this. It was . . ." She shrugged. "It was only one night."

"You spun the gold not a month ago!"

She nodded. "I know. This happened . . . not long after."

He glared at her, looking like he wished he could reach straight into her womb and rip the alien creature out with his fist.

"You summoned, Your Grim?"

She glanced over her shoulder to see a ghostly man in a long-sleeved tunic. Half his face was bloated, his lips fat and tinged purple. Poison? Drowning? Serilda wasn't sure she wanted to know.

Removing the hunting crossbow from his back, the Erlking sank onto his throne and used the weapon to gesture carelessly at Serilda, still on her knees. "The wretched girl is with child."

Serilda flushed. She knew she shouldn't have expected the king to respect her privacy, but still—this was her secret to tell. And for now she was only interested in telling it in order to save Gerdrut.

And, she thought, her child.

Her child.

Again her fingers went to her stomach. She knew it was far too early to feel anything. There was no rounding of her belly, and certainly no movement within. She longed to run home, to talk to her father and ask him everything he could remember about her mother's pregnancy— until she remembered that he was not there, and unspeakable sorrow crashed over her.

Papa would have been a wonderful grandfather.

But she couldn't think of that now, even if the man responsible for her father's death was standing before her. Even if she despised him with every bone of her body. Right now, she needed to think only of saving herself. If she could survive this, then someday she would have a beautiful child to dote on, to love, to raise. She would be a *mother.* She'd always loved children, and now, to be able to care for this innocent baby. To rock them to sleep and tell bedtime stories long into the night.

But—*no,* she reminded herself.

The child would have to be given to Gild.

What would he think when she told him? It was all so surreal, so impossible.

What would he do with a *baby*?

She almost laughed. The idea was simply too preposterous.

"Lady Serilda!"

She snapped her head up, lurching back into the throne room. "Yes?"

To her surprise, the Erlking's cheeks were actually flushed. Not pink so much as a subtle grayish blue against his silvery skin, but still, it was more emotion than she would have thought he was capable of. His right hand was gripping the arm of the throne. His left held the crossbow, its tip rested against the floor.

Unloaded. Thankfully.

"How long, exactly," he said slowly, as if speaking to a simpleton, "have you been in this condition?"

Her lips parted with, finally, an actual lie. "Three weeks."

His sharp gaze darted to the man. "What can be done?"

The man, Redmond, inspected her with arms crossed. He pondered for a moment, before offering the king a shrug. "This early, should be but a tiny thing. Maybe the size of a pea."

"Good," said the Erlking. With a long, annoyed breath, he sat back against the throne. "Remove it."

"What?" Serilda launched herself to her feet. "You can't!"

"Surely I can. Well . . . he can." The Erlking's fingers danced in the man's direction. "Can't you, Redmond?"

Redmond grumbled to himself for a moment as he opened a brown sack at his waist and pulled out a small bundle of fabric. "Never have before, but I don't see why I couldn't."

"Redmond was a barber by trade," said the Erlking, "and a surgeon as required."

Serilda shook her head. "It will kill me."

"We have very good healers," said the Erlking. "I will ensure that it doesn't."

"Probably won't ever carry a babe again," added Redmond. He looked at the king, not Serilda. "Suppose that's all right?"

"Yes, fine," said the Erlking.

Serilda let out a dismayed cry. "No! That is not fine!"

Ignoring her, Redmond paced to a nearby table and unspooled the fabric, revealing a series of sharp tools. Scissors. Scalpels. Wrenches and pliers and terrifying things that Serilda didn't know the names for. Her knees quaked as she stepped back. Her eyes darted around and for the first time she realized that the bloodied gateway was gone. Her path to the other side of the veil.

Surely it was still there. She had opened it once, she could open it again. But *how*?

Then, another sobering thought.

Gerdrut.

She still hadn't saved Gerdrut.

Where was he keeping the child? She couldn't leave her, not even to save herself, not even to save her baby.

"It's been a while," mused Redmond, holding up a tiny blade. "But this should do it." He glanced at the king. "Is it to be done here?"

"No!" Serilda screeched.

The Erlking looked irritated with her outburst. "Of course not. You can use one of the rooms in the north wing."

With a nod, the man started gathering up his tools again.

"No!" she shouted again, louder this time. "You can't do this."

"You are not at liberty to tell me what I can and can't do. This is my kingdom. You and the gifts of Hulda belong to me now."

The words might have been a slap for how they left her speechless.

She drew herself up, solidifying her legs beneath her. She had one chance to persuade him. One chance to save this unborn life inside of her.

"No, my lord. You can't do this because it won't work. It won't bring my magic back."

His eyes narrowed. "If that is true, then best slit your throat and be done with the both of you."

She tried to hide her shudder. "If that is your will, I cannot stop you. But do you not think that Hulda might have an intention for this child? To take its life so soon, you are interfering with the will of a god."

"I care little for the wills of gods."

"Be that as it may," she said, taking a step forward, "you and I both know that they can be powerful allies. If it wasn't for the gift of Hulda, I never could have spun that gold for you." She paused before continuing, "What might the blessing be for my child? What power might be growing inside me, even now? And yes—I know I am asking for your patience, for not just the next nine—eight months, but for years, potentially, before we know what gift this child carries. But you are eternal. What is a few years, a decade? If you kill me, if you kill this baby, then you are squandering a great opportunity. You told me the young princess was also blessed by Hulda. That her death was a waste. But you are not a wasteful king. Don't make that mistake again."

He held her gaze for a long time, while Serilda's heart thumped erratically and her breaths threatened to choke her.

"How do you know," he said slowly, "that your gift of spinning will not return once the parasite is removed?"

Parasite.

Serilda shivered at the word, but tried not to let her disgust show.

She spread her palms, a sign of open honesty that she knew well. "I felt it," she lied. "The moment I conceived, I felt the magic leaving my fingers, pooling in my womb, cradling this child. I cannot say for certain that he or she will be born with the same gift as I've had, but I do know that Hulda's magic now resides in them. If you kill this child, this blessing will be gone forever."

"Your eyes have not changed." He said this as if it were proof that she was lying.

Serilda merely shrugged. "I do not spin with my eyes."

The king leaned to one side, pressing a finger against his temple, massaging it in slow circles. His gaze slid to the barber, waiting with his tools wrapped again in their pouch. After a long moment, the Erlking lifted his chin and asked, "Who is the father?"

She stilled.

It had not occurred to her he might ask this, that he might care. She doubted that he *did* care, but what purpose might he have to wonder?

"No one," she said. "A boy from my village. A farmer, my lord."

"And does this farmer know that you carry his offspring?"

She slowly shook her head.

"Good. Does anyone else know?"

"No, my lord."

Again he leaned forward, mindlessly tracing his fingers along the edges of his mouth. Serilda held her breath, trying not to shake beneath his scrutiny. If she could only buy herself some time . . . If she could only persuade him to let her live long enough to . . .

To do what?

She didn't know. But she knew she needed more time.

"All right," said the king suddenly. He reached down to the side of his throne and took hold of the crossbow. His other hand took out one arrow—one not tipped in gold, but black.

Serilda's eyes widened. "Wait!" she cried, lifting her hands even as she fell again to her knees. Pleading. "Don't. I can be useful to you . . . I know there's some way . . ."

The bow clicked loudly as he loaded the arrow into it.

"Please! Please don't—"

The trigger snapped. The arrow whistled and struck hard.

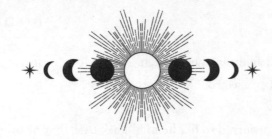

Chapter 54

A grunt. A gurgle. A wheeze.

Mouth hanging open, Serilda slowly turned her head.

The arrow had gone straight into the barber's heart. The blood trickling down the front of his tunic was not red, but black like oil, and reeking of decay.

He collapsed to the ground, his body convulsing as his hands gripped the arrow's shaft.

It seemed to go on forever, before the barber gave one last gasping exhale, then fell still. His hands dropped to his sides, palms open to the ceiling.

As Serilda stared, shocked, he melted away. His entire body succumbed to the black oil, his features dripping down into the rugs. Soon there was nothing left of him but a ghastly, greasy pool and the arrow left behind.

"Wh-what . . . ? You just . . . ," she stammered. "You can *kill* them?"

"When it pleases me to do so." The rustle of leather drew Serilda's gaze back to the Erlking. He lifted himself from the throne and paced over to retrieve his arrow. He still held the crossbow loosely at his side, and when he faced Serilda, she instinctively backed away from him.

"But he was a ghost," she said. "He was already dead."

"And now he has been released," he said in a decidedly bored tone.

He tucked the arrow back into its quiver. "His spirit is free to follow the candlelight into Verloren. And you call me a villain."

Her lips were trembling—with shock. With disbelief. With utter confusion.

"But *why?*"

"He was the only one who knew that I was not the father. Now there will be no one to question it."

Her lashes fluttered, slow and hesitant. "Pardon?"

"You are right, Lady Serilda." He started pacing before her. "I had not contemplated what this child might mean for me and my court. A newborn, blessed by Hulda. It is a gift not to be wasted. I am grateful you've opened my eyes to the possibilities."

Her jaw worked, but no sounds came out.

The king neared her. He looked pleased, almost smug, as he took her in. Her strange eyes, her filthy peasant clothes. His attention lingered on her stomach, and Serilda wrapped her arms in front of herself. The movement made his lips twitch with amusement.

"You and I will be wed."

She gaped at him. "*What?*"

"And when the child is born," he went on, as if she'd said nothing, "it will belong to me. No one will doubt that it is mine. Its human father will not care to claim it, and you"—he lowered his voice into a clear threat—"will know better than to tell anyone the truth."

Her eyes were wide, but unseeing. The world was a cyclone, all the walls and torches blurring into nothing.

"B-but I—I can't," she started. "I can't *marry* you. I am nothing. A mortal, a human, a—"

"A peasant girl, a miller's daughter . . ." The Erlking gave an exaggerated sigh. "I know what you are. Do not give yourself false pretenses. I have no interest in romance, if that's what you fear. I will not *touch* you." He said this as if the idea were beyond repulsive, but Serilda was too flummoxed to be offended. "There is no need. The child grows in you already. And when she returns, I—" He stopped, catching himself. His face shuttered and he glared at Serilda as if she'd been trying to trick him into giving up his secrets. "Eight months you say. The timing is most convenient. That is . . . *if* we have enough gold. No. It will have to be enough. I will not wait any longer."

He moved around her, a vulture around his prey, but he was no longer studying her. His gaze had turned thoughtful and distant. "I cannot let you leave, of course. I will not risk you running away or spreading rumors that this child belongs to someone else. But to kill you would be to kill the child. That leaves me with few options."

She shook her head, unable to believe what she was hearing. Unable to comprehend how the Erlking could have gone from intending to cut the child from her womb to intending to raise it as his own in so short a time.

But then she thought of what he had said, that little hint that had slipped through.

When she returns.

Approximately eight months until the baby would be born.

Eight months would take them nearly to the end of the year.

Nearly to . . . the winter solstice. The Endless Moon. When he intended to capture a god and make his wish. Was it true then? Did he mean to wish for Perchta, the huntress, to be returned from Verloren? Did he mean to use Serilda's unborn child as a *gift* for her, as one might bestow a bouquet of forget-me-nots or a basket of apple strudel?

She frowned. "But I thought the dark ones could not have children?"

"With each other, we cannot. The creation of a child requires the spark of life, and we are born of death. But with a mortal . . ." He shrugged. "It is rare. Mortals are beneath us, and few would abase themselves to lie with one."

"Of course," Serilda said, with a snarl that went ignored.

"The ceremony can take place on the summer solstice. That should be adequate time to prepare, though I hope you aren't one of those brides who fancies elaborate festivities and ridiculous pomp."

She gasped. "I have agreed to nothing! I have not agreed to be your prisoner, or to tell anyone that you are the father of this child!"

"Wife," he snapped. His eyes brightened, as if this were a shared joke between them. "You will be my wife, Lady Serilda. Let us not tarnish the union with talk of imprisonment."

"Whatever words you attach to it, I will be a prisoner, and we both know it."

He approached her again, graceful as a snake, and took her hands into his. The touch almost affectionate, if it hadn't been so very cold.

"You will do as I say," he said, "because I still have something that you want."

Tears prickled at her eyes. *Gerdrut.*

"In exchange for the little one's freedom," he continued, "you will be my doting bride. I will expect you to be very, very convincing. The child is mine. No one is to suspect otherwise."

She swallowed.

She couldn't do this.

She couldn't.

But she pictured Gerdrut's smile, missing her first milk tooth. Her squeals when Fricz tickled her. Her pouts when she tried to braid Anna's hair and couldn't quite figure out how.

"All right," she whispered, a tear escaping her eye. She did not bother to wipe it away. "I will do what you ask, if you promise to let Gerdrut go."

"You have my word."

He beamed and lifted a hand, revealing a gold-tipped arrow in his fist.

It happened so quickly. She barely had time to gasp before he plunged it down through her wrist.

Pain tore through her.

Serilda fell to her knees, her vision going white at the edges. All she could see was the shaft that jutted from her arm. Her blood dripped along its length, down the gilded tip, splattering drop by drop onto the floor.

Still gripping her hand, the king began to speak, and Serilda heard the words from two places at once. The Erlking, devoid of emotion as he recited the curse. And her own story, told in the empty throne room, echoing back to her.

That arrow now tethers you to this castle. Your spirit no longer belongs to the confines of your mortal body, but will be forever trapped within these walls. From this day into eternity, your soul belongs to me.

The agony was like nothing she'd ever known before, as though poison were leaching into her, devouring her from the inside. She felt her bones, her muscles, her very heart crumbling to ash. Left behind was just a shell of a girl. Skin and fingernails and a golden arrow.

She heard a quiet thump as something fell behind her.

And—the pain vanished.

Serilda sucked in a breath of air, but there was no satisfaction to it. Her lungs did not expand. The air itself tasted stale and dry.

She felt empty, wrung out. Abandoned.

The Erlking released her hand and her arm dropped into her lap.

The arrow was gone. In its place, a gaping hole.

She was almost too afraid to look back. But she had to. She had to see it, she had to know.

And when her eyes fell on her own body sprawled out behind her, Serilda surprised herself. She did not cry or scream. She merely observed, as a strange calm overtook her.

The body on the floor was still breathing. *Her* body. The blood around the arrow shaft had begun to clot. The eyes were open, unblinking and unseeing—but not lifeless. The golden wheels on her irises glimmered knowingly with the light of a thousand stars.

She had seen this once before, when her spirit had floated up over her own corpse on the riverbank. It would have kept floating away if she hadn't held tight to the ash branch.

But now there was something else tethering her here.

To this castle. This throne room. These walls.

She was trapped.

Forever.

The pain she'd felt had not been death. It had been the sensation of her spirit being torn from her body.

Not letting go so much as being ripped away.

She was not dead.

She was not a ghost.

She was merely . . . cursed.

She rose to her feet, no longer trembling, and met the Erlking's gaze. "That," she said through gritted teeth, "was not very romantic."

"My sweet," he said, and she could tell that he took pleasure in this act, this mimicry of human affection, "were you hoping for a kiss?"

She exhaled sharply through her nostrils, glad that she *could* still breathe, even if she didn't *need* to. Her hands patted down the sides of her body, testing the sensation. She felt different. Incomplete, but still solid. She could feel the weight of her dress, the path of tears on her face. And yet, her actual body was lying on the floor at her feet.

Her hands made their way to her stomach. Was her baby still growing inside of her?

Or was it now growing inside of . . .

She glanced down at her body, lying there still and stunned. Not dead. Not quite alive.

She wanted to believe that the Erlking would not have used this curse if it would hurt the child. What would have been the point? But she also wasn't sure how much thought he was giving to any of this.

That was when she realized what felt so distinctly different. When it finally came to her, it was obvious, and she wondered how she hadn't noticed before.

She could no longer feel her heart beating in her chest.

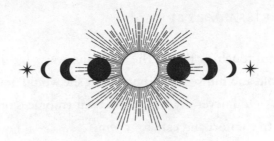

Chapter 55

N ow then," said the Erlking, taking her fingers and tucking them into the crook of his elbow, "let us announce our good fortune."

Serilda still felt dazed as he marched her out of the throne room, through the great hall, beneath the overhang of the massive entry doors that overlooked the courtyard, where all his hunters and ghosts continued to mill about, confused as to what their king expected of them.

The children were gathered right where she'd left them, clutching one another, Hans trying to defend them from a curious goblin who had hopped closer and was trying to sniff their knees.

Serilda crouched down, arms wide. The children hurried into her embrace—

And passed right through her.

It felt like a blast of icy wind cutting through her core.

Serilda gasped. The children backed away, gawking at her wide-eyed.

"I-it's all right," she croaked. Gild had told her that he could pass through ghosts. He had tried to pass through *her* when they'd first met. Squaring her shoulders, Serilda tried to be more conscious of the physical limits of her body. She reached out to them again. They were more hesitant, but as Serilda's hands found their arms, their cheeks, their hair, they again pressed into her.

It was awful touching them. The sensation was a bit like handling dead fish—cold and flimsy and slippery. But she would never tell them that, and she would never shy away from their embraces or from doing all she could to comfort and care for them.

"I am sorry," she whispered. "I am so sorry. For everything."

"What did he do to you?" whispered Nickel, tenderly placing a hand over Serilda's wrist, where the hole from the arrow had stopped bleeding.

"Don't worry about me. And try not to be afraid. I'm here, and I won't leave you."

"We're already dead," said Fricz. "Not much more he can do."

Serilda wished that were true.

"That is enough, children," said the Erlking, his shadow falling over them. As if he'd heard Fricz's comment and was eager to prove just how wrong the child was, the Erlking flicked his fingers. As one, the children backed out of Serilda's embrace, their spines stiff, their expressions dulled.

"Emotional creatures," the Erlking muttered with disgust. "Come." He beckoned for Serilda to follow as he descended the steps toward the spinning wheel in the bailey's center.

Stomach in knots, she stooped to place a kiss on each of their heads. They seemed to relax, whether from her touch or the Erlking's losing interest in controlling them, she didn't know.

With a ruffle of Nickel's hair, she turned and followed the Erlking, daring to glance up toward the wall of the keep. Gild was still there. There was pain on his face, and the hollow place in her chest yawned open.

"Hunters and guests, courtiers and attendants, servants and friends," bellowed the king, drawing their attention. "There has been a change of fortune tonight, and one that pleases me greatly. Lady Serilda will no longer be presenting a demonstration of her gold-spinning magic. After much contemplation, I have determined that such an act is beneath that of our future queen."

Silence greeted them. Furrowed brows and twisted mouths.

Overhead, a puzzled look intruded into Gild's agony. Serilda's hands itched with the desire to run to the top of the keep's steps and tear down those chains, but she remained where she was. She forced herself to look away, to face the demons, the specters, the beasts gathered before her.

As Serilda stared, she realized that while this might be an audience of the dead, there were few elderly among them. These ghosts had met traumatic ends. Their bodies bloated with poisons, scarred with wounds, many still bearing evidence of the very weapons that had ended them. Some were sickly and covered in welts, some swollen and puffy, and others gaunt from starvation. No one here had died peacefully in their sleep.

Everyone here knew what it was to hold fear and pain inside them.

For the first time, Serilda felt how sad it all was, to live an eternity with the suffering of your own death.

And she was to be queen of it all.

At least, until this baby was born.

Then she would probably be killed.

"Lady Serilda has agreed to take my hand," said the Erlking, "and I am most honored."

Confusion reigned over the courtyard. Serilda held perfectly still, afraid that if she moved, it would only be to lunge at the king and try to strangle him. Surely no one would be fooled by such a preposterous notion. That she was in love with him? That he was honored to be her husband?

But he was their king. Perhaps it didn't matter if anyone believed it or not. Perhaps they'd all been trained to accept his word without question.

"We will begin preparations for the ceremony posthaste," said the Erlking. "I expect you will all bestow on my beloved the fealty and adoration due to the one I have chosen for my bride."

He intertwined his fingers with Serilda's and lifted their hands, showing off the gaping hole in her arm.

"Behold our new queen. Long reign Queen Serilda!"

There was laughter in his voice, and she wondered if any of these ghosts could sense it as their voices rose, still uncertain, to repeat the chant.

Long reign Queen Serilda.

She stood dumbfounded, faced with the absurdity of this farce. The Erlking wanted this child as a gift for Perchta. But he had already cursed her, trapped her inside this castle. In eight months, he could take the child and she could do nothing to stop him. He could still tell everyone that the baby was his progeny.

But why *marry* her? Why make her queen? Why put on this charade? Soon he hoped to bring Perchta back from Verloren, and clearly it was *she* who would be his true queen, his true bride.

No—there was more to his intentions than simply wanting to give her newborn child to the huntress. She could feel it. A thread of warning curled in the pit of her stomach.

But there was nothing she could do about it now. Once she had seen Gerdrut to safety, she would try to muddle through whatever secrets this demon still harbored. She had until the winter solstice to figure out how she would stop him.

Until then, she would do what was asked of her. Nothing more. She certainly wasn't going to make charmed eyes at him and swoon every time he entered a room. She wasn't going to giggle and preen in his presence. She wasn't going to pretend that she wasn't a prisoner here.

But she would lie. She would tell them all that he was the father of her child, if that's what he asked.

Until she could figure out how to free the spirits of these children, how to free Gild, how to free herself.

How to kill the Erlking.

As the chant rose in volume, he bent toward her, pressing a porcelain smooth, ever-cool cheek against hers. His lips brushed the corner of her ear and she fought down a shudder. "I have a gift for you."

He turned them back to face the steps. Her horrified gaze swept up to Gild, but his chin had fallen against his chest, strands of red hair hiding his face, almost golden in the sun.

"Every queen requires an entourage," said the king. He gestured toward the children, then curled his finger, summoning them forward.

Hans straightened and put himself out in front of the others, clutching Anna's hand.

"Come now. Don't be shy," said the king, sounding almost sweet.

Serilda knew he could force them to obey, but he waited for them to approach on their own. Hesitant, but with so much courage that Serilda wanted to pull each of them against her and scatter kisses atop their heads.

"I give to you," said the king, "your footman." He gestured at Hans. "Your groom." Nickel. "Your personal messenger." Fricz. "And of course, every queen needs a lady-in-waiting." He tucked a finger beneath Anna's chin. She flinched, but he pretended not to notice. "How do you greet your queen, little servants?"

The children looked wide-eyed at Serilda.

"It will be all right," she lied.

Anna acted first, fumbling into a curtsy. "Your . . . Highness?"

"Very good," said the Erlking.

The boys bowed uncomfortably. Serilda wanted this to be done with. This false spectacle, the appalling pretense. She wanted to go somewhere she could embrace them, tell them how sorry she was. That she would do anything she could to end this for them. She would not allow them to be trapped here forever in this castle, beholden to the Erlking. She wouldn't.

"Well?" said the king. "Are you satisfied?"

She wanted to be sick all over him. Instead, she said, "I will be once I've seen Gerdrut go free."

"Ah yes, the small one. Thank you for reminding me. I give you my final betrothal gift." He raised his voice. "Manfred? The girl."

A groan echoed to them from above and Serilda gasped, her attention darting back up to Gild. He still was not looking at her.

At her side, Anna clasped her hand, her ghostly touch so shocking that Serilda almost pulled away.

Anna looked up at her, tears glistening in her eyes. Serilda tried to smile, when she looked past the children and saw what Anna must have seen.

The coachman was emerging from the crowd. He glanced from Serilda and the children to the king, and Serilda wondered if she was imagining the flash of resentment, even hatred, in his eye. Then he held his hand toward someone who was tucked amid the ghosts. A moment later, he was leading Gerdrut toward Serilda and the king.

This time, Serilda did cry out, a scream that would echo in her thoughts for as long as she was trapped here.

Gerdrut clasped the coachman's hand, tears tracking down her cherub face, her silhouette fading at the edges. A hole where her sweet heart used to be.

"I think," added the king, "that she will make a fine chambermaid. Don't you agree?"

Serilda wailed, feeling as though all her insides had been torn out. "You promised. You promised!" She spun toward him, rage burning up every rational thought. "You cannot expect me to lie for you. I will never tell anyone that you are the fa—"

His mouth descended on hers, one arm roping around her waist, pulling her against him.

Her words were cut off into a smothered scream. She tried to shove at his chest, but it made little difference. His other hand dug into the hair at the base of her neck, immobilizing her as he broke the kiss.

She wanted to retch in his face.

Distantly, she heard the rattle of chains. Gild trying to get free.

"I promised her freedom," the Erlking murmured, his lips brushing hers with each movement. "And that is what I shall grant. Once you have fulfilled your end of the bargain and given me this child, I will release their spirits to Verloren." He paused, pulling away so that he could hold her gaze. "Isn't that what you want for them, *my queen*?"

She couldn't bring herself to respond. Fury was still pounding inside her skull, and all she wanted to do was claw that haughty smirk from his face.

Taking her silence for agreement, the Erlking tipped down her head and placed another cool kiss against her brow.

To their onlookers, it must have appeared a gesture of sweetest affection.

They could not have seen the gloating laughter in his eyes as he whispered, "Long reign the queen."

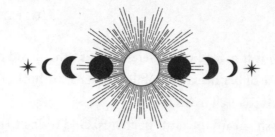

Chapter 56

The children had fallen asleep on top of the massive bed that once seemed like the grandest luxury. Serilda watched them now, recalling how giddy she'd been to see feathered pillows and velvet drapes. How she had marveled at all this castle had to offer.

When this had all seemed a little bit like a fairy tale.

How preposterous.

She was grateful, at least, that sleep was still possible for them. She didn't know if ghosts *needed* rest, but it was a small blessing to know that there would be moments of respite in this tragic captivity.

She wasn't sure if *she* needed rest. She could understand a bit more now, how Gild had known he was different. She was not dead. She was not a ghost, like the children, like the rest of the king's servants.

But what did that make her?

Tired, she thought. She felt so very tired. Yet restless, too.

She found herself thinking about the games that she had played when she was young with the other children in the village. Those whose parents hadn't forbidden them from playing with her, that is.

They were princes and princesses. Damsels and knights. They built castles of twigs and made woven crowns of bluebells and swanned around the fields as if they were nobles in Verene. They had imagined a life of jewels and parties and feasts—oh, the feasts they had dreamed up—the dances, the balls.

Serilda had been so very good at dreaming. Even then, her peers were eager to hear her turn their simple musings into unparalleled adventures.

But never had it crossed Serilda's mind, not for the shortest swallow trill, that it might come true.

She would live in a castle.

She would be wed to a king.

She would be wed to a monster.

And, true, his court might be sumptuous in its own way. Feasting, dancing, merriment, and drink. She might even be given gifts and an imitation of romance—the king would have to feign some amount of adoration for her if he was to convince everyone that he was the father of her child. But she would be a prisoner more than a queen. She would have no power. No one would heed her commands or listen to her pleas. No one would help her, unless the king permitted it.

A possession. He'd called her a possession, and that was only when she was the novel gold-spinner. Now she would be a wife, tied to him in whatever ceremony the dark ones used to commemorate such things.

And amid all this turmoil was still the disbelieving joy, somehow impossible to tamp down. She was going to have a child.

She would be a mother.

Unless that child was ripped out of her arms and given to the huntress Perchta the moment it was born. The thought brought bile to her mouth.

She sighed heavily and sat on the corner of the bed, careful not to jostle the children's sleeping forms. As her fingers brushed a strand of hair back from Hans's brow, then adjusted the blanket on Nickel's shoulders, she hoped with all her heart that pleasant dreams would not elude them.

"I will find a way to give you peace," she whispered. "I will not let you toil here forever. And until that day comes, I promise, I will tell you the happiest of stories to take your minds away from all of this. Where the heroes are victorious. The villains vanquished. Where everyone who is just and kind and brave is granted a perfect finale." She sniffed, surprised when another tear clung to her eyelids. She'd begun to think she was empty of them.

She was tempted to lie down, curl her body into what little space was left for her, and try to let her thoughts settle with all that had happened in a short twenty-four hours.

But she could not sleep.

There was still something she had to do before this disastrous day was over.

A wardrobe had been stocked with fine gowns and cloaks, all of them in tones of emeralds and sapphires and bloodred rubies. All much too fine for a miller's daughter.

What would her father think to see her in such things?

No. She slammed her eyes shut. She could not think of him. She wondered if she would ever be able to properly mourn him. He was just one more jewel in her crown of guilt. One more person she'd failed.

"Stop it," she whispered, pulling a dressing gown from the wardrobe. She left the candle on the nightstand, so that if the children awoke they wouldn't find themselves surrounded by darkness in an unfamiliar room.

Then she slipped out of the tower. She was not sure how to get to the roof of the keep, but she was determined to follow every staircase until she found the right one.

Except, as she rounded the bend of the spiraling steps, she spotted a figure leaning against the doorway.

She froze, bracing one hand against the wall.

Gild stared up at her, clutching a bundle of fabric in his arms. His sleeves were pushed up past his elbows and she could see lines of red welts where the gold chains had wrapped around him. There was tension in his shoulders. His expression was too careful, too wary.

She wanted to rush into his arms, but they did not open to her.

Her mouth opened and closed a few times before she found words. "I was coming to free you."

His jaw tensed, but a second later, his gaze softened. "I was starting to make a bit of a ruckus. Moaning. Chain-rattling. Typical poltergeist stuff. They finally got tired of listening to me and brought me down around sunset."

She eased down the steps. A finger reached for one of the marks on his forearm, but he flinched away.

She pulled back. "How did they do it?"

"Cornered me outside the tower," he said. "They had the chains around me before I knew what was happening. I've never had to worry about that before. Being . . . trapped like that."

"I'm so sorry, Gild. If it wasn't for me—"

"You didn't do this to me," he interrupted sharply.

"But the gold—"

"I made the gold. I designed my own prison. How's that for torture?" He looked briefly like he wanted to smile but couldn't quite figure out how.

"But if I'd told the truth . . . at anytime, if I'd just told the truth, rather than asking you to spin the gold, to keep coming back, to keep helping me—"

"Then you would be dead."

"And those children would be alive . . ." Her voice cracked. "And you wouldn't have been chained to a wall."

"*He* cut out their hearts. He's the murderer."

She shook her head. "Don't try to convince me that I'm not at fault for this. I tried to escape, even though I knew . . . I knew what he was capable of."

They stared at each other for a long moment.

"I should go," he finally whispered. "The king might not like to see his future bride cavorting with the resident poltergeist." The bitterness was tangible, his mouth twisting as if he'd bitten something sour. "I just wanted to bring you this." He thrust the fabric toward her, and it took Serilda a moment to recognize her cloak.

Her old, ratty, stained, beloved cloak.

"I patched the shoulder," he said sadly, as Serilda took it from him. Unfolding it, she saw that the place where the drude had torn the fabric had indeed been mended with a square of gray fabric, almost the same color as the original wool, but softer to the touch.

"It's dahut fur," he said. "We don't have any sheep here, so . . ."

She squeezed the cloak to her chest for a moment, then slung it over her shoulders. Its familiar weight was an immediate comfort. "Thank you."

Gild nodded, and for a moment she worried that he really would go. But then his shoulders sank and, resigned, he opened his arms.

With a grateful sob, Serilda fell into them, tying her hands around his back, feeling the warmth of his hold spreading through her.

"I'm scared," she said as her eyes filled with tears. "I don't know what's going to happen."

"I am, too," he murmured. "It's been a long time since I felt scared like this." His hands rubbed her arms, his cheek pressed to her temple. "What happened in that throne room? When he dragged you away, I thought"—emotion clogged his throat—"I thought he'd kill you for sure. And then you both come back out and suddenly he's calling you our queen? Saying you're going to *marry* him?"

She grimaced. "I hardly understand it myself." She clawed her fingers into Gild's shirt, wanting to stay here forever. To never face the reality of life in this castle, at the side of the Erlking. She couldn't begin to fathom what future awaited her or the children she'd left behind in that room.

"Serilda," said Gild, more sternly now. "Truly. What happened in that throne room?"

She pulled away so she could see his face.

He deserved to know the truth. She was going to have a baby—and he was the father. The king wanted to keep it for his own. He wanted to bring Perchta back from Verloren, and he wanted to gift her the newborn child that was growing in Serilda's womb.

Their child.

But she thought of the children with the holes in their chests. How much they'd already suffered.

If the king ever found out she had not lived up to their agreement, those children would be made to suffer for it. He would never let their spirits be free.

She chose her words carefully, watching Gild's reaction, hoping that he might be able to see the truth hidden in her lies.

"I managed to convince him that I cannot spin gold anymore, but that . . . my child, when I have a child, will inherit Hulda's gift."

His brow furrowed. "He believed that?"

"People believe what they want to believe," she said. "Dark ones must not be so different."

"But what does that have to do with . . ." His eyes darkened with dismay. When he spoke again, there was a new edge in his voice. "Why does he wish to marry you?"

She shuddered at the implication. At the lie she needed him to believe. "So that I can have a child."

"*His* child?"

When she didn't answer, he snarled and started to pull away. Serilda tightened her grip on his shirt, clinging to him.

"You cannot think that I want this," she snapped. "I should hope you know me better than that."

He hesitated. The flood of anger gave way to hurt. But then, finally—horror.

Understanding.

"He's already trapped you. Hasn't he?"

Biting the inside of her cheek, Serilda pulled away from him so she could lift the sleeve of the dressing gown, showing him the hole where the arrow had pierced her.

His expression crumbled. "Part of me feels like this should make me happy, but I don't . . . I don't want this for you. I would never want this for you."

She swallowed. She'd hardly had time to think of what it would mean. To be the queen, locked always behind the veil in this soulless castle, her only company the undead, the dark ones . . . and Gild.

He was right. A part of her might have found some comfort in that, but it was buried so deep it was hard to know for sure. This would not be a life, not one she would ever have chosen for herself.

And she had to assume it would be short-lived. Once the baby was born, and the king saw that Serilda still had no magic, he would rid himself of her without hesitation. He would take her newborn, and if he was successful in capturing a god and wishing Perchta back to this world, he would give that innocent little life to her. The mistress of cruelty and violence and death.

Except . . .

Strangely, unfathomably, this child was already spoken for. She had already promised her firstborn to another.

What did that mean for her bargain with the king?

What did her bargain with the king mean for Gild?

"Gild, there's something else I have to tell you."

His eyebrows lifted. "There's *more*?"

"There's more." She took his face into her hands. Studying him.

He tensed. "What is it?"

She took a breath. "I know how the story ends. Or . . . how it ended."

"The story?" He looked baffled. "About the prince? And the kid-napped princess?"

She nodded, and wished so desperately that she could tell him it had a happy ending. The prince killed the villain and rescued his sister after all. The words would have been so easy to say. They were on the tip of her tongue.

"Serilda, this hardly seems the time for fairy tales."

"You're right, but you must hear it," she said, her hands falling to his shoulders, fidgeting with the wide linen collar of his shirt. "The prince came back to his castle, but the Erlking had arrived before him, and he . . . he killed everyone. Slaughtered the king and queen, all the ser-vants . . ."

Gild shivered, but Serilda gripped the fabric, keeping him close. "When the prince returned, the king tethered his spirit to the castle, so he might be trapped in that miserable place forever. And for his final revenge, he put a curse on the prince, that no one—not even the prince himself—would ever remember him or his family. Their names, their history—it was all ripped away, so that he would be forever alone. So that he would never again know the feeling of love."

Gild stared at her. "That's it? *That's* how the story ends? Serilda, that is—"

"The truth, Gild."

He hesitated, frowning.

"It's the truth. It all happened, right here in this castle."

He watched her, and she could tell the moment when the pieces began to fit together.

The things that made sense.

The questions that still lingered.

"What are you saying?" he whispered.

"It isn't just a story. It's real. And the prince . . . Gild, it's *you*."

This time, when he pulled away, she let him.

"The girl in the portrait was your little sister. The Erlking killed her. I don't know if he kept her ghost. She might still be in Gravenstone."

He ran a hand through his hair, staring into nothing. She could tell he wanted to argue, to deny it. But—how could he? He had no memories of his life before.

"What's my real name, then?" he asked, looking up at her. "If I'm a prince, I'd be famous, wouldn't I?"

She shrugged. "I don't know your name. It was erased, as part of the spell. I'm not even sure if the Erlking himself knows what it is. But I do know that you aren't a ghost. You aren't dead. You're just cursed."

"Cursed," he said, laughing without humor. "I'm well aware of that."

"But don't you see?" She took his hands. "This is a good thing."

"How is being cursed a good thing?"

It was the question Serilda had been trying to answer her whole life.

She lifted his hand and placed a kiss against the pale scar on his freckled wrist, where a gold-tipped arrow had tethered his spirit to this castle, trapping him forever.

"Because curses can be broken."

Acknowledgments

My heart is so full of gratitude that I wish there were more words to describe it in the English language.

Countless thanks are owed to my publishing family at Macmillan Children's Publishing Group: Liz Szabla, Johanna Allen, Robert Brown, Caitlin Crocker, Mariel Dawson, Rich Deas, Jean Feiwel, Katie Quinn, Morgan Rath, Jordin Streeter, Mary Van Akin, Kathy Wielgosz, and everyone who I never actually get to talk to, but I know is working tirelessly to bring these books into the world. I am likewise so grateful to the team at Jill Grinberg Literary Management: Jill Grinberg, Katelyn Detweiler, Sam Farkas, Denise Page, and Sophia Seidner. I am so lucky to get to work with you all.

I am much obliged to my copyeditor, Anne Heausler, for her thoughtful edits and suggestions. To my incredibly talented audiobook narrator, Rebecca Soler, for her brilliant interpretations of the characters. And to Regina Louis for her invaluable input on German customs, traditions, and cultural details (as well as her work on the *Supernova* German translation). Thank you all for helping to make the world of Adalheid glow a little brighter.

I am forever indebted to my longtime friend and critique partner, Tamara Moss. Not only does your feedback always lead to a stronger book, but you also somehow know just the right things to say to help me keep calm and carry on.

I cannot say thank you enough times to Joanne Levy—assistant, podcast organizer and social media manager, Excel expert, and awesome middle grade author. I know I've said this a hundred times, but truly, you are the best.

Speaking of amazing writer friends, it was very strange to be writing this book during the lockdown of 2020, and it has made me appreciate my local writing group all the more: Kendare Blake, Corry L. Lee, Lish McBride, and Rori Shay. I hope that by the time this book comes out we'll be enjoying our regular writing dates again!

I am most grateful to Sarah Crowley for all her assistance with website design and technical conundrums. To Bethanie Finger, host of the Prince Kai Fan Pod, for her unflagging energy and support. To everyone on Instagram who offered suggestions for the *Gilded* playlist—I've been able to surround myself with the most delectably haunting and whimsical music these past months thanks to you. And the readers. All the readers. The booksellers, the librarians, the teachers, the podcast listeners, the fans—everyone who has been so kind, encouraging, enthusiastic, and just really, really lovely over this past decade. I hope you know how much you mean to me.

Lastly, I am full of gratitude, appreciation, thankfulness, and every other synonym for my family. Jesse, love of my life. Sloane and Delaney, close second loves of my life. Mom and Dad. Bob and Clarita, Jeff and Wendy and Garrett and Gabriel, Connie, Chelsea, Pat and Carolyn, Leilani and Micah and Micaela. My life is a little more gold, a little less straw, with all of you in it.